HIGHEST PRAISE FROM AUTHORS AND THE PRESS FOR . . .

SYMPATHY FOR THE DEVIL

"HERE IS THE FACE OF WAR AS IT HAS RARELY BEEN SHOWN IN LITERATURE. The final pages of this book will serve as a metaphor for America tearing its own guts out . . . in Vietnam."

—**Harry Crews,**
author of *All We Need of Hell*

◆

"*SYMPATHY FOR THE DEVIL* . . . WILL TEAR LIKE A BURST OF TRACERS THROUGH THE FIELD OF VIETNAM WAR LITERATURE. A riveting portrayal of hard times survived by hard men who cling desperately to each other—and little else."

—**Dale A. Dye, Captain, U.S.M.C. (Ret.)**
and author of *Platoon*

more. . .

♦

◆

"CHILLING . . . documents the savage evolution of Hanson and his buddies . . . echoes and expands on the nihilism and dread that permeated *Platoon*."

—*Booklist*

◆

"BRUTALLY STARK . . . Hanson writes from experience. He writes not to provoke horror, but to share it."

—*El Paso Times*

◆

"A POTENT STUDY OF MEN AT WAR. . . . There are plenty of passages of power and almost unbearable descriptions in this deeply felt first novel."

—*Library Journal*

◆

"CHARACTERS JUMP OFF THE PAGE TOWARD US. . . . They are wonderful fictional creations. . . . The novel moves unflinchingly through the various ferocious consequences of its equally ferocious assumptions. . . . When we have seen what he has been through, we understand his loyalties and respect the genuine strength and manliness necessary to keep them in place."

—*Peter Straub,*
Washington Post Book World

COVER: From a photograph of
the author. Mai Loc, Vietnam, 1970.

SYMPATHY FOR THE DEVIL

A NOVEL BY

KENT ANDERSON

WARNER BOOKS

A Warner Communications Company

WARNER BOOKS EDITION

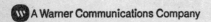 A Warner Communications Company

Printed in the United States of America

First Warner Books Printing: January, 1989

10 9 8 7 6 5 4 3 2 1

This book is for Judith and Jennifer,
who saved my life.

ACKNOWLEDGMENTS

A special thank you to John and Linda Quinn. Without their support and loyalty, and John's clear-eyed reading and advice, I don't think I could have done it.

To Elliott Anderson, who first gave life to Hanson in *Tri-Quarterly*.

To Jim Crumley, for his friendship and for showing me how to survive in this business.

To Bill Kittredge, who taught me to weigh every word, and told me, "You can abandon your work, but it will never abandon you."

To Fred Chappell, my first teacher, who taught me that beauty can be found in anything.

To Nat Sobel, who kept trying when I had given up.

To the National Endowment for the Arts, for giving me some time out of uniform and off the street.

And to all the good men of the 5th Special Forces Group, Vietnam.

SYMPATHY
FOR THE
DEVIL

Part One

THE LAUNCH SITE

A sheet of paper was tacked to the wall over Hanson's bunk:

EVERY DAY IN THE WORLD A HUNDRED THOUSAND PEOPLE DIE. A HUMAN LIFE MEANS NOTHING.

—General Vo Nguyen Giap, Commander-in-Chief, North Vietnamese Army

"IN ORDER TO DESPISE SUFFERING, TO BE ALWAYS CONTENT AND NEVER ASTONISHED AT ANYTHING, ONE MUST REACH SUCH A STATE AS THIS"—AND IVAN DMITRICH INDICATED THE OBESE PEASANT, BLOATED WITH FAT— "OR ELSE ONE MUST HARDEN ONE'S SELF THROUGH SUFFERINGS TO SUCH A DEGREE AS TO LOSE ALL SENSITIVITY TO THEM: THAT IS, IN OTHER WORDS, CEASE TO LIVE."

—Anton Chekhov

Hanson stood just inside the heavy-timbered door of his concrete bunker, looking out. There was no moon yet. The only sound was the steady sobbing of the big diesel generators, but Hanson heard nothing. Had the generators ever stopped he would have heard the silence, a silence that would have bolted him wide awake, armed, and out of his bunk if he were asleep.

He stepped from the doorway and began walking across the inner perimeter toward the teamhouse, a squat shadow ahead of him in the dark. His web gear, heavy with ammunition and grenades, swung from one shoulder like easy, thoughtful breathing. The folding-stock AK-47 in his right hand was loaded with a gracefully curving thirty-round magazine.

As he got closer to the teamhouse, he could feel the drums

and steel-stringed guitar on the back of his sunburned fore-arms and against the tender broken hump on his nose. Then he could hear it.

Hanson smiled. "Stones," he said softly. He didn't have enough to pick out the song, but the bass and drums were pure Stones.

He slid the heavy, light-proof door open and stepped into the bright teamhouse. The song, "Under My Thumb," was pumping out of Silver's big Japanese speakers.

Quinn was pouting and strutting to the music, one hand hooked in his pistol belt, the other hand thrust out, thumb down, like Caesar at the Roman games sending the pike into another crippled loser. His small blue eyes were close-set, cold and flat as the weekly casualty announcement, as he mouthed the words.

Hanson shrugged his web gear to the floor, shouted, "Let me guess," and pressed his hand to his freckled forehead. He pointed at Quinn and shouted into the music, "Mick Jagger, right? Your new Jagger impersonation." His snub-nosed combat magnum glinted from its shoulder holster.

Quinn ignored him, pounding the floor like a clog dancer.

The battered white refrigerator was turned up to high in the damp heat, and gouts of frost dropped to the floor when Hanson opened it to get a Black Label beer. The seams and lip of the black&red cans were rusty from the years they had been stockpiled on the Da Nang docks. Years of raw monsoon and swelling summer heat had turned the American beer bitter. But it was cold; it made his fillings ache when he drank it.

Hanson took a flesh-colored quart jar from the top of the refrigerator, screwed off the top, and took out two of the green & white amphetamine capsules. He knocked them back with the icy beer.

Beats coffee for starting the day, he thought, smiling, re-calling the double-time marching chant back at Fort Bragg: "Airborne Ranger Green Beret, this is the way we *start our day*," running the sandhills before dawn, the rumor that one team had run over a PFC from a supply unit who had been drunkenly crossing the road in front of them. The team had trampled him and left him behind, never getting out of step, chanting each time their left jump boot hit the ground, *"Pray* for war. *Pray* for war. *Pray* for war."

He sat down on one of the wooden footlockers and began thumbing through the *Time* magazine that had come in on the last mail chopper.

The Stones finished "Under My Thumb," paused, and began "Mother's Little Helper." Quinn turned the volume down and walked over to Hanson. He moved with ominous deliberation, like a man carrying nitroglycerin. People got uncomfortable if Quinn moved too close or too quickly.

"Keepin' up with current events, my man?" he asked Hanson. "How's the war going these days?"

"This magazine says we're kicking shit out of 'em. But now," Hanson said, tapping the open magazine, "what about the home front? They've got problems too. Take this young guy, a 'Cornell Senior' it says here, 'I'm nervous as hell. I finally decide on a field—economics—and then I find out I'm number fifty-nine in the draft lottery.' Rough, huh? Just when he decided on economics."

Hanson thumbed through the magazine, softly singing a song from his childhood, "Chicken, *chicken,* don't roost too high for me, chicken, *chicken,* come on out of that tree . . ."

To the west a heavy machine gun was firing, the distant pounding as monotonous as an assembly-line machine. Artillery was going in up north. Three guns working out. They were good, the rounds going in one on top of the other, each explosion like a quick violent wind, the sound your firestarter makes when you touch off the backyard charcoal grill. Normal night sounds.

Hanson read the ads out loud. " 'There's a Ford in your *future.'* 'Tired of diet plans that don't work . . .' "

"Then come to Vietnam, fat boy," Quinn shouted, "and get twenty pounds blown off your ass."

A short, wiry man came into the teamhouse. He wore round wire-rim glasses and had a thin white scar running from his lip up to the side of his nose like a harelip.

"Silver," Hanson yelled to him, then almost said, *how much weight did you lose on the Vietnam high-explosive diet plan,* but changed his mind. Silver had lost half his team, and his partner was in Japan with no legs.

"How's that hole in your ass?" Hanson asked him.

Silver couldn't talk without moving, gesturing, ducking and jabbing like a boxer. He talked fast, and when he laughed it was a grunt, like he'd just taken a punch in the chest. "I like it a lot," he said. "Thinking about getting one on the other side. For symmetry, you know? Dimples. A more coordinated limp," he said, walking quickly forward then backward like a broken mechanical man. Then he stopped and stared at the reel-to-reel tape deck.

"Listen to that," he said, cocking his head slightly. "Background hiss. And that tape's almost new."

"How much longer you gonna be on stand-down, you skinny little gimp?" Quinn asked him.

"Couple weeks. I'll fake it a little longer if I have to. Captain says he's gonna try and get Hanadon up here from the C team for my partner. I don't want to go out with some new guy."

". . . Oh, chicken, *chick*en, *chicken,* don't roost too high for me," Hanson sang to himself as he leafed through the magazine, "Well, *C,* that's the way to begin, *H,* the next letter in . . ."

"And look here," he said, holding up the magazine. "President visiting the troops over at the Third Mech fire base."

Silver had a slight limp as he walked over. He looked at the two-page color spread. "Shit," he said, then laughed. "I was there. After they fixed me up, but before they said I could come back here. The *troops* down there? They spent three weeks building wooden catwalks around the guns so the Prez wouldn't get his feet muddy. Of course, huh, they weren't able to use the guns for fire missions for three weeks, but they *looked* good. Issued all the troops brand-new starched fatigues an hour before The Man was supposed to get there, and made 'em stand around at parade rest so they wouldn't get wrinkled.

"So our main man, the Prez, gets there . . ."

Silver went over to the icebox and got a Coke, then put a mark next to his name on the beer&pop tab on the wall with a red grease pencil. He pulled the pop-top off, put it on his little finger like a ring, and took a long drink.

"The Prez gets there, and they start moving the troops, *processing* the troops past him, and he, like, asks 'em, 'Hi, son, and where are you from?'

"The troop says, 'Uh, Waseca. Minnesota, sir.'

" 'Yes,' the Prez says to him, 'beautiful state, Minnesota. They've got a fine football team at the university there too.'

"Now, I'm hearing all this over the PA system they got. They'd, you know, put me and some of the other people from the hospital out of sight. I wasn't looking too good. Didn't look like I had enough, uh, enthusiasm for the mission."

Silver looked down at his baggy fatigues. "At *best* I don't look like soldier-of-the-month. Anyway, the Prez gives the guy a big handshake and says, 'I just wanted to personally let you know, Private, uh . . .'

" 'Private *Thorgaard*, sir,' this boxhead from Minnesota, this cannon loader, says, and turns so the Prez can see his name tag, but there ain't no name tag, 'cause somebody forgot to put out the word that name tags had to be sewn on the new fatigues. So now, some supply officer's military career is *over. Poor attention to detail.*

"But the Prez says, 'I'm here, Private Thorgaard, because I wanted to let you boys know . . .' "

Silver pulled himself up tight and began strutting and jabbing his finger at the floor, talking angrily to himself in a black street accent. "Boy? You *boys?* Fool up there best not be talkin' 'bout *boys,* one of the brothers up there.

"That's the motherfuckin' truth," he went on in a slightly higher voice, "that aint no boool-shit. Say, gimme some of that *power* now."

Silver took a sip of Coke and went on in his own voice. "The brothers started doing the power handshake and all the white boys moved away.

"So the Prez shakes some more hands, gives out a few medals, and says what a fine job we're doing, and that he, *your president,* was doing everything he could to get us boys home. Then he climbs in his chopper and flies away, all the officers on the ground up there kind of crouching at attention, kind of like ducks at attention, trying to hold their hats on in the rotor blast."

"And you sat through the whole thing?" Quinn asked, "you enjoy the show that much?"

"I was afraid to leave. I was afraid to *move*. I'm glad I didn't have to shake hands with that fucker. I didn't want to get within a hundred feet of him. That was Mr. *Death* standing up there shaking hands. They had gunships flying patterns around there I couldn't fuckin' believe. Then you got MPs all over, trying to look sharp, nervous and trigger-happy as hell. And then there were these *guys*. Secret Service, I guess. All around the Prez. Skinhead haircuts, mirror shades so you can't see their eyes. They didn't look—rational, you know. And they were all packing Uzie's on assault slings under their coats. Anything move too fast or the wrong way, it would've got shot a thousand times. Half the camp would've got wiped out. Would have been like a bunch of Vietnamese in a firefight, shooting at everything."

Silver looked at the wristwatch hanging through the buttonhole of his breast pocket, "Better get down and take the radio watch," he said, "end of the month. Gonna be clearing artillery grids all night. They gotta blow up what's left of the old monthly allotment or next month's allotment will be smaller. That's logical, right? The U.S. Army is logical. It's a logical war.

"Hey," he said, "you want anything blown up? Third Mech's set up a new fire base. 'Fire Base Flora,' in honor of the commander's wife. Got everything on it—one five-fives, one seven-fives, eight inch. Want me to have them plow the ground for you?"

"How about that ridge?" Hanson said.

Quinn nodded.

"You know the one," Hanson said, "about eight klicks north."

"The one where Charles ate up that company of dumbass Third Mech?" Silver asked, "just this side of the border?"

"That's it. Might as well put a little shit on it. South side, kind of walk it from the valley halfway up the side. We'll probably be over that way in the morning."

"Okay," Silver said, "you people watch your ass over there. Charles has got you by the balls when he gets you in Laos. I fuckin' *know*."

He walked to the screen door, stopped, and turned around. "Listen," he said, pointing his finger at Hanson, "listen," he demanded. Then he smiled and sang, "You *must* remember *this* . . .'" spinning around on one foot and slamming out the door, "'a *kiss* is still a *kiss* . . .'" and tap-danced out into the dark, "'a *sigh* is just a *sigh* . . .'"

Silver went down into the underground concrete-reinforced radio bunker and relieved Dawson. He sat at a small desk surrounded on three sides by banks of radios, some of them as big as filing cabinets. They all hummed slightly, each at a different pitch, radiating static and heat like little ovens.

He spent his first few minutes studying "call signs," code names for fire bases and infantry units. The call signs were composed by computer and changed each month in an attempt to confuse the enemy as to what name the units went by. Each call sign was composed of two words, such as "broken days," or "violent meals," and at times the random combinations sounded ominous. Superstitious soldiers were glad when they were changed.

His glasses flashing in the dim yellow and blue dial lights, Silver looked demonic, his face the color of someone dead, as he bobbed his head and shoulders to the rhythm of some stray phrase of code only he could hear.

Up in the teamhouse Hanson was standing next to the bar. "You know," he said, holding a bullet in each hand between thumb and forefinger, "you can get an idea of a country's national character by the bullets their armies use."

"Oh yeah," Quinn said, turning on the bar stool to look at Hanson. "I guess you're gonna tell me about it." He got up and took a beer from the refrigerator, pulled the top off like it was a thumbnail, and drank it all, foam running down his cheeks and neck.

"Now you see," Hanson said, "here's the standard American small-arms round," and held out the bright bullet toward Quinn. "It's slim, lightweight, and fast, but unstable. Look at it," he said, shaking the pencil-thin round. "It's the bullet equivalent of a fashion model—sexy-looking, thin, glittering. But if it gets dirty or damp or overheated, it's liable to jam on you. Temperamental, a prima donna.

"Now here's the Russian bullet," he said, holding out the dull AK-47 round. "Short, thick around the middle. The peasant woman of bullets. Sturdy and slow, not easily deflected by brush, dependable at long range. You can stick it in the mud, put it in the gun, and shoot it.

"We're shooting our fashion models at them and they're firing back with peasant women," he said, holding the bullets out, grinning.

"You know," Quinn said, "I'm used to hearing that kind of shit from you. It doesn't *surprise* me. It even makes a weird kind of sense, sometimes. But," he said, walking over to Hanson and wrapping his big arm around his shoulders, squeezing, whispering now, "let's just keep it between ourselves. You don't want to be telling that to anybody else, 'cause they'll lock you up. And we'd all miss you.'"

They looked at each other, smiled, and burst into laughter.

Mr. Minh walked into the teamhouse, smiling with teeth that had been filed to points, then capped in gold with jade inlays in the shapes of stars and crescent moons. It was part of his magic as a Rhade Montagnard shaman. He had high cheekbones, quick black eyes, and shoulder-length black hair that was tied back with a piece of green parachute nylon. He wore striped tiger fatigues and web gear heavy with grenades and ammo pouches. The little leather *katha* dangled from a cord around his neck. It, too, was part of his magic and could keep enemy bullets from piercing his body.

"I saw a bird fly across the moon," he said. "It is a good time for us to go. We are ready," he said, tapping the pouch at his chest.

"Mr. Minh," Hanson said, "how can it be . . . I have wanted to ask you this—I have seen Rhade shot and killed when they were wearing *katha* to protect them." Hanson called up the images of body after body like slides projected on a screen, little men sprawled in the dirt or curled up, hugging themselves, the leather pouches stuffed in their mouths. "How could that happen?" he asked.

"Yes," the Montagnard said, nodding his head. "Was bad *katha*. Not like mine. Too bad." He went out the door, and Hanson saw the shadows of the three other stocky "Yards." Their eyes and weapons flickered in the starlight. Mr. Minh knew that he would die someday, and he had no fear of death. As long as he lived well and fought bravely, he would be reborn as a hawk, or a hill spirit. Death was only a change of direction.

Hanson began a last-minute equipment check, more a confidence ritual than anything else. He'd gone through his AK-47 the day before, checking for worn or broken parts while cleaning it, then test-fired one clip. He carried the Communist weapon instead of the standard-issue M-16 because the sound of the AK-47 would not give away his position in a firefight, while the M-16 would announce his position to Communists firing AKs. The M-16 used red tracer rounds while the AK-47 used green, and if they made contact at night, the tracer rounds would pinpoint him. On the illegal cross-border operations all equipment was "sanitized." No insignia were worn and all weapons and equipment were of foreign manufacture, most of it acquired from the big CIA warehouse in Da Nang. If they were killed on the wrong side of the border, the North Vietnamese could not "prove" that they were Americans.

Their web gear looked much like a parachute harness. Wide suspenders hooked into a brass-grommeted pistol belt. Two pieces of nylon webbing ran from the front of the pistol belt through the inside of the thighs to the back of the pistol belt. Thirty pounds of weapons and equipment were hung and taped to the web gear. The ammo clips were jammed into the pouches with the bullets facing away from the body in case an enemy bullet detonated them.

Snap links were attached to the suspenders at the shoulders. It was called a Stabo rig. A helicopter could hover 120 feet in the air, drop nylon lines to attach to the snap links, and pull you out, leaving your hands free to fire or drop grenades. They could pull you out even if you were wounded and unconscious. Even if you were dead.

Hanson wore a small survival compass around his neck like a crucifix. In one thigh pocket, wrapped in plastic, having curved to the shape of his thigh, was a stained and dog-eared copy of *The Collected Works of W. B. Yeats.*

Hanson heard a rhythmic hissing, and he shouted, "Hey! Hose, come on in here."

An odd-looking black dog waddled through the door. His skull was warped so that both his eyes appeared to be on the same side of his head, like a flounder. The hissing was the sound of his breathing through a crushed nose.

The dog walked toward Quinn until he collided with his legs, then stood there waiting to be petted. Quinn bent and scratched the dog's ears, then said, "No time now, Hose. We've got to go," and patted him on the rump. The dog waddled back toward the door in a sideways, almost crablike way, then stopped and looked over at Quinn and Hanson.

"See you in a few days, bud," Hanson said.

"Later, Hose," Quinn said.

The dog made a gurgling sound and went out the door.

As a puppy, Hose had been run over by a Vietnamese driving a two-and-a-half-ton truck. It had been rainy season, and the deep mud had saved his life. His flexible puppy-skull bent enough so that it wasn't fractured. Two of his legs had been broken, giving him his odd walk. The sound of his breathing was like a high-pressure air hose, and that's where his name came from. Though he acted normal most of the time, he occasionally had fits of terror or rage and would race across the camp with wild flounder-eyes.

Hose got along with the Americans and the Montagnards, though the Yards would have eaten him if Mr. Minh had not declared that he was a powerful spirit and should be respected. But Hose hated Vietnamese and acted as a watchdog after dark when the inner perimeter was closed off to even the Vietnamese who lived in the camp.

"What an ugly fucking dog," Quinn said, his voice full of admiration.

Hanson pulled a small tin whistle from his pack and tooted a few notes out of it. He put the whistle to his eye and sighted down it, aiming at Quinn.

"Do you know," he said, "that they have whole tin whistle *bands* in Ireland, whole grade schools all playing tin whistles. Maybe I'll go to Ireland when they decide we've won the war."

Quinn threw on his pack. "I'm going back to Iowa," he said. "One fucked-up foreign country is enough for me. Shit, we're all probably gonna die over here anyway."

Quinn carried a crude-looking weapon that seemed to be made of sheet metal and steel tubing. In his huge hand it looked like a cheap child's toy. It was a Swedish submachine gun with a built-in silencer. Quinn had glued felt to the face of the bolt to muffle the clicking of the firing mechanism. It could kill at a hundred yards, the bursts of fire sounding like someone absently thumbing a deck of cards.

Hanson shouldered his forty-pound pack, picked up the AK, and tromped to the refrigerator. He dropped another cap of speed into his breast pocket and stuck a Coke in his pack.

As they went out the door, Jagger was singing "Paint It Black."

The five dark forms crossed through the outer perimeter and headed west. Another heavy machine gun opened up in the distance, and the big red tracers floated gracefully, like glowing golf balls, across the sky. Scores of them hit a hillside and rebounded in random patterns.

Artillery rounds blinked silver and yellow and bluish white against the mountains.

Hanson watched them, his eyes slightly dilated. "God-*damn*, Quinn," he said. "It's always springtime in Vietnam."

Before dawn, they would be across the border.

Seven miles up, the pilot of the lead bomber was tired and bored and worried. It had been a ten-hour flight from Guam, and it would be a ten-hour turnaround, refueling over the South China sea, always a tricky little operation when they were bucking head winds. He swiveled his chair and looked out the thick window. The light coming through had the dead glare of an overexposed photograph.

Cindy wasn't doing well in school, his wife had written him. She needed a real father, she'd written, which of course meant that it was all his fault. She had also mentioned that she was having trouble with the car. It was hard to start now that the weather was turning cold.

Fine, that's fine, the pilot thought. Take it to the dealer, don't tell me about it. Even if it's only the battery terminals. Take it to the dealer and let them fuck you out of a hundred and fifty bucks. We've got the money. No, you want me to diagnose the goddamn thing by mail.

Jesus Christ. I'm seven miles in the air and twelve thousand miles away. I'm flying a fifty-million-dollar aircraft and you want me to worry about the Buick. Everything goes to hell if I'm not right there on everybody's ass.

He'd been thinking of extending his tour if they would let him fly fighters. He didn't need that domestic shit back in Omaha. He decided to talk to the CO when they got back. That made him feel better.

The radar navigator folded back a page in the paperback book he was reading and closed it. The cover showed a cowboy standing just inside a saloon door, right hand poised above his six-gun, a cigarillo in his mouth sending up a thin plume of smoke, looking *hard* at something. A saloon girl with big breasts had her arm draped over his shoulder and was pressing against him. He stuck the book into the leg pocket of his flight suit, made a slight adjustment on the green radar screen, and said, "Comin' up."

"Good," the pilot said. "Let's unload and turn this bus around."

The hydraulics groaned, and four thumps shook the plane.

"All doors open," the navigator said, watching his scope. Two green lines began bending parallel to a central red line; three sets of numbers stuttered along the left side of the screen. He counted aloud: "Ten seconds to release, nine seconds to release . . ."

One hundred and ten iron bombs began to tumble from the belly of the ship. The only signs of their departure were a slight shuddering, a tendency of the plane to gain altitude, and over the radar navigator's head, a small amber light blinking urgently, flashing once for each bomb released.

The three planes in the formation banked and pulled away like sweep hands on a stopwatch, never actually passing over the target, the bombs covering the last twelve miles as they fell.

The radar navigator was still hung over from the night before. He walked to the rear of the plane to get an auxiliary oxygen tank, hoping that the pure oxygen would help his headache. He waved, then held his head and made a face at the tail gunner, a nineteen-year-old boy from San Jose. The tail gunner smiled and nodded his head.

The B-52s cannot be seen or heard through the jungle canopy. The enemy has no warning. They know nothing of the Arclight mission until the bombs begin to detonate and the jungle explodes around them. Though perhaps a split-second before detonation there is a roar of the bombs rushing down like a terrible wind.

It was noon. The heat droned through the jungle like the sound of high tension wires. When Hanson reached up to pull a handful of razor grass down for shade, his canteens and grenades shifted and tugged at him. He had been thinking about time, about how the half-life of radioactive carbon was used to determine the age of prehistoric tools. He glanced at his watch and saw a green fly licking blood from a cut on the back of his hand. The sun whined and chirped in his ears. His crotch and armpits were wet, and the grass cuts on his hands stung. He killed the fly and recalled reading about monks in medieval Europe. It was important, they had felt, to pray to God at very specific times each day. That concern for timely prayer had been important in the development of the clock.

He squinted into the sun again, and the earth began to shudder against his chest and thighs. In the valley beyond the first ridge line, shock waves arced like brutal rainbows, and greasy thunderheads of smoke began to rise.

Far above and to the west, three B-52s winked in the pale sky, but Hanson couldn't see them. He stood and watched the rest of the team rise from the tall brown grass: Quinn, Troc, Rau, and Mr. Minh. The five of them were there on a BDA, a bomb damage assessment. Their job was to move through the bomb impact area and get a body count for the Air Force.

It was quiet in the valley. Sound did not carry in the damp heat but seemed to fall dead to the ground. They moved slowly. Any piece of equipment that might rattle had been taped down or removed. The only sounds were their boots on the baked earth and the rustle of canvas web gear. Dressed for speed and firepower, they carried only water, ammunition, freeze-dried food, and explosives.

Hanson kept losing sight of the rest of the team in the acrid fog—dust, smoke, and the ammonia stink of high explosive. He could taste it in the back of his throat. The jungle floor was torn into steaming furrows. Lengths of vine and tiger thorns were tangled like concertina wire. The craters were as big as bedrooms, smelling of sulfur and freshly turned earth, smoke clinging to their sides like dirty snow. Scorched bamboo groves hissed; patches of brush and grass burned noiselessly.

Hanson watched a fired-mud clinker roll slowly down the side of a crater and disappear in the smoke. His eyes burned, but he didn't rub them. The yellow dust had turned to paste on his face and hands.

Anybody who isn't dead, he thought, is going to be pissed off. He inhaled the smoke and dust, and suddenly had to bite his lip to keep from laughing. He thought about the simple pain in his lip that kept him silent and safe, and he considered the importance of pain in human activities.

Hanson stepped around an uprooted tree and saw the soldier, an NVA regular with a carbine who had been caught in the concussion. He was caked with the same yellow paste that covered Hanson's face and arms. Only his eyes were alive. He seemed to be staring at something far away, or thinking about something puzzling and important. A fine web of bright blood ran from his ears and nose, collected on his chin, and fell to his chest and shoulders with soft *pops.* The blood puddled and ran in red rivulets down his arm through the yellow dust to his elbow, then to his hand, where it dropped from his fingers to the ground, pocking the dust.

His eyes moved slowly until they met Hanson's. Then his feet got tangled up and he sat down *hard.* His eyes had a look of total surprise. His head dropped between his knees, and he toppled to one side.

Rau kicked him twice, once in the ribs and once in the head. When they left him behind, his eyes were dead, and his broken jaw sagged with astonishment.

They found five more in the first collapsed bunker. It looked like a mining disaster, the bodies and sandbags shapeless and caked with dirt, as if they were being reclaimed by the earth. Gouts of cooked rice were stuck to timbers, and there was a heavy smell of fish sauce.

A can of mackerel the size of a smoke grenade jutted from the dirt. The label was bright red with large white letters that spelled EATWELL above a green-and-white fish that was flailing its tail as if in flight, its green-and-yellow eye wide with terror. Blue lines and circles arced back from the fish's head to indicate movement. Beneath the fish were the words, "Product of Alaska."

Another body was a few meters from the bunker. He must have been running while the bombs fell. One gray foot was twisted up against the ankle. His toenails were yellow and torn. The face beneath the stiff black bangs was a patchwork of black and purple and shading blues, like farmland seen from an airliner. Fat green blowflies rose and settled nervously, slapping at the face like a veil. Some of his features were still there, like those puzzles in children's picture books, clouds and gnarled trees that suddenly take focus and reveal a hidden face.

The team continued silently on, finding several more broken bunkers. The only really funny thing that happened was when Quinn spun and threw his submachine gun to his shoulder, having glanced up and seen a body hanging from the crotch of a tree. The rest of the team grinned. Troc whispered, "Fly like bird," and smiled, pleased at his English.

At the edge of the impact area they turned north. The heat seemed like part of the terrain, as solid as the earth beneath their boots. The air was so humid that breathing was difficult. It was like drowning. Hanson touched the compass hanging at his chest and smiled. Alaska, he thought. Good old north. He imagined going north, and north, until the jungle changed to tundra, and mountains, and solid ice.

A tiny deer broke from the underbrush, barking like a dog.

Hanson and the team dropped into a crouch. The barking deer wheeled and went back the way it had come, vanishing in the grass.

The sun was below the hills when they started across the sluggish brown river. The water was warm and oily, and, they found out, full of leeches. They crawled into a peninsula of brush and bamboo to wait for darkness before sprinting across the valley to the first of the foothills, where they would wait out the night.

Hanson pulled down his fatigue pants. Three gray worms with pointed tails hung from the inside of his thigh. He squirted insect repellent on them and they dropped off, leaving bright little dots of blood. He found a bigger one on his ankle, the size of his little finger, gray as the slime in a sink drain. He flicked it off, hissing, "Shitshitshit."

He soaked the leech with repellent and set it afire. The leech rose and writhed like a cobra in the colorless flame, a faint saffron nimbus around its body. Hanson could feel the flame's heat on his cheek and smell the sweetness in the flame and in his own sweat. The leech suddenly turned black and fell into the patch of charred grass around it. Hanson realized that he had been holding his breath.

Just before dusk became darkness they doubled back and set up a night location near a bombed-out family temple on a small clearing awash in the jungle.

Hanson pulled a plug of C-4 explosive from the end of a two-pound brick and pressed it into a ball. He set his canteen cup of water over a chink in the temple floor and rolled the C-4 beneath the cup. He touched a match to it and it began to burn with an orange flame. Patches of gold and bright blue glowed on the flaking temple walls as the C-4 burned like a marshmallow held in a campfire. He poured in a packet of instant coffee that floated on the water like dust.

Out beyond the ornate and shattered temple gate, the jungle and sky were turning gray. Hanson stirred his coffee with a plastic spoon and considered the idea that color was only reflected sunlight, but it seemed just as reasonable that at a given time every day, a part of the world simply turned black.

The countryside had begun to tremble with artillery and heavy machine gun fire. Hanson sipped his coffee and smiled, thinking how the fire bases cough and grumble at night. They pull their men back inside the perimeter and flail the jungle with ordnance. Finally though, they controlled only the land they occupied. At night their control went only to the last roll of concertina wire. They blundered out in noisy convoys every day, but at night they rolled back in like the tide.

Hanson and Quinn slung their hammocks near an artillery crater down the slope from the temple. Quinn's hammock swung gently as he whispered the chant, "Airborne Ranger, Green Be*ret*, this is the way we end the day." Then he laughed, so softly that it sounded evil.

"Hey," he said, "who gets credit for that first guy? Us or the Air Force? He was still alive when we got there. Technically, I think he's ours. Goddamn Air Force anyway."

Hanson listened to the squeaking of his hammock strings.

"I don't like these fuckin' Arclight sweeps," Quinn said. "Body counters. One potato, two potato. That fuckin' *guy* in the tree. Scared the shit out of me. And that first guy. Just standing there. I don't know what he was looking at, but I don't think it's something *I* ever want to see.

"And what about that little deer? The Yards got some kind of thing about them? Even Mr. Minh acted funny after we saw that deer. Seems like the Yards been acting funny ever since we started this sweep."

"Yeah," Hanson said, "that barking deer's kind of like a black cat. If you start a trip and it crosses your path, you're supposed to go back and start over."

"You *believe* a lot of that Montagnard stuff," Quinn said.

"Mr. Minh believes it. It makes as much sense as God with a big white beard up in heaven. Remember those pictures in Sunday school? Like the one of Jesus, long blond hair, *sensitive* blue eyes, knocking at the door of the rustic little cottage, knock, knock, knock?"

Hanson began to speak in a Southern drawl. "An' that's all you have to do, childern, when you hear him knockin'. That is

Lord Jeezus knockin' at your heart, an' you need only to open up the door to receive his blessed love."

It had been while Hanson's father was in Korea, and he was living at his grandmother's. After Sunday school he would go to church, and in the summer they handed out the cardboard fans with the flat wooden handle like a tongue depressor. There was always a funeral home ad on one side and a gaudy color picture on the other—a pair of stocky blond angels hauling a portly man in a business suit into the sky, or a worried middle-aged man standing at a huge podium with a jury of thick-winged angels staring grimly at him. Beneath the pictures a short paragraph told how the artist had been a hopeless alcoholic until he found Jesus and accepted him as his personal Lord and savior, and was now using his talents for the greater glory of God.

After the service everyone stood in small groups in front of the church, the men smoking and talking, the women just talking. Up the street there was a green concrete building, a hospital for crazy people and alcoholics. One Sunday, as Hanson was getting into the car to go home, a wild-eyed man in blue pajamas had come running barefoot from the hospital. Two stocky men in white coats and heavy black shoes were chasing him. The man looked directly at Hanson as he ran past and said, "They won't ever let you finish, will they?" and ran on into the littered little park that smelled like sewage.

One of Hanson's aunts had pulled him into the car and rolled up the windows, but he heard the man scream when the other men caught him.

"What's wrong with them?" he asked as the car pulled away.

"Why nothing, honey. We're just goin' to Grandma's for chicken. Like we always do."

Every Sunday they had cold chicken, biscuits, and mashed potatoes. Then everyone drove to the cemetery—six to a car—to look at Grandpa's grave. Each of Hanson's aunts and uncles had a photograph of themselves standing next to the tombstone, like sportsmen with a trophy kill.

Sometimes Hanson talked his way out of going to the

cemetery; he hated riding in the hot crowded car, the windows rolled up to keep out the dust. It was one of those times that he became a born-again Christian.

He was alone in his grandmother's parlor that Sunday. A big picture of a kneeling Christ caught the afternoon light and seemed to move. His grandfather's open coffin had been put on display in the parlor after his death, and one of Hanson's aunts had lifted him up so he could see, saying to him, "Look at Granpa, honey, he's going to heaven. This is the last time you'll see him till we're all up there together."

His grandfather's face and hands had been powdered, and he looked very small.

Hanson's grandfather was the only corpse he had ever seen until he went to Vietnam.

On that Sunday when he was born-again, Hanson turned on the TV in the parlor so he would feel a little less alone in the house. The Billy Graham Crusade for Christ was on. Hanson had expected the "Good Samaritan" show, where contestants told about their miserable lives, and cried, and the grimly smiling host asked people watching the show to send in donations.

But that Sunday it was Billy Graham. Just when it started to get dark, the music swelled and Billy told the crowd to come down from the stands and give their lives to Christ.

"Come down, come down," he said. "Just look, my friends, hundreds of people are coming down to give their lives to Jesus Christ," he said, throwing his arms up, "and you people out there who are watching from your television screens, get up, get up from your chairs and sofas, get up and walk to your television sets.

"Stand up and witness for Christ there in your living rooms with us. Lay your hands on your television sets and pray with us."

And Hanson had gotten up, terrified, and pressed his hands down on the TV. The metal was warm and the tubes glowed through the grille work in the back.

Hanson looked at the glowing face of his watch. He called the camp and waited.

No answer.

He pulled off the whip antenna and touched the copper contact points with his tongue for a better contact, then jammed and screwed the antenna back down on the radio set. It swished back and forth in the dark air.

He called again. No answer. The radio hissed. A pink flare popped east of the river, dripping sparks and leaving a jagged trail of smoke.

Hanson looked over at Quinn, then called again, "Formal Granite, Formal Granite, this is five-four, over . . ."

Silver's voice crackled through the static. "This is Granite, it's your dime."

"It's a comfort, you know, this instant commo."

"Yeah, yeah. All I get is complaints. Just like the phone company. You're comin' in weak—better change your battery. So, you got a message for me?"

Hanson sent in the body count and two night artillery grids. One grid was H&I, harassment and interdiction fire, a corridor of high explosive to be fired throughout the night around their location. The other grid was plotted directly on the temple, to be fired in the event that they were attacked and had to run.

"I get any mail?" Hanson asked.

"Yeah. Last mail chopper. Three letters from that chick, and one of those Commie newspapers from New York."

"You reading my mail or what? Tampering with mail is some kind of federal crime."

"It's all commo. Part of the job. Your partner there got one of those 'GI Paks' from his church in Iowa. Lotta good stuff. 'What every soldier in the field needs,' it says. Toothbrush, shoestrings, deck of cards—you doing any gambling out there —pair of white socks, little box of raisins, and a plastic packet of Heinz catsup, about enough for one hot dog if you got one, and some Bugs Bunny Kool-Aid. Card says that the ladies' auxiliary is behind us 'all the way.' Yep."

Over the radio, Silver's laugh sounded like a weak battery trying to start a car.

"Any movies?"

"Yeah, a Clint Eastwood flick. He kills a lot of Italian cowboys. The Yards loved it, said that the Italians were VC. Anyway, that's all I've got on this end."

"Okay. Look, things don't *feel* too good here. Have that stuff ready to shoot if we call for it, 'cause we're gonna have to be steppin' right along."

"You got it. Any more traffic? I gotta make radio check with Da Nang."

"Negative."

"Okay. Granite out. Catch you later. Hey, how does this grab you?" A hysterical mechanical laugh came from the radio, the accordionlike laugh box Silver carried around to comment on the absurdity of things.

The radio hissed like a TV after sign-off.

Hanson lay in the hammock listening to the big guns. They fired in pairs or groups of three and sounded like distant box cars slamming to a stop. Moments later he could hear the shells coursing over and past. Some of the explosions sent shudders through the hammock strings. It was strangely comforting.

A voice broke static on the radio, grinding like a gear box. "Granite five-four, this is Night Bird, over . . ."

Hanson looked at Quinn. Quinn shrugged.

"This is five-four . . ."

"Uh, roger . . . Ah just wanted to verify your location an' *advise* you that ah *will* be workin' the area for a while . . ."

Somewhere to the south there was a drone of engines.

"Gunship," Quinn hissed. "Night-vision gunship."

"Uh, roger that," Hanson said into the handset. "Five-four copies."

"Uh, roger. Ah'll be doin' some huntin' then. This is the Night Bird, out . . ."

The engine noise grew louder and passed overhead. Hanson could see the glow from four engines flickering through the propellers, and a dark shape that blotted out the stars.

The engines faded, and the minigun opened up. A solid shaft of red tracers flashed silently from sky to ground like a neon light suddenly switched on, and a moment later they heard the drone of the gun, the sound of a foghorn. Then the red shaft died, burning itself out slowly from sky to ground, eating its tail, and when the sky was black again, the drone stopped. The engine noise was gone. They watched, staring into the dark, and there it was again, flickering and droning in the distance.

The moon had set. Mr. Minh squatted at the temple wall, facing the way they had come, toward the impact zone. He had arranged the contents of his *katha* in a semicircle: a pinch of rice, a green bubble of melted glass—*excrement of fire*—the tip of a buffalo's penis, a tiny piece of quartz, a tiger's tooth, and the bill of a sparrow hawk.

He looked into the darkness and clucked three times, deep in his throat, then three more. All he heard in return were Hanson's footsteps behind him. As the footsteps came closer, Mr. Minh said, "I had a bad dream, Hanson. I dreamed that the sky struck us.

"I know this place. There was once a village where the bombs fell. There were big trees near the village, very strong spirits. It was the year we ate the forest of the Stone Spirit *Goo*. That was a long time ago.

"So. All I do is fight now. Fighting is my work now, not the village. But I know. We must be very careful, tomorrow and the day after tomorrow. The tree spirits are angry. I have tried to call them, to talk, but they do not answer. Go back to your hammock. They do not know you."

Hanson lay in his hammock and watched the stars disappear. A rain squall was moving in. The wind picked up and the rain slanted down like thread on a loom. The artillery reports were muted, grainy, like old recordings. A flare popped across the river, swung up and down with the wind, making a fuzzy, peach-colored arc.

Rain always benefits the attackers; it covers the sound they make as they move into position. When it rains at night in the jungle you are rendered deaf and blind. There is nothing to do but wait.

Whenever a flare popped, the split-leaf palm fronds overhead blinked and raged in the wind, the slits like eyes and mouths squinting and gnashing.

The radio hissed softly.

One summer, long before he had ever thought of the war, Hanson had been hiking near the edge of a large swamp. It was a hot day and the scrub pines gave little shade. He came upon a clearing that seemed to be studded with fleshy horns. They were plants that looked like Easter lilies, but they had no stem or stalk. Each plant rose from the ground like a funnel. No part of them was green.

The plants were a soiled white and seemed to be covered with bruises, though Hanson might have imagined that. The inside of the plants bristled with stiff black hairs. The hairs grew inward and down toward the narrow throat of the funnel, and they were sticky with a thick syrup.

The overall effect was that of hundreds of huge nostrils snorting from the ground.

There were insects inside all the funnels, stuck fast to the sweet syrup, unable to climb through the bristles of hair. As they struggled, they slipped deeper into the neck of the plant— flies, bees, beetles, and butterflies. For a moment Hanson thought about using his pocketknife to free some of the insects, to cut the plants off at the ground, but he realized that there was nothing he could do; there were too many. And anyway, that was just the way things worked in that place. Inside one of the plants he saw what looked like a tiny animal with brown fur, just visible deep in the neck. The sweet smell of the syrup and of rotting meat hung over the field.

They collected their booby traps and moved out at first light as the faint pinks filtered through dark green mountains. It was still cool, but the heat was already seeping in, like an undertow. It was going to be hot. Hanson felt uneasy, like a runner waiting for the starter's gun. The sun rose slowly at first, ponderous, the color of rotten fruit. Then it climbed and got smaller and tighter and bore down on them.

The grave was fresh, probably someone who had survived the air strike only to die of his wounds. A heavy, sweet smell rode the heat from the circular mound of earth. They should have dug it up to check for documents and insignia, but they moved on.

Hanson's cheek itched, but he didn't scratch it. He had a metallic taste on his tongue, and the backs of his hands tingled. He looked at Quinn and Mr. Minh. A patch of split-leaf palm fronds was the wrong color. It was something about the quality of the sunlight. The way the trail curved up ahead. He recalled some odd phrase in his last letter home. His cheek itched. He was afraid that if he touched it, a bullet would strike there.

Someone back in the jungle coughed. There was the soft *pop* of a grenade fuse, and the grenade was floating through the air at him, a grayish green cylinder with cloth streamers. Bullets snapped past him as Quinn fired a magazine and began to run. The grenade went off. Something pulled at Hanson's pant leg. The team was down in a low crouch, facing alternate sides of the jungle. Quinn ran past Hanson and said, "Shit." Troc emptied a magazine and ran. The fire coming from the jungle was ragged. The ambush had been sprung too soon, before they were in the killing zone, because of the cough. Hanson smelled burned powder, fish sauce, and gun oil as Troc ran past him. Mr. Minh emptied his weapon and wheeled around. Rau began to fire. Mr. Minh was putting a new magazine in his weapon as he ran past Hanson, who was pulling the fat white phosphorous grenade from his shoulder harness. The brass from Rau's weapon glittered as it arced out of the chamber. Hanson had to tear the grenade loose with his teeth and his left hand. The electrical tape holding it tasted salty. He fired toward the sound of the cough as Rau ran past. He pulled the pin from the pastel-green yellow-striped WP grenade and threw it over the palm fronds. And he ran. He pulled the quick release on his pack straps and ran. Shrugging off the heavy pack, he ran and tried to keep sight of Rau.

Da Nang

It was almost five, and the NCO club and bar was filling up. Janis Joplin was wailing from the tape deck behind the bar, *uh-huh, UH-HUH, WOAH! uhuhuh, YEOW!*

Two soldiers in the bar were wearing camouflage fatigues. They had gotten off a chopper from the north only ten minutes before. Standing together at the slate-topped bar, they looked like two reflections of the same soldier. The baggy jungle fatigues were mottled and striped to blend with the jungle, the dead browns and greens of healing bruises or of a body left too long in the sun, a nimbus of fine orange dust catching the light. The backs of their hands were crosshatched with small scars and blood-crusted welts. The fine hair on the backs of their hands and wrists had been burned to brown stubble over hurried cook fires. They both had an easy, tireless concentration.

But they were not at all alike.

Quinn was much bigger than Hanson. He was bigger than anyone else in the bar. His features were as small and blunt as his eyes. It was a face that could take a lot of damage and still function. The milky blue eyes seemed to have been set in his head just so he could look for somebody to kill. They were eyes that tourists on back roads have nightmares about—the kind of eyes that watch you from next to the Coke machine in that smalltown gas station, and keep watching as the old pump rings and rings and rings up the sale, while you check the locks on the doors and wish you were back on the Interstate.

His hands looked out of proportion to even his big body, too big to be useful for anything but breaking furniture. They could field-strip an M-60 faster than you could name the parts.

Quinn rarely smiled. When he did smile, it was not a comforting expression.

He'd been a linebacker in college until he'd gotten into

that last fight outside a bar after a game. During the fight the crowd that had gathered, at first laughing and shouting, making bets, slowly quieted as Quinn worked with the same cold anger that filled him when he chopped wood or stacked bales of hay on his father's farm, that drove him to study the textbooks full of useless facts that got him off the farm and into college, where five afternoons a week and every Saturday he would trade blow for blow with others like himself for the entertainment of the same people who were silently watching him outside the bar.

Quinn had stepped back, letting the semiconscious man fall to the ground, kicked him once, viciously in the ribs, and walked away.

"Some of those fuckers started *booing* me. That was the night," Quinn had told Hanson, "I realized I'd been doing shit I hated all my life. I hated the farm, I hated those goddamn books, I hated football—I didn't want to tackle those motherfuckers, I wanted to *kill* 'em. Of course, three months later, three months after I stopped hurting quarterbacks and ends as bad as I could, blindsiding running backs right out of the game, while those college wimps up there in the stands held their weenies and their beers, and their date's tit, three months later, the army had my ass. But what the hell, right? I was big enough, and mean enough, but I wasn't ever fast enough to turn pro. And anyway, little buddy, I've found a home."

Quinn smiled when he told that story.

He finished his Budweiser and looked at Hanson in the big bar mirror. You'll be back . . ." he began.

"Do me a favor," Hanson said. "Shoot me in the head when I step off the plane, okay? If I come back. Save me the trouble of humping the hills waiting for Charles to do it."

"Yeah, you'll be back. You know those killer guard dogs the Zoomies use to guard their airplanes, those dogs that are smarter and meaner than any of the people in the Air Force? They don't let those dogs go back to the States. They just blow 'em away when they're through with them because they're too mean and fucked up . . ."

"Not bad, Quinn. A nice little analogy there. You have the makings of a poet. Now I don't read much poetry—it's mostly

written by women and queers, and doesn't make much sense
—but I think you've got what it takes.

"I'm *already* gone, Quinn. The machinery is in motion.
Time is not the dependable phenomenon you think it is. Look
up there," he said, pointing at the ceiling. "There I am. It's
happening right now, even as I speak the words—I'm up there
in the Freedom Bird. Just another dumb-ass GI at thirty-two
thousand feet. Why, I'm sitting next to a Specialist Four who's
telling me about the year he spent greasing vehicles in the
Third Mech motor pool. Look, Quinn, he's showing me his
snapshots of the Bob Hope show. The captain is talking on the
PA system: 'We'll be cruising at thirty-two thousand feet'—the
Spec. 4 looks out the window—yeah, we're way up there, all
right—'and before the girls show you what to do in the unlikely
event of loss of cabin pressure, I'd like to say that we're real
proud of . . . whatever it was you've been doing, *real* proud
of ya. Girls . . .'

"See," Hanson said, grabbing Quinn's arm and pointing to
where the ceiling and wall met in the bar, "the pretty stewardess is holding the plastic oxygen bag over her nose and mouth,
turning from side to side. Look, you can see her smiling
through the bag. Everybody is smiling and reading *Playboy*
magazine. Hanson is on his way . . ."

Quinn jerked his arm away and smiled down at Hanson.
"You don't want to get too froggy and be putting your hands on
me like that now, or you'll spend the first six weeks at home
listening to your broken bones knit. Sound just like a big bowl
of Rice Crispies.

"If you were having problems getting along with people
before you came over here, like you been telling me, what the
fuck do you think is gonna happen now?"

Quinn laughed, took a drink of beer, and tossed back the
shot of Scotch. "Co Dan," he called to the pretty barmaid.
"Two Chivas, two Budwi.

"You can't even get a letter from back there without getting pissed off anymore. What makes you think you'll get along
any better now?"

"I'll make an effort. I'm through with all the bullshit. I'll
just tell the truth."

Quinn laughed and had to spit out a mouthful of beer. "I like that," he said. "That *had* to be in some movie. You dumb shit," he said, grabbing Hanson, pinning his arms. "You know what those fuckers will do if you tell them the truth?

"You know what they'll do," he whispered in Hanson's ear. "They'll lock your ass *away*. Oh, 'the truth.' I love it, 'the truth.'" Quinn laughed like someone who's just broken your legs and is walking toward you with a knife in his hands. "Look," he said, nodding across the bar, "I see *another* plane. But nobody's smiling because it's going the wrong way. To Vietnam. They all look sad and scared. Wait. One little guy looks almost happy. It's Hanson, on his way back.

"You like it here, my man," he said, releasing Hanson and patting him on the back. "Just like me. You've found a home."

"They're gonna *kill* me if I stay over here," Hanson said. "You recall that last little exercise we went on out of Mai Loc launch site? You remember that one?"

Hanson slapped his open hand down on the bar and laughed. "They had us cold. I was back here somewhere," he said, holding his hand behind his head, "watching myself run in slow motion, looking around at all the plants breathing, listening to the sky like some kind of LSD trip. I just kept running out of habit. My body wanted to fall down and die and get it over with.

"And I tell myself, 'You dumb shit, you're gonna die, and this time it's all your own fault, and it's probably gonna hurt a lot. You don't have to be out here.'

"I can think of three other times I *knew* I was gonna die. I can't even remember how many times I thought I *might* die. I almost laughed at myself for being there. So I decide, well, maybe I'll try praying . . ."

Quinn began to laugh.

"So I say, 'Okay, God, if you really are there, if you get me out of this one time, I'll—I don't know *what* right now, but I promise I'll do something appropriate if you'll get me out of this. Okay?' And I watch myself run some more, and then another RPD starts firing at me, and I think, 'Yeah, I didn't think so.'

"I mean, if there is a God, he isn't making any deals with

me. I'm talking about those times when I've looked around me and said, 'Oh, shit, I'm gonna die now. I hope it doesn't hurt too bad.'

"I'm *already* dead, Quinn. And one of these days, if I hang around here, God's gonna audit the books and come police my ass up when he remembers that I'm dead. I'm one of God's bookkeeping errors. I'm not fool enough to wait here," he said, jabbing his finger at the floor, "for him to get me. I'm going to be a lot harder to find back in the States."

"You got the Hill Spirits looking out for you here," Quinn said.

Prayer hadn't helped them, but the Hill Spirits had, according to Mr. Minh. He had told them that the NVA had somehow offended the Hill Spirits, who had then chosen to help the recon team. It was Mr. Minh who had taken out the RPD machine gun. The stocky little man in the tiger suit had run straight at the gun and its three-man crew, his glossy black hair lifting from his shoulders as he ran through the sparkle of green tracers, and killed them all.

Automatic weapons fire is often erratic. What Quinn and Hanson saw Mr. Minh do was possible, but not likely. It was the kind of thing they had seen him do many times. When they tried to persuade him to be more careful, he only smiled his gold and jade smile.

"You'll be back . . ." Quinn began.

Hanson slowly shook his head.

"Because Mr. Minh said you'd be back. There it is, little buddy. Mr. Minh is never wrong. You know that. If he isn't sure, he says he doesn't know."

Hanson took another drink of beer and watched his own eyes in the mirror. Mr. Minh was never wrong.

Most of the NCO clubs in Vietnam had plywood walls and a sheet-metal roof that kept out the rain but not the heat or the stink of the piss tubes out back.

The Special Forces NCO club in Da Nang looked like one wing of an exclusive mountain resort. The walls were stone. The bar was stone and hand-carved mahogany, and the massive mirror behind the bar was the deep green of a mountain lake. A huge green beret fashioned of thick glass bricks was set in the flagstone and parquet floor, the Special Forces crest inset in chrome and brass. The club was air-conditioned, the Vietnamese barmaids were pretty, and Chivas was thirty cents a shot.

The SKS rifle mounted over the bar had been captured by Quinn and Hanson and traded to the club for two pallets of beer for the launch site. The SKS had belonged to a survivor of an ambush, a ragged straggler who hadn't been in the killing zone when the ambush was sprung.

Hanson and Quinn had gone after him. Hanson threw himself onto his stomach, braced his weapon, and fired two bursts. One round from the first short burst tore the straggler's calf, and he stumbled. Hanson walked the second burst diagonally from the straggler's hip to his shoulder, and he slammed into the ground face-first, bucking like a stunned carp. Hanson ran up to him, ripped another burst across his back to make sure that he was dead, then kicked him over like a rotten log that might have thousands of blind white bugs swarming beneath it. There was an SKS beneath it, an obsolete and rare carbine worth four hundred dollars as a war trophy.

"Food on the *table,*" Hanson had yelled.

"Yeah," Quinn said, "and you almost fucked it up, too."

"What?"

"That's right. Shootin' him up like that. Look."

The last burst of grass-jacketed bullets had gone through the body and torn a furrow through bloody gray-green grass and bleeding shards of sun-baked clay.

"A little lower," Quinn said, "and you'd have hit the SKS. Should have shot him in the head."

"You're right," Hanson said. "You're right. Stragglers like him would be carrying the old weapons. Good to remember. It's like a piece of Asian woods lore. Go for the head."

Hanson put a fresh clip in his weapon, slung the SKS over his shoulder, and started to walk off. Then he stopped, turned, and looked in the dead man's face. Already he was starting to look like all the others. His eyes were gluey and flat; the tiny wrinkles and lines that had made his face different from any other face were beginning to soften and fade. All you dead people, Hanson thought, look alike. Then he leaned over the body and said softly, "But now you don't have to worry about being slow anymore, you don't have to worry about dying."

That's the nice thing about war, he thought. If you win, the other guy's dead. Period. And you're alive. If you lose, you're dead, and your problems are over.

Hanson and Quinn sometimes went after war trophies for trading purposes when they weren't on regular operations. They usually took Sergeant Major's Nung bodyguards on ambushes and sweeps. The sweeps through enemy-controlled areas—which were, in truth, everything outside the camp wire—were the kind of operations officially called "Search and Destroy," in the beginning. But when the American public began seeing nightly TV film footage of dead Asians and Americans on the six-thirty news, when they started seeing bodies while eating their pork chops and mashed potatoes, they began to make unpleasant associations and considered the implications of words like "destroy."

The Army changed the name of the operations to "search and clear." Most search-and-clear operations took place in free-fire zones, large areas of the countryside where everything was considered an enemy (enemy soldier), enemy supporter (farmer), or enemy asset (buffalo, rice, hootch). It was all right to kill or destroy anything in a free-fire zone. Not even Quinn liked to kill the water buffalo, though. It took them so long to die, brain shots were difficult, and they moaned so. But the Nungs liked to kill them, and it was good to keep the Nungs mean and happy. Everyone was afraid of the Nungs, mercenaries of Chinese descent who like the Montagnards, hated all Vietnamese, North or South.

In a free-fire zone you didn't have to wait a fatal second deciding if it was a farmer, a buffalo, or an armed enemy breaking through the brush to kill you. If it moved, you shot it.

As TV coverage of the war increased, the Army changed the name of free-fire zones to "safe zones."

One day while stripping ambush victims of trophies on what they'd taken to calling "kill and supply" operations, Hanson had remembered his Asian woods lore, the SKS rule. He fired a single shot to be certain that one of their ambush victims was dead, and Quinn felt a chubby hand pat his foot. He looked down at the flap of brain stuck to his boot, then thrust his foot out and studied it like the ugliest girl in Iowa coyly looking at her new party shoe. With a scholarly frown, he said, "Hmm, I wonder what he's thinking about right now."

"That's a nine-zero, nine-oh. At *least*. Very nice. Performance *and* degree of difficulty," Hanson said, laughing.

Quinn beamed.

While the Nungs set up a defensive perimeter, Hanson, Quinn, and sometimes Silver would go among the dead, rolling the bodies over, cursing some and praising others for their clothes and equipment.

An officer's pith helmet with an enameled red star was a fifty-dollar item. An officer's belt buckle, recycled aluminum from American napalm canisters, with an enameled red star, would go for seventy-five dollars. A buckle without the star was worth half that. They had to fill in with Montagnard crossbows, plain pith helmets and jungle hats, and the NVA "battle flags" that Co Ba and her daughter made back in camp with their Chinese-made Singer sewing machine.

There were occasional novelty items. Hanson once found a Red Chinese copy of a Scripto fountain pen on a dead lieutenant. It had the word SCRIPTO on the nib. The engraving on the side, Mr. Minh told him, urged the dead second lieutenant to STEADFASTLY ATTACK AND DESTROY ALL AMERICAN IMPERIALISTS.

Hanson studied the engraving and imagined the engraver working on the pen, worried that he would not have room to get the last word on the gift to the young officer from his parents, and thinking how wrong and terribly important even little things oftened seemed.

Cheaper items like plain pith helmets brought *much* more money if you shot a hole in them and sprinkled them with some chicken blood. But it wasn't wise to do that too often. Not that it mattered so much that the buyer might suspect that it wasn't human blood, an authentic result of a soldier having the back of his head blown open. When the buyer showed it off to his wife and friends back in the States, grim or swaggering as he recounted the moment that he blew the enemy's brains out, no one would know. It was simply a matter of economics. Too many of them on the market would lower the price.

Unlike Quinn, Hanson smiled a lot. When he was alone he often seemed to be debating things with himself, nodding his head, narrowing his eyes, smiling. At a glance his eyes seemed full of humor, and they were. They were calm eyes if you were to look his way carelessly. As calm as eighty feet of dead air in a dry well that you don't see until you are about to step into it, a depth of humor that went on and on and got darker and blacker. Most people looked quickly away if they happened to make eye contact with him.

Hanson was average height. He wasn't exceptionally strong, or fast with his hands, but he had adapted quickly and learned fast, as some animals do while others die out, in a world where there are people who will hurt you and kill you for no reason at all.

One night in Fayetteville a good ole boy had thrown Hanson into a jukebox. He had sixty pounds on Hanson and threw him *into* the jukebox. Hanson was wedged into the chrome, plastic, and shattered glass, and for just a moment he almost laughed, thinking that it was like having been in a traffic accident with Dolly Parton, that had silenced Dolly mid-song. Then he pulled himself out of the wreckage, stacks of C&W .45s clattering behind him, wheeling and wobbling away across the dance floor, and he started for the good ole boy, trailing shards of red and blue plastic like a special-effects nimbus.

The good ole boy lost the fight right then. Not when Hanson, head down, was pumping quick lefts and rights into his belly and kidneys, leftrightleft like a machine. Not when he hit the floor like a bag of sand. It wasn't even when Hanson started putting the boots to him. It was when he saw Hanson pry himself out of the jukebox, when he realized that the only way he could stop Hanson from kicking his ass was to kill him. It was then that his guts went flabby, and he just gave up and waited for it to happen and get over with.

The way Hanson walked, a cross between a bounce and a swagger, made him look cocky. He wasn't able to change the way he walked, and he discovered in basic training that he couldn't march.

His drill sergeant would scream, *"Hanson quit bouncin' an' march. You fuckin' up my military formation!"*

Then he'd come up close to Hanson, who continued to march and stare straight ahead, and ask in him a gentle, fatherly voice, "Don't you like me, Hanson? Is that it? Is that why you messin' up my military formation? Sergeant Collins told me that my formation looks ragged and poor. It hurts my feelings when he says that. Is that why, Hanson? Don't you *like* me?

"I asked you a question, Hanson. Do you like me?"

"Yes, Drill Sergeant. I'm very fond of you. I like everything about the army."

"You like me! You sure you don't love me? Is that it? You some kind of faggot tryin' to pass in this man's army? You want to smoke my pole?"

"No, Drill Sergeant."

"No?" the drill sergeant would scream, double-timing in place next to Hanson, his face close to his. *"No? I don't like you, Hanson. I don't like college boys. They so smart, they can't do anything. What can you do, Hanson?"*

Hanson smiled. "Push-ups, Drill Sergeant."

"That's right. That's exactly right. Get your ass out of my formation and drop for fifty an' I wanta hear you sound off like you got a pair."

Hanson would drop out of the formation and do fifty push-ups, sounding off like he had a pair with each one. "One thousand, two thousand, three thousand . . ."

If Hanson smiled when the drill sergeant screamed at him, he'd be accused of thinking it was funny to fuck up the formation, and be told to do fifty push-ups. If he tried not to bounce, he looked worse, and the drill sergeant would say that he looked like a monkey trying to fuck a football, or that he was marching like he had a Baby Ruth bar up his ass, and he'd have to do fifty push-ups.

For eight weeks he did at least two hundred push-ups a day. At the end of basic, he had powerful shoulders and he was the only man in the company who was given PFC stripes.

When he was getting on the bus for infantry training, the drill sergeant told him, "You do all right for a college boy. Don't go and get your ass blown away, Hanson."

Hanson smiled. "Okay, Drill Sergeant."

After infantry training, airborne training, and special forces school, he'd spent eighteen months in Northern I-Corps on long-range and cross-border recon missions without getting his ass blown away. He still smiled a lot, at things that didn't seem funny to most people. He was still alive. In two days he would be home.

Sergeant Major ignored the air policeman on guard duty at the hurricane fence. The AP's job was to demand that you produce ID, that you state your business and write it down in his log book before he motioned you through the gate with his M-16. He was supposed to challenge everyone who entered the air base, even people who worked there, people he knew, even generals. Especially generals, who would demote him and probably put him in the stockade for not challenging the shiny Cadillac with the red stars on the bumper.

The AP didn't know Sergeant Major, and he didn't challenge him. He looked away and pretended not to see him, like someone who has wandered into a tough neighborhood pretends not to notice the stares or hear the insults and just keeps walking, eyes straight ahead.

Sergeant Major was not really a sergeant major, E-9, anymore. He was an E-7. People called him Sergeant Major because that had been his rank before they busted him down to buck sergeant. The reason for his demotion was officially recorded as "conduct unbecoming to a senior NCO." The real reason was never recorded. A number of ranking Army officers had wanted to bust him out of the Army and put him in Leavenworth, but the CIA told them that a court martial would be embarrassing for everyone and not in the national interest. Sergeant Major agreed to accept the demotion quietly. It was a formality that cut his paycheck but not his power. His status as Sergeant Major was affected very little. He knew too much.

He had done two tours of Southeast Asia that were recorded in his Army 201 file. His other two Asian tours were not

recorded in any Army files. His 201 file showed that he had
been in Okinawa during those periods.

He had a slight Southern accent that was very pleasant,
and it reminded Hanson of Billy Graham, who had com-
manded him to go to the TV set when he was a kid, to pray and
be born again. And no one had ever heard Sergeant Major raise
his voice above the level of polite conversation, even in a
firefight. In combat he used hand signals to direct his Chinese
Nung bodyguards.

There was a knotted rope of scar around Sergeant Major's
ankles, as if he had worn leg irons for years on a chain gang. All
the old Southeast Asia hands had the ankle scars. They are
from the leeches.

The 3rd Mech supply sergeant responsible for most of
I-Corps had his headquarters inside the air base. He was in
charge of unloading the big cargo planes and routing the supplies they delivered to bases and warehouses all over the
northern part of the country. The officers and enlisted men
who worked with him stayed just one year, then were replaced
by others interested only in doing their year, avoiding problems, and going home.

The senior supply NCO was big and smart and ruthless.
His name was Kittridge. He had been in Da Nang for four years
in charge of supplies. A decade before he came to Vietnam,
Kittridge had been wounded and lost in Korea. He'd spent
three days alone, trying to find his way back to friendly lines in
the deceptive Korean terrain, using old and inaccurate maps.
He almost bled to death and he almost froze, losing pieces of
his toes to frostbite. During those three days he decided that, if
he survived, the Army would start paying him what it owed
him, what he deserved.

Each year's new batch of supply personnel knew only
what Kittridge wanted them to know. As long as they cooper-
ated with him, they had a pleasant year away from the fighting.
But if any of the officers began checking manifests too closely,
or asking too many questions, life became difficult for them;
their inventory began coming up short, their civilian labor
force began breaking or misrouting things, or not showing up

for work. As a result, they were not promoted, and they were sent home with bad efficiency reports.

Kittridge had highly placed Vietnamese friends who owed him favors. He had large bank accounts in several states back home, and another in Bermuda.

His office was an olive drab mobile home. Inside, it looked like one of those offices tucked way back on the two-acre lot of gleaming single-wides and wood grain and chrome double-wides, the office where you take the wife to close the deal. It was air-conditioned, carpeted, and richly furnished. The handsome walnut liquor cabinet had been manifested for a major general in 1966 but had been misrouted, along with the sectional sofa Kittridge had against one wall.

Kittridge had a pretty Vietnamese secretary. She was more than pretty—she was perfect. Like a doll. Kittridge had paid for the operation that had removed the Oriental eye folds so she would look more American, a "round eye." He had sent her to Japan to get the silicone injections in her breasts. She was wearing a miniskirt and spike heels that had been flown in from Los Angeles.

"Sergeant Major," Kittridge said with the warmth of any successful businessman, "welcome to my hootch. Come on in," he said as Sergeant Major walked through the door and across the wool carpet that had once been manifested for MACV headquarters.

"Wanted to stop by and settle our account," Sergeant Major said, "and see if the beer is ready to go. I'm leaving to go up north in the morning, and I won't get back down this way for a while."

Sergeant Major had ordered two pallets of beer for the launch site. Two pallets was roughly thirty times the amount authorized for the camp, but the beer had been "diverted from normal channels" and on one of the thousands of yellowing supply records the number "897" had been changed to "895." The two pallets of beer no longer existed.

"On the dock and loaded up," Kittridge said. "I got a pilot who's gonna make a 'detour' on his way to Quang Tri. Hell of a detour," he said with a laugh, "but I've got his flight time and fuel records covered."

"Real fine," Sergeant Major said. He pulled an envelope out of the fatigue pocket that had the master parachutist wings on it. "That was two-forty, American," he said, counting out the bills.

"I think we were looking at two seventy-five, Sergeant Major. Rerouting this stuff gets trickier every year."

"No, it was two-forty," he said without looking up, still counting out twenty-dollar bills. Kittridge noticed the scars on Sergeant Major's hands.

"Why don't we check the books?" Kittridge said. "Sugar . . ." he called to his secretary.

"I don't believe there's any need to check the books," Sergeant Major said. "We both know what the books will show."

"What is it you're trying to say?" Kittridge asked, his voice flat.

Sergeant Major laughed softly. "I'm not *trying* to say anything. The price we agreed on was two-forty."

The roar of cargo planes, helicopters, and Phantom jets surrounded the mobile home like rush-hour traffic on a freeway interchange in L.A.

"Sergeant *Major*. Thirty-five dollars. Thirty-five dollars. We've done a lot of business together. I wouldn't care one way or the other, but it's gonna throw my books off."

"It isn't much money, is it?" Sergeant Major said. He pushed a stack of money across the table. "Here's the two-forty, and," he said, counting off a smaller stack of bills, "here's the other thirty-five. Now, if I pay you what we *agree* is the fair and honest price, is that beer going to be at my camp tomorrow? I wouldn't want to have to come back down here to see you about it."

"It'll be there."

"Good." Sergeant Major smiled. He tapped the smaller stack of bills. "Now, if you think that this money belongs to you, just pick it up."

Sergeant Major's eyes seemed to be focused at some middle distance, as though he was mildly interested in something terrible that was about to happen at the far end of a city block.

Though his hands were scarred, there wasn't a mark on his face.

Kittridge had begun to reach for the money when he saw what Sergeant Major saw at the end of that block. His hand stopped and he pulled it back, very slowly, like he'd made a mistake and had reached into the wrong cage, the one where they keep the mean little animal with all the teeth.

"In any event," Sergeant Major continued, "I'll see you next time I'm in Da Nang, and we can take care of new business."

"Of course, Sergeant Major."

"Fine. Why, look at the money still here. It must be mine."

He picked the money up. "See you next time then. *Chao Co,*" he said to the secretary.

A man who's that worried about dying, Sergeant Major thought, should be smarter or in another line of work.

Besides being big, and smart, and ruthless like the supply sergeant, Sergeant Major had the reputation of being a little crazy. He didn't mind that at all. He even did things to keep the rumor alive, like the time he'd cut the liver out of an NVA captain he'd killed, cut it in five pieces, and shared it with his Nungs, eating it raw, the blood dripping down his chin.

"It's good to have people think you're crazy," he'd told Hanson. "Even if they've heard you *might* be crazy, that's enough. They're going to be afraid of you, because crazy people aren't predictable. It's dangerous to try to second-guess them. No matter how tough a man is, he'll usually step aside for a crazy person."

Hanson had grown to love Sergeant Major like a father. He'd learned from him how to stay alive in a place where people try every day to kill you. And Sergeant Major wasn't *really* crazy. Not as long as there was a war.

Back in the bar, there was a screech behind Hanson and Quinn, and they spun around, Hanson going for his shoulder holster.

Sergeant Siebert's monkey was drunk. He was strutting on top of Sergeant Siebert's table in the bar, his arms raised like a furry little acid rock singer, as if he were shouting, "Awright! Tha's right! Let's get it *on* now, *one time!*"

In one of his delicate monkey fists he clutched a french fried potato, in the other a rubbery red Penrose hot sausage. He was wearing diapers. It was a club rule that monkeys had to be diapered or they would not be admitted. The club had few rules, and they were all reasonable.

"Hey, Sergeant Siebert," Hanson asked. "How's the new monkey working out? We heard that the other one crashed and burned."

"Yeah, too bad. Furry little fucker just couldn't get the hang of maintaining altitude. Kept a glide angle of just about dead vertical all the way down."

Sergeant Siebert's other monkey had acquired the habit of masturbating whenever it got excited, whenever it got mad, or hungry, or frightened. All the time. Sergeant Siebert's "A" team wouldn't have minded an occasional hand job, but the monkey did it all the time. It was like having a pervert in camp.

The monkey would grab something solid with his left hand —a chair leg, or an engineer stake—and jerk against it like a strap hanger on a lurching bus, while he pounded away with the other hand, shrieking tirelessly. The "A" team built a wire cage where they could give him a chicken to fuck once a week, like some of the other camps, but he ignored the chicken, grabbed the wire, and began to rock and shriek. It was not considered manly for a Special Forces mascot monkey to jack off when he had chicken pussy available. It was considered even less manly to pull its pud out of fear, but the hiss and flutter of incoming mortar rounds always aroused him.

Sergeant Siebert had the monkey with him one day in a C-130 full of supplies for the camp. He was in the cargo plane's tail section with the supply bundles that were draped with huge blue-and-green cargo chutes. He was the "bundle kicker" and wore earphones so the pilot could tell him when they were close to the drop zone.

The four big engines were roaring as the plane went into a steep dive to avoid ground fire and then leveled off at four hundred feet to hit the small DZ. The slanted tail of the plane cracked, then slowly opened downward with hydraulic whines and groans, the opening filling with dark green jungle.

Sergeant Siebert kneeled at the shining caster tracks, watching the small red light, waiting for it to blink out and for the one next to it to flash green. He didn't see the monkey above him jerking wildly at a piece of nylon strapping, its little monkey eyes full of fear, looking out the wind-roaring open tail.

The light flashed green, the plane went into a steep climb, and Sergeant Siebert started the food pallets and rope-handled ammo crates rolling out, static lines snapping past where they caught, pulled taut, and snatched each chute open as the bundles fell.

Then, as he later phrased it in his Alabama accent, "It felt just like somebody had hawked him up a big goober and spit it on the backside of my neck."

Without missing a bundle, he had grabbed a handful of fur and sidearmed the convulsive monkey out the tail.

"Last I saw of him, the hairy little sumbitch was still whackin' it, getting smaller and smaller."

The new monkey was sitting on the table looking mournfully between his knees like a drunken little king, holding the french fry and sausage like scepters of his authority. He pitched forward, and the sausage skittered across the table.

"Goddamn," Sergeant Siebert said sadly. "An' this little dud can't hold his liquor."

He sat back in his chair and looked at his drink. "I think we're gonna have to have a team meeting back at camp and decide on a new kind of animal for mascot. Somethin' a little more stable."

Sergeant Major strode into the club. He was wearing what he called his fancy fatigues, the ones with all the patches. He wore them because headquarters regulations required that while in Da Nang, "all unit and award insignia *will* be properly displayed." Sergeant Major and the other old hands referred to the patches and wings, all the arrows and lightning bolts, daggers and stars, as "trash" because they all had them, and they weren't interested in impressing anybody in regular army units. Sergeant Major was uncomfortable wearing them because they attracted attention, and he had spent twenty years learning *not* to attract attention. At the launch site he wore camouflage fatigues without any insignia. All equipment at the launch site was "sterile"; it could not be officially traced back to the American military.

"Sergeant Major," Quinn called, "step on over and let young Sergeant Hanson buy you a drink. He's buyin' for all of us today."

"Well now, I'd be pleased. Special occasion and all."

They took their drinks to a table, and Sergeant Major said, "Ah, Trooper Hanson, you wouldn't listen. Giving up the military for a world of slack-jawed, out-of-step civilians who have absolutely no supervision or individual initiative. They're going to be everywhere, and they can't even decide to cross the street unless there's a light flashing on telling them to 'walk.' If it weren't for those lights they'd all die of starvation at intersections trying to make a decision."

He took a sip of Bushmills, looked at Hanson, and said, "And here I had plans to mold you in my own image."

Sergeant Major smiled his pleasant fatherly smile. Hanson and Quinn were his best recon team leaders. When he'd first seen them together at the launch site, he'd thought it would work out that way. He could usually tell. He'd processed enough of them through, and done enough paperwork on the dead ones. He could usually tell now.

Quinn was tough, good and mean, but he'd never have been more than just competent on recon if Sergeant Major hadn't put him with Hanson. Some of Hanson's craziness rubbed off on Quinn, and that was what had made the team so good.

More often than not, Sergeant Major thought, the crazy ones lived through it, even though they took chances that made you think they were trying to get killed. But aggression served them better than caution could. The crazy ones like Hanson killed a lot of Communists, and brought back a lot of good intel. And they were always the ones who knew, just as well as Sergeant Major did, that none of it mattered at all.

It was early the next morning, and the heavy web gear over Quinn's left shoulder swung up, then back as he walked. He carried the Swedish "K" submachine gun in his right hand, the fat silencer on it a dull black. He was wearing his camouflage fatigues and a floppy brown jungle hat he had taken from a dead NVA. They were better than the American-issue hats; they had a plastic insert that kept the rain out. But they were dangerous to wear if gunships were working the area. From the air you looked like the enemy.

Hanson looked like a child next to him in jeans and a green T-shirt. He was singing softly, trying to sound like Dylan. " 'John *Wesley* Hardin' was a friend to the poor, well he ta-raveled with a gun in everee hand . . .' "

Charlie McCoy, Hanson thought. Silver was right. That's who plays bass on that.

But the PFC radio repairman didn't notice Quinn and Hanson approaching. He was watching his baby ducks. He'd bought them from a woman in Da Nang City, paying her twenty times what they were worth, smiling and repeating, "Thank you mama-san." She'd smiled back with her black teeth, hating him for a stupid rich American, and that smile had made the PFC happy for the rest of the day.

He didn't know he'd been cheated, but it wouldn't have mattered if he had known. He was accustomed to being fucked over. He was big, pudgy, and awkward; very pale, and his stiff black hair grew out in tufts, as if his head had been burn-scarred. At a glance there seemed to be something "wrong" about him, the kind of soft, frightened, oversize boy who always wore a slide rule on his belt in high school, and who had no friends.

The five yellow ducklings were swimming in the rubber dishpan he'd bought at the PX.

"The only part *I* like," Quinn slapped the "K" into his left hand, crouched like a bowler as he swept a duckling from the water and rose gracefully without breaking stride, "is the head."

He bit down, pulled with a twist—the delicate grinding crack like a precision machine under an enormous overload—and the body came away. He threw it carelessly over his shoulder, and the fuzzy wings twitched madly as though the ruined bloody little bird refused to believe that it was dead.

The PFC had the same bewildered look that they always have in the newspaper photo with the headline, MASS KILLER SURRENDERS: FORMER TEACHER SAYS HE WAS BRILLIANT STUDENT.

Hanson listened to the erratic little brush and thump of the headless bird behind them as they walked casually on.

When they were out of sight of the PFC's hootch, Hanson said, "The timing. The *pathos* of it. I think we have a nine-five, maybe a nine-seven here . . . as soon as you *swallow* it."

Quinn spit the wide-eyed yellow head out and laughed. "You'll be back. You won't get along with those people, my man. They have no appreciation for that kind of talent."

"Though it's true," Hanson said, "that a nicely structured two or three seconds like that is the sort of thing you can hang your day on over here, I've still got a chopper to catch."

He turned and started to walk away, then spun and grabbed Quinn by the sleeves of his fatigues and began to shake him the way you'd shake a child you were angry with. Quinn's web gear rattled, grenades clacking against each other like pool balls.

"Watch your *ass*," Hanson said, "you and Silver. Don't get yourselves blown away while I'm *gone.*"

Quinn laughed. "No sweat, my man. I plan to skate till you get back. Have a nice airplane ride, sport."

Quinn turned and walked back toward the Special Forces compound.

Hanson walked down to the wide white beach. It was dawn. The black hills across the bay were going to turn green soon. Gray waves began to flush pink and gold, rising endlessly and patiently, crashing back into the surf.

Hanson heard a faint steady drumming, then spotted a black dot over the mouth of the bay. The perimeter gunship.

The door gunner in the perimeter ship was bored. His job was like sitting in a windy open wall locker a thousand feet in the air. The fat Huey helicopter had been circling the huge military complex for four hours. For four hours he had been watching the deserted, dark beach. The door gunner wore a helmet with a tinted bubble face shield that covered everything but his mouth, and a thick ceramic flak vest over his chest and shoulders. He looked like a giant insect. The dead weight of the vest pulled and jerked on its shoulder straps each time the Huey banked around the perimeter.

In front of the door gunner the M-60 machine gun hung barrel down, rocking slightly like an oar in an oarlock. The belted bullets draped down from the gun, folding into a box at the gunner's foot.

He leaned out, into his seat harness, and looked down the beach. There was a single speck moving across the white sand. The door gunner pushed down the chrome nubbin in a black plastic handle and spoke to the pilot through his helmet mike. "Hey, sir. Let's put her down on the deck. Wake that stud on the beach up."

The pilot was bored too. He was a Cobra gunship pilot who had come back to Vietnam for a second tour. They had assigned him to the perimeter ship until his orders for a Cobra unit came through. The Cobra is a fast attack helicopter; flying a Cobra is like driving a Corvette. The fat Huey was like a delivery van.

The paddlelike rotor blades that held the Huey in the air tilted alternately up and down as they spun, stabilizing the helicopter. When the pilot changes the angle of the blades, it is called pulling pitch and causes the chopper to go up or down.

The Huey was a flying chunk of plastic and alloy steel held in the air by the balance and counterbalance of turbine and rotor blades, a bunch of moving parts all working against each other, like a chicken trying to fly. It is almost impossible for a Huey to maintain an exact altitude when it is moving forward.

The pilot pulled pitch, hard, and the Huey dropped like dead weight. He eased back and held it four feet above the sand, bringing his speed to eighty-five knots. He smiled. He could feel it all: the flutter of the rotors, the staggered interacting gears, and the shriek of the jet turbine.

The pilot was flying too fast and too low. He knew that. He hadn't felt so good since his last Cobra mission.

His right earlobe was ragged, as though it had been eaten

away by some disease. It had been torn away on his last Cobra mission by a 7.62 round that had smashed through the canopy of the Cobra, meeting him as he dove directly at the RPD machine gun. The pilot had killed twelve people in less than a minute that day.

He was holding the Huey at four feet by instinct, by feel. It was almost as though he were not involved, that he was watching himself fly. He knew that if he even began to think about making a mistake, interfering with his instincts, the Huey would twitch, dig a skid in the sand, and go into flaming cartwheels.

Hanson watched the Huey grow, slowly at first, then faster. The larger it was, the faster it grew until it was all he could see. It hung there in front of him, the skids at shoulder height, the rotors driving empty air into wedges of sound, jet turbine screaming like pure white light.

He looked up and met the pilot's eyes. The pilot nodded and smiled. But the Huey was moving at almost a hundred miles an hour.

The Huey was moving, and then a huge insect was looking at Hanson. It smiled beneath its dark bubble eye and held human fingers in a peace sign.

The Huey was half a mile down the beach and getting smaller.

The ocean was a deep blue now. Hanson watched an aircraft carrier and two destroyers out on the horizon slowly altering their positions. It was as though they were trying to spell something out to him in sign language.

Freedom Bird

The padded seat tipped back and pulled him down into it. A shudder ran through the 707, Hanson's arms lifted slightly from the armrests, and all the GIs cheered as it rose from the runway at Tan Son Nhut. Hanson looked up at the ventilation nozzle hissing air like a tiny ball-turret gun. In a seat near the rear of the plane, one GI was wearing handcuffs and crying softly.

Later, Hanson got out his *Collected Works of W. B. Yeats*. It was warped to the shape of his leg. It was mildewed, sweat-stained and bloodstained, even though he had kept it in a plastic bag. He turned to "Cuchulain's Fight with the Sea," and skipped to the ending where the warrior-king Cuchulain kills his own son, having been at the wars so long that he does not know him. Afterward the Druids chanted while he slept, making him believe that the sea was his enemy:

> Cuchulain stirred,
> Stared on the horses of the sea, and heard
> The cars of battle and his own name cried;
> And fought with the invulnerable tide.

Hanson always pictured him cursing and slashing with his sword tirelessly at wave after wave as they rolled in at him. He looked out the dark porthole window at the huge wing of the plane, outlined by the blue-yellow glow of the jet pods.

So, he thought. Well.

The Tokarev was in the carry-on bag between his feet, a heavy Russian automatic the size of an Army .45. A red star was set in the center of the black plastic grips. Much of the bluing had been worn down to bare metal by the stiff military holster, and there was some rust-pitting on the side, but it had been well cared for over the years.

The pistol had a yellow tag attached to the trigger guard with a metal seal, authorizing him to take it on the plane. Like everyone, Hanson's luggage had been searched, and he had been frisked before boarding the plane. The search was for narcotics and weapons, explosives and ammunition. An MP had glanced at the Tokarev, then stared Hanson in the eyes and barked, "You got any rounds for this weapon, troop?"

Hanson blinked. He leaned slightly forward and said, "Pardon me?" It had been a long time since anyone had spoken to him that way.

"That's right. If you're carryin' any rounds for that weapon, you're in big trouble. You got it now?"

Hanson watched the delicate machinery of tendons and cartilage, like tiny ribs, working the MP's throat as he talked, the vocal cords throbbing like a heartbeat. It would crush in his grip like a sparrow. He smiled and said, "I'm going home. I don't want any trouble."

The MP gave him one last hard look, then said, "Okay, troop," and jerked his thumb toward the door.

Outside, Hanson said to himself, "Big trouble." He smiled and said it again, changing the inflection. *"Big* trouble. Big *trouble."* Halfway across the tarmac he was laughing. "Got some *big trouble* here at the boarding gate," he said as he walked to the end of the line to board the plane, still laughing.

The PFC in front of him turned around and said, "Yeah, Sarge. I feel the same way. Gettin' on that freedom bird."

"Yeah," Hanson said. "Let's go home."

Hanson reached up and turned off the reading light. He put the book away, careful not to disturb the corporal asleep in the seat next to him. He leaned back and closed his eyes.

The NVA captain had been propped in a sitting position against a bamboo grove, badly wounded in the legs. His men were gone. The hatchet team Hanson was with had been after them all morning. But the captain had led his men well; the hatchet team had taken casualties.

It had been a nice morning, not so hot. A slight breeze made the bamboo grove clatter softly. The brown stalks were the size of a man's leg; the smaller stalks were green.

The captain got off one shot with the Tokarev. It blew Hanson's canteen up, snatching him to one side as if someone had pulled at his pistol belt. For a moment Hanson thought that he'd been hit, that the canteen water was blood.

He met the captain's eyes and saw no fear in them.

He put two six-round bursts into the captain's chest.

Then he stripped the body of its pistol belt and picked up the Tokarev. The body had a letter in its shirt pocket, and a picture of a woman and child, wrapped in a plastic bag. Hanson put the letter and photograph back in the shirt, wrapping it well because the shirt was soaking through with blood.

He looked at the body and said, "Well . . ." but there really wasn't anything to say. It was the best ones who died, he thought.

Hanson reached down into the carry-on bag between his feet and popped the clip out of the pistol. He slipped past the corporal and walked down the narrow aisle past the rows of sleeping GIs, some of them softly spotlighted by reading lights, their cheeks and eyes hollow. The plane hit a pocket of turbulence, and all the green-clad GIs leaned to one side, rose slightly, then sank back down into their seats as one.

When he reached the tail of the plane, a pretty blond stewardess wearing a blue cap looked up. He smiled at her, and she looked back down at the paperback book she was reading.

Inside the lurching little bathroom—glaring light and stainless steel—he loosened his web belt and unbuttoned his trousers. There was a wide strip of white adhesive tape across the inside of his thigh. He slowly pulled the tape away and the bright bottlenecked bullets dropped, one by one, into his other hand. He threw the tape away, buttoned his pants, and pulled the Tokarev clip from his pocket. Each round made a solid *click* as he thumbed it into the clip. He loaded the rounds the way a man might deposit dimes in a pay phone.

Back in his seat, he slid the loaded clip into the butt of the pistol and stuck the pistol between the armrest and the side of the plane. For eighteen months not a minute had passed when he did not have a weapon in his hand or within easy reach.

Outside the porthole the silver and black wing shuddered slightly. The muffled jets sounded like a waterfall.

Well, Hanson thought. He smiled slightly, then had to squint to keep his eyes from watering. He leaned his head against the roaring skin of the plane and was asleep in seconds. He dreamed about the skull.

It had been a year and a half since Hanson had reported for duty at CCN. The gate into the compound was a narrow path cutting through the wire: triple-strand and engineer stakes, coils of concertina piled shoulder-high and head-high, two-layered webs of tanglefoot with trip flares hanging in it like beer cans littering the ground cover along a highway. Triple-strand, concertina, tanglefoot all the way in like jagged steel hedges.

Claymore antipersonnel mines perched on little folding legs, facing the gate—almost jolly-looking, like fat little Keep Off the Grass signs. But the words stamped across their faces were FRONT TOWARD ENEMY.

There was no grass in the wire. It had been burned away with mo-gas so often that the fired red clay smelled like over-heated machinery.

Two sandbagged towers inside the compound could rake away the gate and sweep the entire perimeter with interlocking heavy machine gun fire.

But it would not be the wire, or the claymores, or the gun towers that Hanson would remember about that day; they became familiar and comforting, as welcome as the outskirts of the old neighborhood after an exhausting trip to a vicious city.

Hanson would remember the skull.

There was nothing crude or clumsy about the skull; it had been skillfully cut out of plywood and painted: a huge grinning death's-head wearing a green beret. Taller than a man, it looked down from a heavy cross-timber above the entrance to the compound. It was the black-socket eyes that had stopped Hanson; the way they pulled wryly down toward the jagged nose hole. The skull seemed amused at itself. Below the skull,

painted in large block letters, were the words, WE KILL FOR
PEACE. Sometimes at dusk, when the light was right, the skull
seemed to be screaming.

The plane landed at Fort Ord and they were all processed
through the replacement center in a matter of hours. The
planeload of GIs stripped out of their jungle fatigues and ex-
changed them for baggy dress uniforms in a windowless concrete building. On the other side of a low wall, another planeload of soldiers was reversing the process, leaving their dress
uniforms in a pile and putting on stiff new fatigues for their
flight to Vietnam. Hanson imagined the two groups lining up
on the runway according to size and simply trading uniforms.

The wall was high enough that neither group could see or
talk to the other. A skinny kid on Hanson's side jumped up,
grabbed the top of the wall, and began shouting to the soldiers
dressing for Vietnam, "You'll be sor-ree. You'll be sor-*reee*.

"You'll be sorreeeee . . ."

Hanson left his fatigues and jungle boots in a pile, took a
cab to the airport, and caught the first plane headed east.

The FASTEN SEATBELT sign blinked on above Hanson's head as
his plane lost altitude over Illinois, but he didn't notice. He was
thinking about Barker, the time he'd bought a bicycle in Da
Nang and brought it back on the mail chopper, remembering
the way he rode it around the outer perimeter road, doing
tricks that got the Montagnards to line the road and laugh at
him.

"Sir."

Hanson looked up to see the stewardess standing over
him, her face tight with anger. The plane was empty.

"Sorry," he said, smiling, picked up his bag and walked
toward the front of the plane.

They'd found Barker at dawn after a sapper squad had probed
the camp. He was draped over the big four-deuce mortar tube,
never having gotten his first round off. The NVA sappers were

good. They'd had all the mortar pits bracketed before they came through the wire.

An RPG rocket had hit Barker in the back of the head. There wasn't much blood. The explosion had cauterized most of the veins and arteries. There was nothing left of his head except the lower jaw hanging from his neck like a huge, ragged lip. When they carried him to the teamhouse to zip him up into the talcum-and-rubber-smelling body bag, the jaw flopped as if he were trying to say something.

He hadn't thought about Barker since the morning they found him. It was better not to remember dead friends. He was glad he wouldn't have to worry about seeing Silver and Quinn die.

The sheet-metal exit tunnel, curving from the plane to the boarding gate, rocked and shivered beneath Hanson's jump boots. It was painted a stark white, with fleshy plastic accordion pleats where its sections were joined. He was alone in the tunnel, and the wind moaned down its length. He smelled hot machinery. The tunnel had begun to close in on itself. He could feel the shudder through the soles of his boots, and he fought the urge to run.

The boarding gate was still under construction and he had to go outside and walk to the main terminal. It was foggy, and the air smelled of mo-gas and hot metal. Beyond the far runway, refinery burnoff tubes flared dirty yellow in the dark sky. Hanson thought he could hear a faint roar each time the flame pulsed. White smoke boiled under hundreds of floodlights.

A red fan of light swept through the fog like a rotor blade. Hanson could hear it hiss each time it passed over him, and he couldn't keep from ducking his head.

He hurried toward the terminal. Over the entrance a banner announced, WELCOME HOME GIs—CHICAGO IS PROUD OF YOU!

The first thing he saw after pushing through the glass doors was a car. A gleaming metallic blue Ford LTD. It turned slowly around with a mechanical groan. The headlights and bumpers winked, windows flashed as they turned through blue spotlight beams. Glossy color posters showed elegant men and women gazing at each other across the hoods of automobiles. Muzak droned from hidden speakers.

He turned and began to walk down the concourse, following the arrows. It smelled of sweat, perfume, and cigarette urns. He passed men in suits carrying briefcases, angry-looking women in tailored dresses, bracelets, and bright lipstick, exhaling smoke, security guards with pistols on their hips and black men pushing brooms and shining shoes. He felt that they were staring at him, but they glanced quickly away if he looked back at them.

Gift shops, snack shops, Hertz, bars, all cut into the side of the corridor like bunkers. Arrow-shaped signs saying R-11 or GIFTSBOOKS, posters of beautiful women smoking cigarettes or running along white beaches. A loudspeaker boomed, asking someone to "report to the Eastern ticket counter *please.*" He passed a door that had a bull's-eye painted on it with the silhouette of a man spread-eagled in its center like a target.

Hanson felt like an immigrant or a refugee in his baggy uniform. Everyone he saw looked healthy and rich, but no one smiled. The last time he'd seen anyone laugh had been back at Fort Ord.

He saw a young soldier and could tell by the insignia on his uniform that he was on his way to Vietnam. He stepped into one of the little bars to avoid him. The bartender was Hanson's age. He was wearing a loose-fitting silk shirt and a gold link necklace. When Hanson ordered a Scotch and water, the bartender frowned at him and said, "Eye dee."

"What?"

"ID. I've gotta see some ID."

"Oh. Right. ID. You have to know who I am."

The bartender didn't change expression.

Hanson handed him his Army ID card. The bartender looked at it, laid it on the bar like it was something that smelled bad, and walked away.

Hanson looked at the photo on the card. It had been taken three years before, in basic training. It looked like a mug shot of a criminal. The person in the photo had a shaved head and was staring dully somewhere beyond the camera.

The bartender set a drink in front of Hanson and said,

"One fifty." Hanson laid some bills on the bar. The bartender took two and walked away as Hanson sipped his drink and thought about what had happened in the past three years. He was thinking about the skull when the young soldier walked in.

"Okay if I sit down, Sarge?"

He was infantry, eleven-bravo, grunt, sixteen weeks of training. The kind of kid who gets killed in the first two months, before he learns what to be afraid of, what to look out for, before he understands that there are people out there who are *really* trying to kill him. It would probably happen in the first or second operation. In the regular infantry units they don't worry about new guys. The troops who have survived a few months look out for themselves and their buddies.

"Sure," Hanson said.

"I don't want to bother you . . ."

"Sit on down."

The kid set a thick manila folder on the bar. His 201 file, a record of his life for the past sixteen weeks, medical history, uniforms and insignia issued, inoculations, pay vouchers, unit clearance forms, next-of-kin insurance forms, rifle qualification, Geneva Convention training certificate, and, right on top, his travel orders for Military Assistance Command Vietnam—MACV. He was going to the Third Mech.

Hanson looked at him in the dim light, and he saw the basic Army-issue dead eighteen-year-old. When Hanson looked at him, he saw him as he would look when he was dead. They all looked alike when they were dead.

"Look," Hanson said, "I've got to catch a plane, but let me give you some quick, free advice."

"Sure, Sarge," he said, trusting Hanson because of the green beret and the ribbons on his uniform.

"Okay. When you get to your unit you look around for someone who's been there six or eight months. Do what he does. The reason he's still alive is because he knows what he's doing. Try and stay in the middle of the column on operations. The middle is good. And don't be afraid of being scared. People start shooting, you get down on the *ground*, okay? Give yourself a chance to figure things out. You make the first two months alive, and you've got it made."

Hanson stood up and said, "Don't sweat it, you'll be okay. I can tell." He pushed the bills lying on the bar over in front of the kid. "Buy you a drink. When you get back a year from now you can buy somebody else one. Take care now."

As he walked out of the bar, the kid said, "Thanks a lot, Sarge."

"Thanks a lot, Sarge," Hanson muttered to himself as he walked quickly away. "Thanks a lot for lying to me, for not telling me that I'll be dead in six weeks. Thanks for the *drink*, Sarge."

As he walked toward his boarding gate, he passed a huge bank of TV screens set into the wall. They were all turned to different channels, mostly game shows and soap operas. The sound was off, and the whole wall flickered and blinked like a monstrous computer screen as the camera angles jumped and cut from scene to scene. On the game shows people were laughing and jumping up and down, hugging TV sets and ovens, people dressed like clowns and vegetables.

A little boy walked up to Hanson, watching him hard. "Were you in the war?" he demanded.

"Yes, sir, young man."

"How many people did you kill, then?"

"I don't know. It's hard to tell. Sometimes you shoot at them and they shoot at you, and you can't tell if you killed anyone or not."

The boy was disappointed. He looked at Hanson for a moment, then said, "Well, was it a lot?"

"Yeah, I guess it was."

The little boy grinned savagely. "I knew it was a lot," he said.

"Matthew," a thin, angry woman called from down the concourse, "come here right now."

The little boy ran to her, and she took his hand, glaring at Hanson. She walked on down the passageway, and the little boy twisted away from her like a demon and grinned back at Hanson.

One screen on the bank of TVs stood out like a blind eye. It was black and white, and it kept showing the time, temperature, humidity, and wind speed, one fact indifferently replacing the next.

It was raining when Hanson's plane began to taxi down the runway. The tiny raindrops pulled themselves across the round window, lurching sideways toward the tail. The domes and spires of the refinery gleamed under thousands of floodlights. They floated in the boiling white smoke and bursts of yellow flame. It looked like a city in the act of destroying itself. Hanson couldn't hear any explosions. He wondered what it would be like if he were deaf. But you can *feel* the explosions that come close enough to hurt you.

The brakes squealed as the plane stopped. It sat back and shuddered as the engines began to rev. Hanson touched the window lightly with the back of his hand and felt the pitch of the engines.

They began to move. A black and white sign flashed past that said K-4 RUD CLOSED. Then the blue runway lights were snapping past like bursts of memory or foreknowledge of events you can't prevent, and the plane was in the clouds.

It was black outside the window, and Hanson watched the raindrops drag themselves across the glass. He wondered if it was the jet exhaust or the wind speed that made them act that way.

The pilot announced that it was seventy-two degrees below zero outside the plane.

In the seat behind him a child began to cry. A woman's voice said, "Jason, if you don't stop that I'm really going to give it to you when we get home."

He kept crying.

Hanson couldn't remember ever seeing any children cry in Vietnam, not even the ones who were wounded, who had flies crawling on their wounds and faces. He tried to think of at least one, but he couldn't.

As he thought back, recalling face after face, he met the same listless stare each time. Not that they seemed to blame him for whatever had happened to them, but they expected him to *do* something. Most of the time all he could do was wait for the medivac and watch them die.

The Bluffs

Hanson was running the bluffs. Sixty feet below him the surf bore in on the cliffside, booming into the gray rock. Past the breakers and beyond the kelp beds, the sea folded into the horizon. The land rose slowly on his right. Tall blond grass covered the hill, curling away from the sea, up into the shadows of gnarled evergreen windbreaks. He ran the winding lip of the bluffs at a steady pace, relaxed, head slightly back. He ran toward the pain. It came dully at first, in his calves and chest, swelling until it pumped through his blood, until it filled him. He smiled, his eyes the color of the ocean, and began chanting softly:

> Here we go
> all the way
> Airborne.
>
> All the way
> Airborne, hunh!
>
> I can run . . . Airborne
> I can jump . . . Airborne
> I can kill . . . Airborne.
>
> Hunh! I can kill,
> Airborne.

"I can kill . . . Airborne, Airborne, Airborne," until the pain began to fail and fall away. It came at him like ragged gusts at the edge of a powerful wind, and then he was through pain into the pure violence that breaks just beyond. It was raw oxygen and adrenaline and he could run forever. The wind was at his back now. The wind cupped around him, took him in.

"Airborne Ranger, Green Beret . . . Make my money blowin' gooks away, hunh, here we go, all the way . . ." When the whole team ran together they slowly increased their speed, almost sprinting the last lap around the perimeter of the launch site. Montagnard team members watched them, laughing at the Americans for running in the heat.

"Come on, ladies," Quinn roared. "Pick up the step. Charles is gonna have your ass for sure, you that slow. That fish-breath little rice burner gonna be runnin' behind you with his hand in your panties."

Dawson, out of breath and laughing at Quinn's accent, shouted, "Quinn, quit playing nigger drill sergeant and slide your paddy ass back in formation. You fuckin' up my timing. Don't nobody talk that way. Maybe they talk that way in some weird place, in Australia or some shit."

No one got out of step, and the pace kept getting faster, the left jump boot slamming down harder than the right to keep time, pounding out the rhythm of the team in tight formation.

"I'll double-time down Tu Do Street . . . Kill more Cong than I can eat . . . Ha! Here we go, all the way . . ." Running with the team was being one of the bricks in a flying wall that could crush anything that opposed it, miles of slamming that left jump boot down, running beyond endurance: not through thinking, but through the assurance—held so long and confirmed with each thud and push of that high-topped, spit-shined paratrooper boot that it was never even put into words, certainly never questioned—that none of them would ever die.

Silver yelled back over his shoulder, out of breath, his wire-rim glasses flashing in the sun. "Quinn. Probably some people talk that way. In California. Whole neighborhoods, probably. They got everything in California. They got everything there that you don't want."

Hanson eased his pace, watching one of the small hawks that hover against the offshore winds of Mendocino, California. The hawk's wings and splayed tail feathers quivered as it held like a kite on a string, searching for movement in the sea grass. As Hanson slowed to a walk, the wedge-shaped bird tipped one wing, tucked its talons, took the wind and was gone.

Hanson walked halfway up the hill and lay down in the waist-high grass. He tore a piece from one of the broad blades and put it in his mouth. It tasted of sea salt. He bit into it and the saltiness gave way to bitter juice. Hanson thought of the two tastes as a fragile sandy brown suddenly masked by a thick wipe of dark green.

He cut his eyes sideways. Something was moving toward him through the grass, not a field mouse or thrush, something much bigger than that. The grass dipped and popped back up.

A badger pulled himself out of the grass, his head weaving strangely from side to side, and started across the little clearing that Hanson had beaten down. He staggered into Hanson's foot, then lurched on out of the clearing.

Hanson rose slowly. Something was wrong with this animal—thirty pounds of muscle, teeth, and claws that even bears go out of their way to avoid. He had read about a species of badger that was the only animal, except man, known to kill for no apparent reason. Not for food, nor defense, but out of some sort of anger or simple, ruthless joy. "He is a puzzle to scientists," the article had said. Hanson smiled, recalling the phrase, and followed behind the badger as it floundered on through the grass. Clusters of swollen ticks hung like dusty grapes from the badger's jaw and throat.

Weak from loss of blood and the toxin that ticks produce to keep the blood flowing, the badger looked up at Hanson and hissed. All his teeth were fangs. An animal with teeth like that, Hanson thought, has no fear, no mercy, and no regret.

Hanson took off his shirt and wrapped it around his left hand. He held the groggy badger down with that hand and began pulling the ticks off with his right, carefully working them loose so as not to leave the heads in the badger. One by one he pulled them out of the coarse brown fur, their tiny black heads and pincers flailing blindly, and squeezed them between his thumb and forefinger, slowly, until they popped. When he'd removed them all his hand was sticky with black blood, pale shards of burst bodies, and, scattered across the back of his hand like seeds from crushed berries, the black flesh-boring heads of ticks, still alive though ruined, groping for purchase on the freckled skin.

The cabin was chilly and damp. She was in the bedroom reading. Though it was getting dark, she still wore the gray-tinted wire-rim glasses. She had a handsome, wide-featured face and was wearing a long cotton dress and a hand-knit shawl. Everything about her—the tasteful, expensive clothes, her calm brown eyes shaded by the gray glasses, her slow, calm voice and easy logic, reflected a life in which there had always been enough money, and time, and room to move away from anything unpleasant. She had spent the previous summer in Taos, New Mexico, where an aura balancer had read her tarot. "You will always have young lovers," the woman had told her. She had picked Hanson up in a bar the month before, and he'd been living with her since then.

The money he'd saved in 'Nam was gone. He'd drunk it up, given it away, spent it on airplane tickets and rental cars. The cabin had been good at first. He'd been glad to be away from the cities where there was too much noise, too many people who didn't pay attention, who talked too much and got in his way. In the cities he'd provoked fights with strangers whose faces he couldn't recall, for reasons he didn't remember, and found himself sobering up on a bus or plane, trying to remember what he'd done. He would finger the cuts on his cheek, or suck his skinned knuckles, and try to remember, sore and hung over. When it did come back to him, he'd try to forget again, glad to be clear and not in jail. Two assault charges, one in Denver and the other in Palo Alto, were gathering dust in the inactive files of the two police departments, the "Suspect Information" boxes empty except for the words "Male Cauc, 5'10", 150#, med brn hair, dk jacket, blu jeans." Another box on the forms asked, Weapon/force used, and was filled in, "Hands/to hit. Feet/to kick."

It had been better since the cabin. He'd begun to watch himself, watch for the signs, and avoid people when he felt it coming on. But the winter rains were beginning; things seemed to be closing in. The omens were unfavorable.

Hanson scooped the ashes out of the Franklin stove and swept it clean of soot. He stuffed newspapers under the grate, then carefully laid Xs of small kindling, crossed and interlocked sticks of larger kindling over that, balanced two wedges of dry fir on top, and touched it off.

The paper flared, burning away a full-page ad for power mowers; the kindling caught, and in a minute the big chunks of fir were flaming. The logical progression of fire always pleased him. A slow, controlled explosion.

Then she was in the room talking about her weekend—another encounter group "mini-marathon": two days without sleep in a geodesic dome back up in the redwoods, with twenty other people and "Jonathan," the group leader. That summer in Taos, when she found the aura balancer, she had stopped taking LSD.

"God," she said, "it was fantastic. Really. Something *very* real happened this time. Spaces opened. You could feel the *spaces* open."

She laughed, took a drag on her cigarette, and flung her arms wide, her shawl swirling gracefully.

"I was surrounded by people attacking me because they cared about me—as *me.* Then that space opened and it was full of support, sharing with them, getting in touch with ourselves and our feelings. Like . . . even if I don't like someone, that's fine because it opens things up for honesty."

She was smoking furiously.

"There I was the first afternoon with everyone watching, and Jonathan asks me, 'What do you feel?'

"And I thought, and said, 'Nothing. I feel nothing . . . I don't *trust* what I feel.' And Jonathan just smiled—he has a wonderful smile—and he said, 'We hear what you're saying, and that's how we begin to really feel, by admitting that we feel nothing.'"

As he turned to go into the kitchen, Hanson said, "Jonathan wants to *feel* something in your panties."

He walked through the kitchen door, and a cluster of roaches broke like a lacquered sunburst, fanning out as they ran for safety behind the sink.

"Nice maneuver, roaches," Hanson said, speaking to the dark space between the sink and the wall. "Precise and coordinated. I'll give you that."

He didn't like the roaches, but he felt that since they had been there before he'd moved into the cabin, they had as much right to stay as he did. He went out of his way not to step on them, and refused to let her put out poison for them. "Can you imagine what it must feel like," he had told her, "to swallow that shit, and then have to crawl off and wait for it to eat your guts out? How could you sleep knowing they're in agony all over the house, dying all around you in the dark. *Listening* to them die."

Hanson did like the snails that had invaded the cabin when the winter rains began. He kept track of their slow, sure movements across the windows and redwood walls. When they found their spot, they would seal off the edges of their shells. Scattered about the walls, they looked like little knots of muscle pulling the house tight. Even in the heaviest rain the cottage no longer leaked as it had before they came. Their shells were all slightly different—striated earth colors, creams and browns—and very delicate. She had wanted to put them back outside, but even if she was careful, trying to slide them loose gently, once they had sealed off, the shells cracked and they died. Hanson had told her to leave them alone. Things had been better for him since the cabin, and the snails held the cabin together.

Hanson glanced in to see how the fire was doing, and smiled.

"Really real, really real, oh really really really really *ree*-al," he sang, shuffling from foot to foot, flopping his head like a puppet. He turned and, looking through the empty doorway into the kitchen, smiled more broadly, nodded his head, and said in a hearty voice, "Hi, I'm Hanson. Is your encounter card filled? No? You know, there's these *feelings* I have, that I've been, well, keeping bottled up. You see, I did these *things*. . . . Could I, you know, *share* them with you? Really? That's very supportive of you."

He looked in the cupboard where he kept his wineglass, but it wasn't there. His wine-drinking glass was a tall, thin jelly jar with fluted sides and a flaw running from lip to base like a transparent scar. He looked in the sink and through the other cupboards.

"Where's my glass?"

Reaching farther back in the cupboard, he knocked a dime-store coffee mug off its hook with his elbow. The heavy white mug dropped harmlessly to the shelf.

"Goddamn!" he shouted, snatching the mug up, and pitching it over his shoulder. White dust and slivers of glass exploded from the far wall.

"Where's my fucking glass?"

He burst through the bedroom door as if an enemy were waiting for him. She was lying on the bed reading an orange paperback titled *ATLANTIS: The Third Eye?* in block letters on both covers.

"You really are childish sometimes," she said, not looking up from the book.

He slapped the book out of her hands and it flapped across the room into the wall. "That's right. I'm one childish son of a bitch." He spun and drove his fist through the cheap hollow-core door, gashing his hand. He slowly turned back to her, sucking on his fist. He smiled at her, his teeth pink with blood, and asked in a pleasant voice, "Well now, that was even more childish, wasn't it?"

Then his voice hardened. "Wasn't it?" he asked her. "Isn't that right?"

He grabbed her by the shoulders and shook her. "Right? Say it. Right! You goddamn well better say it. Say it now!"

She said the word "right," and he let go of her.

"Right," he said. "That's right. Absolutely. Right! Aren't you pleased that we were able to clear that up?

"And you don't know any*thing!* Nothing!" he yelled, splintering the door again, then again, "Nothing!"

He stepped back from the ruined door, out of breath, and stood looking at his bloody hand.

"I know that I'm tired of your moods and rages," she said softly.

"So am I, lady."

Hanson sat with his face close to the fire, drunk on White Mountain wine. He thought now how fire was like the ocean, colors changing and flowing into one another. The fire was hot on his face, and the lump on the bridge of his nose throbbed, still tender where it had been broken when a Hell's Angel had sucker-punched him in an Oakland bar. The iced white wine made his tooth ache, a tooth that had gotten chipped in a fight with a black staff sergeant back in Da Nang, a fight that had grown out of a drunken argument about what Hanson had called the "realities" of integration.

The crescent scar over his right eye seemed to pull tight. An old friend had thrown a full Budweiser across the kitchen at him, the lip of the can splitting his scalp open. It had been a party the woman had thrown for a visiting poet only a week after Hanson had gotten back from 'Nam. The poet, a woman in her forties, wrote about "The Revolution" in lines like, "Be warned amerika, your friends/enemies wait to bring you to justice."

The cut had bled a lot, blood running down over his eye, dripping from his chin. Hanson had cupped his hands and caught the blood, lapping it up like tap water, laughing crazily. He spotted a pretty girl, a graduate student, he supposed, her face smooth and perfect. She had on jeans, ninety-dollar hiking boots, and a patched work shirt. She was watching him in horror.

"Hey, momma," Hanson had called to her. "Hey, my little alternative-life-style dumpling," he'd said as he walked toward her, fixing her with his bloody eye. He snatched her by the hair, bent her head back, and kissed her full on the mouth, forcing his tongue between her lips. She broke loose, her lips bloody, retching, and ran for the door.

Now, sitting in front of the fire, Hanson thought, A person's scars are a dossier of his dealings with the world. He smiled, pleased with the phrase, and studied the flaw in his wineglass, the firelight opalescent through the wine.

He passed out in front of the fire, sweat on his face, dreaming that he was on a hillside in Vietnam, taking a break in the midday heat. Beads of sweat tickling like green flies down his neck, the fire rustling like elephant grass. He could feel the web-gear harness across his left shoulder and the compact submachine gun under his right knee. If anything happened he could be up and running with all his gear, sprinting the first few yards in his sleep.

It was winter. The tourists were gone, and the tidal pools were healing after being trampled and littered by the summer people who clogged the roads with their campers and rec-vees.

Hanson stepped carefully from rock to rock above the fragile life of the tidal pools. He crouched occasionally to study one of the clear basins: starfish, green and purple spiked anemone, small striped fish flashing in the shadows. Pieces of abalone shell shifted and turned in the currents, one side like an old scab, the other side a smooth, pearly blue.

Anyone watching from the bluffs might have thought he was studying a road map, shifting from one leg to the other, inclining his head, studying the highways for the best route, the fastest, the most scenic, one that would take him through a particular town perhaps.

But Hanson was looking for what he called clues, some pattern in the tidal pool that might explain something or part of something, might hint at what he should do, or forecast an event. The patterns and movements of larger masses—the ocean, wind in the grass, the quality of the light, hawks and clouds—he called them omens. They were no more or less important than clues, but he watched them differently. Omens moved around and over him; they came and went suddenly, and he could only hope to realize their meaning before they were gone. They could not be studied like tidal pools. The world was alive with omens and clues, like dust sparkling in the sun. Hanson felt that if he could discern the pattern in time, he could leap into it and take his place in the world, like leaping into a complex and manic dance.

He found a shark's tooth in the sand, a big one, shaped like an arrowhead. The body of the tooth was a glossy dappled gray, the edges serrated. The root, the part that had pulled somehow from the shark's jaw, was wedge-shaped, a thick wing, porous, the color of driftwood. The tooth was flawless, not a crack or chip in it. He placed it carefully back in the depression in the sand where he had found it, setting it in like a puzzle piece.

On the way back to the bluffs he stopped to watch a sea gull peck at the white eye of a large fish head. The head was thick and gray, set in the sand like a lead maul.

The gull pecked mechanically, without malice or relish, tearing off a small scrap of eye, tipping his head back to swallow, then pecking some more. Hanson walked toward the fish head, and the gull side-waddled to the edge of the surf, fixing Hanson fearlessly with its bright black eye.

The fish had a heavy, low-slung jaw that Hanson prodded open with the toe of his blue track shoe. The jaw flanges were thick with pearly mucus and gave way slowly to perfect rows of needlelike teeth.

Hanson sat down on an outcropping of rock and looked out to sea. On the horizon a big seagoing tug was towing the hulk of an old freighter north to the scrap yard up the coast. The freighter had no king posts or booms, no bridge or wheelhouse, and it rode high in the water. It was too far away to see the tow lines, so the freighter seemed to be stalking the tug, maimed and blind, neither gaining nor falling behind.

"Ah," Hanson said, smiling, "the omens are many and confusing this night," thinking of Mr. Minh, who had taught him how to read the omens.

It was getting on toward dusk when Hanson started back to the cabin. The gull was still pecking tirelessly at the fish head. The lighthouse out on the point blinked, and Hanson could feel the faint, insistent wind begin to blow, howling faintly in his ears, chilling him, reminding him that he was supposed to be dead, that there had been a mistake in Vietnam. The space that his body was supposed to occupy in the world had closed over while he was still alive to fill it, shutting him out.

The pile of snails was just outside the back door. They were dying, but still trying to move. Their shells were split and torn like thumbnails, and they grated softly against one another, whispering to Hanson. In the dim light the pile of snails moved more slowly, and then not at all. Hanson heard the whispering, and the old terror rose in his chest and up into his mouth.

She was sitting inside at a folding table, writing. As she took a drag off one of her thin brown cigarettes, he kicked the table over, catapulting paper, books, and half a cup of tea against the wall, leaving her sitting in the chair in the middle of the room. He placed one hand against her chest and, very deliberately, pushed her and the chair over backward.

"Don't move," he said.

She was in an awkward position, her legs straddling the back of the chair, braced on one arm, about to scramble back and away from him.

"Don't. Fucking. Move. I'll kill you if you move. I'll break your fucking back. Jesus Christ, you're crazy—"

"I don't think—"

"Shut the fuck up. You can't *do* things like that. The snails know what they're doing. They pull their shells along until they find the place they're supposed to be. They *know* where it is when they find it, and they stop there and seal off. You start fucking around with things like that—they been around for a million years—they *survived* because they know when to stop and seal off and when to move—you fuck around with patterns, with constants, don't you see," he put his foot on her chest, "don't you *see?*"—she nodded her head—"and it's all over—it's too late now—and that is when the bad shit begins."

The tavern, The Uncommon Good, was crowded and noisy; all the regular winter people were there. Commune hippies in bib overalls were nursing their beers. There were people who ran the boutiques and crafts shops, students and teachers at the small but well-financed art center. Always there were a few women, in their thirties and early forties, who had a desperate enthusiasm for everything, who favored peasant dresses and shawls, who made weekly trips to the post office to pick up checks sent by their husbands.

The kid had a pitcher of beer and a glass in his hand, looking for a place to sit down. He was Hanson's height, but thinner and several years younger. His hair was light brown and shoulder length. He was wearing jeans and a brown satin cowboy shirt embroidered with roses. He had a wide leather belt with a big silver buckle in the shape of a peace symbol.

The only empty chair was at Hanson's table, and the kid walked over to it.

"Anybody usin' this chair?" he asked.

Hanson stared straight ahead as if he hadn't heard.

The kid stood there.

Hanson looked up at him with a neutral, almost benign expression, then looked past him. "Nobody's using it," he said.

The kid stood there, looking uncomfortable.

"It's okay," Hanson said. "Go ahead and sit down. But *can't take a hint* just took on a new depth for me."

The kid, who had started to sit down, stood back up, spilling some beer. "Look," he said, "I'm sorry, man, if you're into something. I didn't mean . . ."

"No, it's okay, Gypsy Cowboy. Siddown, I'm not *into* anything. Sit down! I'm almost out of beer. Pour me a beer." Hanson laughed. *"Into* anything."

Hanson drained his glass and held it out for the kid to fill. "See," he told the kid, "I learned this trick somewhere. You're on a bus, right, and there are only two empty seats left, one of them next to where you're sitting. And here comes some big fat woman with a bunch of shopping bags. Here she comes now, dragging all her shit up the aisle. Or it's a wino who stinks and is gonna tell you what a great guy he was in the old days. Or some pimply-faced PFC home on leave, wearing his baggy uniform with his pants tucked into his boots, all his friends away at school or married. All through basic training he's been thinking how great it's gonna be to come home, and after two days of it he wants to go back to the barracks.

"Here they come now, the PFC tripping over his boots, feeling self-conscious and out of place, the wino sucking his teeth, the woman grunting and sweating, all headed right for that empty seat next to you. And you don't want them to sit there. No, you can do without that. So what you do, see, is just stare straight ahead, not at anything in particular—what they call a thousand-yard-stare—and keep thinking, Die. Die. Die! and they'll go past every time. They'll *stand up* before they'll sit next to you."

"Maybe the lady is tired," the kid began. "The PFC could tell me about the Army. The wino might have a story."

"Maybe," Hanson said. "The lady can take her bags and sit in the other empty seat. The PFC isn't going to tell you the truth about the Army, he's gonna tell you what a hero he is. All winos have the same story: 'It's a hell of a life, kid. If only I was your age again, whole life ahead of me, coulda been something.' "

Hanson gripped the edge of the table and glared at the kid. "Coulda *been* something," he shouted. "Maybe, huh!" People at other tables looked over.

"You know! Don't ya? Huh. Huh. Yeah, I know you. No 'maybe.' *I* don't forget."

More people looked over. Hanson made a clumsy grab at the kid, who jumped back, knocking over his chair.

"Yah," Hanson growled, "dirty son a bitch. Oughta *kill* ya!

"That's the wino story," Hanson said, sitting back and laughing. "Starts out telling you a lot of lies, giving you advice,. then forgets where he is, thinks you're somebody else, somebody who fucked him over once, and you got a madman next to you for the whole bus ride.

"On the other hand," Hanson said, "you should pay better attention to who you sit down next to.

"Thanks for the beer," he called to the kid, who was edging up the stairs to the second floor of the tavern.

Hanson ordered another beer and carried a chair to the back of the room, setting it down in a narrow space between the jukebox and the doorway opening to the stairs. He rocked on the back legs of the chair rhythmically, lightly thumping the back of his head against the wall, holding the beer in his lap with both hands. He smiled. His back was to the wall and both sides were protected.

He'd changed from the nylon track shoes into heavy work boots. In his hip pocket he had a flat-handled lock-blade knife. The first three inches of the blade could shave the hair off the back of his hand and lift a gray powder of dry skin. The last two inches were dull, so he could pop the blade open with his thumb. A trick he'd learned from a merchant seaman in—

where was it now—Mobile? Yes. Mean Mobile, Alabama, where a knife was called a Mobile boxing glove.

Knife fighting. Yes, an interesting topic. An excellent topic, he thought, reciting to himself as if he were giving a lecture. "The most important rule," he went on, his lips moving slightly as he half-pronounced the words, "is never to let the other guy know you've got a knife until you've cut him." But, he thought, taking a drink of beer, even if he knows you've got a knife, try to keep it just out of sight, behind your leg. That way he won't be able to kick it out of your hand, and when you move, he won't be able to anticipate the angle of your lunge.

A guy with a red beard and a girl in a tie-dye blouse walked through the front door, laughing. The guy bent his hands into his armpits and flapped his elbows like wings, shouting, "Whoop. Whoop."

Also, Hanson thought, also, it makes the other guy nervous, psychs him, knowing you've got a knife but not being able to see it.

Now some people say, if you get into a knife fight, you might as well plan on getting cut, but you decide *where*. Offer the other guy your left forearm, and while he goes for it, you can move inside and pick your spot. But I don't know about that one. He'd seen what the pain and loss of blood from a deep cut could do.

He remembered the black PFC who'd gotten his cheek laid open with a case cutter in Fayetteville. The Circus Lounge. A place where you go to the bathroom in groups, for protection. "Gorier than a white man," he mumbled to himself, looking at the moisture rings on his table. Smooth black skin peeling open, white fat tissue underneath and red muscle beneath that. The blood bright and startling against the black skin.

Well . . . he thought. His eyes had begun to work independently. He closed one and watched people in the bar talking. He couldn't hear what they were saying. The jukebox drowned them out. Some bullshit song by some guy with a voice like a woman. Some *sensitive* asshole, he thought.

The jukebox paused, whirred, and began another song:

You got yer army an' yer CIA . . .
I got my rainbow an' a sunny day,
You gotta boogie-woogie,
You gotta boogie-woogie . . .

Hanson bought another beer and went upstairs to a room with two pool tables and a pinball machine. The kid was playing eight ball with three guys in their twenties. The leader seemed to be the one wearing a black T-shirt. It was too cold for just a T-shirt, but his big arms and chest showed nicely through the thin cotton.

Hanson planned to take the leader out first.

One of them was wearing a plaid shirt, jeans, and logger's boots. He didn't look like a logger.

The third one had shoulder-length blond hair and was wearing a gold ring in his left ear. He had on a denim vest with silver studs across the back and a wide leather watch band with three buckles.

A twelve-year-old boy, one of the local kids, was playing the pinball machine that rang and chattered as Hanson pulled a chair over to a corner where he could watch the whole room.

The boy was good. He knew just how much he could shove and knee the machine before it would "TILT" and end the game. The machine was named Round Up, one of the old kind that fire silver ball-bearings with a spring-loaded plunger. Pink plastic flippers, like little stubs of amputated limbs, twitched as if stung and batted at the ball as it rolled past. When the ball dropped into one of the holes, the machine shuddered, big-breasted cowgirls etched into the glass flickered with light, and the box score added up with mechanical grunts.

The boy had already won two free replays when the one in the T-shirt yelled at him. "Hey, that's enough of that noise. You're fucking up my game. Take off."

The boy looked up from the machine.

"Yeah, you got it. Take off. Now."

The boy left, his two games unplayed.

Hanson sipped his beer and tapped his foot to the jukebox below. The Gypsy Cowboy kid smiled and said to the one in the T-shirt, "Frank, you're shooting so bad tonight an *earth-quake* couldn't hurt your game."

"Hey, punk, when I want your opinion I'll stomp it out of you, okay?"

The other two laughed.

"You got that," Frank said.

"Yeah. Okay. Didn't mean anything."

"Then don't *say* anything. That's your problem. When you say something, you better mean it. That's something you gotta learn."

Hanson was drunk. The pool table looked like a smooth green parallelogram, and that made the rebound of the balls, the physics of the game all the more interesting. While he watched the players, he idly rolled a cue ball along the top of his leg. He tapped his foot to the music downstairs and sang softly to himself, ". . . I got my rainbow and a sunny day." He smiled broadly, like a person who is about to buy something that he has waited and saved a long time for.

The one in the T-shirt was bent over the table, lining up a shot. Hanson walked over, as if to watch, and sidearmed the cue ball just below his ear. He fell sideways, sweeping a mug of beer off the table, his stick clattering across the floor. The cue ball seemed to stick to his jaw for a moment, then fell to the floor and rolled under the table. Where the cue ball had struck the jaw, there was now a shallow depression slowly turning from white to red. Hanson didn't see it. He'd felt the jaw give way when he palmed the ball into it, and he knew that the one in the T-shirt was through for the night. He was already turning toward the plaid shirt who stood facing him, holding his cue stick, feet braced wide. Hanson kicked him between the legs and took the stick from him as he fell.

The one in the biker outfit swung his cue stick, but Hanson saw it coming and it only glanced off his arm. Hanson snatched a striped ball from the table and threw it at him. The ball hit him high in the chest, and when he flinched, Hanson snapped his pool cue into the wide watch band. The man dropped his stick and stumbled back, holding his wrist.

"Why—" he began.

"Why," Hanson said to him. "You want to know why?"

then drove the stick into the V of his ribs and watched him fall and hit the floor, where he began making little *whoops* and throwing up.

"Because things are too fragile out there," Hanson said, pointing toward the dark window, "and I don't know what to do about it. Because," he said, "I wake up scared every morning."

The kid, the Gypsy Cowboy, hadn't moved. He stood staring at Hanson, half a glass of beer in his hand.

Hanson smiled at him, laid the cue stick down, and thumped the heel of his hand on the rubber bumper of the pool table. "Good," he said to the kid. "Just don't move. Be cool, and you'll be okay. Finish your beer. Drink up, podner."

The kid drank down the beer, watching Hanson over the rim of the glass.

"Set it down," Hanson told him, and the kid set the empty glass down on the pool table.

"Now. You too may wonder why I did what I just did."

"Oh no, I, no—" the kid began.

"Whoops," Hanson said to the kid. "Don't move now."

The one he'd kicked was groaning and pulling himself around on the floor in a circle.

Hanson waited until he pulled himself a little farther around, studying him like a piece of defective machinery. He cocked his leg back slightly, then snapped it straight, sending his heel into the man's jaw. "Boogie-woogie, motherfucker."

"Now, let's see. The *reason,*" he said, sweat dripping down his cheek. He looked quickly around the room. "I wake up scared," he said, lowering his voice and walking closer to the kid, "and then I get pissed off because I'm scared, and I want to kick somebody's ass. I don't know the difference anymore between being scared and being pissed off. It's all connected. Like the tidal pools. You change one thing around and that makes it so that everything else has to change, and pretty soon it's all fucked up.

"I don't usually trust myself to get drunk in public places anymore. Hell, you *see* what happens," he said, wiping his hand across his face.

"God*damn* it," he shouted, swinging the pool cue and

shattering the beer glass off the pool table, then bringing the stick down, splintering it on the table.

The one who had asked him why groaned and rolled over.

"Shut up," Hanson snapped, kicking him. Kicking him again, then spinning around and grabbing the pool table, trying to lift it, growling and crying down in his chest.

The kid started moving slowly toward the door.

"Hold it. I'm not through yet. See, I get around other people, and they're talking and making noise, and I start getting mad. Because they don't pay *attention*. They got to be quieter and more careful."

"Anyway," he said, breathing hard, but calmer, trying to smile, "don't move now, or make any noise, and I won't hurt you."

The kid nodded.

"Do you believe me?" Hanson asked him.

The kid looked at him and nodded.

"Good."

The kid heard a quick metallic snap, and Hanson had the knife an inch from his throat. "See, you just never know where things will come from. That's why you got to pay attention.

"Now listen up. If you cut a man's throat below the larynx, the vocal cords, don't you see, he can't make any noise. You take the carotid artery—it's strange, the guy keeps breathing through the hole you cut in his neck, blowing like a fucking bellows—and in a second he faints and dies. But you got to have a sharp knife."

Hanson cut the buttons off the kid's shirt, popping them off one by one, from top to bottom, as the kid stood perfectly still.

"The throat, see, it's pretty tough meat. Friend of mine always called it the ee-so-*fay*-gus. He's dead now, though.

"But that's pretty useless information, isn't it. Interesting, I think, huh, but useless."

Hanson smiled. "Getting cut doesn't even hurt if the knife is sharp enough," he said, and laid open a three-inch gash on the back of his own forearm, snapped the knife closed, and slipped it into his pocket. Blood seeped down the arm and in between the webbing of his fingers. He looked at the blood collecting on his fingertips and dripping onto the floor.

"Did you ever think about the devil—because I have— about what a hard job he's got? He does all the work and God just sits around and takes all the credit for everything. The devil's got to jump around and hiss and sneer," Hanson said, then jumped up, rubbing his hands together, jumping, holding his bloody hands like claws, sticking his tongue out, jerking his head from side to side, "like some fuckin' asshole, 'cause that's the job he got stuck with. Go out there every fucking day and deliver the pain. Deliver the pain for that slimy asshole God. And everybody hates him for it. Well fuck that, right?"

"Yeah," he said, his voice almost normal. "Fuck that." He exhaled slowly. "Boy, I'm tired. I gotta go. I'm really tired."

"Look, you better stay up here for a few minutes till I'm gone. People are gonna be mad about this. I know it. So you stay right here, okay? If you don't, what with all this stuff I've taught you and everything tonight, I'm gonna be pissed off, and I'll come back and get you. Do you believe me?"

The kid nodded.

"Good. Take care, now," he said, snapping the fingers of his left hand at the kid, speckling him with blood.

It was a cool night, and the fog collected on Hanson's face like sweat as he walked the dark road. He picked up his step, a staggering double-time. "Gotta go," he chanted, dropping one shoulder. "Gotta be," then the other, loosening up like a boxer. "Airborne. Infantry.

"Gotta go. Gotta be. Airborne. Infantry.

"Gotta go, gotta be, Airborne Infantry . . ."

The lighthouse on the point didn't blink. Through the fog he could see the edge of the light, anticipate it as it began to swing around. It would glow brightly for a moment, dispersed and indistinct, as if it were behind frosted glass, then fade out and swing away.

Hanson stopped and watched the light.

Out beyond the surf a blowhole boomed and sighed with each wave, like a man who has stopped running for a moment to catch his breath and decide which direction he should go next.

Da Nang

Three weeks later Quinn was standing at the NCO club bar in Da Nang staring at a point somewhere deep inside the big green mirror. He was remembering an early morning in February, his senior year in high school, when he'd had to walk seven miles back to Mason City, hiding from the police. He could feel the numbness in his toes thinking about the frostbite. Using grain silos to plot his course home, he'd crossed the miles of frozen cornfields that rustled in the wind. He lost the feeling in his feet, and blowing snow stuck to his eyelashes and hair as he stumbled through the ice crust and bamboolike corn stalks, scaring up little gray sparrows and field mice. But it had been worth it. Worth the late-night drive to the Clear Lake High School homecoming dance—their chief rivals—where he and some other football players crashed the party with sawed-off pool cues. It was his fondest memory of high school.

Quinn was in a good mood.

The door swung open behind him, and he watched Hanson through the mirror as he walked to the bar and stood next to him, seeming, as Quinn watched, to walk through a small door in the mirror and grow to normal size.

Hanson ordered a beer, poured it into a glass, and took a long swallow.

"There's something about a bar, first thing in the morning," Hanson said, looking at Quinn in the mirror. "No cigarette smoke—the light's different—there's the smell of stale beer and Lysol. A new world every morning."

"I got your new world *hangin',*" Quinn said, slapping a copy of the orders assigning Hanson back to CCN down on the bar.

Behind them, a bitter warbling laugh rose and fell hysterically. Silver, wearing a Grateful Dead T-shirt, jeans, and a red bandana, stood behind them, holding his mechanical laugh box. He smiled and tipped his hand, and the laughter began again, sobbing, out of control.

"Some fun, huh?" Silver said. "We got a laugh riot here."

"Tell us about your trip, sport," Quinn said. "We've got a chopper laid on to take us back to the site tomorrow. We even stashed away your gear so you won't have to break in a new set."

"So tell us," Silver said. "How was it, man? How was it back with all those people?"

Hanson laughed. "Not too good . . .

"But then," he went on, "I remembered that phone number Sergeant Major gave me before I left . . ."

The dark mountains, their tops still hidden by fog, rose behind Hanson as he took the sandy path to the beach and the transient barracks. The parchment-brown dune grass brushed his hands and hips as he walked. He had forgotten about the lowland heat, the way it rode the air, as tangible as the wind and rain of the monsoons.

He stopped at one of the crumbling French gun emplacements and looked through the firing port. The sea was calm, the same pale blue as the simmering mid-morning sky. A few small boats were out tending the fishnets on the far side of the bay.

The wide white beach was dotted with jellyfish that had been stranded by the tide. Weakly pulsing, they looked like transparent blue brains, or thoughts, random bits of memory caught on the sand. Sea gulls coursed woodenly above him in the thermal currents. Gold flecks of mica moved over the sand with the surf, flickering in the sun. Sea grass and bright blue flowers blanketed the sandy hills toward shore, and a bank of clouds was pushing into the mountains to the north.

Each step he took on the damp sand compressed it so that it flashed beneath his feet like bomb bursts seen from the air.

Hanson sang softly to himself against the sound of the surf, and it occurred to him that Mr. Minh had probably never seen the ocean.

The transient barracks were pleasant bungalows on the

beach. Hanson went inside the one he'd been assigned, dropped his duffel bag in the corner, and lay down on the bunk. The surf hissed as he looked up at the ceiling.

Lizards on the walls moved in sudden flurries of speed, then stopped dead still, and it was difficult to actually see them move. As soon as Hanson detected movement, the lizard had frozen again, its shiny eyes focused somewhere beyond him. It was like trying to watch your eyes move in a mirror. The lizards lived on the walls, eating flies and mosquitoes.

Bars of sunlight fell through the shutters onto the concrete floor. They moved slowly, imperceptibly, relentlessly with the angle of the sun.

Hanson lay on the bunk and inhaled the odor of Vietnam. Why was it so different from the smell of his home back in the States? Was it the plants, the earth itself, or was it the breath of the people and animals who lived there? Was he inhaling the same breath that had warmed their lungs and fed their blood?

Outside, two of the maids were talking in the high wail and whine of Vietnamese.

He drifted off to sleep in the cool hootch dreaming of the South Pole, blue-white and motionless.

Later, when the sun had touched the horizon, there was no breeze at all. Outside the NCO club, on the patio, beneath the big green cargo-chute canopy, the Hustlers had set up. The Hustlers were a Vietnamese rock band that had learned their songs by listening to record albums that were diverted from the Army PX and sold on the streets in black market stalls along with Kool cigarettes, Ivory soap, and combat boots. They were young Vietnamese who had spent their adolescence immersed in the war and in American rock&roll culture. They spoke little English, learning to sing the rock lyrics phonetically, with heavy accents. Squeezed through another culture to entertain soldiers, the songs were strangely disturbing, showing at times the dark side of their energy. They were all six months out of date.

Their costumes were taken from record album covers— shoulder-length black hair, bandanas, aviator sunglasses, unzipped leather jackets, tight tailored jeans and boots, cigarettes and surly expressions. Asians in the midst of a bloody civil war parodying the rebellion of middle-class American adolescents.

The two dancers had beautiful waist-length hair and wore fringed bikinis and heavy eye makeup. They were sultry, sexy in a cheap way, an Asian version of the Playboy bunnies that the soldiers had grown up masturbating to. The band was like a disturbing dream in a language that almost makes sense—should make sense—but does not.

When it was dark, Hanson looked up at the stars, the same stars he always looked at when he was on ambush. A sky full of stars, not the ones he used to look at back home, a place he used to call home.

And he was getting drunk, sitting at a table with Quinn and Silver, sharing two pitchers of beer, glowering at the band. The acrid smoke of Vietnamese cigarettes, like smelling salts popped under his nose, kept waking him to the fact that he was back in-country.

"All right, all right, is everybody feeling *good?*" the band-leader shouted, pacing across the stage, grinning.

"We are happy abou' being in Da Nang tonight. We have two be-*u*-tee-ful girls for you . . ."

The drummer popped the snare drum, both girls did a bump and grind, and the band leader did a double-take at both of them. "Awright," he yelled, clapping his hands. "What about *that?*"

The audience broke into cheers and whistles. Most of them were headquarters personnel—clerks, typists, quarter-masters—though Hanson spotted a few people from the other teams.

"Awright!" When the band leader shouted the word, it sounded like "our eye."

One of the dancers did another bump&grind, the snare drum popped, and the bandleader shouted, "What you think abou' that? I don' know abou' *her,*" he said, rolling his eyes.

The audience whistled and cheered.

"This is what you call your easy-to-please crowd," Silver said.

"A bunch of dumb fucks," Quinn said. "And somebody ought to shoot that slimy little fucker up there on the stage," he said as the bandleader introduced the song "Hang On, Sloopy."

"Our eye! Now we like to do one favorite songs, 'Hay Naw *Soopey!*"

"Hay naw Soopey, Soopey hay naw, yeah, hay naw . . ."

The dancers began doing a double-time version of "the swim," jerking and grinding through the song, shaking their hair, bending backward, throwing their arms and hips toward the audience. When the spotlight hit the dancers at the right angle, beads of sweat glistened on their chests and down the curve of their bellies.

Like everyone else there, Hanson wanted to go up and grab one of the dancers and throw her down, rip her clothes off and fuck her right there on the floor, looking into those black eyes. It would be more like assault and battery than making love, more like murder. He was breathing tight, shallow little breaths, everything in him focusing on the dancers, nothing but the sight of the dancers filling his head and the ache in his chest.

It didn't matter that the band was bad. It was loud, and the dancers were humping and sweating. The smell of cigarette smoke, and sweat, beer and a taste of marijuana hung in the air. Hanson began to look at the laughing and shouting faces of the other soldiers. The roar in his head drowned out their noise. He watched their jaws moving up and down, streaming smoke. Their lower jaws and noses began to look like angry little Punch-and-Judy dolls, whining, barking little faces that he wanted to smash. The hot, rank air pulsed with lust, rage, and loud music.

Soldiers crouched in the aisles, snapping flash photos with Polaroids and Instamatics, jockeying for position. Scuffles broke out when people stood up, or bumped against each other, straining to get a better view of the sweating, panting dancers.

"Our *eye,*" the bandleader shouted at the end of the song. "Hay naw, *Soopey . . .*"

"Hanoi Soopey," Silver said. "The Commie version of the American favorite. That drummer's so fuckin' bad. . . . I know, he must be drumming in Vietnamese. Some kind of language barrier.

". . . How you like to hay now to one of our be-yu-tee-ful gulls, huh? Our *eye*. Now, one mow song we know you aw know . . ."

The drummer popped his drums. The dancers began to grind and hump sideways as the band launched into the song that every Vietnamese band played at every performance. The guaranteed hit, "We Gotta Get Outta This Place."

The audience began to cheer and make the peace sign, jumping up, thrusting their fingers into the air like crippled Nazi salutes, shouting, "All right!" "There it *is*." "We owe it to ourselves!"

"Fuck *you*," Quinn shouted, and held up a "fuck peace" sign, the index, middle and ring finger.

Hanson grinned. If they didn't like the war, what were they doing here? He began to laugh at the stupid peace sign. It was good to be back in a world that made some sense, with Quinn and Silver.

He was back home. He could do anything he wanted to now that he was home.

"What a bunch of fucking fairies," Quinn said. "Let's get outta here and go find a bar." When he stood and pushed his chair back, people around him gave him room. He spotted a fat, pale soldier wearing a drip-dry PX sportshirt who was crouched in the aisle taking photos with a Polaroid camera.

"Hey, doofus," he yelled at him. "Hey," he shouted, prodding him in the back with the toe of his boot. The soldier looked around, annoyed, then looked up and almost fell over.

"Hey," Quinn said, "take our picture," jabbing his finger at his own chest and nodding at Hanson and Silver.

"Uh, jeeze, Sarge, I'm really short on film."

"Take the picture or I'll kill you. I'll fuckin' kill you, okay? I'll beat you to death."

Hanson and Silver nodded, agreeing. "Uh huh."

They posed for the picture, standing with their arms around each other.

"Now *take* the fucker," Quinn said.

He snapped the picture, peeled it off and give it to Quinn, then started to walk away."

"Wait one, bud," Quinn said. "I want to be sure this one came out okay. These goddamn Polaroids fuck up half the time."

They watched the image float onto the film, then sharpen. The three of them standing close, with boozy smiles, captured as they had been thirty seconds before. It had that quality of having happened long ago to three people Hanson didn't know. Quinn, the biggest, in the middle, his chin thrust toward the camera. Silver, his glasses flashing, laughing like a blind man. And Hanson, slightly out of focus, looking at something over the photographer's shoulder, wearing civilian clothes, blue jeans and a green Hawaiian shirt.

The three of them found their way to the 3rd Mech NCO club and started drinking boilermakers, shots of Chivas and Budweiser. Silver sat studying the photo of the three of them.

"You guys want this picture?" he asked.

Hanson shook his head, and Quinn said, "Naw, it's fucked-up looking."

Silver held a corner of the photo over the red candle on the table, watched it burn, then dropped the last bit of it in an ashtray.

"There were days back home," Hanson said, breaking the silence, "when I wouldn't go outside. I was afraid to go outside. Afraid I'd kill somebody and go to jail. Somebody would break in front of me in line at the grocery store, or bump into me, and I was ready to kill 'em. And nobody even *noticed*.

"Sometimes I'd get out the door and down the steps, and think, Huh-uh, no, not today, and kind of ease my way back up into the house. I mean, some goddamn dog could bark at me and I'd be pissed off the rest of the day, wanting to kill the dog. If I got drunk enough, I could go out after dark, but I stayed inside during the day."

Quinn had turned even gloomier and sat staring from the table toward the crowded bar. "Fuck 'em," he said. "You shoulda just kicked all their asses."

Quinn slumped there in silence, then said, "You know what I fuckin' hate back there? You know? I hate it when some motherfucker you don't even know says hello. You're walking along and some dipshit you never even *saw* before walks past and says 'hello.' Hello my ass. What am I supposed to do? Say hello, nice *weather*, or some bullshit like that? If you don't know me, you got nothing to say that I want to fuckin' hear. Right? Shit!"

Silver and Hanson looked at each other, and Silver rolled his eyes.

"Who do you want me to punch out?" Quinn said, looking at Hanson, then back to the bar.

"Nobody."

"Come on. For a coming-home present. Pick one."

"Forget it."

"Hey. Don't tell me, 'forget it.' Am I supposed to just go 'Hu, click, buzz, oops, okay, boss, I'll just forget whatever the fuck I was thinking' because you *told* me to? Nobody tells me, 'forget it,' when . . ."

"Okay, okay. I'm sorry. I apologize. I didn't mean it like that."

"And don't be interrupting me like that, either," Quinn said.

"Yes sir, your honor."

"How about that college boy up there in the pretty blue shirt?"

"How do you know he's a college boy?"

"Come on. I know. I *know.* He talks too much. He thinks he's hot shit when he don't know zip. Because he's got that pretty peaches-and-cream complexion."

Hanson dimpled his cheeks with his forefingers.

"That's right," Quinn said, patting his own cheeks with his huge hands, a gesture that made Hanson think of a crowded cattle pen. "*Sensitive*-looking, just like you. Except something went *right* with you. You got rehabilitated over here or something.

"You ever notice how, in the paper, when somebody gets arrested, or kills somebody, the paper always says, 'So-and-so, high school dropout.' What does that have to do with anything? Huh? Tell me that? They never say, 'So-and-so, college boy.' Always the same old bullshit, 'High school dropout arrested for senseless murder.' It's the college boys who must commit the *sensible* fucking murders, I guess, 'cause they do it with a college degree.

"That guy up there's the kind of fuck that used to come and watch me play football, then talk to his fraternity buddies about what I did wrong, after the game's over. When he don't know *shit*. That fuckin' pisses me off," he said, crushing his beer can.

"Jesus," Hanson said, "go ahead then, before you jump on *me* and I have to stomp you."

Quinn stood up, grinned, and said, "Never happen, little buddy. You know you don't have enough sand in your pockets."

He strolled over to the bar where the "college boy," a Specialist Four, was talking to two other radio technicians, his back to Quinn. Quinn jabbed him in the back, said, "Hey, fraternity boy," and braced himself.

The Spec Four turned, and Quinn hit him square in the face. Spit and snot sprayed his friends as he fell against the bar and then down on the floor, where he began to moan and bleed.

"What have you got to say about that, then, *Mister* College," Quinn shouted, kicking him. "Try this on."

Then Hanson and Silver were there.

"He's just drunk, just drunk," Silver said to the Spec Four's friends. "We'll take care of it."

"Come on, man," Hanson said. "That's enough."

Quinn straight-armed Hanson against the bar and kicked the Spec Four again.

Hanson jumped on Quinn's back and wrapped his right arm around Quinn's neck, catching his throat in the V of his elbow. He grabbed his own right wrist with his other hand and began to squeeze, cutting off the blood going to Quinn's brain. Quinn bucked like a horse and swung backward with hammer blows to Hanson's kidneys, but he began to weaken, then fell over on top of Hanson.

Hanson and Silver picked Quinn up and walked him out of the bar, where he began to straighten up, then swing wildly at both of them. He shook his head and said, "What happened?"

"You almost killed him, man," Silver said. "Let's get the fuck out of here before they call an MP or some goddamn thing."

"Fuck him," Quinn shouted. "Fuck him. Good. Pretty little college prick knows what it feels like to be scared now. He asked for it and he fuckin' got it."

He walked a few steps, then said, "Did you see that little doofus's nose when I connected? It *exploded*. Like a fuckin' tomato."

As they passed the mess hall, a shadow detached from the building and followed them, then raced past Silver, snarling and barking. Silver spun and kicked at the dog as it ran back into the dark.

"God*damn*," Silver shouted. "Scared the shit out of me. Goddamn mess sergeant's dog. Eats better than the troops in the field do. Lard-ass mess sergeant keeps it 'cause it's the only thing in the world that could love him. A dog lover. You can be ugly and stupid, lazy and a liar. You can be a goddamn child molester and if you feed a dog, it loves you. Blackie, that's his name. Lot of imagination. If it was white, he'd be Whitey. Old Blue. Old Yeller. Blaze. Red."

They heard the dog growling in the dark.

"I mean, what is the dumb mother growling at, man? Fucker always growls at *me*. I'm gonna kill him one of these days, man. And he can see it in my eyes!

"Who you growling at," Silver screamed, then ran into the dark toward the sound of the growling, waving his skinny arms and shrieking, vanishing into the sound of his own footsteps and the softer, quicker rhythm of the running dog.

Then he came walking back, out of breath, muttering, "We'll see, man. We'll see." He was shivering, though the temperature was in the nineties. "I'm gonna get that goddamn dog," he said, a slight quiver in his voice.

They walked the rest of the way to the cadre barracks, and Silver unlocked the door of one of the bungalows. "Dawson's gone on a little R&R," he told Hanson. "Left us the key to his place."

It was a small, pleasant room with a bed instead of a bunk and comfortable rattan furniture. There was a Japanese stereo, a Japanese TV, and a small Japanese refrigerator stocked with Budweiser beer. Silver put on an album, an eerie electronic blend of harmonica and violin and a woman's voice singing of hot summer days. As he listened, Hanson imagined he could hear the swish and hiss of elephant grass moving around him on patrol.

Silver stood for a moment, playing an imaginary bass guitar, but his heart didn't seem to be in it. He stopped and walked over to the door, where he stood looking out.

The room smelled of incense. An M-16 hung from one wall, three red Christmas tree bulbs dangling, one from the stock, one from the muzzle, and one from the receiver. Above the weapon, Che Guevarra stared down at them from a popular poster, a red star set in his beret.

"*Que paso*, Che," Hanson said to him.

"You know," Silver said, "I miss old Dawson. But after two tours I guess he got a little tired of getting shot at. He lost a couple of teams out there, and that bothers him. Sergeant Major got him a skatin' job here. He does some courier work for Sergeant Major. Goes on R&R a lot."

Silver opened the little refrigerator and a blue-white light came on inside, lighting up dozens of red, white and blue Budweisers. He threw beers to Quinn and Hanson and passed them a yellow and green fifth of Cutty Sark.

"Wait one," he said. "Give me a taste of that," and he swallowed a couple of times from the green bottle of Scotch.

"That's it," he said. "That's it, man. Good-bye Blackie and *adios* motherfucker. He's gone, man. *Fini*. He's dog meat."

He walked over to a big teak chest and unlocked it. It was full of weapons. There was a Thompson submachine gun, a Swedish "K," a folding-stock AK-47, an Army .45, a Colt Python, claymore mines, and trip flares. He took a grenade out and held it in his hand, then put it back in the box. "Dawson likes to be prepared," he said, banging guns and ammo boxes against each other. "He's almost a little paranoid," he said, holding up a fourteen-pound satchel charge of C-4 explosive.

"Dog meat," Quinn muttered, standing up and walking over to the chest. He handed the Scotch to Silver, who took ther long swallow.

"This," Silver said. "Yes!" and held up *A LAW*.

"Piece of shit," Quinn said. "You remember Lang Vei."

"Might not kill a tank," Silver said, "but it'll kill a dog," he said, looking at the three-foot-long metal tube.

The LAW, a light antitank weapon, fired a 66-millimeter rocket. The tube telescoped open to five feet, and was thrown away after it fired the single rocket packed inside. During the NVA tank attack on the Special Forces camp at Lang Vei, they proved almost useless, failing, again and again, to detonate when they hit the tanks' armor.

"Dog meat," Silver said, pulling the LAW open to its full length, the clear plastic sight popping up. He went out the door and the dark swallowed him up.

Quinn and Hanson looked at each other. "He's too drunk to be firing LAWs," Quinn said, and the two of them went out after him.

Hanson was having trouble with his vision. At times it was like looking through a tunnel. Everything in the tunnel was clear while everything around it was distorted. He took a capsule of speed out of the pocket of his Hawaiian shirt and swallowed it.

"Here, Blackie. Heeeere, Blackie." They could hear Silver calling for the dog. "That's a good puppy. Come on, pup-pup, I got a doggie treat here . . ."

Hanson tripped and fell, catching himself with his hands. He heard Silver moving slowly toward the 3rd Mech compound, singing, " 'Walkin' the *dog,* I'm walkin' the dog . . .' "

Quinn stumbled over Hanson and fell down on top of him. "Shit," he said. "We're all gonna die drunk in Da Nang."

"Heeeere, puppy, come on, puppy. Got a surprise for you . . ."

"Let's get him," Hanson said. "We gotta help each other up."

The two of them locked arms and got to their knees, then to their feet. They lost their balance for a moment, staggering around in a circle, holding hands like square dancers. They steadied themselves and walked toward the sound of Silver's voice.

"Heeeere, Blackie. Come on, boy . . ."

Hanson heard the dog bark, then growl.

"That way," he said, and the two of them ran clumsily toward the sound.

"That's a boy . . ."

The dog growled, then began whining.

"That's a boy . . ."

The back-blast from the rocket almost knocked Hanson down. He hadn't realized that he was so close to Silver. It came at him like a red-orange funnel, and he covered his eyes with his arms. Quinn stumbled into him just as the rocket caught the rear wheel of a jeep, and a black and orange explosion sent it cartwheeling in the air. Hanson thought he saw a furry shadow racing toward the beach.

Just as they got to Silver, the sirens started wailing. Silver was laughing and shouting, "Body count, body count!" The jeep was upside down, its tires aflame, the rear ones spinning and throwing demonic shadows. Hanson grabbed Silver, and the three of them ran from the jeep. They threw themselves behind a Conex container just as the gas tank blew up. The sirens continued wailing and spotlights flashed on as the three of them grabbed each other and began laughing.

"They think it's incoming," Silver said between laughs.

"Whose jeep was that?"

"Third Mech's. We're on their compound."

Then, as they laughed, they were rocked by more explosions, *real* incoming, as North Vietnamese 122-millimeter rockets hit the airstrip. A soldier ran past them shouting, "Incoming, incoming," and Quinn slammed a forearm into his stomach, knocking him down, his helmet flying off.

Quinn put the helmet on backward and ran in a tight little circle shouting, *"In*coming, *in*coming, we're all gonna die in Vietnam," until he fell down laughing, still shouting, "Oh no, oh, my goodness, *in*coming." He was shirtless, his heavily muscled shoulders and arms rippling in the flame and moonlight as he pounded the ground with his forearms, laughing, shouting, "Isn't this a *great* fucking movie? Incoming, oh, it's incoming . . ."

The rockets walked down the airstrip and into the civilian ~~arter~~ of Da Nang City, roaring and gnashing overhead, ex-

ploding flame and shrapnel through the tin and cardboard
hootches of the town.

"All *right*," Quinn shouted, shaking both fists over his
head. "*Get* some, rockets! Get you some slant-eye, gook, Vi-*et*-
namese motherfuckers," cheering at every explosion.

Hanson couldn't remember how they'd gotten to the 3rd
Mech hootch. It was adjacent to the Special Forces compound.
It seemed to be the only place left where anyone was still
awake. An E-5 was celebrating his last weekend before going
home, but most of his friends had left.

The big E-5 was standing behind the homemade plywood
bar, talking to a pair of E-4s who were sitting on the floor.

". . . five more days and I'm on the freedom bird and
back to the world. I'm glad to go, but I don't regret a minute
I've spent here in the 'Nam. Not a minute. We've done a hell of
a job here. I watch those demonstrators, and I can respect their
right to protest, but they don't know what it's all about. We had
a job to do . . ."

"That's right," one of the E-4s said, slurring his words.
"Freedom of speech is one thing, but impersonating the rights
of others is another."

At a glance, Hanson looked harmless enough, sitting on
the floor, his back against the wall, in his jeans and Hawaiian
shirt, but a bad smile had begun to take over his eyes and
mouth. He felt the speed beginning to work. The air was cool,
but he was sweating slightly, a faint tremor in his hands, all the
high-octane liquor he'd drunk burning away. He could smell it
in his sweat, and he felt good and mean.

"Well, yeah," the E-5 said. "Irregardless of what those
demonstrators think, we've done a damn fine job here, something I, personally, believe in, and when I see my wife
again . . ."

Hanson had to squint, concentrate to hear him over the
acid rock coming from the stereo. The music and the speed
made him shiver pleasantly in the warm night air.

Silver was playing an imaginary guitar to the music, feeling better since firing the antitank rocket at Blackie.

". . . and when I get back," the E-5 went on, "when I leave mortar alley here . . ."

Silver looked at Hanson and rolled his eyes. He pumped his fist up and down by his crotch and silently mouthed the words, "Mortar alley."

Jimi Hendrix's guitar was sneering and cursing from the speakers.

". . . just gonna lay back, you know, just lay back and do my own thing for a while. Hey, I owe it to myself, right? That's what your Eastern religions are all about, doing your own thing.

"I've learned a lot watching these Vietnamese. That's where I'm different from most of the guys here. I may be living on mortar alley, but I'm taking the time to watch and learn. A man can learn from any situation, any situation, if he tries."

Hendrix sang like a howling wind. Far to the west, H&I artillery grumbled, backing up the bass line.

"I'll tell you one thing," the E-5 said, "I'm proud of what I've done over here."

"I'll tell you one thing," Hanson said as he pushed himself up from the floor. "I'll tell you *one* thing. Uh-huh. You know what? I never heard anybody say that when they didn't have a whole *lot* of things to say. Did you?" he asked, looking over at Silver.

"Do your own thing," he said with a snort, walking over to the E-5. "*Free*dom bird. What did you do that you're so proud of, man?"

"Hey, partner," the E-5 said, "I don't know what your problem is, but why don't you take it for a walk."

" 'Partner,' " Hanson said. "He's a cowboy." He grinned enormously, looked at Quinn and Silver, and said, "Do you believe this guy?"

"You don't," Hanson said, grabbing the E-5 by the collar and shoving him into the wall, "talk to *me* that way," slamming him again against the wall, "over here." He kicked the plywood bar into him, splintering the top loose from the sides, knocking the E-5 down, beneath the plywood top.

One of the E-4s stood, but Quinn was suddenly on his feet.

He grabbed a handful of the E-4's shirt and slung him against the wall.

"Sit back down, dickhead," he told him.

Hanson kneeled on the plywood and the E-5's eyes bulged. "Can't. Breathe," he said.

Hanson shifted his weight and said, "What do your *Eastern religions* tell you about *that?* I might have to listen to bullshit back in the States, but not here. Not *here,*" he shouted, grabbing the E-5's shirt with both hands. "Not here," he said, standing the E-5 up, the splintered wood tearing his fatigue shirt. He let go of the shirt and shoved him back against the wall. "Now stand there. You got that?"

"Yes. Sir," he said, trying to catch his breath.

"Well, hell," Hanson said, turning to look at Quinn. "You were right. How'd I ever expect to get along back there?

"The *third* day I was back," he said, brushing splinters off his shirt, "I went to a party. This woman, a psychology professor, comes up to me—she's a little drunk—and says, 'I heard that you were in Vietnam, is that right?' I said, 'Yes, ma'am,' and she starts screaming at me, 'How could you do that?' So I tell her I don't really want to talk about it, and she yells, 'Well *I* do. *I* want to talk about it.' She's screaming in my face.

"So I walked away, and she followed me, yelling, 'Did you enjoy it?'

"She wouldn't leave me alone. I went into the bathroom and locked the door, and sat on the edge of the tub for a couple of minutes. Real nice bathroom. Ceramic tile and mirrors and soap shaped like sea shells." He laughed. "I thought about you guys while I was sitting there. Hiding in the bathroom.

"I got up and opened the door, and she was waiting for me. She started yelling again, so I said, 'Yeah, I enjoyed it,' and pushed her out of the way and went home. She fell over a hall stand or a table or something chasing me out the door. Somebody started the story that I beat her up. Things just went downhill from there.

"Back in 'the world,' huh?" Hanson said, turning to the E-5, who was still breathing hard, his shirt torn. "Back in the land of the big goddamn PX, huh? Well good luck, pal. It's all yours."

And then they were lying on the beach. Quinn was passed out and Silver was talking. The moon was low in the sky, red and lopsided.

"They'll never be the same. Those guys," Silver said, "who walked on the moon. What else could they ever do after that?

"I watched 'em on TV that night in July," he said, gesturing with his head as if July were just back *there* somewhere. *Back in July,* as if time and space and distance were all the same.

"Grainy black-and-white picture, couldn't tell what we were looking at, at first. They were taking pictures of their feet. On the moon. It was like sugar they were stepping in. And the shadows, man, they were sharp as fucking knives.

"We were all fucked up and tripping. Laughing at it. 'Oh wow,' you know, taking pictures of their feet on the moon.

"What would they ever be able to *do*, after that. Work in an office? Make commercials for shaving cream? Get old. We put them up there and then . . .

"We brought them back. Just brought 'em back, man. Congratulations, and thanks a lot, and see you around sometime.

"They must look up there—like this—and try to see where it was that they stood. Maybe they wonder if they're still up there, looking back at themselves. Like it's all still going on and there's two of them, one up there and the other down here. They must get scared, right? Worried that they're going crazy. Real straight-arrow dudes, too. Always had some kind of goddamn machine, where they push a button and it does what it's supposed to do.

"I wonder if they call each other up, like they're the only guys in the world who have this rare disease—the only ones who know what it feels like. Call up and ask, you know. 'Hey, are you all right? You okay, man? I'm feeling kind of weird tonight.'

"Probably not, huh? Too macho to admit something like that. Too hard-ass. Good goddamn troops.

"There must be nights when it's like the moon looks in at them through the window, calling them—'Come on back, brother.' " Silver's voice was crystalline as he sang. " 'Come on back now,' and they have to close the shades and hide under their blankets, or turn on all the lights until morning while the moon hangs in the air outside and waits.

"All their lives, you know, that's all they wanted to do. Go to the moon. It was what they dreamed about. And all the time it was dreaming about them. And they get back and . . . Whose dream was it, anyway?"

The surf rolled in, black and silver under the moonlight. Hanson thought that Silver had passed out. But then his voice came again, as if he'd never paused.

"I've seen things here. You know. I never even suspected. Those guys on the moon. They get there and it's like it's all been waiting for them all their lives. They never should have gone, but they didn't have any choice. Like when you step into an ambush, into the killing zone, before they start to fire you up, and for an instant, you *know* what's gonna happen, like your life started there, and it's gonna happen over and over. Like that time in Laos. Sometimes I feel like it's still happening, it's always happening, and if I fall asleep, I'm gonna be back there."

Silver rolled over onto his elbow and looked through the dark at Hanson, the South China Sea hissing in behind him on the sand—silver-blue winks of phosphorescence in the blackness farther out. Yellow smears of light from the fishing boat lanterns bobbing, and farther out still, the rows of porthole lights from the destroyers and carriers, like lights of a frontier settlement on the prairie. An image they'd grown up with at the Saturday matinee.

The stars were perfect points of light. Hanson could feel the cough of artillery coming up from deep in the ground. He settled his head into the sand and went to sleep.

Part Two

THE BEGINNING–
FORT BRAGG

The induction center had the dirty glitter of a bus station. It smelled of sweat and stale cigarette smoke. Rows of chrome and plastic chairs shared the floor with overflowing aluminum ashtrays. It was hot. There were vending machines for candy, cigarettes, and bitter coffee. But it was the mood of the place, the pervasive resignation, the defensive impersonality that gave the concrete-walled building the atmosphere of a Greyhound station.

When he looked around, Hanson realized that most of the people in the room would be the ones who couldn't afford an airplane ticket, who would wait with their shopping bags, cardboard boxes, and taped-up suitcases while a recorded announcement of the next departure reeled off the list of dying farm towns and industrial suburb slums, ending with a hearty, "All aboard, *please*."

Hanson was hung over. His mouth tasted tinny. He was sick to his stomach and had a headache. He'd reported to the center at 8 A.M., and he was still there at three in the afternoon.

Very little had happened during the day. A cadre assigned to the center had made a joke about Hanson's long hair, but no one had laughed. They weren't in a mood for easy jokes. The other thing that had happened was that a Marine sergeant had walked into the room, pointed at seven people, saying as he pointed, "You, you, you . . ." then said, "Stand up."

They did. Then he said, "Follow me. You are now United States Marines."

One of the seven said, "But you can't . . ."

The Marine sergeant, who looked like he'd already put in a long day, smiled at him, the way you'd smile at a willful, irritating child.

"Son," he said, "I just did. So why don't you just shut up

and try not to step on your dick again. Cause if you piss me off, you're gonna be a whole lot unhappier than you already are."

They marched off, and Hanson didn't see them again.

Just before five the rest of them were sworn in in a small carpeted and paneled room. An aging captain greeted them from behind a plywood podium. On the wall behind him there was a gilt device the size of a wagon wheel. In the center of the wheel was what seemed to be the limbless torso of a stocky woman, clad in armor, with cannon, spears, and flags blooming from her breasts like growths. The words, THIS WE SHALL DEFEND ringed the rim of the device, symbol of the Army Training Command.

The captain's uniform hung on him like a baggy business suit, and he looked like an unsuccessful salesman. A miniature of the wheel behind him was tacked to his lapel like a lodge button. Hanson imagined him being patronized at an Elks Club luncheon by more successful members. If he'd worked for an automobile agency, he'd have been the guy who sits in the little building at the back of the used car lot, a half-pint of liquor in his desk drawer.

He swore them in, telling them that they did not have to include the words "under God" if they did not want to. Hanson and the others raised their right hands and recited the oath after the captain like a grim responsive reading. Hanson did not say the words "under God," and felt immediately foolish.

"Congratulations. You men are fortunate enough to serve your country in the uniform of the United States Army, the best-trained, best-equipped, and most-motivated fighting force in the world today."

They boarded the olive drab buses, more like schoolbuses than Greyhounds, for the 120-mile trip to Fort Bragg. Graffiti, bloated women with spread legs, penises like rocket ships were scratched into the metal backs of the seats.

Hanson watched cars passing, farmers and cows in the fields. The sun was setting, and the taller trees turned orange. Cars began to turn on their headlights, and the temperature dropped. Dim lights came on in the bus, throwing the passengers' faces into shadow. None of them spoke, rocking together with the movement of the bus. It grew dark outside, and the seams in the concrete road thumped through the bus like flak around a bomber.

Out across the dark fields he could see winks of blue static. Boxes containing electrical grids were mounted out there like little phone booths. Insects were attracted to the boxes, and when they flew into the grid they were electrocuted. Hanson imagined that if he were close enough, he could have heard the dry *snap* of the current and the burned husks and wings falling into the pile of dead below.

Something touched his shoulder and a voice behind him asked, "Well, what do you think about it?"

It was a pudgy kid in the seat behind him, his face moon-like in the dim light.

"I don't know," Hanson said, smiling, "but I'm not too happy about the way things look so far."

"Have you had any college?"

"Yeah. I came home from my Shakespeare class and there was the letter."

"I thought so. You don't look like the rest of these guys. I could tell," he said happily. "Me too." His voice hardened. "But I had to drop out my sophomore year. Mono. I told them that, but they still drafted me. No one even listened to me.

"But hey," he said, suddenly smiling, "it's great to run into another college man. Billy Riley," he said, extending his hand across the back of the bus seat.

Hanson twisted in his seat and awkwardly shook hands, introducing himself.

The bus dimmed its headlights, and all the reading lights went out with a tiny *click*.

The first DI stalked silently to the back of the bus, then turned to face the front, staring straight ahead as if the bus were empty. He was a wiry man, not much older than Hanson, but his pale face already showed a tracery of broken veins across his nose and beneath his eyes. He had a tattoo on his forearm, but just as Hanson was about to look back to see what it said, the DI snapped at another recruit, "Don't look at me, shitbird," and Hanson cut his eyes toward the front of the bus, grateful that it hadn't been him caught looking.

The second DI stepped up to the front of the bus and stood with his back to the windshield, hand on hips, glaring at the recruits from beneath the brim of his Smoky-the-Bear hat. He was big and black, his starched fatigues tailored for his weight-lifter's build. He had a wide nose and small, deep-set eyes, and he looked down at the recruits as if he were genuinely, personally angry with them. Hanson could see a vein in his neck throbbing, and the bead of sweat that appeared at his temple and slid down his cheek.

"People," he said, "I am Staff Sergeant Jones. I don't want to be here tonight, but my captain said I had to be here. You already fucked up my night.

"You all are some sorry-looking individuals, but they scrapin' the bottom of the barrel for bodies to fight this raggedy little war, so I got to take you.

"You gonna be sorry you ever got on the bus. You gonna hate this place. I'm gonna make you people *pay* for the trouble you caused me. You got one minute to get your shit and be standing at attention out there on the blacktop. Now *move!*"

Two more drill instructors leapt into the bus, and then all of them began screaming, *"Move. Move. Move,"* tendons cording their necks, faces red.

*"God*damnit get your ass out there," one yelled, grabbing a kid by his high school T-shirt—"Wilson Wildcats"—jerking him out of the seat, and slamming him against the opposite side of the bus.

"Move your ass. Gonna knock your dick stiff . . ."

"Don't you raise your hands at me, boy," one of them screamed at a kid who tried to shield himself from a blow. "I'll kill ya. I'll tear your fuckin' heart out. You *hear* me? You *hear* me," he screamed, slapping the back of the kid's head with his open hand.

"Yessir, *yes* sir!"

Another body hit the side of the bus, shaking it on its suspension.

"Damn you . . ."

"Yes sir!"

"*Out.* Get outta my bus, this is *my* motherfuckin' bus . . ."

"They're *crazy*, they're really crazy," Riley said as Hanson clawed his way to the door, worried that he might get trampled. A DI kicked a skinny black kid out the door, where he landed on all fours. Then Hanson was out, and they were all trying to line up on the parking lot. There were yellow patches of streetlight across the asphalt, ragged with shadow from swarming bugs.

Hanson looked up at the bus and saw Riley coming off, one DI lifting him to his toes by the seat of his pants, another walking alongside, screaming in his ear and slapping him on the back of his head. ". . . my fat boy. You my fat boy. I get one every busload. They always *mine* 'cause I like fat boys. I'm gonna *fuck* you to death."

He hit Riley in the stomach, dropping him to his knees.

"Get up, you tubaguts, getonyerfeet," he shrieked at Riley, silver spittle flying from his lips. "Youan'you," he yelled at two other recruits. "Take charge of this fucker, get him outta my sight. I can't kill him now, I wanna save him for a couple of days. Take him, take him . . ."

They took Riley under his arms and half-walked, half-dragged him to the end of the formation. One of them called him fat boy and slapped him on the side of the head. "You're causing trouble for all of us," he shouted.

As they marched the terrified column off the parking lot, two of the DIs looked at each other and grinned. It was good training.

The room was bleak and harshly lit, like an interrogation setting. Illustrated posters of "The Soldier's Creed" lined the walls, one of them declaring, "*I will never surrender of my own free will.*" The "Last Chance Table," a scarred plywood platform, stood at the front of the room. A black and white sign, posted above it like a lunch menu, listed prohibited items.

One of the DIs addressed the recruits from the front of the room. "Gentlemen, when you leave the induction center you will have nothing on your person that is not U.S. Army issue. You will not have any of these items," he said, pointing at the sign, and then began reading off the list: "Firearms, narcotics, controlled substances or medication of any kind—"

Billy Riley raised his hand and said, "But sir, I had my prescription filled just before—"

One of the DIs shouted from the back of the room, "If you passed the Army physical that means you don't need any pills."

Riley looked like he was going to say something more, but the recruits sitting near him hissed and cursed him, and he lowered his hand.

". . . alcoholic beverages, candy, knives, condoms—rubbers, gentlemen, you won't be needing them—pornography— No *Playboys* or fuck books or dirty pictures—we don't want you getting all hot and bothered 'cause your buddy might start looking good to you—any reading matter except the Bible, playing cards . . ."

The room stank of sweat, farts, and fear. In the harsh light, the recruits, exhausted and frightened, looked like psychotics in the day room of an asylum.

They lined up and filed past the table, dropping linoleum knives, hawkbills, case cutters, yellow-handled straight razors, chewing gum, paperback Westerns, Trojans, a ragged paperback with the title *Coeds with Hot Pants*.

"Put it *all* on the table, gentlemen. Don't take it out the door. We *will* find it and you'll go to barbed-wire city. Think about it."

. . . half-pint bottles, pills and multicolor capsules, a pair of brass knuckles, marijuana cigarettes, a Polaroid photo of a skinny, naked girl with bad skin squatting on a motel bed, her knees parted to a hairy black pubis and dead white thighs. The camera flash had turned her eyes into red points of light.

A muscular, stocky kid with a tattoo of an impish red devil on his bicep, already drunk, finished off a half-pint of grain alcohol in a shaky show of bravado and dropped the empty bottle on the table. The DIs ran him around the building until he didn't have anything left in his stomach to vomit up.

The DIs kept up a running commentary as the contraband piled up. "Brass knuckles? What kind of recruit they sending us?"

"Dig *way* down in those pockets. Get that last pill. You men gonna like it here, won't be needing to take no dope."

"How long you been carrying that rubber around, boy?"

"All right, another bottle of that Thunderbird wine. I heard that back on the block you people can still have a big night for a dollar, enough for a bottle of wine and a rubber."

"God*damn*. That girl is ugly. I mean she's some kind of serious ugly. Look at that twat. Goddamn, man, anybody'd fuck that would fuck a dog. I'd sooner slam my dick in a car door than put it in that thing."

At 3 A.M. they were lined up outside still another buff-yellow wooden building, waiting to get their shots. Riley peeked around from behind Hanson at the line of recruits feeding into the brightly lit doorway.

"How many do you think we'll have to get?" he hissed.

"I don't know. Maybe they'll give us all the stuff in one shot."

"No. It'll be at least two, maybe three. They can't mix some of those serums. Oh, damnit, probably three. I *told* them that my vaccinations were up to date. There's no reason for me to have these shots. It's on my record."

"Yeah," Hanson said, "but it doesn't seem like they're set up to give much individual attention."

"They don't *care*," Riley went on, irritated by Hanson's irony. "I mean, they don't care about anybody. How hard would it be for them to just look at my records, verify what I told them, and excuse me from this. It's a waste of vaccine. You know, if they'd treat us more as individuals, they'd get better results in the long run, the recruits would work that much harder . . ."

The smell of antiseptic drifted out the open door and hung heavy and sweet in the warm night air.

"This is senseless. Anybody with a brain can see that it's counterproductive. But not them, no, they—"

Riley's anxious monologue suddenly stopped, and something soft and heavy hit the backs of Hanson's legs.

Riley's head was bleeding where it had hit the concrete, and he was moaning softly. Hanson and another recruit took him under the arms and carried him to the door, his feet dragging behind him. They sat him in a chair, and a medic popped an ammonia capsule under his nose. Riley snorted and straightened up in the chair, saw blood dripping from his cheek and fainted again, toppling sideways and taking the chair over with him.

"Fuck *this,*" the medic said. "He's gonna give his life for his country right here. Fuckin' blood donor is what we got."

Hanson went back out in line, and in a few minutes he saw Riley emerge, looking shaky and foolish with a pink Band-Aid on his forehead. His face was grim as he walked down the line to Hanson.

"I've just about had it with them," he whispered. "They can't treat us like dogs. I mean, I expected some discipline, some harassment. That's okay. I understand the need for it, and it would be kind of a challenge. But this is ridiculous. These people are completely out of line. The command people must not have any idea that we're being treated like this. We're *individuals.* Some of these people, maybe they *need* this kind of treatment, but we're intelligent guys. Why do they want to humiliate us? What good does it do anyone? All they have to do is tell me what they want me to do, or show me, and I'll do it. Why humiliate us?"

"Looks like it's all part of the process," Hanson said.

"I don't know," Riley said. "I think they're jealous. No, suspicious of intelligent people, threatened by them. No, not intelligence so much, some of these guys are intelligent enough, in their own way. I mean, there's a lot of mechanics and truck drivers and farmers who are *smart* people, who we could learn from. That's one of the things I was looking forward to. Talking to people like that. No, what it is is education. It's our education that threatens them."

The line had moved them to the outside of the door. Inside, the room was so bright that there didn't seem to be any shadows, just various levels of glare. The medics were giving injections with little pneumatic pistols that literally blew the serum through the skin, popping each recruit in the arm like spot welders on an assembly line. Riley bared his arm and looked away, grimacing.

"Don't flinch," the medic said. Then, as he was about to shoot the serum, Riley jerked his arm away.

"Don't flinch, or it'll cut you," the medic said, and jammed the serum gun against the arm as Riley stiffened. The gun went *snap*, and a bright patch of blood appeared on Riley's arm, mixed with sweat, and ran down to the elbow.

"Get him out of here," the medic said to Hanson, "before he falls down again or bleeds to death. Do it outside. I don't need the paperwork."

They were issued pillows and gray wool blankets, then marched to a transient barracks. The soiled mattress cover on Hanson's bunk smelled like dirty feet. He could hear Billy crying into his pillow across the aisle. Outside, loudspeakers whistled and chattered until dawn.

Three hours later they were marched to a mess hall where they waited in line for half an hour, then had five minutes to eat chipped beef on toast and watery scrambled eggs. Hanson forced himself to eat the warm, salty breakfast, and then they were marched to the barber shop.

Five civilian barbers stood behind their chairs, ankle-deep in dull, dead hair of all colors and textures.

"Here's one for you," one of the cadre said, and pointed Hanson to a chair. "He'll be needing a little bit off the top there," he said to the barber, who didn't crack a smile. He drove the clippers deep into Hanson's long hair, digging the hot metal into his scalp, pulling hair out as well as cutting it, driving the shears through, over and over. It was like sitting in a dentist's chair while he drills, then pauses, drills, then pauses.

Handfuls of his hair dropped softly on Hanson's shoulders and thighs, and the shears kept digging in, their buzzing almost a roar in his ears, smelling of hot oil and electricity. He held the sides of the chair and tried not to think about killing the barber who twisted his head to one side and dug in, cocked it to another angle and dug in, gripping Hanson's head with nicotine-stained fingers.

"Next," the barber said, and Hanson got out of the chair, turning to look the barber in the face, to look him in the eyes, let him know that someday he was going to pay for treating him the way he had. But the barber didn't even notice that Hanson was looking at him. He was staring out the window, waiting for the next recruit.

The recruits, too tired and intimidated to complain, were then marched to a warehouse and issued uniforms, T-shirts, boxer shorts, socks, fatigues, web belts, hats, helmets, and two pairs of black combat boots. A seedy civilian with slicked-back hair squinted through the smoke of his cigarette as he marked the hem in Hanson's baggy dress uniform.

The recruits were each given a cardboard box and tape to package all their civilian clothes for shipment home.

"And gentlemen," one of the cadre told them, "if you have a high school ring, or a wedding ring, you ought to send it on home. Nobody cares where you went to high school, or if you got a wife. Nobody *cares*, gentlemen. I seen a recruit once jump on the back of a deuce an' a half, and he caught his wedding ring on a wooden slat. Tore his finger off at the knuckle. Think about it, gentlemen."

Dressed now in stiff, wrinkled fatigues and heavy boots, they were marched to another building. It was a hot day, and the smell of sizing in the new fatigues was smothering.

They had their photos taken and were issued laminated ID cards. Hanson looked at the bald, gaunt, hollow-eyed image of himself. He looked like a refugee, or like one of those stricken faces in a Civil War tintype. He recalled that aborigine tribesmen refused to let anyone photograph them, fearing that it would take their soul away. Hanson had never before felt so alone, so without any sense of who he was or who he should be.

Hanson's nose had blistered, peeled to pink skin, and blistered again. His whole body ached, and his head was throbbing. His eyes were gritty, the sun in his face.

Riley had dropped out of the two-mile run again, and the two biggest recruits in the class were dragging him the rest of the way around the dirt track, dragging him by the legs at a fast walk while Riley moaned and drooled, his head and arms bouncing along the ground.

The rest of the class was watching at attention while the

captain strode back and forth in front of them. He was a short man with black hair and a face that was almost pretty.

"Gentlemen," he was saying, "when I accepted the responsibility of turning you into soldiers, I did not do so lightly. It is my job to see that every one of you, when you leave here, is ready for combat. That is my mission, and I *will* carry it out. It behooves each and every one of you individuals . . ."

Out on the track behind the captain, Riley bounced along, leaving a faint cloud of red dust behind him. Sweat and dust had collected in Hanson's eye, stinging it to tears that attracted more dust. He blinked the eye and twitched his cheek.

And then he was face to face with the captain, who was saying, "What's your problem, young man? Is it that hard for you to maintain a position of attention? Get that chin up!" he said, twisting Hanson's head by the jaw. Then he walked back down the column, continuing his speech, already having forgotten Hanson.

At that moment Hanson thought that if the captain, or anyone, laid hands on him again, he would quit. He'd walk out of the formation, sit down beneath a pine tree, and just go away, stop talking or responding for a week or a month until they declared him insane and discharged him. There seemed to be no other way out of the heat, humiliation, and, most of all, the brutal indifference.

As he considered it, he noticed four soldiers walking on the far side of the parade ground, heat rippling from the sandy soil and eddying around their legs. They were wearing jump boots, the green and black patterned fatigues called tiger suits, and green berets. Special Forces soldiers from the school over on Smoke Bomb Hill. Their aviator sunglasses flashed in the sun as they laughed about something, one of them gesturing elaborately with his hands. Yet even while they laughed and clowned, they moved with absolute confidence, not the lockstep of the training cadre, but with the ease of professional athletes, or royalty. They were the first free men Hanson had seen since he had been sworn into the Army.

"This, gentlemen," the wiry black DI announced, "is the bayonet." He held the bayonet-tipped M-14 rifle out at arm's length.

"This afternoon," he continued, his voice as smooth as a radio announcer's yet abrupt as an auctioneer's, a hypnotic cadence, "you will have an opportunity to put what you have learned in bayonet practice to use."

As he spoke, the DI snapped the heavy rifle into different positions, holding each one until his sentence caught up to it, holding, then snapping into a new stance, his words following the movement.

The sky was overcast, a huge pewter bowl, but it was hot. There was a hint of yellow in the sky, like an old bruise, a storm moving in. Hanson noticed how colors changed, very subtly, in the light beneath the moving clouds; the sand, scrub pine, and the faces of the men, their relationships and relative importance shifting in the greasy light. Only the DI, crouching and striking, seemed permanent, his cadence and inflection as precise as his movements, wheeling and striking, in the middle of the circle of men, beneath the silver-yellow sky.

"This. Gentlemen. Is the on-guard position. A position you are all familiar with. The . . .

"*Butt*stroke. Can be delivered in this manner. Or . . . in an *up*ward movement. Catching the throat and chin. It is effective, gentlemen. It can ruin your opponent's whole day, or," he said quickly, moving forward, then backward, then spinning to face the opposite direction, "at the very least . . . fuck up his concentration. And. After repeated blows to the side*ofhishead* . . . lower his level of self-confidence. At which point, young troops, you jab. Jab! Jab! Taking him to . . .

"The *ground*. Where you kill him some more . . ."

Fat C-130 transport planes took off from the nearby airfield at regular intervals, endlessly, it seemed, the pitch of their engines rising as they lifted heavily from the runway like stunned bugs into the hot, thin air.

One of the PT instructors for another class was shouting, "Eye gouge, groin chop. Eye gouge, groin chop."

Another training company was marching down a dirt access road calling cadence. "I picked her *up*—I threw her *down*

—I stomped her *face* right in the *ground.* Left—left—left
. . ." The voices were happy. They were marching well.

"And this, ladies," the DI shouted, "is what we call a pugil
stick." He held it out and began to turn slowly so that all the
men in the circle around him could see. It was a thick wooden
staff as long as the DI was tall, each end wrapped with heavy
padding.

As the DI turned, still speaking, he began to spin the staff
like a baton, then snap it into the various striking positions.

"As I said earlier today," he went on, turning and striking
like a dancer, "you are going to have an opportunity, to put
into practice, what you have learned today." He completed
the circle and snapped the stick up to port arms, holding there
at attention while the junior DI walked into the circle dragging an equipment bag.

"All right then," the junior DI shouted. "Since the Army
doesn't want any of its valuable young recruits injured or
fucked up in any way, because they *care* about your safety,
ladies, you will wear this protective equipment.

"We want you to stay as pretty as you are," he said, pulling
a football helmet out of the bag. "And, we do not want you to
hurt your fingers," he said, pulling out a pair of heavily padded
hockey gloves, which he threw at Riley. Riley flinched and
dropped them, and the others in the circle groaned and
laughed.

"Where do they find these people?" he said, turning to the
DI.

"They out there," the DI said. "Civilians walkin' the
streets."

The junior DI shook his head and reached back into the
bag. "Now, some of you girls," he said, holding a plastic groin
cup above his head, smiling at Riley, "may not have any use for
this. But the Army says that you will wear it anyway. For those
of you individuals who *do* have anything between your legs to
protect, we don't want you to go home and disappoint little
Susie, or little Fred, or whatever it is that makes you people
happy back on the block.

"You know what?" he said to the DI. "Some of these fat

boys got tits. Just like a girl. *Bigger* 'n a lot of girls. Ain't that some shit, now? To have tits hanging off your chest?"

There was laughter around Riley as people goosed him.

The DI threw the pugil stick at Riley who didn't even manage to get his hands up before it bounced off his chest. "Riley," the DI said, "get out here and put this shit on."

Riley was matched against Bobby Ray Corn, a mean little squad leader from Yazoo, Mississippi. He was smaller than Riley, but all bone and muscle. Poor white and stupid, he found his pleasure in meanness. He liked to hurt people. It was the only kind of victory open to someone who seemed to fail at everything else. The DIs had spotted his potential immediately. He was a bully and he followed orders to the letter. He was made a squad leader. Just as there always seemed to be a fat-boy Riley in every company, there was always a Bobby Ray Corn.

Corn had a tattoo of a cute, grinning little devil on his right bicep. He talked a lot about going back home, in uniform, driving a new car.

Corn was a bully, but not a coward. He didn't have enough imagination to be afraid. No one had ever hurt him enough to show him that there was anything to fear. The black DIs despised him as the kind of dumb cracker who used to make their lives difficult, but that didn't stop them from using him like a training aid. Corn had written home about how nice the nigger drill sergeants treated him. Corn was as much a pawn as Riley, part of the performance the DIs directed to show the recruits that if you don't fight back, you're doomed. To demonstrate that a belief most of them had grown up with, the assumption that if you are nice to people, they will be nice to you, was a lie, to show them that force was the best response to force, to prepare them for the moment, a few months away, when people they didn't even know would start trying to kill them.

Riley entered the circle awkwardly in his equipment. Someone shoved him, he stumbled, and Corn was on him, hitting him at will. One of the first blows knocked Riley's helmet askew so that he could only see out of one eye. Corn danced around his blind side, hurting and humiliating him. Finally Riley tripped over his own feet and refused to get up.

The DI stopped the match, and when he pulled the helmet and face guard off Riley, everyone could see that he was crying, tears cutting furrows down the dirt on his cheeks.

As he had expected, Hanson was paired off with Henry Johnson, a black kid from Newark who slept in the bunk below him. Henry wrote his mother regularly, never used obscenities, yet was well liked by the other black recruits. He and Hanson were almost identical in size and endurance and had become regular rivals, yet they had, grudgingly, come to like each other.

They put on the equipment and began circling toward each other as the circle around them tightened and roared, "Kill him!"

The inside of Hanson's helmet was slick with sweat and smelled like a locker room. Through the grid of the face mask he could see his own hands on the pugil stick, Henry Johnson moving toward him, and the brutal ring of screaming faces. He felt as though he were inside a machine, powering it with his arms and legs—looking through the face mask was like peering out of a ventilator grid. His hands felt numb in the padded gloves, and his legs sank into the sand.

But he discovered that he was able to read Henry Johnson's moves and get out of their way or block them. It was easy. His senses were heightened to the point that everything was very clear and moving slowly. It was as though he weren't even involved. As he moved and blocked the blows, he studied the faces of the other soldiers and watched the gray and yellow storm clouds boiling toward the parade field.

It was interesting, countering the blows while handicapped with the equipment and loose footing, watching Henry's eyes through the shifting grid of the face mask. The crowd was shouting for more action, but Hanson was working out a rhythm, his defense shaping Henry's attack. For the first time since he had arrived at the induction center, he felt that he was in control of his life.

Then something hit him flat on the side of his helmet—he tasted his own salty blood—and his legs were kicked out from beneath him. He looked up from the sand and, through the grid work of the mask, saw the DI standing over him, filling up his field of view. His face was wide and angular, hard, a pulse beating on the side of his nose. The DI placed one jump boot in the center of Hanson's chest and slowly began to put his weight behind it. His lips were moving, but Hanson couldn't hear him at first. The sun was glaring down behind the DI, and sand grated against the back of the helmet as Hanson tried to shift his head.

". . . ain't no game," the DI's voice said, the words and the movement of his lips beginning to make sense. "You ain't playing tennis. This is practice at killing people. This ain't *golf*, or some bullshit sport for polite people.

"You got something going with Johnson? You two been playin' in the shower? You supposed to *kill* him. That's all, not play with him.

"Young man, you *best* work at killing, 'cause that's how you gonna stay alive. You think too much, Hanson. You know that? You think too much an' make what's simple, complicated.

"Now take off that shit and get back in the circle."

The DI turned and looked around the circle from beneath the wide brim of his hat. "That's what it all about, people," he said. "The little man tryin' to kill you. You got to understand that now—ain't gonna be no time to figure it out when he's comin' at you.

"You people think I'm *lyin'*? You think I'm standing out here in the sun tellin' stories? You people got to learn it. You got to mentally prepare yourselves to dig in and kill old Newyen van Newyen before he kill you. You got to do it quick—ain't got time to think about it.

"Now remember that when you out here with those sticks."

Hanson began watching the other fighters in a different way. He could read them. By their eyes, by the way they shifted their shoulders and hips, he could tell how and when they were going to strike. He was surprised, and he wondered if everyone could do it. He'd felt good in the ring with Henry for that minute or so when he held the pugil stick. For that minute he felt that he *had* "dug in," that he had, for the first time, held his ground against the Army. For a minute he had risen above the grinding anonymity of the past weeks. He felt strong.

After everyone had fought, Vernel Friday stepped into the ring. "Drill Sergeant," he shouted, "Private Friday requests permission to go again. I didn't even break sweat that first time."

Friday was the biggest, strongest man in the training company. He was black, he was from Detroit, and he was alive with rage. He had been a gang leader "back on the block" in the city, and he was a squad leader in the company. When he broke into chow lines and PX lines, no one tried to stop him.

"All right," the DI said to the circle of men, "Friday says he wants to"—and he looked at Friday and smiled—"hone his skills with the pugil stick against another opponent. Who wants to try him on?"

Friday stood in the middle of the ring, shoulders back, looking contemptuously at the other recruits.

Hanson knew he could beat Friday if he did it right then. He could picture himself doing it. He felt as if he were in a movie and he was the only actor who had seen the script.

"I'll go again, Drill Sergeant," Hanson said, his own voice startling him as the words came out. For an instant he was dizzy with fear, but it was too late to back out. He turned away from the fear as he might turn away, finally, from the endless complaining of a lifelong companion. He looked at Friday and felt solid on his feet again.

The DI looked at Hanson and grinned. "You got something against Vernel, Han-son?"

"No, Drill Sergeant. I just thought I should go out there and beat him."

"Well, then," he said, still smiling, "you better get started.

"Throw him that gear," he said to his assistant. "We don't want him to lose any, you know, mo*men*tum.

"He's all yours, Hanson."

Vernel Friday stood easily at the far arc of the circle as Hanson walked slowly toward him. Hanson could see, though, that he was disappointed. He'd expected a better match than a quiet little white dude. Beating Hanson was no problem, but he'd have to look cool doing it, knock his dick in the dirt and not break a sweat.

Hanson broke into a run, holding the pugil stick across his body with both hands. He slammed into Friday, driving him through the ring of recruits, catching him low, before he'd had a chance to get set, and knocking him on his back.

And then he was standing over Friday, swinging the stick like a club, slamming down at his head and throat as Friday tried to block the blows with his own pugil stick, crabbing away from the blows through the sand.

The DI grabbed the pugil stick from behind as Hanson brought it up for another blow. "That's all," he said. "You won."

After the company was dismissed, the white recruits gathered around Hanson, laughing and slapping him on the back. Hanson enjoyed the attention, and it had been easy.

There was talk of forming a "security guard" for Hanson in case the blacks went after him for humiliating Friday, and Hanson realized that it was a possibility.

When Hanson left the mess hall that evening, Riley was slumped beneath the overhand bars, a long horizontal ladder that the recruits had to traverse before they could eat. They had to jump up, grab the first rung, then go hand over hand, rung by rung, to the opposite end.

Hanson watched as Riley jumped, grabbed the first bar, and hung there, rocking slightly with each ragged breath.

An olive-drab tractor-trailer made a sharp left turn behind the mess hall. It moved slowly, black smoke boiling from the twin stacks on the cab. The heat was tainted by the smell of half-burned diesel fuel and the stink of old grease blowing from the back of the mess hall where the "outdoor man" on KP was hosing out the heavy garbage cans. The blue sky was cloudless except for the smeared contrails of a high-flying jet.

The land rose slowly behind the mess hall. Past the clusters of barracks and buff-yellow Quonset huts, beyond the check points and chain-link fencing, on the only hill in sight, the huge water tower dominated the base, its red and white candy stripes wavering in the heat. Marching columns moved across the landscape like figures in an epic mural. Hanson could hear, over the sound of Riley's breathing, the faint cadence of a training company marching somewhere out of sight. ". . . ain't no use in goin' home, Jody's got your girl and gone, ain't no use in goin' back, Jody's got your Cadillac—left, left, left . . ."

Riley, his fatigues dark at the armpits and crotch, was unaware of any of it, conscious only of the heat and humiliation, lost in the overwhelming indifference of the world he had somehow stumbled into.

Riley only showed the weakness and fear that all the other recruits felt but managed, most of the time, to hide. It was as if he was burdened with the weakness of the whole company. In a way, he was the most important person there. Just as a hero must live out other men's dreams of triumph, Riley lived out their failures.

As Hanson watched, Riley lost his grip and collapsed in the dirt.

The barracks smelled of paste wax, gun oil, sweat, and paint.

"Hey. Hanson. Mister New Hero."

Hanson looked down at Henry Johnson in the bunk below. "Yes *sir*, Private Johnson, sir. What can I do for you?"

"Vernel says not to sweat it. He told the brothers to leave you alone. But he says to tell you that you were just lucky. I told him that you were okay compared to most of these crackers."

"Well thanks, Henry. I didn't know you thought so."

Henry laughed and said, "That ain't no *big* compliment."

Hanson was reading when Canada and Bostic, two of Vernel Friday's protégés, burst into the barracks, drunk on sour three-two beer. Canada was a short, stocky kid, inarticulate and always on the edge of rage over real or imagined wrongs done to him. Like some of the other black recruits, he was paranoid and almost psychotic with anger. He was likely to respond to any request, suggestion, or order with hysteria and violence, as if he could flick a little switch in his head and say, "Now I get to go crazy." He used rage as a narcotic, as a means to shut out frustration and doubt. He was, Hanson thought, a scary guy.

The blacks in camp knew that they were going to Vietnam as infantry troops in a matter of weeks—there had never been any question about that—and they had nothing to lose. A familiar, bitter comment to disciplinary warnings was, "What the motherfuckers gonna do, send me to Vietnam?"

Hanson was trying to read a collection of movie reviews, a paperback book he'd found in the dog-eared little camp library. He had not seen any of the films discussed, but he read anything he could find as an escape from the routine of the camp. He'd even taken to ripping sections out of paperbacks and carrying them concealed in his fatigue pockets to read out in the field. He often carried sections of poetry books for the times when they had to stand the hour-long inspections, slipping them out of his pocket back in the third rank of the formation and holding them down at his waist, hidden by the soldier in front of him. He'd memorize stanzas to dull the pain of cramping muscles when the sun drove down into the sand of the parade ground and up into his face, when the steel helmet he wore got heavier and tighter around his head. "I will arise and go now," he'd say to himself, memorizing Yeats, "and go to Innisfree." It was a practice that had earned him the name "Pageman" for a while.

"Reading. My man here, he always reading something," Canada said, stopping at Hanson's bunk. "Mr. Pageman. What you reading now?"

"Book about the movies," Hanson said, not looking up from the page. "About how to make movies."

"Shit," Canada said. "You crazy, you know that?"

"Yeah, I know. The Army made me that way."

"But you all right for being crazy. Vernel says you were lucky, but you all right. Hey," he went on, "you make a movie, I'm gonna be in it, right?"

"Right. Absolutely. Roger that. I'll make you the hero."

"Awright, man here gonna put me in his movie," Canada said, then he spun around to Riley, who was lying on the top bunk across the aisle from Hanson.

"Hey," he said, suddenly enraged, "you cracker motherfucker, how come you been talking about me?"

Riley tried to smile as though they were sharing a joke, his mouth twitching into a shit-eating grin. "Aw, come on, Canada, you know I didn't—"

"Shut up, boy. You don't be tellin' *me* what I *know*. You been talking about me, and I'm telling you to apologize."

Riley held the tight smile and licked his upper lip. He glanced quickly over at Hanson, moving only his eyes.

Three different record players were on in the barracks. After the first payday, the PX had been stripped of Polaroid cameras and battery-powered record players. The Beach Boys were singing "California Girls."

Hanson looked down at Henry Johnson and Henry met his eyes, shaking his head.

A Puerto Rican band was going heavy on drums and maracas, and at the far end of the building, James Brown screamed the song "I'm Black and I'm Proud," over and over.

Neither Canada nor Riley moved. Two doomed boys. Canada knew it and was trying to wield all the power, get all the revenge against the world he could, while he still had time. Riley didn't know it, and he was a coward, afraid of getting hurt and not knowing how to avoid it.

"You apologize to me, boy. Nobody talks about me," Canada said, by then believing the accusation he had invented.

Riley was still trying to smile when Canada hit him on the side of the head, the sound of bone against flesh almost lost in the music.

"Apologize, motherfucker."

"Okay. If that's what you want," Riley said, close to tears. "I apologize."

"*That* ain't what I'm talkin' about," Canada said, hitting Riley again. "I want a real motherfucking apology."

"I'm sorry. I'm sorry. I apologize."

"Awright then. Awright. Shit," Canada said, hunching his head down into his shoulders like a boxer. "Shit! Motherfucker, you *through* talkin' about me."

He smiled at Bostic, then said to Riley, "Hey, my man. Since we friends now, how about lending me five dollars?"

"Well," Riley began, "I don't think—"

"Sure you do. Take a look. If you my friend. You sayin' you don't want to be my friend?"

Riley, his ear red and already beginning to swell, took out his wallet and Canada jerked it out of his hand.

"Look here," he said, holding the wallet open, "it's *ten* in here. I'll just take that. I'll be sure to pay you back as soon as I get the money, my man."

He pocketed the money, then removed a photograph of a girl from the wallet and held it at arm's length, frowning. "Say, look at this ugly bitch. She your girl? Or your momma? One thing for sure, she *ugly*. Look like a chicken. You been *fucking* this bitch? Shit! You a braver man than me, 'cause I'd be afraid to put my dick in that."

"You some kind of bad dude," Canada said, laughing. "And I been thinking you just a punk."

He tossed the wallet on the bunk and said, "We gotta be going. Thanks for the loan."

Canada and Bostic walked out of the barracks, laughing.

Hanson looked back at his book but couldn't concentrate. There was nothing anyone could have done for Riley. If he'd tried to defend him, it would have been worse the next time. In a way, Hanson thought, Riley deserved it.

He reached under his pillow and felt the reassuring, solid handle of the entrenching tool he kept there. In the Army, he had finally learned, all you have is the space that you fill up with your body. That's all they allow you to own, and there is nowhere else to go. So if somebody fucks with you, they are fucking with everything you have. At some point Hanson had decided that he'd die before he'd let anyone do to him what Canada had done to Riley. They'd have to kill him. They could tell that, and they left him alone.

Later that night the fire guard found Billy Riley in the latrine, lying on the floor with his wrists slashed. He ran and got the duty DI, who, after seeing that Riley's life was in no immediate danger, woke up the whole company and marched them into the latrine.

Riley lay crying on the red concrete floor. Toilets and sinks gleamed in the harsh light, the old plumbing whining and thrumming with water pressure.

"Gentlemen," the DI said to the assembled company,

"think of this as a late training session, getting you out of your bunks because of this fat pussy laying on the floor. A training session on the correct, Army-approved procedure for committing suicide."

He reached down and grabbed Riley's arm, wrenching it up and holding it so the company could see the blood-crusted cuts across the wrist.

"You do *not* cut across the wrist like this. It is *not* effective, gentlemen, no!" he shouted, throwing the arm to the floor. "The blood will co*a*gulate before you can bleed to death. All you will accomplish is to fuck up the tendons in your arm.

"Make a fist, Riley," he shouted. "Make a fist," he said, grabbing Riley by the hair, "or I'll pull your fucking head off."

"I can't," Riley sobbed.

"That's right," the DI said, flinging Riley's head to one side. "You're gonna have a hard time jacking off from now on."

He turned back to the company and said, holding up his own wrist, "Cut your wrists this way, up and down, the long way. Open 'em up good, and you won't end up like this pussy here.

"Now, get this sorry piece of shit off the floor and outside while I call an ambulance to haul his fat ass away. And this latrine had better gleam when I come back."

Several of the recruits grabbed Riley's shirt and dragged him to the door, cursing him on the way. He was sobbing, and his feet bounced and bobbed on the floor.

Hanson lay in his bunk, looking out the window at the steel hedge of concertina wire that the recruits had to jump over when they took turns chasing each other with sections of rubber hose each night before dinner. Down at the end of the barracks, a Korean war vintage reciprocating fan droned to the end of its circuit, hesitated, then began swinging back.

He was thinking about the Special Forces soldiers he'd seen, how they seemed untouched by the bleakness and oppression of the base. He wanted to find out whatever it was that they knew. Find out. It wasn't that he wanted to *become* one of them, whatever that really was. But they had something he thought he wanted. He did not want to go to war with the bullies and sadists and cowards around him.

Hanson didn't know that he had decided to do exactly what the Army hoped some of its men would do, what the best ones do—try to beat them at their own game. The game was war, and if you get too close to war, if you look in its eyes it will take you, muscle, brain and blood, into its heart, and you will never find joy anywhere else. Outside it, love and work and friendship are disappointments.

The god of war was pleased that night. He had gotten an initiate into his priesthood. He loved the common soldier, the battles of massed infantry, not much changed from the times they had gone at each other, drunk and terrified, with pikes and farm tools. He loved them all. But the priests, the sorcerers, the ones who met his eyes were the ones he loved most, and Special Forces was where they were. Hanson didn't realize it that night, but he would realize one day that it is not possible to soldier with an army's free men and best killers without becoming one of them.

Hanson looked out the window at the wire coiled around the barracks. The fan pushed dead air, twitching after each arc and changing direction, as the shadow of the fire guard passed the window. The fire guard was carrying a pump shotgun and singing softly to himself, "I'd be safe and warm, if I was in L.A. . . . California dreamin', on *such* a winter day . . ." It was midnight, and sweat beaded his face. While the company slept, he thought about Vietnam.

Hanson took the Special Forces test from a staff sergeant wearing jeans, tennis shoes, and a red shirt with hundreds of yellow hula dancers on it.

Night Jump—
Pisgah National Forest

Hanson tried not to look directly at the bare bulbs in the sheet-metal Quonset hut, but after two nights with little sleep, the glare went into his eyes like grit. The last briefing was almost over, the captain in charge of the insertion going through the prejump procedures, reviewing the correct body positions for the water landing, tree landing, and power line landing. He illustrated each position with a watercolor cartoon of the same terrified parachutist the instant before he hit the water or tree or web of hissing high-tension wires.

". . . and, gentlemen," he went on, "if, when you exit the aircraft, your static line should tangle and you find yourself attached to the aircraft by the static line, place one hand on your helmet so we know you are conscious, and we will cut the static line, allowing you to fall free and utilize your reserve parachute. If you are not conscious, or if, for some reason, we are unable to cut you loose or pull you back inside the aircraft, we will radio ahead and have the runway foamed before we tow you in for a landing. Gentlemen," he said, grinning, "you will be in a world of foam."

Out on the dark tarmac, Hanson got in line behind a two-ton truck where a rigger in a red baseball cap gave him his main chute and another rigger gave him a reserve from another pile. He carried them to a spot on the edge of the runway, beneath the drooping wings of a C-141 jet transport, its engines droning like the night wind through a canyon. He shouldered the main chute, running the harness over his shoulders, under his arms, then carefully adjusting the straps through the inside of his thighs. He tightened the webbing through his crotch for the moment when he would leave the plane at 120 miles an hour, the chute snatching him up and slinging him backward, eight hundred feet above the forest.

He snapped the reserve chute onto the D-rings across his chest, attached the forty-pound equipment bag beneath the reserve, and strapped on the padded rifle case. He tightened the combination of buckles once more. Then he relaxed and let the main chute pull him over backward, hitting the ground in a sitting position, to wait, looking like he had been buried under a pile of green luggage.

The operation was a full-dress rehearsal for something they would probably never do—a night parachute jump into the mountains where Hanson and the other "insurgents" would link up with civilian members of the resistance movement against the aggressor forces, a rehearsal for a jump into Eastern Europe in the event of a Russian invasion there, to organize the underground against them. They would soon be going to Southeast Asia, not Eastern Europe. They would not be organizing a civilian resistance, but training aboriginal tribesmen to fight with carbines instead of the bamboo crossbows they had used for centuries.

An hour later he was packed into the big C-141 with 150 other soldiers, squeezed in tight on the collapsible benches made of aluminum tubing and yellow nylon webbing. It was hot inside the plane, stuffy with the anxious breathing of the troops, whose faces were shadowed by the dim red light. The plane smelled of sweat, electricity, and farts.

He could feel the plane bucking in a crosswind as it crabbed in to approach the drop zone eight hundred feet below, the jet engines sobbing and whining as the pilot throttled up and down, through the wind, into the correct azimuth and altitude. The door at the front of the plane was opened, letting in a rush of cool sweet air.

Hanson was weighted down with a hundred pounds of equipment; a rucksack, an equipment bag between his legs, and the padded rifle case strapped to his leg like a splint. He was sandwiched between the main chute and the reserve, strapped so tightly that it was difficult to expand his chest to breathe. He fought the feeling of suffocation and claustrophobia, breathing calmly and shallowly.

Up near the door, the jumpmaster's shout was drowned

out by the engines as he motioned "up" with both hands, like a minister inviting the congregation to stand.

Hanson and the others pulled themselves to their feet and snapped their static lines over the steel cable running the length of the plane. They stood bowlegged for balance as the aircraft rocked and bucked, throwing the soldiers into one another. Hanson was anxious to get out the door before he got airsick, or before the man behind him did.

The dim red light in the plane turned green and the line of soldiers, Hanson trapped in the middle of the column, pushed, staggered, and then began to run with short, shuffling steps toward the wind-sucking door like some overburdened chain gang, the jumpmaster screaming, *"Go, go, go!"* Yellow static lines whipped back from the door as the jumpers grunted and shouted, pushing forward. It seemed as if the planeload of men was taking a terrible mechanical beating.

As he went out the door into sudden silence, Hanson could see a forest fire off to his left, a dirty orange flame with a ragged perimeter of white smoke. An instant later it was gone as the chute snapped open and slung him back and up. And then he was flying backward through the dark.

The moon had not risen, but he could make out the shadows of other canopies and hear the ruffling of nylon in the air. A canopy sideslipped beneath him and he felt it brush his leg. Voices muttered and called out in the air above and below him like spirits as he pulled the release on his equipment bag and felt it fall away. For a moment the hiss of the wind gave way to the pine-scented silence of the ground. The shadow of the earth rushed up and hit him and he heard himself grunt as though it were another person making the sound. All around him there were the thuds and clanks and groans of others hitting the ground.

He had been avoiding the roads, cutting across fields, paralleling the roads when he had to. The night was chilly, spicy with the smells of wood smoke and rotting leaves, and Hanson was still soaring on the adrenaline of the parachute jump, warm in his wool sweater, sweat beading the acrid camouflage paint on his face. He checked his map with a red-lensed flashlight.

The compass declination in the North Carolina mountains, the difference between true north and magnetic north, was exactly the same as that of Vietnam on the other side of the earth. It was a handy coincidence. Twelve hours and twelve thousand miles from where he stood on that mountain, Vietnam waited, a mirror image of geography and polar lines of force.

The stars will be different, he thought. He looked up, found the North Star, and felt elation and something like homesickness rising in his chest. The air made him think of the beginning of school and the smell of a girl's sweater, brushed with perfume and cigarette smoke and a hint of musky perspiration. The stars above him, in their turning, were indifferent as diamonds.

The farmhouse looked small and lonely against the foothills, a soft light glowing in the front windows. He approached it carefully, circling it once before knocking at the door.

A big man in bib overalls and a blue work shirt opened the door. He was a tobacco farmer who worked two fields, the legal one that he had an allotment for, and the one hidden back in the hills, concealed like a moonshine still from federal agents. He had a faint smell of black soil and sawdust about him.

"Come on in, son," he said. "We been waiting supper for you. You have any trouble with those aggressors?"

"No, sir. There was a roadblock down the road there at that bridge, but I just went around it. They were mostly concerned with staying warm and comfortable."

The man laughed. "It's the same every year," he said. "Come on in here and get you something to eat."

An electric line ran from the road to the house, but the dining room was lighted with kerosene lamps. "This is my wife Tracy," the man said.

She was a handsome woman with high cheekbones and dark red hair. Premature crow's feet set off her startlingly clear green eyes that made Hanson almost dizzy when he met them, embarrassing them both in a moment of unexpected sexual contact.

"Pleased to meet you, ma'am."

"And this one here is our girl Helen." She was in her early

teens and looked like her mother, with the same cheekbones and eyes, auburn hair, and a dusting of freckles.

In the burnished lamplight they looked, Hanson imagined, just like their Anglo-Saxon ancestors who had settled the mountains before the Revolutionary War, or the ones who, a century later, walked down from the hills to die for something called the Confederacy.

They prayed before they ate, closing their eyes and bowing their heads, the father saying, "Dear Lord, we thank thee for this, thy bounty we are about to receive, and ask your blessing on this house, and also on this young man who will soon be fighting for our country. Amen."

They passed plates of fried chicken and squirrel, biscuits, green beans and cold mashed potatoes. There was buttermilk, dark brown molasses to go on the biscuits, and coffee from a blue enamel pot. The dishes had a faded tracery of a floral print, the kind of dishes that come free, packed in large boxes of detergent.

The family and others like it scattered around the mountains had been playing the role of insurgents for a decade, getting a token payment from some CIA/Special Forces slush fund but doing it mostly out of simple patriotism. They knew as much about guerrilla warfare as anyone in the Army. But before they started playing the role of insurgent, that was what they had been, in the Revolution, in the Civil War, in their fights against federal agents to keep from paying taxes on moonshine and bootleg tobacco.

In the World Wars, and police actions, and border skirmishes, their own sons had always gone, not simply out of patriotism or adventure, though that was part of it, but because they still recognized the human need for the blood and redemption of warfare.

Hanson wondered how many other Special Forces soldiers had eaten at that table, and how many of them were dead now.

As they ate, the woman and the girl glanced up from their plates to look at Hanson. He was a romantic character that night, wearing jeans, a black turtleneck sweater and black knit cap, green and black paint on his face, and he wished that he could enjoy it. Wished that he could be fighting for these people who had no TV and whose water came from a hand pump beside the kitchen sink, people who heated their dish water on a wood stove in a time of pollution and men walking on the moon.

"What part of the country are you from?" the woman, Tracy, asked. "You don't sound like you come from around here."

"No, ma'am, but my grandmother lives up in Virginia. We lived out in Oregon for a while, but now we're up near Chicago. My family's moved around a lot."

"We got some cousins moved out there to Oregon," the man said. "Oregon's where the Davis boys moved to, wasn't it?" he asked his wife. "Dewey and his boys. Somewhere, didn't he say, near Portland? He drives a schoolbus and works in a sawmill out there."

"We hated to see 'em go," he said, "but they just couldn't make a living back here. I know somebody who was sad to see 'em go," he said, looking at his daughter and smiling. "That Ronnie Davis still writing you letters?" he asked her.

"Oh, Daddy," she said, blushing in the lamplight.

"Why don't you clear the table and bring us some of that pecan pie, sugar," her mother said.

"Do you think we're winning that war over there?" the man asked Hanson as his daughter cleared the table. "Seems like we been at it a long time, and we keep seeing new faces come through here. I hate to sound like one of those protesters, but we've met some nice boys out here and I hope we're doing the right thing by them."

"I don't know, sir," Hanson said. "It's hard to know what to believe. I guess I'll find out when I get over there."

They heard the whine of a big truck's transmission, getting closer, grinding up the dirt road. The girl hurried in from the kitchen.

"That's some of those aggressors," the man said. "Helen, go hide him in the cellar.

"Don't worry," he told Hanson. "They'll just ask me if I've seen any strangers around here lately, and I'll tell 'em no, give 'em some biscuits, and they'll go on back where they came from. They're nice boys, but it's pretty hard for them to catch you all when everybody who lives around here is on your side. That," he said, getting up and motioning Hanson toward the rear of the house, "is what bothers me about that war over there."

The girl led Hanson to a trapdoor in the back of the kitchen that opened to a root cellar beneath the foundation of the house. Down in the musty darkness he could hear the sound of boots overhead, walking, stopping, turning around and going back the way they'd come in. He heard indistinct voices and laughter. The truck started and he listened to it grind and clatter back down the road until he couldn't hear it any longer.

The door above him opened, and Helen looked down. "They're gone," she said, smiling. "Daddy told them that he'd come down to the bridge and let them know if he saw any strangers."

He had a cup of coffee before he went to bed, and he watched the girl in the kitchen as she pumped water and heated it on top of the wood stove to wash the dishes. He thought about the girls at the marches and peace vigils, fashionable and sure of themselves, burning with self-righteous anger. They seemed a long way off.

The weathered wood of the barn where he spent the night glowed like pewter in the moonlight. It was a lopsided old building, and in the hayloft he could feel it sway in the breeze. An owl was hunting from the air near the barn, and Hanson could hear, from time to time, the muffled sweep of his wings. Somewhere out of sight was the faint sound of the Interstate, of downshifting trucks, the ringing hum of tires. The sound of the real world. The owl dropped to the grass and something squealed. Hanson covered himself with straw, pulled his rifle close, and went to sleep.

He awoke early the next morning, the sunlight banded as it came through the slats of the hay door into the dusty loft. The morning was crisp, but it would be warm by noon. It would be another day before he was to link up with other guerrillas, and he had offered to clear an old garden plot that had been overgrown with blackberry vines and Johnson grass.

Down in the tool shed he scoured the old machete with

steel wool and oil until the pitted blade shined, then worked on the edge with a file. He put on leather gloves with pictures of donkeys on the cuffs, and waded into the blackberry vines that were ten feet tall and dense as a bamboo grove. The stalks were the thickness of broom handles at the ground, and they slapped back as he hacked into them. He found that they severed smoothly if he cut down into them rather than swinging from side to side, and he began to take each stalk down with two cuts, one at eye level, then, turning his wrist, backhanding the rest off a few inches above ground level.

The sun warmed his back and drew the cool scent of the earth up through the severed stalks. He changed the machete from hand to hand, cocking his wrist, focusing his strength into the blade as he drove it down, the stalks parting and falling before him.

He heard a sound like cloth being torn, inch by inch, *rip— rip—rip*—behind him, and turned to see the farmer cutting the Johnson grass with a bentwood scythe, pulling the silver crescent blade into the grass in short easy strokes, shocks of grass falling with the ripping sound, the farmer seeming only to shrug his shoulders, turn his wrists, and another bundle of grass dropped. His tireless concentration reminded Hanson of the martial arts instructors he'd had in training.

"Good morning," he called. "Got done with the tobacco sooner than I expected. Thought I'd give you a hand with this. She's been after me for weeks to do it so she could get that garden planted. The vegetables are sure good, but I think her flowers are more important to her."

And they worked together, keeping pace, Hanson chopping through the vines, the farmer working through the Johnson grass, parallel to him, the ringing chop of the machete and the *rip* of the scythe developing a rhythm as they worked faster, gradually turning it into a race to the far edge of the plot. Hanson's arms and shoulders began to ache, but, exhilarated, he worked still faster, more efficiently, occasionally looking up and exchanging grins with the farmer.

They raked the lengths of blackberry vine and the wide-bladed grass into a single pile the size of a small car. The thorny vines looked like huge crab legs stuck and snarled with sea-weed, washed up from some hostile ocean.

The farmer's wife brought them fresh lemonade in flow-ered glasses. "Well," she said, her eyes shining, "I can start thinking about planting some of these."

She reached into the bag over her shoulder and pulled out a handful of seed packets. They had wonderful paintings of flowers and vegetables on them, cucumbers, cabbage, Brussels sprouts, light greens and dark greens, beans and carrots, pumpkin and yellow squash, round red tomatoes. "Here," she said, taking a yellow and gold packet from the bunch. "Crack-erjack marigolds. It says they'll grow this high," she said, hold-ing her palm straight out. "As big as snowballs. We'll put these in for you," she said, smiling at Hanson, "and whenever we look out at them, we'll think of you."

Hanson blushed, grinned, and said, "Well, thanks. That's nice to know."

Later that day the farmer was sitting at a scarred workbench, looking out the dusty window at the cottonwoods in back.

The shed was full of tools: shovels, axes, bucksaws, picks, sledgehammers, splitting wedges, pulley blocks, pry bars—all hand tools that had cutting edges or that offered extra lever-age. An old 45-70 government rifle was mounted on a rack of elk horns, and beneath it hung an old calendar with a painting of a butternut-brown elk. The farmer liked the picture too much to throw the calendar away and had kept it so long that he sometimes transposed the current date with those on the calendar.

A photograph tacked to the wall showed the farmer as a young man, a staff sergeant, standing in front of a gutted tank with two other NCOs. Another figure was visible in the back-ground, but out of focus and blurred. The sergeant to the left of the farmer had been killed a week after the picture was taken. The other one taught school up in Virginia now.

The three of them had been together in the retreat from Chosen Reservoir, the freezing wind and thousands of Chinese soldiers screaming down after them. The farmer still shivered when he thought of the sound the Chinese bugles made before night attacks.

There was a time, the farmer thought, when he'd hated the human race. He'd never suspected that people could do some of the things he'd seen them do. But that was a long time ago, he thought; his life was good now.

He took a last look at the photograph and went back to sharpening the sickle in his hand, filings glittering as they fell to the floor, the curved blade taking on a shine.

When Hanson came in with the machete, he showed him where to hang it on the wall. A row of big steel traps with spikes set in the jaws hung along the length of the rafter above.

"What do you use those for?" Hanson asked him. "Is there anything that big around here?"

"Wolf," the farmer said. "Those are Newhouse number fourteens. I did some wolfing after the war. They were still paying bounty up in Wyoming and Montana—that's where those elk horns came from. Things weren't working out too good for me when I got back home, so I decided to leave this part of the country for a while.

"It was pretty good money too, back then, but it was terrible hard work sometimes. It got cold, and boring, and the dogs would try to kill you if you turned your back on 'em. I never liked dogs much after that, but I got to where I liked the wolves. They killed some range stock, but not nearly as much as people blamed 'em for. It was a few that were into the cattle, but mostly it was wild dogs and bad farm dogs that did it. Besides, the wolf was just trying to stay alive like anything else. The smarter they were, the harder I tried to trap them, then felt kind of bad when I did. That was a bad winter. All I remember about it is the cold and all the dead, frozen wolves.

"You know, I was there the day they trapped the last wolf —what they *said* was the last wolf—in western Montana, up by Cut Bank. They strung that animal up, shot its legs off, then set it on fire with gasoline.

"Far as I knew, that wolf never bothered any livestock. It's just that he was the last one. When there's just one of something, people seem determined to kill it. Maybe it's just as well. What do you do if you're the last wolf out there, everybody trying to hunt you down? Like one of those Jap soldiers holed up in a cave all those years after the war was over, holding out for years, and nobody even knows he's there."

He looked at the photograph on the wall. "You know," he said, "after a few days of digging into the snow over there, with shells dropping around me, I didn't care who controlled Korea. I didn't know anybody over there, none of those Koreans, and the few I'd seen I didn't much care for.

"There was some who liked the war, though, who went kind of crazy for it. They'd volunteer to go out at night, past our lines, and try to kill a few Koreans. As if it mattered. I used to wonder what became of them. If they lived to come home again.

"They gave us a couple of parades when we got back, but nobody was glad to see us after that. There weren't enough jobs to go around, or women for that matter, and even folks who knew us before were kind of, well, afraid of us."

He finished the sickle and hung it on the wall. "Must be about time for supper," he said. He glanced up at the traps.

"Went to a zoo once," he said, "over in Charlotte. They had an elephant there, chained to a pipe. Said he'd been there forty-three years. Had a wolf in a concrete pit. Gone crazy. All he did was pace around and gnaw at his own leg. Wish I hadn't gone."

After supper Hanson looked out the window at the dark, as he had been doing all through the meal. He was going to have to leave in the morning before dawn. He could feel the cold flow from the rippled window glass like a faint, icy wind.

"Let's go burn that pile of brush we cut today," the farmer said. "It should make a real good bonfire."

They poured gasoline around the edges of the brush and touched it off with a rotten cottonwood branch. The gasoline caught with a soft *boom*, and yellow light poured toward the center of the pile, spread and grew brighter, then began to rise, the pile of brush burning from the inside out, towering over them and dappling their bodies with light.

The lengths of thorn-studded vine twisted in the fire, and for a moment it seemed that the mound of dead vines was not being consumed but was taking on a life of its own. Then the first flames tore away from the yellow glow in the middle of the pile and swaths of fire were everywhere sweeping up through the vines into a single gold flame that turned into and against itself at the top of the pile, curling slowly to a tip where ribbons of flame tore away, apart and burning free in the air for an instant before they flared black and became part of the dark. The fire rushed through the vines, cracked them like seeds, and sucked away anything that would burn. But just beyond the edge of the light, it was still dark and cold, as unchanged as if the fire had never started.

The next morning he watched from the wood line as the aggressor forces, an 82nd Airborne unit from Fort Bragg, interrogated captured members of the unit he had planned to link up with. In a soupy, flooded parking area they tied the prisoners to a jeep bumper with ten-foot lengths of rope and drove through the shin-deep mud while the prisoners tried to keep up, stumbling and finally falling, to be dragged slowly along, kicking up wakes of mud, turning and bouncing at the end of the rope.

They tied one prisoner's arms behind him and shut him up in a metal wall locker. They kicked the locker and it toppled over, sending up a wave of mud. They walked around the locker, pounding on it with sticks, then raised it up and toppled it again.

Another group was using a technique that had been turning up on the six o'clock news from Vietnam, laying a prisoner on his back, his arms bound behind him, then stuffing the corner of a towel down his throat, pinching his nose shut, and pouring water over the towel until the prisoner felt as if he were drowning.

Hanson watched for a while, then turned and went back downhill through the shade-dappled woods, his feet slipping on the layers of pine needles. He came to a creek that bordered a pasture of knee-high grass, where he waited and watched for several minutes before crossing the creek. The water was clear and cool as he waded through it, his legs splitting the water into silver-brown rivulets that caught the sun.

As he climbed the far bank, he was startled by a scream, a sound with the terror of a wounded rabbit and the mockery of a crow, yet almost human. He froze on the riverbank, and when he heard the cry again he inched his way up the bank and looked across the pasture.

What he saw seemed to be a giant snake, an iridescent green and blue snake slipping through the grass, undulating, dipping up and down as it moved, its scales shimmering, fixing Hanson with its black lidless eye. It seemed to slip out of focus for an instant, and as Hanson squinted to bring it back, he heard the cry again and the snake shuddered, became a blur and blossomed into a peacock, its tail quivering, gleaming in the sun, crying out.

Fort Holabird

Fort Holabird was a pleasant, well-manicured little army base that hadn't changed much since World War II. It was outside town, and when the wind was right you could smell the paper mills down the river. A small, polluted stream ran through the center of the base. There was a post movie theater, library, USO club, and snack bar, all built of whitewashed ship-lap siding. The officers' club was elegant, with a circular drive, covered walkways, and a golf course.

The base was the U.S. Army Intelligence Headquarters, where MP detectives and CID officers were trained to do background security checks and drug investigations. Those detective trainees were easily picked out on the street because of their short hair, black low-quarter military issue shoes, and the tan raincoats they all bought at the PX. It was almost a uniform. "Agent handlers" were trained there, too, and you could see them following each other around in downtown Washington, taking their coats off and on, switching hats, backtracking and watching the street reflected in store windows, playing at being spies.

In many ways it was a relaxed base. Most of the personnel wore civilian clothes, and those in uniform were not, as they say in the Army, sharp-looking individuals. Their uniforms were sloppy and poorly maintained. Most of them were college graduates, draftees who had volunteered to serve an extra year in order to attend the intelligence school and so avoid the possibility of being assigned to the infantry.

Several times a year the base reluctantly played host to a class of Special Forces intelligence sergeants, offering courses in interrogation, terrorism, propaganda, lock-picking, counter-security measures, sniping, selective assassination, aerial photography analysis, and psychological operations.

Most of the Special Forces people attending the courses were old Southeast Asia hands with three or four tours behind them, and they considered the two-month school a vacation. They had only to listen to second lieutenants tell them things they already knew, that they had themselves discovered and developed years before, and the rest of the days and nights were theirs. They had a tradition of terrorizing the regular personnel and cadre at the base, swaggering around in tailored, starched fatigues with all their patches and badges, spit-shined hundred-dollar jump boots, and, of course, their green berets.

Because of the number of intelligence sergeants being killed in cross-border operations in Vietnam, a group of younger soldiers were allowed to take the course as replacements. Hanson was one of them. He had finished basic training, infantry training, jump school, and seven months of Special Forces training. Vietnam would be next.

The march to the classroom building involved crossing a small steel bridge over the polluted stream. A sign at the bridge said Break Step When Crossing Bridge, but the twenty-five Special Forces troops never did. They stayed locked into step, and the bridge bellied and quivered and swayed from side to side under their boots. It was a small gesture of contempt for the rules, for a warning sign, for caution, for the regular Army, for any soldiers who weren't hard-chargers, ass-kickers, eye-shooters, and hard core widow-makers.

It was a crisp morning. The only clouds were contrail streaks from high-altitude aircraft. Hanson was at the rear of the formation, with the rest of the junior NCOs. The SFCs and master sergeants were up front, some of them big and barrel-chested, some small and wiry. There were red-veined whiskey faces, hard-eyed Chicanos, a Korean, a couple of mustachioed ladies' men, and a pair of businesslike sergeant majors. Every one of them was genuinely tough, physically and mentally, the kind of men Hanson had, not long before, disdained, but whom he now admired. It was seductive, the kind of blunt threat they carried with them everywhere, and Hanson was learning how it was done.

He liked it that people stayed out of your way, gave you

room. He liked the way it simplified arguments, the way The Threat said, You may be right in your argument, it's an interesting idea and I've enjoyed talking to you, but I can still kick your ass anytime I want to. And the way women, no matter how they might deny it at first, were attracted to it.

What had surprised him most was that those tough soldiers at the front of the formation knew what they were doing with The Threat. They understood it and used it the way a diplomat uses protocol. They were smart, tough, and articulate. And, most of all, they got things done.

The classrooms had red and white SECRET placards slipped into brass frames on the door, and armed guards stood outside the door while classes were in progress. It was not uncommon to see men in Russian or Red Chinese uniforms walking the halls. Notes taken during the lectures had to be left in the classroom, and at the end of the day they were stamped with the appropriate security classification and locked in a safe.

". . . simple isolation combined with random beatings takes a little longer, but is extremely effective. The subject has no opportunity to anticipate the beatings and so cannot prepare himself psychologically for them. After a beating he might be subjected to another one ten minutes or ten days later. He is alone, with no one to confide in, no one to share his misery or to help him evaluate the situation, and he finally must turn to the interrogator for this.

"With adequate facilities, the subject loses any sense of time, of night or day, while waiting for the next interrogation session. Anticipating the next session or the next beating, he is unable to sleep, and he quickly weakens.

"We do not, of course, approve of or advocate these interrogation techniques," the lieutenant continued from behind his podium, "but we feel that you should be familiar with them in the event that *you* are subjected to them."

"Right, L-Tee," one of the E-7s in the class said. "We wouldn't do any of that *bad* shit."

The class laughed, and the lieutenant tried to smile.

"Hey," a big master sergeant said with a grin, "don't let

these guys bother you, sir. They're just a bunch of fun lovers. Go ahead, sir, please continue."

There was more laughter, and the lieutenant's face flushed. It was like a classroom full of tough kids who have a substitute teacher.

"Sir, go on ahead. We'd like to hear more about those techniques, how to keep that little fucker from evaluating his situation."

"Wire him up," a Chicano SFC said. "Sit him in a puddle with a TA-312. A couple hundred volts through the head of his dick will get his attention right away."

The lieutenant attempted another smile. "I say again, gentlemen, these methods are neither advocated, recommended, nor approved of by the U.S. Army. Aside from the fact that they go against the Geneva Convention and simple humanity, they are not reliable. I'm sure that you all agree that they are not reliable. You know that the subject will tell you anything he thinks you want to hear in order to terminate the session if you use those techniques."

"Yeah, that may be, but it still makes me feel a lot better about having to listen to the little bastard lie to me."

"You know how I can tell when the little bastards are lying to me?" another SFC said from the back of the room. "Whenever I see their lips moving."

"Hey, sir, what do you do if you need information in a hurry? You know, when you don't have time to win his heart and mind."

"Give him to the ARVN, let *them* torture the asshole," another student offered.

"Unless they've got money, or relatives with pull," a red-faced sergeant major said. "I took this prisoner once, my first tour, this slack-jawed gook who just happened to be in the area before we got ambushed. I know the little fucker fingered us for the ambush. But I gave him to the ARVN.

"Couple months later I picked him up again in our AO. I gave him to the ARVN. A month later I found him hiding in a hole in a riverbank, down where we'd been running into a lot of booby traps. He came out, didn't even have his hands up, grinning like a possum eating sweet potato, like me and him were old buddies. Pretty funny. Third time I'd picked him up. I grinned back and put about ten rounds through his scrawny chicken chest. Last I saw of him, he was floating south. I decided not to bother the ARVN anymore."

Someone had written, "Get 'em by the balls and their hearts and minds will follow," on Hanson's desk. An old joke. He checked his watch and looked out the window. In the distance a smoke stack rose above low clouds. The red lights at its tip blinked like beady little eyes.

Late that afternoon Hanson went to the NCO club with Bishop and Gallager, the two other junior NCOs in the class. The club had a garish Hawaiian/Tahitian motif—Tonga torches, bamboo, wicker, and dark wood tables that had been beaten with a ball-peen hammer and blowtorched to give them a weathered look, then coated with a quarter-inch of clear plastic. A soupy string orchestra version of "I Wanna Hold Your Hand" was coming out of speakers in the ceiling.

There were fishing nets and cork floats on the wall behind the bar, the parchment-yellow light coming from half a dozen spiny blowfish with lightbulbs inside their distended bellies. The bar specialized in Mai Tais, Planter's Punch, Zombies, and Coconut Rum Sunsets. The women in the bar, the wives, girlfriends, mistresses and secretaries—satellites to the men, soldier groupies—drank the specialties, while the men drank bourbon and blended whiskey.

It was warm outside, but the bar was cool and dark. Each table had a little red candle on it.

"Real classy place," Hanson said. "Tonga torches, Chinese lanterns, illuminated fish, you know?"

"I think it's pretty nice," Gallager said.

"Growing up in West Virginia like you did, you probably are impressed," Bishop said. "Fuckin' coal miner. You're the kind of person this place was designed for. Promise you cheap drinks and a Hawaiian shirt and you'd re-enlist."

"At least they'd *let* me re-enlist," Gallager said. "Perverts are not asked to stay in."

Bishop saw something over Hanson's shoulder and quickly

looked down at his beer. "Speaking of perverts," he said, "don't look now, but Larkin just walked in."

"Must have worked him up a thirst," Gallager said, "kissing ass back at the barracks." He took a drink of beer and set the mug down. "You know what he does whenever somebody calls 'attention'?" he asked. Then he threw his head back, rigid, the veins in his neck standing out. He curled his lips into a wet pucker, his mustache bristling over the upper lip, and muttered through his teeth, "Yessir. Yessir. Lemme kiss it, sir."

The lanky soldier who had come into the bar stood next to the jukebox, his shoulders hunched, squinting against the cigarette smoke and dim light. When he saw Bishop, he straightened and sauntered over to the table. "So *here* you are," he said.

"Yeah," Bishop muttered into his beer, "here we are."

"Mind if I sit down?"

Without looking at him, Bishop said, "There's the chair."

Larkin sat down and looked across the table at Hanson. "You're the one I was looking for," he said. "I heard a little piece of news you might be interested in."

"Oh yeah?" Hanson said. "What did you hear?"

"A friend of mine," Larkin said, "saw a set of orders assigning you to the permanent training cadre back at Bragg. As soon as we finish the training cycle."

Hanson looked at Larkin, looked across the bar, then looked down at the candle flickering on the table. He felt dizzy. The puddle of melted wax feeding the flame was littered with blackened match heads.

"Fuckers must of found out you can type," Gallager said.

"I hear it's good duty," Larkin said. "The nights and weekends are all yours."

A woman at the bar laughed and shouted, "Honey, I told you about that," to the bartender. Hanson squinted and watched the candle flame.

"Hey," Larkin said, "at least you know you'll be alive a year from now."

"Fuck that," Hanson said. "If I was worried about that I could have gone to Canada. I'm *ready*. I'm ready to go to

Vietnam. All this shit . . ." He could taste the sausage he'd had for lunch.

"Maybe after a few months you could put in for a transfer," Gallager said.

"I think—" Larkin began.

"He might as well put in for a transfer to Mars or Beverly Hills, California, for all the good it's gonna do him with that college on his record," Bishop said. "You seen these dumb motherfuckers they're drafting these days? The sergeant major at training group needs somebody with a brain to keep his paperwork lookin' good."

"You know," Larkin said, "I think—"

"What," Bishop said. "Okay, what?"

"Well," Larkin said, "if you're really serious about not wanting to go to training group, I've got an idea."

"You gonna tell us what it is," Bishop said, "or do we have to ask you or what?"

"Mrs. Dunaway," Larkin said.

Hanson looked up from the candle. "You got the phone number?"

"Just call the Pentagon and ask Information."

"Let's go," Hanson said, looking at his watch. "She might still be there." He stood, started for the door, then said, "Quarters. Quarters." He bought a red roll of quarters from the bartender, and the four of them went out the door.

Mrs. Dunaway was a GS-14 who worked somewhere in the Pentagon. She handled the records of all the Special Forces troops in the Army. All the orders, transfers, and promotions were routed through her office.

No one Hanson knew had ever seen her. Some liked to imagine her as a voluptuous dragon lady, studying their ID photos and licking her lips, manipulating their lives according to her mood.

As they jogged across the parade field, Hanson pictured her as a kind, blue-haired little old lady. Like his grandmother. She had a tiny office somewhere deep in the concrete heart of the Pentagon, where she did needlepoint. There were photos of her grandchildren on the filing cabinets.

The phone booth was in front of the whitewashed little

post library. A soldier wearing low-cut Army shoes, jeans, and a Ban-lon shirt was using the phone. He was leaning against the glass, looking up at the ceiling and smoking a cigarette.

Hanson pulled open the folding glass door and said, "Tell her you'll call her back in a minute. I've got an emergency."

The soldier looked down at Hanson. "Hang on a minute, hon," he said into the phone, then to Hanson, "What the fuck's *your* problem, man . . ."

Gallager stepped from behind Hanson, grabbed the soldier's arm, and jerked him stumbling out of the phone booth. The phone bounced and spun at the end of its cord, banging against the glass walls of the booth as if it were trying to escape. Hanson caught it, pulled the door closed, and pumped the chrome receiver until he got a dial tone. The soldier in the Ban-lon shirt was saying, "Okay, man. Okay," his voice muffled by the glass. He grunted and said, "All *right* . . ."

A voice on the phone said, "Operator." Hanson asked for the Pentagon and she said, "One fifteen for three minutes." As he dropped them in, the quarters rang—*bong-bong-bong*—tolling ominously—*bong-bong*—like an iron clock. Hanson listened to the phone ringing on the other end. Cigarette smoke was still thick in the booth and it burned his eyes. He jerked the door tight and the little fan in the ceiling began to hum, sucking the smoke up. It washed over his arms and face like fog. A woman's voice said, "Please hold."

Hanson held the receiver to his ear, listening to the static, the clicks, the musical phrases whistling and tooting in quick, random patterns. He imagined the armored phone cable snaking north under freeway traffic, and bedrooms, and arguments in neighborhood bars, turning along the bottoms of rivers and bays, covered with mud, humming beneath the dark water.

"Hello? Yes? Hello?" he said, and saw his voice, a blue spark jumping across microwave relays, beamed over swamps and herds of cattle, hissing through windowless switching stations.

No one answered, and he waited. The sun was going down. High overhead a B-52 caught light from the curve of the earth.

"Thank you for waiting," the woman said, breaking the static. Hanson explained who he wanted to speak to and she said, "Please hold."

"That will be another one fifteen," the operator said, coming on the line.

Bong-bong-bong—the phone began to ring again beneath the sound of the quarters—*bong-bong*.

A woman's voice said, "Hello." A husky voice. It was more like a greeting than a question, the way a blind date might say hello when she opened the door to her apartment, then smile, look over her shoulder, and say to her roommate, "Don't wait up."

Hanson smelled hot wiring. The fan rattled in the ceiling. He could see sparks behind the grillwork.

"Hellooo there," the voice said, throaty and seductive. "Are you out there?"

Hanson kicked the door ajar. "Yes. Yes, ma'am," he said. "Is this Mrs. Dunaway?"

"Here I am," she said, sounding like she was smiling. "At your service."

"The Mrs. Dunaway in charge of Special Forces?"

"The very one, darlin'. What's *your* name?"

Hanson gave her his name and ID number. "I'm sorry to bother you so late in the day," he said, "but I've got a real problem and you're the only person who can help me. I hope."

"No bother," she said. "That's why I'm here. I hope I can *handle* your problem, Hanson. Let me pull out your file here."

The fan had stopped, but the smell of burning wires was strong. It was mixed with a faint smell of perfume and sweat.

"Here you are, darlin'," she said. "Why, you're almost finished out there, aren't you? You've done real well."

Hanson felt himself getting an erection.

She laughed and said, "You're a good-looking young man. But you don't look very happy in this photograph." It sounded like she was smoking, the way she exhaled her words. "Big shoulders," she said, and Hanson pictured her lips forming the words. "But now," she said, "what can I do for you?"

"Mrs. Dunaway, I was drafted, but I volunteered for Special Forces. I didn't mind the extra year. I worked hard, and I like it. I just found out that they've cut orders at Bragg assigning me to Training Group . . ."

"I see here that you have three years of college," she said. "That's wonderful. Hanson," she said, "we need more young men like you.

"Hanson, are you there, darlin'?"

"Yes. Yes, ma'am. What, uh, I mean, I volunteered to go to Vietnam. All my friends, the people I trained with, are going. Is there anything you can do to help me?"

"To see that you go to Vietnam?" she said. "Of course. I can just put your name on the next manifest before those other orders get here. Is that what you'd like, Hanson?"

"Yes, ma'am. Could you do that?"

"I'm doing it. I'm doing it right . . . now," she said. "I've entered your name."

"Thank you. Thank you very much."

"Oh," she said, exhaling into the phone, "it was my pleasure. What else can I do for you?"

"That's all I need."

"Well, good. I'm so glad you called me. Have a good trip . . . Hanson."

Her voice vanished and all Hanson could hear was the static and drone of the dial tone. He held the warm receiver to his ear. His mouth was dry and he could feel his heart beating.

Cam Rhan Bay

The chartered World Airways 707 bucked and shuddered like a boxcar on the way to the Western front. The FASTEN SEATBELTS/NO SMOKING sign came on. Hanson could feel the plane slowing, his body lifting, floating away from the seat back, as the engines changed pitch. They dropped into heavy cloud cover, and Hanson watched the mist flow over the rivet-studded wing. He studied the forward edge of the wing, then looked back at the flaps, big and small, as they moved slowly, tentatively, like the heel and fingers of a hand feeling for something in the fog. A silver-white strobe light on the tip of the wing flashed through the mist. Everyone on the plane strained to see through the fog, finally to see Vietnam.

Vietnam. A myth. It was the place they'd seen on the six o'clock news all through high school. The sound of teletypes, Walter Cronkite's fatherly voice as he said, "Good evening" and gave the weekly body count as stick figures, each representing a hundred dead men, appeared on the TV screen. It had become as much a part of their lives as homework and drive-in movies. Jungles, hootches, rice paddies, punji stakes, booby traps. Ambushes. The jumpy film footage of men running and falling in fear of an invisible enemy, the camera swooping, out of focus, from the treeline to the ground, shouts and puny popping noises in the background. Then the pictures of bodies, of writhing, bandaged men, and the sound of medivacs.

Charlie. Charlie was down there, Victor Charlie, *Mister* Charles.

"Gentlemen," they had been told, again and again, "Charlie is the best jungle fighter in the world today. He has been fighting for twenty-five years. Think about it, gentlemen. Twenty-five years. He knows every trick there is, and, gentlemen, if you do not have your shit together, he is going to kill you. Look at the two men sitting on either side of you." And they would act as if they were not looking, but they would look. "One of them is going to come home dead or seriously fucked up. Graves registration will tie off his dick, shove a rubber plug up his asshole, and ship him back in a reusable aluminum coffin."

And yet it was hard to believe that Vietnam *really* existed. It would be like going through the looking-glass into a familiar movie, to become actors, directors, prop men, in a long-running TV series in which you became the characters you had grown familiar with, comfortable with, over the years. Roles that had been waiting for you with lines you already knew.

"The first thing you'll see is the shit fires," one private said to the man next to him. "That's what they do over here. They burn the shit. A buddy of mine told me."

Hanson imagined a country ablaze, shadows and sweet black smoke.

A grinding noise and two thuds shook the airliner, and the passengers stiffened, but it was only the landing gear dropping down.

A dim image of ocean and rocky cliffs floated beneath the last layer of cloud, and then the plane broke through. The ocean was overcast, a dark blue breaking gray and white against the rocks. A few shacks flashed past below, faces looked up, and the plane touched down on a gray, skid-streaked runway.

As the plane taxied toward the terminal, two stewardesses walked the length of the cabin spraying small aerosol cans at the ceiling. The cans emptied with a faint hiss, and the sweet stink of insecticide settled on the soldiers. It was necessary to fumigate the aircraft to kill any American insects that might upset the ecological balance of Vietnam.

The air base was not much different from McChord AFB, where they'd taken off eighteen hours and twelve time zones away, leaving there in mid-morning, having waited with their gear since 5 A.M., landing in Vietnam in the early afternoon of the same day, having flown with the sun but having lost a day and a night, according to the calendar, somewhere over the ocean. Cam Rhan had the same busy little trucks on the runways, the same camouflaged C-130s, the same olive drab buses which they boarded on the tarmac.

But the buses in Vietnam looked like prison buses. They had heavy wire screens over the windows to deflect grenades. The C-130s were housed behind wedge-shaped steel walls that were five feet thick at the base. And out on the far runway, F-4 Phantom jets were landing. Hanson watched them coming in as the bus crossed the runways and he listened to their faraway furious shrieking until the sound was lost in the drone of the bus.

The buses bounced along in a sullen little convoy, cutting through a sea of sand dunes veined and crosshatched with rusting concertina wire that seemed to have no pattern.

The replacement center was neatly laid out on the sand, falling-down two-story barracks whose walls flaked cream-colored pieces of paint the size of maple leaves. There was a bunker between each row of barracks made of corrugated four-foot-wide drainage pipe. The pipe was heavily sand-bagged on the sides, the sandbags thinning out toward the top where there was little danger of shrapnel penetration. The sandbags were rotten; many of them had burst and washed away in the rain.

The buses stopped at a large open-sided building much like a covered loading dock. A young buck sergeant shouted, "Everybody out and line up over there at the hard stand," pointing to a large open area bordered by a low wooden fence. Inside the fence, the sand was covered by hundred-pound sections of PSP, perforated steel plating, the stamped-out three-by-five sections that are linked together to form temporary roads and runways.

The busloads of men walked over to the hard stand, and Hanson recognized two Special Forces soldiers, Bishop and Hanadon. They were standing across the street, their arms folded across their chests, watching the group of new men. Hanson had gotten drunk with them two days before at Fort Ord, and they had left on an earlier flight.

Hanson had his beret stuffed into his fatigues pocket. He'd found out long before that it didn't pay to stand out in a formation, especially in a temporary duty station. If there are four ranks, slip into the third one and look like everyone else. That's how you avoid work details.

Hanadon spotted Hanson and grinned. He nudged Bishop and walked over. Hanadon was half-Filipino, but he was bigger than Hanson. The two of them had gone through infantry school, jump school, and a year of Special Forces school together. Hanson had once stopped Hanadon from killing another soldier.

"Say brothuh," Hanadon said, grinning. "Welcome to *The Country*, my man," and the two of them slapped hands.

A pair of dented loudspeakers that were aimed down at the hard stand began to shriek and chatter from atop a miniature guard tower. They quieted to a low hum, and a bony staff sergeant in the tower began to speak, his voice metallic, with a slight mechanical echo. "All right, gentlemen, *every*body down here on the hard stand. You can talk to your buddies later."

He waited while the new troops grumbled. "Man, an' I thought it was gonna be different here, but it's the same old Mickey Mouse bullshit."

"What that fool think he gonna do? Send me to Vietnam? I ain't hurryin' for *no* motherfucker."

" 'Less it's Charles, holdin' some shit."

"Shitman, you tellin' the truth now."

"But for that Mickey's Monkey bony motherfucker—my *momma's* gonna catch a flight over here and play soldier for him before I do."

"There it is."

"Gentlemen," the staff sergeant went on, "if you cooperate with me, we can get this over in a short time. If you do not cooperate with me, that's all right too. You'll be here all night. It doesn't matter to me. I get off at six o'clock."

"I'll catch you later," Hanadon said. "Barracks C-Charlie. Me and Bishop got a bottle. You the only SF guy on this manifest?"

"Just me."

"Okay. We'll fill you in on this dump after you process in. Look out for work details. This place is falling apart 'cause there isn't enough cadre to maintain it. They're snatching everybody up for details. Catch you later."

Bishop grinned at Hanson and gave him the finger.

Special Forces was like a small fraternity within the Army. All the members looked out for each other. At any new base an SF soldier could go up to the first Green Beret he saw and find out who and what to avoid, what he could get away with and what he couldn't.

"Okay, gentlemen, cover down there," the staff sergeant announced through the loudspeaker feedback. "Let's get in some kind of formation. You're in Vietnam, but this is still the Army. Let's dress it up a little there," he said, then waited while the troops shuffled into a ragged formation.

"Gentlemen, on behalf of Captain William Fenners, I would like to welcome you to the Three hundred eighty-fifth Replacement Company . . ."

"Fuck Captain Fenners."

"And his hard stand."

"And you too, Jack."

The staff sergeant picked up the rest of his speech just as the last insults had been spoken. His pauses were as perfectly timed as if he and the troops had been rehearsing, pausing for insults. He had given the same speech several hundred times.

". . . while you are here, at the Three hundred eighty-fifth Replacement area, there are a few rules that you *must* follow, in order to make your stay as brief and pleasant as possible . . ." And he began listing the rules in a tired, bored voice while jet lag, fatigue, and anger rose from the troops on the hard stand like an acrid wind.

"Gentlemen," he went on, droning through the buzzing, hissing PA system, "while you are here, if at any time you hear sirens, that means that we are under enemy attack. When you hear the sirens, get up and put on your boots. Make sure that the men on either side of you are awake, and then go quickly—quickly, gentlemen; move out! The little man is trying to kill you—to one of the bunkers between the barracks. You will stay in the bunker until morning. I say again: You *will* stay there until morning. If you have to shit, shit in your pants, shit in your sock, shit on your buddy's back, but do not leave the bunker for any reason whatsoever until morning.

"The more people in the bunker, the safer you will be. People soak up shrapnel. So pack on in. The fat boys soak up shrapnel real good, so if you get in a bunker with a fat boy, talk nice to him and squeeze up next to him until he starts to smile . . ."

On the hard stand a muscular black soldier patted a chubby white boy on the ass and said, "Sugar, me an' you gonna be bunker mates. I already know that I'm gonna like you a lot."

The chubby boy pulled away as the soldiers around him laughed, and the black soldier moved up next to him and put his arm around him. "Now, baby," he said, "jus' be cool. You gonna like your daddy."

". . . and gentlemen, if you do not hear sirens, but you hear a lot of loud noises, and buildings start falling down, you may assume that we are taking incoming rounds. In that case do not wait for the sirens. You may go to the bunkers on your own.

"Okay. That's all I've got for you. Are there any questions?"

A young soldier raised his hand, and everyone groaned. A few people nearest him cursed him and shoved him. He lowered his hand, and the staff sergeant pretended that he hadn't seen it.

"Okay, if there are no questions, Specialist Peterson will take charge of you from here."

Specialist Peterson, a clean-cut clerk/typist, seemed annoyed as he spoke. "All right, as I call your name, I want you to answer up and file into the building on the left," he said, pointing to the left without taking his eyes off the troops. "Fill *all* the seats up from front to rear. *All* the seats from *front*—to *rear.*"

"How'd that go now, *Jim?*" one of the soldiers near Hanson said, loud enough for Peterson to hear, but just soft enough so he could pretend *not* to hear it. "Maybe you oughta whip that on us one more time, we all a little slow."

"Say, I'm a specialist too," said another, tough-looking soldier. "I specialize in kickin' ass. When you reckon that little white boy up there had a good ass-kickin'? I mean, something he could write home to his momma about."

"*Too* motherfuckin' long."

"Awright!"

"There it is."

They started laughing, then went through the ritual, open hands, fists and elbows, the black power handshake.

Charlie barracks was lit by three bare bulbs hanging above the aisle between the rows of bunks. All the bunks were filled, and people were sleeping on the floor. The barracks looked like a skid-row flophouse. Somewhere a radio was playing. ". . . and now, here's a request for all the studs in Bravo Company, First of the Ninth, and especially for Abnormal Norman in fire team Delta . . ."

Hanadon and Bishop were lying on the bunks at the end of the barracks, apparently already asleep. Hanson stood between the bunks, his bed linen draped across him like a toga. In a conversational voice, he said, "Anybody who can't tap dance is queer."

Hanadon and Bishop leapt out of their bunks and began kicking, pounding the floor in their jungle boots. Voices from across the barracks, from the shadows, shouted at them to "Knock it off," "Get some sleep."

"We're tap-dancing," Bishop yelled. "We'll sleep when we're dead."

"You want to come on down here and try us on?" Hanadon yelled, doing a heel and toe with one boot, "or you want to just shut the fuck up?"

The voices grumbled, then stopped.

"Yeah!" Bishop said, "They don't want to fuck with three heroes."

"Three 'Fighting Soldiers from the Sky,'" Hanadon said.

"Three motherfuckin' legends in the making," Hanson added.

The three of them roared with laughter, grabbing each other's shoulders and shaking them, like football players in a locker room.

Hanadon pointed to the only empty bunk in the piss- and sweat-smelling barracks. "Throw your shit there, Brothah," he said. "There was another guy sleeping in it, but we convinced him that it was a good idea for him to find another bunk."

"Offered to qualify him for one in the hospital," Bishop said.

"And," Hanadon said, holding up a half-full bottle of Jim Beam, "SF looks out for their own."

The night was hot and restless. Loudspeakers announced the arrivals and departures, calling roll. Throughout the night Hanson could hear the PA system clicking on, rough background static and whine, and he waited for the names to be called before trying to go back to sleep. With each announcement there was a stir in the barracks as someone stood, shouldered his rucksack, and walked out the door, headed for the flood-lit hard stand.

When the wind was right, he could smell the stink from the piss tubes.

Da Nang Airport

The red and white sign in the busy concrete-block air terminal was matter-of-fact, like a reminder to have your ticket ready for better service. IN CASE OF MORTAR ATTACK DO NOT PANIC. LIE FLAT ON GROUND UNTIL ALL-CLEAR IS GIVEN. Hanson had processed through the replacement center and had been sent to Da Nang for assignment to a Special Forces unit. Hanadon and Bishop had processed through two days before, and Hanson hoped he would catch up with them before the next training cycle at Hon Tre Island.

One wall of the terminal was lined with souvenir booths. One of them offered hand-painted watercolor scrolls with the words "Memories of Vietnam" at the top and simple sketches of peasants and water buffalo beneath. Another booth had paintings on black velvet of vaguely Oriental-looking Caucasian soldiers glaring, knife in teeth, from the frame, but they were outnumbered by fantastically voluptuous Oriental nudes. There were jackets made from black-market poncho liners— camouflage nylon quilts— a map of Vietnam embroidered on the back and the words "When I Die I'll Go To Heaven I've Spent My Time In Hell—Vietnam." Display cases of Vietnamese-made "Zippo" lighters bore the inscription, "Yea, Though I Walk Through The Valley Of Death, I Shall Fear No Evil—For I Am The Baddest Motherfucker In The Valley," on one side, an enamel image of Snoopy, the cartoon dog, on the other, Charlie Brown's cute, innocent, and enthusiastic Beagle pup who, in the States, acts out his charming and harmless tough-guy fantasies. In Vietnam he was a popular symbol of the American soldier, the Grunt, arrogant in ragged fatigues, a cigar in his mouth, a smoking M-16 carelessly braced on his hip.

The terminal looked like a shelter for the homeless survivors of some disaster. The floor was crowded with GIs lying on their rucksacks, sleeping, reading, or just smoking and staring at the ceiling. Hanson had to walk carefully to avoid stepping on an arm or a leg.

Dozens of tape decks and radios pumped out noise, Vietnamese and American. It sounded like an argument, a shouting match between two opposing mobs. The Vietnamese music keened and sobbed and mourned the dead while Jimi Hendrix and Jim Morrison—who would not survive the war—strutted and sneered at it all.

The air seethed with the smell of terror and lust, adolescent rage, and the burnt almond stink of sweat, mo-gas, fish sauce, Vietnamese cigarettes, gun oil, wood smoke, urine and stale beer, high explosive and freshly turned earth, the salty sweetness of blood and meat, a gang-rape musk that was always there in Vietnam, a smell that, later on, would seep into Hanson's dreams, warning him that a nightmare was beginning.

The snack bar attached to the terminal was humid and thick with cigarette smoke. The Young Rascals were singing "It's a Beautiful Morning" on the jukebox.

Four American soldiers wearing faded jungle fatigues were eating cheeseburgers and french fries at one of the tables. They wore 101st Airborne TIGER FORCE RECON patches and were armed with AK-47s that they cradled across their knees. Hanson thought that he recognized one of the soldiers, but he wasn't sure until he heard him laugh. It was Henry Johnson. Hanson thought back to infantry school, where they'd both been sent after basic.

It had been early autumn. The mornings were cold and the afternoons hot. Their huts were heated by sheet metal gasoline stoves. A gallon can mounted on a wooden pole dripped gasoline through a spigot onto a hot steel plate. Each drop of gasoline vaporized in a tiny explosion the instant it hit the plate. The stoves burned through the night, glowing a dull red, their pattering explosions like a pulse. Each hut slept thirty-two men in rows of double bunk beds and the quick measured hiss of the stoves entered their dreams as the scrape of footsteps, or the sound of their own exhausted breathing.

The CQ runner woke Hanson for KP. He lay in his warm bunk and listened to the sound of the stove, the ragged breathing of the sleeping men, and static from the Little Rock radio station that had gone off the air during the night. He turned his head and could see the glowing radio dial two bunks away. He pulled his fatigues under the covers to let them warm up for a few minutes and listened to the wind bang the screen door at the end of the Quonset hut, wishing he were somewhere else, somewhere warm and private, far from the Army.

After dressing, he went outside and stepped into the cold, dark, phone-booth-size chemical toilet that served as a latrine.

As he walked toward the KP tent, the lighted phone booth in the center of the company area looked like a stage prop. Hanson passed it and imagined that the phone might ring. When he answered, a strange voice would give him instructions.

He stopped at the company duty roster and checked his name on the KP list, knowing it was there but hoping nonetheless that it had somehow been deleted during the night. The neon light above the roster buzzed and snapped, and fat, cold-stunned flies staggered across the Plexiglas.

KP started before dawn and lasted until well after dark. Dish water was heated in the cast concrete sinks with immersion heaters that worked on dripping gas like the stoves in the huts. The tent had wooden sides and duckboards over the dirt floor.

As he approached the tent, Hanson heard Henry softly singing, ". . . Open my eyes that I may see—glimpses of truth you have for me . . ."

Henry was inside, sitting on a pile of fifty-pound bags of potatoes, brown burlap bags with a dark blue outline of the state of Idaho and the words FAMOUS POTATOES. He looked up and laughed when Hanson walked in.

"Hanson, my man," he said. "You don't look happy."

"Damn," Hanson said, looking around the tent. "I hate KP."

"Yeah," Henry said, "but my momma used to tell me that a person can get used to anything. Even learn to like it."

The waxy-smelling tent was almost comfortable, a lighted

little island in the dark, warm from the steaming, still-clean dish water. By the time the first batch of partitioned plastic trays had been washed, the dish water would look like minestrone soup, but early in the morning Hanson could watch the little silver bubbles rise from the bottom of the gray concrete sink as he cut curling slivers of lye soap from the thick tan bars.

It looked like it was going to rain. The sunrise was gray and sodden. But it was almost cheerful inside the tent with the popping gasoline heaters, the clean steaming water, drinking strong coffee from a paper milk carton. And there were the eggs to break, hundreds of eggs to break into big stainless steel bowls. Hanson could crack them four at a time, two in each hand, flipping the shells into the garbage can without breaking his rhythm. He liked to drop them from a foot above the bowl so that the bright yellow yolks soared heavily down through the whites.

Through the canvas doorway Hanson could see a section of the chow line shuffling past. They did their ten chin-ups on the pair of bars on either side of the wooden-plank sidewalk, shouting out as they did the chin-ups, their voices ringing and overlapping, ". . . . eight airborne, nine airborne . . ."

". . . . airborne, three airborne, four . . ."

". . six airborne, seven . . ."

The smells of bacon and coffee, gasoline and lye soap, damp earth and wet canvas, mixed with the green bite of Georgia pine on the breeze.

After lunch they finished the pots and pans, cleaned the sinks, and scrubbed down the floor. The unpainted wood was silver with daily scrubbing, and it steamed under the soapy water. The sun had burned through the clouds, turning the day hot and humid, and Hanson watched the steam rise from the floor, his wet fatigues sticking to his back and legs.

In the late afternoon they began shucking the crates of corn. The ears were freshly picked, their light green husks fragrant and crackling as they pulled them off like skirts. The husks and silk piled up quickly, and they stacked the heavy ears. The cornsilk looked like golden brown pubic hair, and Hanson absently brushed the side of his hand against it as he worked. Once, when Henry was looking away, he pressed his lips against the cool, smooth kernels.

"I could do this for the rest of the day," Henry said. "KP's not so bad. I can think of worse things. Like momma said, you can get used to anything, once you get your mind right."

The husks snapped and crackled open, and the fresh sweet smell surrounded them. The yellow-brown silk came off in Hanson's hands, and the ripe kernels squeaked.

"Check out this little dude," Henry said, holding an ear of corn out to Hanson. A white worm was burrowing through the fat kernels, splitting slowly through the meat.

"Now this young man of a worm knows what he's doing— eatin' and movin'," Henry said, carefully stacking the ear so as not to crush the worm.

The night after KP was warm, and Hanson and Henry Johnson jogged the three miles down to the showers, a big reinforced concrete installation that hung like a balcony out over the river. It was pleasant to walk back and drink beer and watch the fog rolling in with the cold. Hanson spotted a rabbit hopping tentatively across the road and saw its eyes blink red in the light of an oncoming truck.

"Hey, Henry," Hanson said. "How long you been in-country?"

The soldier turned, and for a moment Hanson thought that he'd made a mistake. The flat hard eyes he found himself looking into weren't Henry Johnson's. Then the soldier smiled.

"Hey. Hanson! Come on over here and sit down, my man."

"I been here awhile," he said. "Took my thirty-day leave after infantry school, and I was gone. Assigned to the One-oh-First. Three days later the little man was shootin' at me. It was fucked up. Nobody in the unit knew much more than I did. So I volunteered for long-range patrol. They know what's goin' on."

The three soldiers with Henry acted as though Hanson were not quite there, as if he were an idea someone had brought up that they did not want to acknowledge. A new guy. Hanson was suddenly uncomfortable and self-conscious about his stiff OD fatigues and his shiny new jungle boots. He hadn't even been issued a weapon.

"Well goddamn," Henry said, turning to the other three. "Hanson here's a partner of mine from AIT. Introduce yourselves."

The soldier with the drooping mustache was Martinez. The other two were Orski and a big black guy named Jones.

"So what's it like?" Hanson asked, feeling foolish as he spoke. "You know, the war?"

"Like a fucking movie. That's no shit. It's a TV show out there. There's the jungle, there's a fuckin' trail, and sometimes you look, and there's Charlie."

"There it is," the one with the mustache said. "The war's a movie and we *are* the stars."

"We're on stand-down, the four of us," Henry said, "trying to get transportation to Vung Tau. Killed five Charlies last operation. CO gave us a seven-day leave."

"Yeah," Jones said. "Four cunts and an old man."

Orski laughed. "Are we *bad* or what? Four cunts and an old man. Are we cold? Are we some stone killers?"

Henry laughed. "There was these four women coming up the trail. The one in front had an old 1906 Springfield strapped to her back. The two in the middle didn't have weapons. The last one had an SKS. We could have taken them prisoner, no problem, but this old poppasan behind them had an AK. Didn't want to take a chance with him. So we laid back and hit the claymores, had six of them set up on the trail. Blam! All the women went down . . ."

"I hope to shit they went down," Orski said in his southern accent. "Had to be God invented the claymore. It is an instrument of his retribution. Thought of it one day when he was pissed off 'cause he wasn't getting any."

"God can get some whenever he wants it," Jones said. "He was just drunk when he thought of the claymore."

". . . poppasan beat feet down the trail," Henry said, smiling. "We let him go about fifty meters, then we burned his sorry ass *down*.

"One of the women was still alive, all fucked up and moaning. I mean to say, my man, I never heard anybody make a noise like that. Sound like an animal. 'Ski there emptied a magazine into her head. I've still got her hair someplace, hung down to her ass.

"We took 'em out with us on the extraction chopper. Crew chief was pissed about getting blood and shit on his chopper, but we talked him into it. When we were about five hundred feet off the chopper pad, we kicked 'em out . . ."

"Those clerks at headquarters like to shit," Orski said. "I mean, they never saw *nothin'* like that."

Henry sat back and laughed. "Raining Cong. 'Ski was hanging on to a strap, leaning out the door, yelling, '*Get* some motherfuckers, getsome, getsome.'"

"Fucking clerks were going crazy," Orski said. "Those bodies kinda turning in the air, real slow, doing goddamn cartwheels through the air. Fuckers bounced when they hit."

"We thought the CO was gonna be pissed," Henry said, "but he's a hard charger. Said it was good training for those people in headquarters company. 'Those people need motivation,' he said. 'Bought us a vacation."

Later Hanson sat on his duffel bag at the air base, waiting for transportation to the Special Forces replacement center, and from there to Hon Tre Island for a final week's training before being assigned to a unit.

Out on the far runway F-4 Phantom jets were landing, coming in hot, parachutes snapping and popping out behind their tails to slow them down. They seemed to strut on their landing gear, the 'chutes rippling behind in the jet's blue-yellow heat. Hanson stood and watched as one of them taxied closer, the furious shrieking power of it buffeting his chest. The canopy slid back and the pilot, his face covered by a shiny black bubble, turned his head slowly so that he seemed to be looking at Hanson. Then his gloved hand came up, and he gave Hanson the thumbs up, as if they knew each other and shared some secret.

And then he remembered that on the plane from California, he'd been dreaming about the field survival exercise back at Special Forces school, the first one, the one where they'd killed small animals with their hands and used knives on the goats.

It had been on the fourth or fifth day, February in the woods, where there had been a steady cold rain since the night they parachuted in. They'd had no food at all and less than three hours' sleep each night in the mud, forced marches through the swamps, planning ambushes at night with red-lensed flashlights hidden beneath the dripping shelter halves. It was the week they used to wash out Special Forces recruits who couldn't or wouldn't suck up the pain and keep going. The week that won them the right to wear the green beret.

The chickens were simple. You just pulled their heads off, then held them quickly away from you, like a champagne bottle you've just uncorked, while the neck pumped blood.

The rabbit they gave him was big, the size of a small dog, white with glittering pink eyes. He held it by its hind legs, its head toward the ground. It struggled in his hand at first, then arched its back, suddenly rigid, its head back, clearly exposing the muscled V where the neck fit into the shoulders. He held the rabbit up with his left hand and chopped down hard with the edge of his right hand into the V. The head, with its thick, delicately pink-veined ears, popped off, spinning to the ground, while the heavy warm body shuddered and leapt in his hand like a bird trying to take flight.

But it was the goat that he remembered most clearly. It was tied between two trees, bawling and lunging against the ropes as tirelessly as a machine. A lot of animals had been killed that day. The blood smell was riding the cold rain, and the goat was wild with panic. He kept bleating and running out the little slack he had, the ropes stopping him, slinging him back into the mud.

Hanson tried to look into his eyes as he walked toward the goat, but the animal refused to make eye contact, looking away, refusing to acknowledge what he knew was about to happen to him.

Hanson went around behind the goat, straddled it, and twisted one of its ears to keep it from bucking. The animal was warm and wet between Hanson's legs as he dug his heels into the mud to keep control, the wet wool stinking of musk, mud, shit, and wood smoke. The goat arched its neck, and for an instant Hanson saw, reflected in the animal's wild, dark eye, the pine trees, the watching soldiers, and his own distorted face.

An icy rain fell steadily, hissing through the trees, turning the ground and sky a yellowish green. Hanson pulled up and back on the goat's jaw with his left hand and drove the heavy blade of the K-bar knife into him, through the muscle between spine and windpipe and out the front of the neck.

The goat stopped bleating because the vocal cords had been cut away from the air supply. He began to blow steam and gouts of blood through the severed windpipe, a fine red mist, its breathing loud, wet, and ragged. Then its legs buckled and it dropped beneath Hanson, twitching and kicking, one of its hooves bruising Hanson's shin, and it died.

"All *right*," the instructor said. "Good job. You 'bout took that mother's head *off*."

It would be a long time before it occurred to Hanson that there were no goats or rabbits to eat in Vietnam, that they had not been training him to butcher livestock.

A clerk-typist and a radio operator picked him up in a jeep. They were wearing white tennis outfits, and they argued about their game all the way to the replacement center, another of the many stops on the way to his permanent assignment.

Hon Tre Island

Hanson watched the blue waves purl back along the slab-steel hull of the LST, turning into themselves and vanishing as the landing craft worked its way through merchant ships and Navy destroyers anchored in the channel. The destroyers were a uniform gray, as if they'd come off an assembly line like Buicks or Fords. Their decks were empty except for gun turrets as flat and sullen as snake's heads.

The merchant ships were from all over the world, painted red and black, buff and electric blue. Most were in poor repair, hulls streaked with brown rust, great scabs of paint flaking off, oil drums full of garbage piled on the fantail. They looked as though they had been designed as they were being built, booms, winches, and generators attached as afterthoughts.

The steel bow of the LST slammed down with a splash and clattering of chains, just like he'd seen them do in World War II movies. The island's two jagged peaks rose three thousand feet out of the ocean. It was midday, and the peaks were still shrouded in fog.

The boatload of fresh soldiers was greeted by two master sergeants. One of them was bare-chested and tanned, with a blond crew cut and a handlebar mustache that was waxed and curled out to his ears. The other was a huge black man with a woolly mustache, a deep rolling voice, and a savage smile.

"Gentlemen," he said, "welcome to Hon Tre Island, home of the in-country Special Forces training group and the Two forty-eight-B Vietcong Marine Sapper Company. I am Master Sergeant Burns, the NCOIC here. This is *my* island. There are a few officers here on my island, but they are here simply as a formality. The U.S. Army had to put them somewhere, but we don't bother them, and they don't bother us. So if you have any problems, gentlemen, bring them to me. You will find that I have a warm and sympathetic nature.

"And this," he said, nodding to the other NCO, "is Master Sergeant Krause."

Krause looked at each of the troops with mild curiosity, humming softly to himself and nodding his head slightly.

"Well now," he said in a pleasant voice, "good morning men."

"Good morning, Sergeant," the new troops shouted in unison.

"You know," he said, "I was just looking to see if I could guess which ones of you all were gonna get yourselves killed in this low-rent war we got going here. Sometimes it happens through plain bad luck, but a lot of times bad luck is just you or your buddy fucking up, getting careless or sloppy, losing your cool and forgetting what you know.

"Gentlemen," he went on, "you can step dead in the middle of a shit storm, and if you just keep thinking, keep doing what you know how to do, what you've been trained to do, you're probably gonna get out okay. But it's something you have to learn out in the field. It's our job to teach you as much as we can so you can stay alive out there long enough to learn the rest.

"Most of the regular Army troops get blown away during the first two months because they don't know what the fuck they're doing. They've had sixteen weeks of training. You people have had over a year of training and you're gonna have one more week here. In about ten days those little people are gonna be shooting live ammunition at you. Learn it now. When the little man is coming at ya, it's too late."

"Gentlemen," Sergeant Burns said, "we are goin' to be practicing our patrolling techniques here on the island. We don't expect to make any contact, but if we do, here's some advice. The best time to search a prisoner is after he's dead. And, gentlemen, if you blow away any Vet-namese personnel here on the island, and he doesn't seem to have a weapon with him, if you can not *locate* his weapon, he *will* have a weapon on him before the body is brought in, at least a grenade. We do not shoot unarmed civilians. He *will* have a weapon."

"I'll try to make this as brief as possible," Krause said, "so you can get some chow and find a bunk. We'll start fresh in the morning.

"You *are* in Vietnam, and there is a war going on over here. Do not base your impressions of this country on what you saw over there in Cam Rhan. They got ice cream parlors, they got tennis courts, and they got Air Force personnel sunbathing. That is *not* what it is like in the rest of the country. I can assure you that you will see death and destruction when you are sent to an A-camp. You will see some of your friends dead before you leave this country because it's a place young men come to die.

"In the event of an enemy attack while you are here, get up and put on your boots. I say again, put on your boots. Most of the casualties we get during alerts come from barefooted individuals who jump on engineer stakes. Gentlemen, they tell me that it is painful. So put on your boots.

"In the event that we do come under an enemy *ground* attack, we will throw the Vietnamese personnel out of the machine-gun towers and man them ourselves. All weapons positions *will* be manned by American personnel. If you encounter a Vietnamese who refuses to leave a weapons position, shoot him—shoot him several times—be sure he is dead, and throw him out.

"You'll be pulling some guard duty here. You will report to the sergeant of the guard, draw a weapon, and man your post until relieved. No Vietnamese personnel will enter or leave after nineteen hundred hours. While on guard duty, check the gun towers every hour. Throw rocks at them to wake the Vietnamese guards up. They go right back to sleep, but it gives you something to do while you walk the perimeter. Again, the towers will be manned by Americans in the event of a ground attack.

"The Vietnamese personnel are assigned to this camp because this is *their* war. We are only here to assist them. That's what we are told. Ten to twenty percent of our Vietnamese personnel are Vietcong. Be polite, gentlemen; win their hearts and minds, but watch your backs. It's a funny kind of a war."

The barracks was a large two-story building, clean and

pleasant, unlike the rundown transient barracks of the regular
Army units. From his window Hanson could see a large rice
paddy, then low hills and the sea. The barracks was separated
from the rice paddy by rolls of concertina wire and a system of
slit trenches, bunkers, and machine-gun towers. At dusk the
yellow floodlights snapped on, turning the paddy into a flat
pattern of green and black shadow.

The farmers had begun work before dawn, and when
Hanson looked out the heavy wire screen, past the concertina,
the slit trenches and gun towers, he saw dozens of people in
the rice paddy. The old men were hoeing, the women herding
huge flocks of ducks that flowed over the green paddy like the
shadow of a passing cloud. Small naked boys watched the water buffalo, keeping them out of the rice by beating them with
bamboo sticks, slashing savagely at their flanks until the lum-
bering animals snorted and bolted away.

One of the gunships on perimeter security low-leveled
over the paddy, its shadow racing crazily across the ground.
The flock of ducks flattened against the green rice, then exploded in all directions. The old men didn't look up at the
helicopter pounding past only a few feet above them. They
didn't even break rhythm with their hoes. They knew that
they might be shot as an enemy for running and had learned to
ignore a steel machine the size of a dump truck racing just
overhead at eighty miles an hour. In Vietnam one of the most
important things you had to learn was what to ignore.

He could see a Special Forces A-camp out on the mainland, peaceful-looking, set into the dark green hillside, mist
clinging to the ravines around it like snow. The tops of the hills
were solid white, the whole scene like a Japanese watercolor.

Hanadon, who'd gotten there the day before, came to
Hanson's bunk and the two of them went to have lunch in the
air-conditioned mess hall, where the tables were covered with
white linen and set with fresh flowers. Dark wood speakers
were bolted to the walls, and from them came the sound of
radio station AFVN, Armed Forces Vietnam. The other stations, Hanson would find out, were Vietnamese, and all they
seemed to play were endless wailing ballads of death, grief,
and mourning.

After he ate Hanson rolled up the mattress at the end of his bunk and used it for a pillow, lying on the bare springs. He read, looked out the window, and thought about all the choices and accidents that had led him to where he was. The sky was a very pale blue, as though the color had been thinned out by the heat. Sometimes a shit smell would drift in from the paddy.

A white stone Buddha the size of a two-story house overlooked the city on the mainland from the hills above. At dawn he caught the first rays of the sun and seemed to emerge from the dark. At dusk he was brighter than the sky or the gray-green hills, the first thing to appear and the last to fade each day. He had not yet been damaged by the war, and his peaceful face was clearly visible from the barracks through the wire grid of the window. At night Hanson would look out and see the blinking lights and red exhaust cones of the gunships swarming the sky around him. The Buddha had great dignity, and the gunships seemed as inconsequential and vexing as insects.

But in the noontime heat of that first day Hanson drifted in and out of sleep and dreams, sometimes bolting awake, not knowing where he was in the midst of radio music and the conversation of other soldiers.

". . . counting 'em down and rocking 'em out on a beautiful Thursday *in*-country with a weekend on tap . . ."

". . . an' so the captain says to me, 'Is that prisoner still alive?' Now, this Charlie layin' there is *all* fucked up. He's hurtin'. You know, he's gonna die anyway, man. An' to medivac him I'm gonna have to hump his sorry ass all the way up to the LZ. Dig it, that sorry fucker gon' die anyway. So I walk over and put a burst into him and say to the captain, 'Naw, sir, he's dead.' Captain just nods and walks off. He's a cool dude."

". . . and here's a request for all the guys at the fourth support battalion, Charlie Company of the Third Mech, and especially for Ringo and *Big*-time . . ."

That afternoon all the new arrivals were marched to a small auditorium for orientation. A movie screen was pulled down, the lights turned off, and the audience groaned as the film began. They had all seen it several times since joining the Army, but MACV regulations stated that no soldier would be assigned to a combat unit until he had seen it, and they were showing it one more time to catch anyone who might have missed it.

The film opened on Lyndon Johnson sitting at a massive desk, absorbed in paperwork. The camera moved in closer and the narrator's voice said, "The President . . . of the United States."

Johnson looked up as if this were an appointment he had forgotten about in the midst of the duties of his office. He paused thoughtfully, took off his glasses, and looked directly into the camera.

"The other day," he began, speaking slowly in his Texas accent, "I received a letter from the mother of a boy who had died in the jungles of Vet-nom. She had sacrificed her boy to a war she didn't understand in a strange land thousands of miles away. So she wrote her President and wanted to know, *'Why . . . Vet-nom?'*

"History has taught us that force must be met with strength. Munich taught us that. When Britain sacrificed the peoples of a few small countries to a tyrant in the hopes of 'peace in our time,' they found that a tyrant will never be satisfied until he has everything. Those that do not learn from the lessons of history are doomed to repeat its mistakes.

"As your Commander-in-Chief, I pledge to meet force with strength, and as your President, I give my solemn oath to support the struggles of the freedom-loving people of Vet-nom."

The President's long, gloomy face was replaced by the words "WHY VIETNAM?" The words faded to newsreel footage of North Vietnamese troops marching to the sound of pounding kettle drums, intercut with jerky footage of fleeing refugees. There followed scenes of American troops handing out food and medical supplies, giving candy to children, and helping old villagers walk to aid stations, all to a sound track of french horns and violins. It was a battle of the bands, the ominous kettle drums and oboes of the Communists versus the french horns and violins of the Americans.

Hanson, Hanadon, Bishop, and some others walked to the "Playboy Club" after the film to get a beer.

"I see what it's all about now, thanks to that film," Bishop said. "We're not going to let those Nazis take over Vietnam *this* time."

"Fuckin' tyrants in the jungle, man."

"Why Vet-nom. Why?" They laughed as they walked.

"Why, why?"

"Oh, why Vet-nom."

A sign taped to the mirror at the Playboy Club said, No One under 21 Years of Age Will Be Served Alcoholic Beverages.

After supper Hanson, Hanadon, and Bishop sat on sandbags drinking beer, eating popcorn they'd gotten from the small Special Forces bar, and watching the war in progress at an A-camp across the bay, whose yellow lights looked like a ship passing in the distance. They were able to pick out an occasional blink of a green or red tracer at the edge of the camp and hear the sporadic chatter of the firefight that was going on.

The A-camp finally called in Spooky, the C-130 gunship, and requested mortar support from the island. Hanson watched the crew fire the four-deuce mortar just down the hill from where they were sitting, the tube bursting with a hollow explosion and pale yellow flame. If he judged its trajectory right, and stared out at a point where he estimated the shell might pass, Hanson could sometimes catch a glimpse of it as it flashed toward the mainland.

The A-camp began popping flares, showing itself against the hills, a high-contrast black-and-white scene jogging in and out of focus as the flares swung and twisted beneath their little parachutes. Hanson could hear the voice of the A-camp commander directing the mortar fire on the radio, while a rock group on the jukebox in the bar sang, "American woman, stay away from me-eee . . ."

Spooky came in from the right of the camp, a solid slab of shadow in the black sky, the glow of its four engines flickering behind their props. Its minigun opened up, the flickering column of tracers boring down into the camp, moaning in the distance.

"American woman, just let me be-eee . . ."

The next morning a chaplain was leading the morning prayer on the radio as Hanson walked into the mess hall. Someone farted skillfully. The sound of knives and forks on plates did not slow down. The prayer ended with a background of violin music, then a cheerful, glib voice shouted, "Gooooooood *morning, Vietnam. It's seven o'clock right here *in*-country," as though Vietnam were a great place to live and work and raise a family. It was the same voice you'd hear on the car radio, on the freeway, on the way to work.

Then Archie Bell and the Drells began to sing "Tighten Up," clapping their hands and rapping to quick little trumpet riffs.

After breakfast they formed up outside the barracks and were issued battered little M-1 carbines that wouldn't knock a man down unless you shot him in the head or heart. They threw on forty-pound rucksacks and began the double-time march up the steep mountain road, sweating out their fatigues in the damp early morning. It was the only time, that first half-hour of dawn, that you could distinguish the delicate jungle smells. After that the sun boiled them together into green heat.

The outside edge of the road dropped off a thousand feet to the dark blue ocean. It was low tide at that time of day and the big fishing nets, bellying on stilts off the beach, were full of silver fish trapped there by the outgoing tide.

One of the primary rules of jungle warfare is never take the same trail twice, never return over the same route you took out, yet they came back down the mountain on the same road. Hanson asked Sergeant Burns why the Vietcong Sapper unit that was based on the island didn't just set up a bank of claymore mines along the road and blow the whole column into the sea.

Sergeant Burns smiled and said, "Now Charles ain't gonna do nothin' like that. He do *that,* you understand, and he *know* we gonna police his ass up, and he ain't gonna be able to blow up no more of the Navy's boats, which is his job. We have, don't you see, an *understanding* with Charles here on the island.

Long as he don't fuck with us, we ain't gonna fuck with him.
He's the Navy's problem, not ours."

There was more map reading review, but no one minded. Very
soon they would be calling in artillery and gunships, and
medivacs. The radio was the most powerful weapon they had.

The U.S. Army Corps of Engineers maps were beautiful—
the white valleys shading off into light green hills, blue river
lines twisting through ravines and into the little double-smoke-
stack symbols of rice paddies. But dominating the maps were
the big hills and mountains, convoluted brown contour lines
like thumbprints and palm prints stitched with the dotted blue
lines of intermittent streams. There were the towns, clusters of
black squares representing neighboring villages that once ex-
changed goods and services, working together in harvests,
celebrating marriages between their children. But now most
of them had the word "destroyed" or "abandoned" beneath
them:

Kong
Dang   Plei Bon (1)   Plei Bon (2)
(destroyed)   (destroyed)   (destroyed)

And there was more first aid.

"Today I'm going to teach you how to keep yourself or
your buddy alive until you can get a medivac. Thousands of
troops die over here that don't have to because their buddy is
too stupid or too fucking squeamish to keep him alive. You're
gonna see a lot of blood over here, gentlemen, a lot of real bad-
looking shit. You're gonna have to get used to it fast. No matter
how bad he might look, you can probably keep your buddy
alive.

"The first thing you want to do is reassure him. Say, 'Hey,
Bill, medivac's on the way. You're gonna be okay. That doesn't
look so bad.'

"Now even if he knows you're lying, that's what he wants
to hear, and he *wants* to believe you.

"What you don't want to do is something like this," he said,
putting his hands over his ears and screaming, "Oh my god!

You're *all* fucked up! Your guts are all over the ground. I don't think you're gonna make it.

"Gentlemen," he went on, in a normal voice, "he's gonna roll his eyes back and die. You've just killed him.

"You've always been told that the first lifesaving step is 'clear the airway,' but that is not the first step. The first step is 'calm down.' Pretend it's just a movie if you want to. That works for some people. Then get down there and do what has to be done.

"*Then* clear the airway. Just reach in there with your first two fingers and pull out any teeth or pieces of bone that might be in the way. Turn your buddy over on his side so the blood and mucus will drain and he won't drown in it. Give him mouth-to-mouth resuscitation. Gentlemen, a little vomit and blood is not going to hurt you. There are hundreds of dead soldiers who would be alive today, but their buddy wouldn't give them mouth-to-mouth because of a little blood and puke.

"If you can't clear the airway, or if the lower face is destroyed so badly that you can't get a seal to give him mouth-to-mouth, give him a tracheotomy. Get him breathing. A buddy of mine over at CCN was breaking contact with a WP grenade when he got shot. The grenade took most of his face off. A tracheotomy kept him alive. Last time I saw him in the hospital, he was drinking Jim Beam through a tube."

He jammed his thumb against his throat. "Right here. Stick a hole right here in this little hollow below the larnyx. Everybody find it? Okay, punch a hole through there with a knife or a ball-point pen, or a fucking can opener. Anything. Don't worry about keeping it clean, just get it open and get him breathing. The cartilage is tough, so you've gotta push hard. Once you've got the hole made you have to keep it open. You'll have a ball-point pen with you. Cut off a section of the plastic tube and stick it in the hole.

He held up something that looked like a tiny silver toothpaste tube with a small needle at the end.

"One half-gram of morphine. All you have to do is stick it in an arm or leg, right through the fatigues, and *squeeeeze* it in. Just like Pepsodent. If your man's lost an arm or a leg, you don't want to put it too close to the stump because it will just drain out. You don't use it for head wounds or chest wounds. You want to keep the brain and the lungs working, and this stuff will just slow them down and kill your man.

"If he's hurting, well *sin loy*, sorry about that, your job is to keep him alive. If you got ten casualties and only one styrette of morphine, *you* take the morphine and go to work. You're gonna need it worse than them. This stuff," he said, holding up the tube, "makes everything seem okay. The last time I had to take it I looked down at my fucked-up leg and thought, Wow, that leg is hurting like a sonofabitch. Interesting.

"The pain is still there, but it doesn't seem very important.

"If you hear a loud noise out in the field and the man next to you falls down, he's probably dead or wounded. If he's dead, fine, no problem, but if he's wounded, you have to find the wound. Once you find the wound, do what you can to patch it up, then start looking for the *other* wound. Don't find one wound, patch it up, and say, 'Lookin' good now, Jim,' and wait for the medivac. What probably put your man down is shrapnel or automatic weapons fire. That shit comes at you in batches, not one at a time. Look for multiple wounds.

"A sucking chest wound is another one of nature's ways of telling you that you've just been shot. If the hole in the chest is frothing little pink bubbles, your man has got it through the lung. Get that hole sealed off so it's airtight, or both lungs are going to collapse. You die if your lungs collapse. And, gentlemen, don't seal the hole in the chest, then sit back and wait for the medivac, because your man is probably blowing little bubbles through a hole in his *back* where the bullet went out. Your man's gonna be a corpse when the medivac gets there. 'Oops, forgot that exit wound.'

"Pills, gentlemen. We have pills for everything. Pills for pain, for fatigue, diarrhea, infection, water purification, gonorrhea, coughing, uppers and downers."

He held up a green and white capsule. "Special Forces popcorn, gentlemen, dexamphetamine. It makes you mean. It makes you want to go out and kill Charles with a knife, with your hands and teeth. It makes you want to go out and have *fun* with Charles.

"It will also get you over a hill after your troops have deserted you and Charlie is on your ass. When your body tells you to stop, but your brain *reminds* you that Charlie is on your ass, this will help you run faster, see clearer, and hear better.

"Lomotil. Keeps you from shitting your pants if you pick up some dysentery. And it's good to give to your little people before you go out with them on night locations and ambushes. They have dysentery all the time, they were born with it, and all they eat is rice and fish covered with fermenting *nuoc mam*. If one of your people takes a shit on an ambush site and Charles is downwind, he's gonna know where you are.

"Most of your troops also have tuberculosis . . ."

The rain had started again. It swept through the heat a dozen times a day, violent, then gone as quickly as it had come. Water poured down in steady streams from the lip of the corrugated roof, and beyond the roof the wind-driven rain slanted down at a forty-five-degree angle, the streams of water seeming to mesh like silver-gray yarn being worked in a loom.

Monkey Mountain

Hanson walked across the helicopter pad kicking up little red mushroom clouds of dust that blossomed and faded behind him. He stepped into the operations center and continued down the long hallway, through the stale refrigerated air and the smell of floor wax and duplicating fluid. Soldiers sat typing on both sides of him, behind glass partitions. He passed a wizened Vietnamese woman who was sifting cigarette butts out of a brass urn, then stopped at a gray steel door with the words Authorized Personnel Only stenciled across it in black. The woman grinned up at him accusingly with black teeth, then flashed the peace sign.

He knocked, and a voice on the other side of the door said, "Enter." He walked in, and a big warrant officer looked up from his desk at him but said nothing. He was wearing the green triangle patch of the 3rd Infantry (mechanized), the 3rd Mech.

The 3rd Mech was the conventional unit responsible for northern I-corps, coexisting with the isolated Special Forces camps and sharing intelligence with them. Hanson, because he'd been to college, had been assigned as liaison with the 3rd Mech headquarters after leaving the island. Hanadon, Bishop, and the others had been sent to A-camps throughout the country.

Special Forces despised the 3rd Mech as a bunch of bungling amateurs, and the 3rd Mech hated Special Forces as elitists who thought they were a law unto themselves.

"I'm Hanson," he said after waiting for the warrant officer to speak. "They sent me over here."

The warrant officer sat looking at Hanson for a few seconds, then said, "Right. Been lookin' for you, Hanson. Come on in," in a Texas accent, lowering his voice to what is known in the Army as a command voice. "I'm Mr. Grieson. Be with you in a minute," he said, turning to a chattering teletype pumping out an endless sheaf of paper that coiled and writhed on the floor. The white drone of neon lights made Hanson squint. A round TV screen displayed a flickering green bar graph to the right of the teletype.

A framed Polaroid photograph of Warrant Officer Grieson stood on one corner of his desk. It showed him sitting in a swivel chair, looking sternly at the camera, one arm slung over the back of the chair to expose the .45 he was wearing in a shoulder holster.

Grieson spun around in his chair and stood, a head taller than Hanson. He extended his hand, a star sapphire ring and a gold Rolex watch catching the light.

"Glad to have you aboard," he said, squeezing Hanson's hand and fixing him with a straight-from-the-shoulder look. "You'll be working with me here in collection. Your job, basically, will be to help me interpret and disseminate intelligence on enemy units. It's an important job, and a demanding one, but if I'm any judge of character, I think you'll be able to handle it. Am I right?

"Sure I am," he said. "You're a college man, aren't you?"

"Some. Before I got drafted."

"I never had time for college myself," Grieson said. "Wish I had. But I've done all right without it, I think. Well," he said, "I think you're going to like it here. You'll be helping me cross-reference enemy unit designations, their strength and movements, weapons and personnel. Over here," he said, walking across the room, "is something I'm kind of proud of."

He flipped up a large window shade, the word SECRET across it in red block letters, exposing a large map of northern South Vietnam on the wall. Dozens of little boxes with tiny flags were drawn in crayon on the map. They looked like the stubby ships in a kid's game of Battleship. Grieson pulled the chain on a light fixture, and the Day-Glo crayon lit up, throbbing with electric reds, greens, and blues. Grieson stepped to one side, folded his arms, and grinned.

Hanson thought about Linda, back in school, and almost smiled. She had the same kind of black light in her bedroom, the light that made her body glow blue in the dark, her lips and nipples black, that lit up the peacock feathers and the Jimi Hendrix poster.

Grieson pulled down a clear overlay with more boxes drawn on it, and another, until the symbols began to overlap and obscure the map.

"Here, for instance," he said, tapping three of the glowing boxes with a bullet-tipped pointer, "we think that these three units are really only a single unit that uses different names and radio call signs and has two extra commo units that make radio transmissions from decoy locations. But we aren't sure. Sometimes a unit will just vanish when we think we have it pinpointed, then turn up fifty miles away under another name. It's our job to find and fix these units . . ."

Hanson leaned his head against the wall. He could feel the hum of the radio components against the back of his skull as Grieson talked. He looked down at Grieson's desk, at the carefully printed sign beneath the Plexiglas top that said, the difficult we can do right away—the impossible takes a little longer. It shared the space beneath the Plexiglas with some yellowed newspaper clippings, a photo of a small dog sitting on a sofa, and a faded color print of a woman standing in front of a Chevrolet.

". . . using POW reports, visual sightings, radio intercepts, sensors, and other—classified techniques you'll soon be familiar with.

"I know," he said, "that some people laugh about us being 'armchair commandos,' but I've got over a thousand confirmed kills since I've been here. B-fifty-two strikes. Arclights. That's confirmed. A thousand kills confirmed by BDA.

"The troops out in the field do a good job, but it's this," he said, sweeping his arms wide, taking in the teletype, maps, banks of radios and filing cabinets, "that kills the gooks out there. Believe it.

"You know, Hanson, war is like a business at this level. Expense versus profit. But I've got more power than any corporation president." He laughed. "Welcome to the corporation."

After the briefing, Hanson was dismissed for the day. He

thanked Grieson, walked back down the shotgun hall, and when he stepped outside the air-conditioned operations center, the noonday heat struck him like a sudden illness. The only sound was the *tweet-tweet-tweet* of a chopper that had landed while he was inside. It was empty, its rotors drooping as they turned slowly around to a standstill. The whole compound was deserted, everyone holed up in air-conditioned buildings. The presence of the empty helicopter was the only indication that time had passed while he was inside. He left the compound through the main gate and began walking down the road toward the granite hill known as Monkey Mountain.

Dust from the red clay road collected on his face and the backs of his hands, turning to mud with his sweat, the color of the road. A squad of Navy SEALs ran past in formation, wearing ragged cutoff fatigue pants and combat boots, barking at him and laughing as they passed. Though there was a rivalry between the Navy SEALs and Special Forces, Hanson felt a kinship with them. They had volunteered for hard training and dangerous duty, and they stuck together.

Off to the right, a military junkyard was piled with olive-drab and soot-black wreckage scabbed with rust. Behind the barbed-wire perimeter, there were jeeps, trucks, APCs, tanks, and a John Deere tractor with one rear wheel blown off, like a civilian casualty mixed in with the military hardware. A giant cargo helicopter hovered over the junkyard like a praying mantis, sucking up a column of dust.

Hanson squinted against the glare and the roar of the helicopter. A wrecked APC dangled beneath the hollow belly of the chopper, smoke-blackened, a jagged hole just visible in its side. The smell of mo-gas, hot metal, and dust blew across the road.

A family of four Vietnamese passed him, balanced like a circus act on a Honda motorbike, the transistor radio that hung from the handlebars wailing a Vietnamese song.

A Huey gunship loped along the perimeter like a green steel wasp, and farther off, at the base of the green hills, a C-130 transport leveled off like a big crop duster and trailed a silver mist. The sunlight made an oily rainbow in the defoliant.

A jeep passed him, slowed, and stopped. The driver

turned and called back to Hanson, "Where you headed?" He was wearing a green beret, but he had a strange yellow patch on his fatigue pocket, a yellow skull with a jagged leer.

"CCN," Hanson said.

"Hop in. That's where I'm going."

The jeep rattled down the road, a tape recorder on the floorboard playing a Beatles tape. ". . . the magical mystery tour is waiting to take you away, *die*-ing to take you away, take you today . . ."

The driver turned to look at Hanson, laughing, his eyes dancing. "Sound track," he shouted, pounding the steering wheel, the jeep lurching off the shoulder of the road. "What a war, huh? Rock 'n' roll war.

"Hey, what you going to CCN for?"

"I think I want a job."

"Ha. We got some openings. We got openings. Go talk to Sergeant Major, he'll fix you up. Tell him Silver sent you. Abadabadaba," he said, flicking an imaginary cigar. "Say the magic word and get a job. No. As you were. Better not mention my name."

They barreled down the road, Silver bobbing his head to the bass line on the tape recorder.

"You believe in reincarnation?" he shouted over the music.

"Sometimes."

"Me too! I want to come back as an electric bass guitar. Plug myself in and just, you know, vibrate!"

The Vietnamese guards at the gate waved the jeep through. They drove down an alley of barbed wire, beneath the skull with the green beret, and up to the wood-frame operations center.

"Here it is. Sergeant Major's in there. Huh!" He laughed down in his skinny chest. "Maybe you two can make a deal."

Hanson hopped out and thanked him.

"That's okay. That's all right. Probably see you around." He popped the clutch and disappeared in the dust.

Hanson walked through the last of the wire and beneath another grinning skull and the words WE KILL FOR PEACE. There were rows of barracks behind the operations center, each with a skull over the doorway and the name of a state beneath it: Kentucky, Minnesota, Montana.

A soldier walked out from behind one of the barracks. He wasn't American or Vietnamese. He was stockier and darker than a Vietnamese, and his handsome features were broader. He was a Montagnard, a "Yard," an aboriginal hill tribesman. The Yards were the niggers of Vietnam, despised for centuries by the Vietnamese who called them savages and who methodically killed them off whenever they could. Special Forces had been recruiting Yards, training them, and paying them to fight since the early sixties.

He looked like an Eskimo in jungle fatigues and combat gear, wearing a pack as big as his torso and carrying an AK-47 assault rifle. His body was hung with green hand grenades, and he wore a silver peace medallion the size of a hamburger patty around his neck.

Another Montagnard, this one with shoulder-length hair and wearing only a loincloth, watched from the shadow of a gun tower as Hanson walked up to the operations center. His name was Rau. He had been watching for Hanson, the new one Mr. Minh was expecting. The one he'd seen in his *katha*.

Hanson knocked at the screen door of the operations center. Back in one of the barracks someone was playing "Summertime" on a bugle. He knocked again and thought he heard a voice inside.

The room seemed black as he stepped in out of the shrieking, hallucinatory noon sun. He could hear a reciprocating fan in a corner of the room, whirring, thumping to a stop, then turning back. He could feel the hot air it was pushing touch his face. The smell of hot wiring and oil was strong in the room, and he could hear the squeal and bark of a single sideband radio somewhere.

He made out a dark form behind a desk, came to attention and saluted. "Specialist-Four Hanson, sir. Request permission to speak to the sergeant major."

"At ease, son. You're speaking to him. What can I do for you?"

"I want a job with CCN, Sergeant Major."

The man behind the desk smiled, and Hanson could just make out his eyes and cheekbones and the white of his teeth.

"Do you know what we do here, Hanson?"

"I have a general idea, Sergeant Major."

Hanson began to see more clearly, his eyes adjusting to the room. The sergeant major looked to be in his early forties, with the strong jaw and high cheekbones of a Southerner. He had a pleasant Southern accent, and his voice was mild, almost fatherly, the voice of an interrogator.

A narrow blackboard ran the length of the wall behind the sergeant major, and it was sectioned off in green boxes. The name of a different state topped each box, and beneath each of the states there were six smaller boxes with names written in them in chalk: two American names at the top and four Montagnard names below those. Several of the boxes had been erased, a smudge of white chalk where a name should have been. Hanson could just make out parts of the erased names, ghostly in the smeared chalk dust.

"We've got jobs, Hanson. See those empty boxes behind me?"

"Yes, Sergeant Major."

"They're all dead or medivaced." He watched Hanson for a few seconds, then laughed. "Do you have some kind of death wish, son? Do you have something against Communists? Do you think you can help," he said with a smile, "win the war? Do you think it matters *what* you do over here?"

The door opened and closed behind Hanson, lighting the room for a moment so that he could see Sergeant Major's dark, ironic eyes. Someone moved a chair and sat down on the far side of the room.

"Who are you, Hanson?" Sergeant Major asked him. "You don't look like you belong here. You look like a nice, intelligent, sensitive college boy." A laugh rose from the far side of the room and Hanson felt himself blush in shame and anger.

"Why aren't you back home taking part in student antiwar self-criticism sessions, going to rallies and getting laid? That's where I'd be.

"Okay," he said. "I'm listening. Why do you want a job with us? Give me your best pitch."

"I think I can contribute more to the Special Forces mission—"

"Why don't you save that for the captain?" Sergeant Major said, interrupting him. "It's a nice opening, and he likes that kind of speech, but I want to know why you want a job with us. We're talking about hundred percent casualties, and nobody really cares. Talk to me, son."

"Sergeant Major, I was drafted. I was doing fine without the Army or this war. They put me on a bus, shaved all my hair off, issued me baggy clothes, and put me into a barracks full of seventeen-year-old juvenile delinquents where NCOs screamed at me for sixteen weeks. I didn't want to go to war with those people.

"So I signed up. I *signed up* for an extra year in the Army so I could volunteer for Special Forces. I went through all the training—I *was* a nice college boy. I was happy being a college boy, but they said I had to go. It wasn't my idea.

"But when I went through the Special Forces school, I kind of got to *like* it. Which surprised me more than anybody. I liked the people I met there. I spent over a year with them getting ready for combat. Then I finally get here, my friends go off to A-teams, and they assign me to work with some regular Army warrant officer in the S-Two shop, drawing circles and arrows on maps."

"Ah," Sergeant Major said. "Mr. Grieson. He runs an efficient S-2 shop. A thousand confirmed kills, as he likes to remind people in the NCO club."

The voice on the other side of the room said, "Immaculate violence. And very nicely charted on his Day-Glo map collection, too. 'Some may call us armchair commandos,' " the voice said, imitating Grieson's Texas accent, then laughed.

"Too neat for you, Hanson?" Sergeant Major said. "You just want to go out there on the ground and see how it feels to kill folks?"

"Sergeant Major, I didn't go through all that training to work in an office. I'm *ready.* If I come all the way over here and don't get into combat it'll be like getting into bed with a beautiful woman, then rolling over and reading a book. I'm a good soldier. I'll do a good job for you. Get me out of that S-2 shop."

"Why don't we give him a chance?" the voice behind him said. "Rau sent me over here. He says that this might be the guy Mr. Minh was expecting."

"Going native on me, Lieutenant?" Sergeant Major asked him.

"Who knows, Sergeant Major? But God knows we need some names on the blackboard if we want to get some of these operations moving again."

"Okay," Sergeant Major said to Hanson. "Be back here at fifteen hundred hours to talk to the captain. Put on some fresh fatigues. All you have to do is say 'Yes sir' and 'No sir.' I'll handle the details.

"I don't think I have to tell you not to mention this to anyone. Go ahead and do what your warrant officer wants, and smile when you do it. I'll have your orders cut by tomorrow, and by then it'll be too late for them to do anything about it. We have priority on personnel procurement."

"I'll walk him out to the gate," the voice said.

"Okay, Hanson, take a walk with Lieutenant Andre. I'll see you this afternoon."

"Come on, college boy," the lieutenant said, laughing. He was a dark-haired, wiry man a few years older than Hanson. "I had to put up with that 'college boy' shit, too. They get tired of it after a while," he said as they stepped out the door into the blinding sunlight.

"Where do you think they'll send me, sir?" Hanson asked him.

"You came at a good time. We're setting up a base camp near the DMZ. It's still under construction. We've got two companies of Vietnamese strike force and two companies of Yards for security. We'll be doing some patrolling with them. It's a good place for you to get your feet wet. There's enough people on a strike force patrol that you're just one of many. On a cross-border team, when the little man is shooting, he's shooting at *you*. The only problem—they probably told you about it at Bragg—is the Vietnamese and the Yards hate each other, but we've got to use the Vietnamese and run them on patrols because of the politics over here. We're hoping we can get rid of them once we go operational as a launch site."

"What was that you said in there about someone 'expecting' me?" Hanson asked him.

"Well," he said, and took a few more steps. "Okay," he said. "Here it is, take it or leave it. There's this Montagnard up at the camp. He doesn't have any rank, but he's basically the head honcho of the Yards. The Yards call him Chicken Man, but we just call him by his name, Minh. Only we call him *Mr.* Minh. The man has got some balls. He also . . ."

The sound of rotors drowned him out as a pair of Cobra gunships pounded past overhead.

"He also is kind of a shaman, a priest, to them. He can predict things sometimes. That's what the Yards say. He said that a new guy was going to show up here today, looking for a job, and that we should give him one."

They walked toward the gate and the grinning skull.

"Yeah," Lieutenant Andre said, "like I said, you can take it or leave it.

"Anyway, welcome to CCN."

CCN, Command and Control North, was one of the units under SOG, Surveillance and Observation Group. The names of the illegal cross-border units were kept as vague as possible and changed from time to time. The individual soldiers in the units might be referred to in official reports as "detection operation systems personnel," or "border control structure components."

The soldiers in the units usually operated in six-man teams, two Americans and four Montagnards, and were members of the U.S. Special Forces. No Vietnamese were involved in the real workings of the unit.

The units went on reconnaisance patrols and prisoner snatches into Laos, Cambodia, and North Vietnam. Approximately 80 percent of the reliable intelligence about enemy troop movements came from these patrols but was attributed to other sources, such as captured documents, friendly villagers, aircraft spottings, and enemy defectors. Vietnam, some said, was a "polite war," and it was illegal to cross borders.

Most of the security precautions were not taken in an attempt to confuse the enemy. The enemy knew the day a unit had its name changed or when a new launch site was planned. Their spies and sympathizers were everywhere, from maids to field grade officers. No, the complex, often ridiculous security measures were part of an effort to protect the Special Forces operations from American political and military investigation.

Public opinion about the war could change in the time it took to look up from your potatoes at ten seconds of garbled film footage on the evening news, and some hustling young congressman would be out to get the truth, once again, on the controversial Green Berets. By the time he got the necessary secret, top secret, and need-to-know clearances to start sorting through hundreds of confusing, euphemistic, and sanitized reports (sentences and entire pages would be missing, blank pages might have been inserted, stamped "pages 12 through 15 have been removed in accordance with letter, MACV 246 HQ US Military Assistance Command, Vietnam, dated 15 June 68, as not relevant to debriefing requirements") in an attempt to get publicity as a "concerned American" or a peace candidate, the operations would have new names, and all information would have been refiled under "Terrain Studies During Monsoon Conditions."

Field grade and general officers in the regular Army who wanted to see all Special Forces operations discontinued—and the majority did. The regular Army has always distrusted elite units—had almost as much difficulty as the congressmen. With only a year in Vietnam, they had to devote most of their time to trying to devise some tactic novel and flamboyant enough to justify their promotion, or to orchestrate an operation big and bloody enough to make the headlines, ensuring their promotion *and* a medal.

Most of the Special Forces units were inserted by helicopter near an enemy-controlled area. They worked their way through the area until they found the enemy, and then directed air strikes on them.

Sometimes the enemy found the team first, and the team had to run. Drop everything but ammo, and run.

Mai Loc
Launch Site

The lined yellow legal sheets fluttered in Hanson's hands in the rush of air from the open chopper door. He kept looking past Linda's black felt-tip writing to the jungle passing below. It was almost cold at two thousand feet. They were skirting the city of Hue, and in the river below he could see the staggered Vs of fish traps. An area on one side of the river was pocked with hundreds of craters.

"What's that?" he asked the staff sergeant next to him, shouting over the wind and the roar of the jet turbine. "Bomb craters?" He pointed down.

"No. Cemetery. They bury them in round graves," the staff sergeant shouted back, cupping his hands. "Put 'em in the ground sort of sitting down. That's the kind of fucked-up people they are."

Each of the circular graves appeared to be marked with a triangular flag on a pole.

"What . . ." Hanson shouted, his voice lost in the wind and noise.

The staff sergeant pointed at the microphone/earphone hanging above Hanson, then took down another one for himself. After they put them on, he said, "Better than shouting, eh?" his voice shuddering with the pounding of the chopper, like someone with palsy.

"What are the flags for?" Hanson asked him.

"Land-clearing operation. They put flags on the graves so the 'dozers don't plow 'em under."

Then the pilot's voice, quivering and metallic, came through the earphones. "Are you ready, Sarge?"

"Right," the staff sergeant said. He reached into his ruck-sack and pulled out two 60-millimeter mortar rounds, little iron bombs the size of Thermos bottles. "Ready," he said. "Mr.

Smith, you are now driving an aircraft with the rough configu-
ration of a fighter-bomber."

The chopper dropped toward the river.

"Hanson," the sergeant said, his voice shaking over the
intercom as if someone had him by the throat, "we're going in
on a little unauthorized mission. There's a machine gun just
about there"—and he pointed at a bend in the river—"that
fucks with Mr. Smith every time he comes up this way. We're
gonna see if he's still around."

The chopper dropped to a couple hundred feet, and Hanson felt his ears pop as he lifted slightly from his seat. The
sergeant pulled safety pins from the noses of the mortar
rounds.

At their altitude, the river threw the sunlight back like a
mirror set in the dark green jungle.

Something flickered at the elbow of the river.

"There it is."

"Mark, mark."

Green tracers arced slowly up toward the helicopter,
growing out of the darker green of the jungle, growing bigger
and faster, then blinking past the open door.

The door gunner on that side began firing, adding another
shudder to the chopper, the ride bumpy as a station wagon
speeding down a dirt road. Red tracers from his M-60 arced
down to the jungle, and he began walking them toward the
spot where the green tracers clustered like bubbles before
floating up at the chopper.

"Bring some peel!"

Gleaming brass poured from the breech of the machine
gun and was torn away by the wind.

The chopper banked, and the other gunner began to fire.
The staff sergeant leaned out the open door into a safety strap,
holding the mortar rounds in each hand like iron footballs.

"Comin' up," he said. "Good . . . good," and he spiked
the rounds down, giving then a spin as he let go.

"Bombs gone," he said with a laugh. Then he began slapping at his chest, shouting, cursing.

"You hit?" a voice said over the intercom.

"No. No, dammit. Got some hot M-60 brass down my shirt."

Suddenly Hanson's earphone was full of electronic, shuddering laughter. The bend in the river looked peaceful, distant. Two columns of black smoke rose from the jungle and spread downriver. A short burst of green tracers rose from the jungle and fell away behind them.

"Goddamn, Sarge," Mr. Smith said, "looks like we missed. He's a ballsy little gook. We're way out of range now. He just wanted us to know he's still there. I ought to call in an air strike on his ass, but I'd kind of miss him. He's *my* gook."

They climbed still higher to cross a range of mountains, and it got colder.

Wire surrounded the raw launch site at Mai Loc like a barrier reef around an island, gray triple-strand wire lashed around engineer stakes, piled coils of concertina, and webs of tanglefoot. The concertina was a new design. Instead of the knotted barbs there were little galvanized bow ties of raw-edged tin pinched onto the wire, designed to cut rather than scratch. It was a design that couldn't be used to fence in livestock because it would hurt them too badly.

The wire was littered with paper and plastic and cardboard, like a parking lot hurricane fence, cluttered with silver trip flares, squat claymore mines, and rusting beer cans filled with pebbles. Out in the wire it smelled of kerosene, burned grass, and hot metal.

Quinn was squatting in the wire, twisting tanglefoot around short steel stakes. He was wearing heavy leather gauntlets, the palms studded with staples. His face and bare chest were slick with sweat and red dust, and he had bright little cuts on his forearms. The bottom layer of wire was cutting into his ankles, the other into his knees, and sweat was stinging his eyes. As he twisted the wire, he tried to shake off a fly that was walking on his cheek.

He tossed his head, snorted, then bolted upright, tearing one leg of his fatigue pants from knee to ankle. He threw down his wire cutters and began swinging at the fly, unable to move in the wire, swaying awkwardly with each of the blows that, in the studded gloves, would have broken a man's jaw, but which the fly easily avoided.

He took off the gloves and stood catching his breath. "Goddamn flies," he grunted. "Goddamn slopes." He'd started out that morning with a work party of Vietnamese to repair the wire. As usual, the Vietnamese had played dumb and worked so slowly that Quinn lost his patience and did all the work himself because it was faster than trying to coax and threaten them into doing it. Two of the Vietnamese who were supposed to be helping him lay wire were sitting in the shade of a water tank. They waved at him, then looked at each other and giggled.

"Lazy little bastards, little thieving scumbags," he muttered. Quinn didn't like the way the Vietnamese looked, or talked or smelled, or the mincing feminine way they moved and sometimes held hands like slant-eye faggots. He'd be damn glad when they left and the Yards took over all the company areas.

Once the camp was finished, the Vietnamese would leave, and only Montagnards and Americans would work out of the launch site. All the South Vietnamese were security risks, so classified documents that came through camp arrived in two versions. One set was shared by the Americans and Vietnamese, but a second set marked NOFORN was seen only by the American personnel. The NOFORN version contained all the facts, while the other set was used to maintain the illusion that the Americans were only advising the Vietnamese in conducting their war, when in fact the Americans seemed to be fighting the war in spite of the Vietnamese.

Quinn tugged at his pants leg to free it from the wire and heard a soft *pop* behind him, not unlike the sound of someone opening a beer, and Quinn froze. He reached for the .45 holstered at his hip. Then he crouched as though he was going to dive into the wire, then he said "Shit," and stood slowly, having realized what he'd done. His pants were still snagged on the trip wire.

A loud hissing erupted behind him, and he turned to watch the brilliant white glare and thick smoke boiling up from the trip flare that he had triggered, its fuse having made the same *pop* that a grenade fuse makes five seconds before it explodes. The flare was bright even in the sun, burning furiously, urgently as a false alarm that won't turn off.

Quinn kicked his leg free and walked out of the wire, ignoring the laughing Vietnamese, past the inner perimeter bunkers and the final defensive firing positions, beneath the sandbagged gun tower that looked like an old wooden oil derrick, and on into the teamhouse.

The teamhouse was a long tin-roofed building. Screened windows ran the length of the two long sides, covered at night and during rainy season by heavy wooden shutters. It was divided into three sections: a kitchen/pantry, a narrow dining area dominated by the big picnic table where the team took their meals, and the largest section, taking up half the building, where the team spent their free time. Big wooden footlockers, one for each team member, lined the walls. There were book and magazine shelves, a card table with heavy handmade chairs, and another crude table near the back door that supported all the backup commo gear. Web gear, weapons, and pouches of grenades hung from nails along the walls. A bar was set in one corner, and Silver's gigantic stereo speakers were mounted on the wall over the bar, the reel-to-reel tape deck on a shelf behind the bar.

A battered old refrigerator hunkered down behind the bar, and next to it, on the wall, a plastic-covered chart listed each team member by name and job. An eight-by-ten close-up of a woman's crotch was taped to the door of the refrigerator and at a glance looked like an aerial photo of some strange jungle terrain.

Quinn took a beer from the refrigerator, put a slash next to his name with a grease pencil, and sat down on one of the wobbly bar stools that they'd had made for them in the nearby village they called The Ville. Pictures from pornographic magazines had been sandwiched beneath the Plexiglas bar top, and months of spilled beer had seeped beneath the acrylic, bloating and discoloring the already contorted women.

Quinn was sketching in a little spiral notebook when Silver and Dawson came in.

"Hey, Mr. Bob Wire," Dawson said, "you been givin' those

little people some of that on-the-job training? Teachin' 'em, you know, how to help their own selves against those bad old Communists?" He started laughing.

Silver got two beers and threw one to Dawson.

"I thought the little bastards had fragged me," Quinn said, still sketching. "I tripped a flare, heard that fuse pop, and thought my ass was blown up. Thought it was a grenade. They thought it was real funny. Lazy little bastards.

"You know what I like about them? Huh? Nothing. Not one fuckin' thing. I don't like their skinny, bony faces, or their ass-tight fatigues and the faggy way they walk, or their rotten goddamn fish breath when they get up in your face like they're gonna kiss you, to talk to you in that whining, for-shit language of theirs, and blow that stinking rice and fish breath past their rotten teeth into your face, only they don't know how to talk in any kind of fucking normal human voice, all they know how to do is yell. I hate a gook motherfucker to get in my face and yell at me, and wave their scrawny arms around."

"You got to learn how to *communicate* with the people," Dawson said. "Remember, you a kind of ambassador, winnin' hearts an' minds, like the man said in the movie."

"Right," Quinn said. *"Why* fuckin' Vet-nom?"

"What you drawin' there, my man?" Dawson said, putting his arm around Quinn. "Looks like some kinda trick radio."

"You got it right. Something for those thief motherfuckers to find next time they break into my bunker. What you do, see," Quinn said, showing Dawson the drawing, "is take a little transistor radio, scoop out all the guts except the battery and the on/off switch, and replace 'em with half a stick of C-4. Put in an electric blasting cap and hook it up to the battery and the switch, then leave it sitting where one of those rice-burning little zips is gonna be sure to steal it."

Quinn tapped the sketch with his wire-cut knuckles. "Huh? Is that all right or what? Thievin' little fuck gets him a radio next time he rips my bunker off. He gets back to his bunker with his dope-smoking asshole buddies, and they're gonna listen to that whining and moaning they call music, and turns it on. His slack-jawed, slant-eyed head just—goes away. His buddies lose their eardrums and start bleeding from the nose. And nobody knows what happened." Quinn was grinning hugely.

"Kay, Bee, Oh, Oh, M, Kay-Boom," Silver said, holding his hand up to his ear like a headphone, imitating a disk jockey, "Comin' to you like C-4 at forty thousand feet a second. News, weather, and sports, and, my friends out there, the top-forty countdown—the sounds that made us what we are.

"Hey, GI. Have you taken your 'damtril' today? That's right, the little orange pill. Sure, it's easy to forget, but you're no good to your buddies out there if you have *malaria!* So think about it. You owe it to yourself, *and* your buddies. Awright, this one's goin' out for Honcho and the guys at the Forty-first radar company . . ."

They could hear or feel the faint disturbance in the air that was the mail chopper coming in.

"Hope they've got some movies," Silver said. "I don't want to watch *The Night They Raided Minsky's* again."

The chopper was a black dot to the south of camp, like a speck of dust in the eye.

"New man comin' in," Dawson said. "Lieutenant Andre says we're getting a new intel man who can take over when Myers leaves."

"Good," Quinn said. "We could use another experienced hand up here."

"Nope. It's his first tour. He's an E-Four fresh from training group."

"When did they start putting E-Fours in intel slots?"

"Just lately. They need the bodies. They been using too many people up across the border," Silver said.

The thudding rotor blades became more distinct as the chopper circled the camp and began to spiral down to the landing pad, dropping quickly to avoid possible sniper fire.

Red dust corkscrewed through the rotors as the chopper set down on the pad. The staff sergeant from Da Nang got out with two orange mailbags, followed by a soldier wearing stiff new jungle fatigues and shiny new boots.

"There's the new guy," Dawson said.

"Hey," Silver said, "I know him: I gave him a ride to

Monkey Mountain to ask Sergeant Major for a job. I guess he got it."

"Great," Quinn said. "Shit. A fuckin' college kid. Just what we need."

"How can you tell that?" Dawson said.

"I got eyes. Look at that peaches-and-cream college-boy face. Look at the cocky goddamn way the little fucker walks. Thinks he's hot shit. He's gonna last about a week, then they can send him back to Da Nang where he belongs and send us somebody who knows what he's doing."

"Hey," Dawson said, "give the dude a chance. He might be okay."

"We'll see," Quinn said, watching Hanson walk toward the teamhouse. "We'll see soon enough."

The next day Hanson was on a work party building new, mortar-proof bunkers. The heat was stunning. There was the sound of steel on iron as shovels chipped at the baked clay earth. Clouds of gnats floated through the heat, dropping down over men's heads like nets. They couldn't be waved away or outrun. They moved along with you as you ran, getting inside your nose and ears with a whine that was almost too high to be heard, that you could almost taste. If you tried to breathe through your mouth, they flew down your throat. It was like drowning in heat and bugs.

Hanson was trying to forget the heat, and bugs, the loneliness and uncertainty that shaded off into fear as he shoveled sand off the back of a deuce-and-a-half. The shovel hissed and thudded as he drove it into the sand, polishing the blade, working out a rhythm with the long-handled shovel; filling it, lifting, pivoting toward the cement hopper, tipping the blade of the shovel just as it reached the apex of its climb so that the sand hung, weightless, for a moment, then splaying the shovel, sending the sand to the ground in a sparkling tan curtain. It was reassuring, the rhythmic hiss and thud. He could ignore the ache in his arms and shoulders, the sweat in his crotch and under his arms, working out variations of the rhythm, the pivot and release.

"Hey, I *said*, you want to give me a hand here," Quinn

shouted up at him, startling him out of his rhythm. "We got enough fucking sand."

"Right," Hanson said, speared the shovel into the sand, and jumped down. Quinn walked away without saying anything, took hold of a strap on an aluminum pallet, and stood glaring at Hanson.

"Over there," Quinn said, gesturing with his head, and began to pull the heavy pallet. Hanson snatched up another strap and began to pull. But Quinn pulled against him, and each time Hanson tried to adjust the direction of the pallet to compensate for Quinn's movement, it seemed as if Quinn tried to work against him in a new direction. It was like moving bulky, sharp-edged furniture with an angry stranger.

The pallet banged Hanson's shins with each step. Sweat stung his eyes and a fly bit him on the back of the neck.

"Hey, Quinn," he said, dropping his end of the pallet. "Something bothering you?"

"Nothing bothering me, man."

"About me," Hanson said. "Something bothering you about me?"

"Like I said, nothing bothers me. Not for long. Something bothers me, I just squash it. No problem."

Quinn gave the pallet one last tug, then let it drop, almost on Hanson's foot, and walked away.

It took Hanson's eyes a minute to adjust to the darkness in his new bunker, to see beyond the dusty shaft of light from the sandbagged entrance. He sat on his bunk and began unlacing his boots by feel. When he saw the cobra, he started up to reach for his rifle, but the snake wasn't moving. It didn't look right. He backed toward the door, fumbled for his red-lensed flashlight, and shined it on the packed-clay floor. It was an empty cobra skin as long as a man and thick as his arm.

He checked every corner of the bunker with the flashlight in one hand and an entrenching tool in the other, throwing black and red shadows, but he found nothing. The snakeskin rustled like paper when he prodded it with the entrenching tool. As he bent to pick it up, a voice behind him said, "He stayed here in the night, but now he is gone. He left you his skin."

Hanson spun around and saw a Montagnard framed by the heavy-timbered doorway. He smiled, and Hanson saw that his teeth were capped in gold, with jade insets of stars and crescent moons.

"He left you his old life," the Montagnard said. "The snake is a very powerful person, and now you have his old life. He is a powerful person, but he is not a man. A long time ago, in the dream time when the animals could still talk, man had to choose between being a man and being a snake. It was a hard choice. The snake never dies. He just sheds his old life and grows a new one. Man chose to stay a man, and walk and keep the pain of his life, and finally to die. The snake thinks we are fools. We try to kill him whenever we can. It's hard to tell who is right."

Then he stepped back out into the sun, out of the shadow of the doorway, where he took on sharp definition: a small, dark-skinned man in a tiger suit, wearing a green bandana and a small leather bag around his neck. His eyes seemed black in the sunlight, like little caverns with a light deep inside. He had a handsome, broad face, Mongolian as an Eskimo in the shimmering heat, and he could have been anywhere between the ages of thirty and sixty. He smiled, waved, and walked away.

Hanson picked up the snakeskin and looked at the diamond pattern of gray-green scales. It hadn't been there the night before, and he thought about the cobra . . . , and he thought about the cobra, blind and ready to strike at anything that moved, shedding its skin in the bunker while he slept.

He took off his boots and socks, put powder on his feet, and lay on the bunk staring up at the timber and sandbag ceiling. The doorway shimmered like a movie screen set into the dark wall of the bunker, shapes warping and bloating in the heat.

Above his head, the firing port looked out over the rows of tanglefoot and concertina, the field of view spreading until it reached the jungle. The claymore firing devices on the ledge below the firing port looked like swollen green clothespins. Squeezing them generated tiny sparks of electricity that would travel down the wires that disappeared into the grass and blow the bank of squat little antipersonnel mines.

Hanson looked at the light on the ceiling and wondered what it was he'd done to piss Quinn off.

Quinn spent most of the next day with a squad of Vietnamese, trying once more to show them how to string tanglefoot, putting in two layers of short engineer stakes ankle high and shin high, then running barbed wire in random webs around them, on two different levels so that to walk through it you had to step high and carefully, exposing yourself, cutting your ankles and shins and the backs of your calves. The Vietnamese stood around and smoked Salem cigarettes, joking about the big American who always lost his temper and did the work himself.

The angrier Quinn got, the more he nicked himself on the wire, little cuts on his forearms mixing blood with sweat and dust. He squatted carefully to inspect a claymore mine set in a base of rotting sandbags, and when he picked the mine up, he found a nest of mice, blind furless babies. They were pink and translucent, webbed with purple blood vessels, their blind eyes just gray bulges under the skin.

"Goddamn dumb mice," Quinn muttered. "Even the fuckin' mice in this country are dumb. Gook mice. Build a nest under a claymore, sure. What kind of shit-for-brains parents have you got?" he demanded of the squeaking, wriggling pile of tiny bodies.

He checked the blasting cap and wiring, set the mine back on its little folding metal legs, and re-covered the nest with grass, the high-pitched mewling barely audible.

Quinn looked up at the little blue Buddhist shrine out in the middle of the wire. The Vietnamese still sneaked out to visit the shrine with incense and little food offerings, out in the perimeter wire with claymore mines and trip flares surrounding it, refusing to move the shrine because, they said, that was where it had always stood. Just like the mice, Quinn thought. He looked at the group of Vietnamese who were supposed to be doing the work he was doing. They were laughing, talking loud in their high, singsong language. Quinn wished he could shoot them, kill every one of the whining zipperheads.

Fuck it, he thought, and bent to twine the wire onto an engineer stake. The heat and smell of hot grass reminded him of the cornfields around Mason City in the summer.

That evening Hanson was sitting in the teamhouse reading a copy of *Rolling Stone* that had come in on the mail chopper. As he looked at the pages, he listened to Dawson tell Silver about killing someone in a bar on his last thirty-day leave. He glanced at the laughing Dawson, who had high cheekbones and an ash-colored scar streaking up beneath one eye, giving him an expression of satanic amusement.

"Then this fool come up out of his pants with a piece," Dawson said. "Little twenty-five auto. Just flashing it around, you understand, impressing the ladies. I'm checking this all out from where I'm sitting at the bar, and I don't *like* this dude. I mean, that's no way to act, lettin' people see what you got. That's just asking for it. I mean, what kind of bullshit is that? Pisses me off. So I say to myself, 'All right. This one's for free—this fool is bought and paid for.'

"So I walk over to where he is . . ."

Hanson looked up from his paper and saw Dawson poised on his toes, simulating a pistol with his thumb and forefinger, holding it above his head. He jabbed his finger down at the floor three times, grinning, and said, "Pop. Pop. Pop.

"So what they gonna do," he said. "Dude pulls a piece and I shoot him in self-defense, right? I say, 'I thought he was gonna *shoot* my ass.' Besides, I'm a motherfuckin' *war* hero. One tour of 'Nam behind me, my orders already cut to go back and fight the bad ole communists some more. *Adiós,* motherfucker."

When Quinn came banging into the teamhouse a few minutes later, he was still cursing the Vietnamese. He went behind the bar to the refrigerator and got a beer. He took a swallow and stared at Hanson. "The team hippie taking it easy?" he said to Dawson and Silver, gesturing at Hanson. "Or is he on some kind of special enlistment?"

Hanson looked up and noticed that Quinn was wearing a .45 on his hip. Quinn glared at him while the other two waited to see what would happen. Hanson went back to his reading but twice looked up and found himself trading stares with Quinn. Hanson deliberately held the stare, as if considering it with minimal interest, then unfocused and went back to the paper, reading the same sentence over and over as he considered his situation. As he turned a page, he wondered if there wasn't some way to avoid a showdown, but he knew there wasn't.

It wasn't the sort of place, either, where people are quick to rush in and break up a fight. The threshold between anger and violence was low. He couldn't avoid it, and he couldn't expect any help.

"What kind of fucking hippie college boy are you?" Quinn demanded.

"Pardon me?" Hanson said.

"Pardon me," Quinn said, mocking him.

"If I'm a hippie, I am a strange one. Up here in northern I-corps, wearing a green beret . . ."

"You got *that* right," Quinn said. "A strange one."

"What's your definition of a hippie?" Hanson asked him.

"A hippie, in your case, is somebody who *thinks* he's hot shit. Somebody who walks funny, and says 'pardon me,'" Quinn said, walking over to where Hanson was sitting, "and who reads hippie shit like this newspaper," he said, tapping the paper with his finger.

"Excuse me," Hanson said. "I gotta go piss."

Quinn didn't move, standing in front of where Hanson was sitting, and Hanson bumped into him, face to face as he stood up.

"That's twice now you've bumped into me, little man. Number three's gonna be a pisser. You ain't got enough sand in your pockets for number three."

Hanson walked outside to the piss tubes, metal shipping tubes pounded into the sand. Out on the perimeter someone popped a hand flare, and it swung slowly from its parachute, dripping sparks squeaking and barking like a loose fan belt.

He listened to the country grumble with artillery fire. He'd been there only a couple of days, and it was his one chance to avoid the S-2 shop. If he fought Quinn, who had already established himself here, he'd likely be labeled as someone who couldn't get along and get his ass shipped back to Da Nang. But if he didn't fight Quinn, he'd never last either. He'd run into guys like Quinn before, who didn't like the way he talked or walked or what he said.

He decided to go back into the teamhouse.

Jefferson Airplane was flying out of Silver's big stereo. The three of them had been into a bottle of Jim Beam, drinking boilermakers. They were over at the radio table, laughing, hardly noticing when he came in. He got a beer out of the refrigerator, picked up the *Rolling Stone*, and sat down at the far end of the bar on one of the high bar stools. He was reading an article about a war protest in Brooklyn, where demonstrators rubbed pig's blood on their nude bodies, rolled in the street, and then "made love," when he felt something jammed into the small of his back and heard Quinn's voice saying, "What do you think of *this*, my man?"

Jefferson Airplane was singing "White Rabbit." Quinn had stuck the muzzle of his .45 against the base of Hanson's spine. Hanson felt the tiny shudder and click of the gun being cocked, felt it quiver through his spine and the tight muscles in the small of his back.

Once cocked, a .45 goes off with just a touch of the trigger, just an accidental twitch of the finger. Hanson could smell the liquor on Quinn's breath. The refrigerator shuddered and began to hum. Then the pressure was gone. He heard the click of the hammer dropping to half-cock. Quinn said, "Yeah, that's what I thought."

Hanson turned on the stool, stepped down, and walked out the door, listening to them laugh behind him. He sat down on the waist-high sandbag wall that ran from the teamhouse to the piss tubes. A flare popped, then another, the two of them barking as if they were calling to each other in the dark, swinging two sets of shadows across the camp. He touched something leathery next to him and jerked his hand back.

It was one of the wire-laying gloves Quinn had been wearing. He put it on, made a fist, and jabbed the heavy glove in the air, then tried it against the sandbags. He put the other one on and moved back to the side of the teamhouse door and waited.

He heard Quinn laughing on his way to the door, and he set himself just outside the door, legs shoulder-width apart in a slight crouch. When Quinn stepped out, drunk and laughing, Hanson drove his left fist into Quinn's solar plexus, bending him over, then snapped a right into his kidneys, sending him down. Quinn raised himself up on his elbows, vomited, then slumped back down.

Bending over him, Hanson said, "Quinn, I want to get along in this camp. Let's not underestimate each other and maybe it will work out. But I'll kill you before I'll leave."

He hid the gloves under a pile of sandbags and smiled in the dark. It had felt good. He repeated the two punches he'd used on Quinn and walked grinning out of the faint light coming from the teamhouse, to his bunker, where he slept.

Quinn woke up with a couple of cracked ribs, pissing blood. He found Hanson filling sandbags and walked carefully over to him, hung over, trying not to wince. If he were to hit anybody, it would hurt him more than the person he hit.

"Hey," he said.

"Yeah," Hanson said, gripping the entrenching tool he'd been using.

"Come on over to the shade here. I want to talk to you."

As they walked to the shade of the gun tower, Quinn said, "Those were pretty good shots for a dude your size, but I was drunk. Sober, I'd pound your ass into the sand."

"You better kill me if you do," Hanson said, " 'cause next time you're drunk or asleep or looking the other way, I'll be there.

"But we don't need that shit. Let me buy you a beer."

Quinn looked down at him, smiled, and said, "I believe you. We'll see. Let's go get that beer."

Quinn never did figure out what had caused the little parallel rows of dashlike lines that patterned the bruises on his side and chest. He never realized that they were the same size and shape as the staples in wire-laying gloves.

The Orchard

It was past seven, still cool, but Hanson could feel the heat beginning to seep in like an undertow. Shreds of milky fog clung to the green folds of the mountains to the west like spiderwebs in wet shrubbery. The sun was just beginning to warm the red clay, concrete and sandbags, the wood and wire of the camp, teasing out the odors of mo-gas, urine, smoke, and waxy canvas. He could smell the sizing in his new tiger suit. It was dyed in swirls and rivulets of green, black, and brown and was as stiff as a Halloween costume.

His web gear and harness were almost new. They had belonged to the dead man he was replacing, but he didn't know that yet. It had been the dead man's first operation. He'd stood and charged the tree line where a small ambush had been sprung, and was shot dead. Afterward, the team had sent him back to Da Nang in a body bag, still a stranger to them, and the heavy-weapons man, who'd been with him at the ambush, had said, "Now why do you suppose he did that?"

It had been a small, routine ambush, and no one else had been hurt. The three local Vietcong villagers who had initiated it with AK-47 fire had run away while the rest of the patrol stayed under cover and called in artillery. They were surprised and delighted that they had actually killed an American.

The young soldier they'd killed hadn't known what was expected of him, and he didn't want to look like a coward. When the shooting started, he had looked around—no one gave him any orders—and attacked the tree line, bewildered as he ran, the 7.62 rounds stinging, then deadening his leg and shoulder and chest and hand, lifting him up and letting him drop. The last thing he'd seen was the top of a gray-green tree and the bright blue sky, worried that he'd done the wrong thing and looked foolish.

"Damn it, Chung," Lieutenant Andre said to his Vietnamese counterpart, "I told him last night that we needed three machine guns. Three."

"Company commander say no more M-60."

"Look. It's past dawn. Charlie should be able to see which way we're going and stay out of our way. The company commander can probably find one now. Okay?"

"Okay. I go see."

Lieutenant Andre turned to Hanson, smiled, and said, "You might as well take your rucksack off. It'll be a while yet. On an operation this size, the Vietnamese usually manage to stall until they're sure Charlie has all his ambushes in and knows which way we're going so they can stay out of our way. There's no Vietcong units out there big enough to mess with us, but *our* Vietnamese want to be sure we don't surprise anybody who might shoot at us.

"Nothing usually happens on an operation this big, but you never know. Sometimes the stalling backfires and Charlie's waiting. I'll be glad when we get this launch site hardened so we can get rid of our Vietnamese." He laughed. "But, like they say, it's the only war we've got right now."

He reached into his fatigue pocket and pulled out a roll of black electrical tape. "Let me see that weapon a second," he said, taking Hanson's M-16. "It's a good idea," he said, tearing a piece of the tape loose, running it up the last two inches of the barrel, over the muzzle and down the other side, "to tape the muzzle up." He ran another piece over the barrel, making an X of tape that covered the muzzle. Then he ran a third piece of tape around the end of the barrel to secure the first two pieces.

He handed it back to Hanson. "Keeps water and dirt out of the barrel, but blows right off if you fire a round."

The Vietnamese were all bunched around their teamhouse, smoking Salems, playing grab-ass, strutting and preening. The Montagnards stayed apart in groups of four or five, smoking their acrid tobacco in tiny curved pipes fashioned of wood and water buffalo horn and pieces of brass from M-16 and AK-47 rounds. In those groups only one person spoke at a time, the smooth cooing and flow of the Rhade dialect so much more pleasant to American ears than the nasal whine of the Vietnamese.

"First operation for you, yes?" a voice at Hanson's elbow said.

Hanson turned to see the man who had told him about the cobra. "Yes," he said.

The man smiled at him, his gold and jade teeth catching the sun. "Good," he said. "It is the first operation for my nephew's son. I am going along to . . . how do you say it, Andre?"

"Watch out for him?"

"Yes, thank you. To watch for him. How are you today, Andre?"

"Very good, Mr. Minh, and you?"

"Very good, thank you, sir. But we must *watch out* very good. I killed a chicken today, and something was wrong. I don't know what it means," he said, gesturing with his hands.

Hanson noticed that dark dried blood rimmed his fingernails and outlined the creases on the backs of his hands.

He smiled again and walked over to a group of Rhade in which there was a boy of ten or twelve, hardly taller than the carbine he carried. His black canvas Bata boots were so big that they flapped at the toes like clown shoes. His baggy green pants were gathered below the knee and gartered with shoelaces. He had all the best features of his race—broad forehead and high cheekbones, long black hair and dark eyes, and skin the color of his rifle stock. The older men were helping him adjust his rucksack and gently teasing him. They could have been getting him ready for a Little League game or his first date.

"That was Mr. Minh," Lieutenant Andre said. "And the guy over there with the long hair is his nephew, Rau. Rau's the one who saw you down at Monkey Mountain."

"What was that about killing a chicken?"

Lieutenant Andre smiled. "Well, like I told you, the Rhade call him Chicken Man. He can read the entrails of chickens and, they say, find things out that way—find things that are lost, tell if somebody is lying, predict the future. I don't know, but I'm willing to believe a lot more now than when I was in law school. He's a hell of a good soldier."

"His English is pretty good," Hanson said.

"His French is better. He used to work for them. He knows what he's doing."

Lieutenant Andre looked over at the Vietnamese teamhouse. "Where the fuck is Chung?" he said. "I'm ready to get this circus on the road."

There was no one uniform worn by the company of troops but random combinations of green American fatigues, cut down or rolled up to fit, brown leopard-spot fatigues, green and black striped tiger suits, black pajamas, and even an occasional pair of faded bluejeans that cost the Vietnamese a month's pay on the black market and that they tailored skin-tight.

Headgear was even more varied and personal—flop-brim hats patterned with greens and browns, narrow-brim hats that a golfer might wear, some of the brims raveled into fringe or cut in a sawtooth pattern, some with the brim torn off and worn like skullcaps; olive brown NVA bush hats, green baseball caps, conical straw hats and Fiberglas helmet liners. Some of the young Montagnards had thick, shoulder-length hair that they tied back with strips of tiger suit material, and they wore red bandanas around their necks. They were the best soldiers, cocky and reckless, and the Americans called them Indians.

"Remember what I told you," Andre said. "If we make contact, find a hole and keep an eye on me. If anything happens to me, you're the only person who can use the radio to call in air support. Don't get killed. Your first operation, you're just there to see how things work."

Chung had worked his way back through the troops. "Okay, *Trung Si*," he told Andre. "Lieutenant Van get M-60 from one-o-one company. No sweat. We can go now."

"Well thank you very much, Mister Chung," Andre said.

"No sweat," Chung said. *"Dee,"* he yelled into the crowd, swinging his arm in a circle above his head. *"Dee."*

If anyone had been watching from the hills to the north, they'd have seen the camouflaged brown and green troops begin to swarm, the red dust rising to their knees, then up to their shoulders like smoke as they formed into a ragged line feeding out the inner perimeter gate. The thud of boots and rucksacks might not have reached the hills, but the clink and dull ringing of buckles and belts of ammo would have carried like the sound of wind chimes.

Hanson bucked his rucksack higher on his back and slipped in near the middle of the column, keeping Chung and two riflemen between himself and Lieutenant Andre, the way he'd been drilled to do, through more than a year of twelve- and sixteen-hour days, so that only one of them would be likely to be hit by shrapnel from a single grenade or the first burst of automatic fire initiating an ambush. He did it without thinking, as a sailor might close and seal a watertight door behind himself as he walked through a minesweeper in enemy waters. Hanson glanced back at the teamhouse and saw Quinn and Silver watching. They gave him a "thumbs up" and he returned it, feeling like an imposter.

Outside the main gate, a worn and rutted section of airstrip pointed north–south, ending abruptly like a misplaced section of two-lane country blacktop. Red clay showed through the asphalt like raw meat in a third-degree burn. Once across the airstrip they were officially in hostile territory, and a metallic rattling rose from the column, tentative at first, sporadic, growing to a sustained static, the sound of a platoon of soldiers chambering rounds with heavy, spring-loaded rifle bolts.

A unit of American troops from the 3rd Mech stopped to watch them from atop APCs and an open-sided truck mounting a Quad-50 machine gun, the truck's name professionally lettered along its sides: CHUCK WAGON.

A quarter-mile beyond the airstrip they passed between a pair of guard bunkers, mounds of rotting and ruptured sandbags that looked like Iowa hayricks after a bad winter. A cheerful old man, smoking a pipe and carrying a carbine over his shoulder like a rake, pulled back a sagging concertina-wire gate, and the column entered the Vietnamese village, The Ville. As Hanson and Lieutenant Andre passed, the old man pulled himself erect and saluted. Hanson hesitated, then gave him a quick return salute, not wanting to hurt the old man's feelings. Two of the Vietnamese behind him laughed.

The first building inside the wire had slab-sided concrete walls and a flat tin roof. A tall bamboo flagpole was flying the

South Vietnamese flag, a yellow field with three horizontal red stripes. It was the village chief's house, a sign over the door reading, VIETNAM CONG HOA. The rest of the village consisted of bamboo-frame hootches roofed and walled with thatch and a montage of American military garbage: pieces of tin sheeting, C-ration cases, their sides broken down and folded out into fat cardboard crosses with the words RATIONS COMBAT INDIVIDUAL and a mysterious crescent moon logo printed across them. Shutters were made from the thin wooden slats of ammunition crates, stamped with the lot number and the type of warhead, HE WP CN, a cryptic alphabet. Flattened beer cans were used as hinges and fasteners. *Blue Ribbon—Black Label—Schlitz.*

A ditch alongside the road served as a gutter and an open sewer. No one else seemed to notice the body in the ditch. Bullets had pounded its face and crotch into a dark pudding, and one leg was twisted at the knee, the foot pointing backward. The body, the uniform it was wearing, and the mud in the ditch were all the same color. The body seemed to be trying to take shape, to emerge from the mud, to evolve into a human being. Hanson had never seen a body before. The perfumed corpse at his grandfather's funeral, rosy-cheeked and pillowed in velvet, had been different.

Villagers lined the road, watching the troops pass. Old people smiled, but their shiny black teeth and raw gums turned the expression into a grimace. Children, infants barely able to stand, wearing shirts but no pants, identical except for their tiny exposed sexual parts, gave the soldiers peace signs or "thumbs up" with chubby fingers, chanting "Huh-low, huh-low," like doves, a spooky, accusatory cooing.

A beautiful little girl watched sullenly, holding her naked brother propped against her outthrust hip.

There were few men or boys of military age. They were all in the Americans' camp, in the hills with the VC, or dead.

A retarded boy with a club foot ran toward Hanson, grinning, then began lurching alongside, marching with them as the villagers laughed. A shiny pink burn scar on the boy's neck pulled his head to one side so it looked as if he were listening for something. A woman ran up behind the boy, shouting and slapping him, chasing him back into the crowd.

The column slowed, stopped, then bunched up, the Vietnamese soldiers shouting and laughing, pointing up at a leafless, dead tree that had tatters of uniform and pieces of meat and intestine draped over its splintered limbs. One of the soldiers threw his arms up and out, made a sound like an explosion, then laughed madly, hopping bowlegged from foot to foot.

The hootches at the far end of the village were deserted and collapsing. The edge of a village was not a safe place to live in Vietnam.

The soldiers stopped in groups to buy noodles, rolls, and cans of Japanese mackerel, the younger soldiers strutting and cowboying for the village women.

Then they repacked their food, point men were sent out, and the cowboys took their rifles off their shoulders. The patrol wound out of the village, down the single trail snaking through terraced fields of pungi sticks, sharpened bamboo stakes set in the ground, pointing out toward the jungle. The pungi sticks, Hanson thought, looked like corn stubble bending beneath a monster wind.

A single gunshot cracked on the far side of the village. Chung turned to Hanson and said, "VC shoot. Say now we leave The Ville." It was a signal to other VC somewhere outside the village.

The trail curved to the left, bordered by thick jungle on one side, dropping off with a sharp bank on the other to a system of tiered gardens. The people weeding the gardens went about their work as if the soldiers weren't there.

They passed a temple set back in the jungle, orange poppies growing around it. It reminded Hanson of a Rousseau painting. Then it was gone, and he was staring into the jungle, recalling the phrase from training, "A few feet inside the treeline will hide you." He could be looking at a claymore mine or an enemy soldier and not realize it.

Farther ahead, the trail narrowed even more before it disappeared, skirting around behind a large rice paddy that looked like a lake, flat and silver in the sun.

Hanson felt excited, nervous, but not really afraid, the way he used to feel waiting for the starting pistol at a cross-country meet. He had real trouble believing that he was actually on patrol in Vietnam. He watched his feet moving, looked at his hands around the black rifle. He drummed the fingers of one hand against the rifle butt to be certain that he was still in control of them.

The column stopped, and a moment later Lieutenant Andre motioned for Hanson to follow him and Chung on up ahead. The Vietnamese platoon leader was questioning two boys, both of them twelve or fourteen years old. The taller of the two was thin, almost gaunt for his height, a blue nylon shirt hanging straight as a sack from his shoulders. The side of his face was flushed and already swollen, the eye literally bloodshot, all of the white a dark red. He stood stiffly, his arms and opened hands pressed tight against his thighs, fighting the impulse to shield himself from another blow, an act that would only invite a more severe beating. His head was bowed and he was crying silently.

Chung spoke to the platoon leader, who stepped aside. Chung's face pulled tight, lacquered with light sweat. He spoke to the boy, not loudly, but low and sharp, then hit him in the face. The boy stumbled half a step backward and regained his balance without looking up or raising his arms. Chung walked up close to the boy and spoke softly to the side of his head, then hit him again, almost knocking him down.

A soft cry escaped the boy the next time Chung hit him, which earned him another blow.

Hanson tried to look impassive. He didn't know whether to watch or look away. Lieutenant Andre walked back to him. "Watch this," he said, and walked over to the smaller boy.

He pointed the muzzle of his Car-15 at the boy's face, less than an inch from his right eye, and insisted, with sudden fury, "VC. You VC!" He leaned into the submachine gun, almost touching the boy's eye with it. "VC!" he shouted. "Now I kill you."

Terrified, the boy said, "No. No VC. No VC."

Lieutenant Andre turned and walked back to Hanson, shaking his head, a wry smile on his face. "Power," he said.

"That was a power demonstration. Did you see the look in his eyes? He thought he was going to die. That's what power comes down to when you get serious about it. No wonder people want it.

"I'll have to tell you about law school sometime. This," he said, holding up the mean-looking little gun, "and that," gesturing at the boy, "is what the law is based on. But they don't tell you that. They neglect to mention that part," he said with a laugh.

"See that tree over there?" he said, pointing off to the side of the trail. "They were up there and the point man saw them. They're trail watchers. One of their buddies back there in the village fired that shot when we left The Ville to let them know we were on our way. When we passed the tree, they were going to signal to their partners who were waiting to ambush us somewhere up there. They want to kill us.

"We're gonna use them to break trail for us in case there are any mines up there, and as a kind of ambush shield. All in violation of the Geneva Convention, I might add."

Chung and the platoon leader tied the boys' arms behind them, cinching their wrists and elbows tightly together so their bony chests were thrust out, and put them at the head of the column.

The trail cut sharply around a hedgerow, a dense peninsula of bamboo and thornbushes, and Hanson lost sight of the boys as they rounded the hedgerow while he was still parallel to it. The space between the trail and the hedgerow was thick with grass, the wide, saw-edged blades a grayish green about three feet tall, the height of grass in a vacant lot unmowed all summer.

It was getting hot, and for the first time that morning Hanson was conscious of the weight of his rucksack. The straps were like a tightness in his chest, making breathing difficult, and his right arm was going numb as the strap cut off circulation. He bucked the pack up on his shoulders and tried to adjust the straps, realizing that he had left too much slack in them. He took a second to look at the grenades hanging at his chest, still feeling as if he were in a movie, then began fumbling with his pack straps, trying to tighten them and watch the trail at the same time.

The two explosions overlapped, the second following like a quick echo, though much louder than the first. *BooBOOM!* The wooden pop of a few rifles surged to a furious lashing fire, gusting and rattling like hail in the wind. The air around Hanson was alive, boiling with tiny sonic booms and brass-jacketed slugs, little cones of lead rabid with energy that, if they only touched him, would tear away gouts of muscle and splinter his bones.

It was as if he had taken hold of a high-voltage cable and become part of the circuit. His old life burned out of him, replaced by this new power. His eyes dilated and he could taste the adrenaline as it stung up into his nose and pushed through his skin as sweat.

He dropped into the grass, the wind clubbed out of him as his chest hit the ground. Flicking the safety switch on his rifle to AUTO, he fired eighteen rounds, the electrical tape on the muzzle shredding away in a colorless strobe of heat, the black gun shuddering in his hands, pistoning shells in and out, spent brass arcing gracefully away, glowing tracers blinking out in the dark green hedgerow. Twigs and bits of bark exploded from a tree above him, landing on his back, and a bullet tugged at his rucksack.

His new bush hat, a self-conscious piece of war fashion, unreal as a stage prop, fell over his eyes, and he pushed it back on his head. He reached back and fumbled at one of the stiff new ammo pouches, feeling the canvas against his thumb and fingertips as if the sensation went directly from his hand to his brain. While pulling a fresh magazine loose, he studied the breathing blades of grass in front of his face, smelled the sunlight in the dirt.

He snapped a new magazine into the rifle, fired it off, and reached back for another. It took a conscious effort to pay attention to the basic things that he was supposed to do, but the months of training he'd had, the habits he'd learned, took over and his body did the simple tasks that were required of it to stay alive—eject the magazine, remove a fresh one, insert it into the rifle, point the rifle in the direction of the enemy, pull the trigger—doing it all as mechanically as scratching an itch in the midst of a complex emotional debate. The tracers seemed to be the only dependable measure of passing time, every fifth round, blinking out of the muzzle of the weapon, vanishing in the same instant into the hedgerow, as regular as long seconds being counted off.

He heard Lieutenant Andre calling his name. "Yeah," he shouted, smiling. At least he thought he was smiling, but he wasn't really sure what his face was doing, trying to smile to show that he hadn't been shaken by the ambush. He felt self-conscious and foolish to be doing something as silly as responding to his name, something as superficial and ordinary as that.

He raised himself off the ground so that he could see Lieutenant Andre, who was lying on his side, looking at a map and holding the radio handset to his ear.

"What?" Hanson yelled.

"Get back down! I just wanted to see if you were okay."

The firing died down to a few nervous bursts like scattered showers at the end of a storm, and Lieutenant Andre hobbled over in a crouch. "You stay here," he said, "and help the medic. I'm going up ahead to see what's happening."

"Right," Hanson said. "Okay." It was an immense relief to be told what to do. He had no idea what was going on or what he was expected to do, as if all the rules he had learned all his life were no longer valid. He felt as if he weighed five hundred pounds. His knees and mouth were twitching, and it took him several seconds to gain control over them.

Right, he thought, the lieutenant knows what to do. Stay here and help the medic. That's it.

He stooped to pick up the three empty magazines he'd fired, and then stood there stupidly trying to think of what to do with them. Pinning his weapon against his side with one arm, he fumbled with the buttons at his chest, thinking to stuff the magazines inside his shirt and deal with them later. He reached over for them with his free hand, and the barrel of his weapon burned a pink welt on the inside of his forearm. He thought he could smell the cooked skin, a sweet, delicate odor almost lost in the burning plastic and pepper smell of gunpowder.

His leg began to tremble at the knee, and it felt good. He stood there and let it quiver. It was as if all the terror and confusion built up inside him were pouring out of his body at the knee. He let it drain out, almost urinating as his muscles suddenly relaxed.

He looked at the three empty black magazines in his hand and flung them away into the grass.

Just off the trail a chunky Vietnamese sat in the grass holding his side, his long face a picture of comic surprise, like the little fat man in a slapstick comedy whose chair has just been pulled out from beneath him. He was holding a pressure bandage against his ribs, a square wad of cotton and green gauze, like a small fat book, olive drab cover with the title, OTHER SIDE AGAINST WOUND across it in big red letters. Frayed gauze tails dangled from each of its corners.

A Vietnamese medic, kneeling beside the surprised man, looked up at Hanson, *"Dau,"* he said. *"Dau."* Hanson was sure that it was a word he was supposed to know, *Dau? Dow? Tau?* But it made no more sense than anything else seemed to. His knee was still shaking, and it felt very good. The plastic wrapper from the bandage lay next to his foot. Cartoon soldiers printed on the wrapper demonstrated how to apply the bandage.

"Dau," the medic said. *"Dau."* He opened his mouth wide, jabbed his finger in it, then pointed at the wounded man. *"Dau."*

"I don't know," Hanson said, holding his palms up and out. "No *Biet.*"

The medic spoke to the wounded man and gently pulled the bandage away. The man watched mournfully as the wound appeared, dark jellied blood, ribbons of muscle, a white splinter of bone. He looked up expectantly at Hanson.

"Dau," the medic said. He pointed at the wound, pointed at Hanson's pill kit, opened his mouth and jabbed his finger inside.

"Oh. Right!" Hanson said. *"Biet Roy. Dau. Beaucoup dau.* Pain. Pain."

He took the pill kit off his web belt, removed it from the green plastic bag, and worked the top off. He considered the morphine for a moment, then took out two small foil-wrapped codeine tablets. He'd keep the morphine. Next time he'd bring an extra. He looked up the trail and saw a man's legs sticking out from beneath a poncho. Red and greenish-black fluids puddled to one side of them.

Lieutenant Andre came back grinning and excited. "How about that," he said. "An hour out on your first operation, and you lose your cherry. How's it feel?"

"Not exactly what I expected."

Lieutenant Andre laughed. "It never is," he said, then jerked his thumb toward the body in the trail. "One of the trail watchers. Took a dose of gas from his own people. What goes around comes around. Yes. Yes it does, I'm here to tell you that. We only took the one slightly wounded. Good beginning, Hanson, excellent beginning . . ."

And then the medivac chopper was coming in, getting bigger and bigger, coming down like it was riding a cable, its rotor blast bending the grass and hedgerow, blowing dirt and debris, the jet turbine shrieking, a machine the size of a bus falling out of the sky.

The wounded man hobbled to the chopper and got on board while Lieutenant Andre talked to the pilot on the radio. Chung and one of his squad leaders walked the shorter boy, the one Andre had threatened, blindfolded and bound, up to the chopper and threw him in.

Two Vietnamese carried the poncho-wrapped body to the door, the edges of the poncho flapping demonically in the prop blast, but the crew chief jabbed his finger at the body, shaking his head *no*. Chung walked over to the two men, spoke to them, and they let the body drop. Then they argued, their stiff black hair blowing back from their heads. They looked like two drivers arguing after a fatal accident on a freeway, yelling at each other over the traffic noise. Finally one of them, rigid with anger, pulled a poncho out of his pack, and they used it to double-wrap the body. They slid the body over the lip of the door, and Lieutenant Andre waved the chopper away.

It dipped its nose and rose to tree level, then banked away. The grass around where it had landed was littered as if there had been some kind of bloody picnic there: used field dressings, puddles of blood, mackerel cans, plastic rice bags, and a couple of Coca-Cola cans. Some of the troops had taken advantage of the break to have an early lunch.

Hanson watched the chopper go, the sound of its rotors fading, and wished he were on it. The first hour of the first day in the field and he was ready to quit. He hadn't expected *this*. And he had a year to go.

"Crew chief was pissed about the body," Lieutenant Andre said with a smile. "Said he didn't want a bunch of 'body fluids' on the floor of his airplane."

"Hey," he said, "come and take a look at this."

Hanson followed him, thinking that somewhere close by there were people, people he didn't even know, who had tried to kill him.

Lieutenant Andre showed him where the B-40 round had hit, the bazooka-type weapon that had made the double explosion—the first bang when it was fired, the boom when the rocket exploded. Just a shallow crater the size of a dinner plate scorched into the baked mud of the trail. Scattered around it were jagged pieces of tin, shredded bits of gray sheet metal smaller than dimes, like bits of a letter ripped up small enough so that no one could piece it together and read it.

"Not very dangerous unless it's a direct hit," Andre said. "A piece hit me in the leg once and didn't even break the skin. No purple heart for the El Tee. Designed for tanks, not people. Real good for initiating an ambush, though. Makes a lot of noise. Throws you off balance. Noise superiority," he said with a laugh.

Hanson was looking at the muzzle of Andre's weapon. It was still taped up.

The lieutenant held the weapon up and said, "Yeah, I didn't bother to fire the thing. Too busy on the radio. Remember, that's the most powerful weapon we've got out here.

"Well," he said, "we better be moving out."

Hanson waited until Andre had turned and was walking away. Then he looked quickly around, scooped up a few bits of tin and slipped them into his pocket. He'd look at them later.

They followed the trail for a short while, with point and flank security, then angled off into the bush.

The brush got thicker and taller, shading, then blocking out the sun until it seemed like dusk. Tangles of vine, thorn-bushes, and fallen trees had to be stepped over or crawled under. It was difficult for Hanson to keep up, and it got worse. The Vietnamese and Montagnards slipped easily through the brush, but Hanson had to work his way through, his rifle and pack hanging up on branches the smaller soldiers could ignore. Soon he was out of breath, desperately trying to keep sight of the man in front of him, catching only an occasional glimpse of a boot or an elbow slipping out of sight in the gloom.

A red and silver fireball burst in his eye as a twig slapped it. He stumbled and fell, losing the man in front. He listened for someone behind him but no one came.

He wasn't sure which way he'd been going when he fell, and could not pick up a trail. He tried to bulldoze his way through, break through the vines, but they wrapped him like a web and he had to free himself vine by vine, falling even farther behind.

Talking the panic away, he listened for the sound of the others over his heavy breathing, turning slowly, not at all sure which way they'd gone.

Please, he thought, please, when someone touched his elbow and he spun around to see Mr. Minh smiling at him. "This way," he said, leading Hanson over a route that was easy to follow, finding a passage through growth that seemed impassable, a passage that seemed to open in front of the little man whichever way he turned, until they had slipped back into the column.

"Thank you," Hanson whispered to him, and Mr. Minh touched his shoulder and vanished again into the bush.

The patrol stopped to eat at a small clearing, an artillery-ravaged hilltop whose edges were awash in the jungle. A small family temple, shattered and roofless from decades of war, stood at one edge of the clearing. Its walls were pocked with bullet holes and the deeper hollows gouged out by artillery shrapnel. Inside there was a rubble of concrete and C-ration cans, pieces of foil, cellophane, playing cards, newspapers, and

sun-baked piles of human shit. Spent cartridges told the history
of the war. The oldest, tarnished and scabbed with green, were
from M-1 Garands. The short fat carbine rounds were more
recent, but most of the wasp-shaped little .223-caliber M-16
casings were still shiny. Hanson wondered what some future
archaeological dig would make of it.

They put security out, three-man groups just beyond the
edge of the clearing, hidden in the jungle. Hanson and Lieutenant Andre found a slight depression near the edge of the
tree line where they took off their rucksacks, propped them up
for back rests, and sat facing out toward the jungle. It was a
beautiful day, still not too hot, the sky a pale blue with fleecy
clouds that broke up the blue so that it didn't look like a great
suffocating inverted bowl.

"Give me a little wad of C-4," Andre said, "and I'll heat
some water for both of us in my handy-dandy marine stove
here." He pulled a blackened mackerel can from a side pocket
of his rucksack. The top was cut off, and triangular can-opener
holes had been punched around the sides.

Hanson handed him a wad of C-4 plastic explosive, and
Andre pulled off a piece and gave the rest back. He tore his
piece in half, set one piece in the middle of the can, and lit it
with his lighter. It hissed and flared up as he set half a canteen
cup of water on top of the can.

Yellow jets of flame escaped through the triangular holes,
then shrank back into the can as the flame died down. Andre
lifted one end of the canteen cup and popped in the other
piece of C-4. The flame rose and the light at the vent holes
jetted back out.

Hanson settled back against his pack, watching the flame,
and realized that he was gritting his teeth. He had to concentrate to unlock the muscles in his jaw. Then they heard the
shouting over at the temple.

Five women, who had walked into the perimeter, were
squatting in a circle, facing out, their shoulders and backs
touching. They had taken off their conical straw hats and set
them on their knees. Three of them were in their teens, one
just barely, and the other two were middle-aged.

Chung was standing over one of the older women with a

two-foot length of bamboo in his hand. The woman stared at the ground. Her black hair, pulled into a bun, was streaked with gray. Her hands were in her lap, palms up, her shoulders and arms rigid, prim as a schoolgirl.

"They say they come here to get firewood, but I do not think so," Chung said. "Too far. Beaucoup wood near village, no reason to come here."

He turned and questioned the woman in Vietnamese, punctuating his questions with the piece of bamboo. If the woman hesitated, even slightly, in answering, he struck her in the hollow between her neck and shoulder. *Whap.* When she answered with what he thought was a lie, he struck her, *whap*, repeated the question, and before she could answer, hit her again, *whap.* He hit her skillfully, patiently, without anger, and with an elusive kind of rhythm. He reminded Hanson of a dentist drilling, pausing to ask without real concern, "Is there any discomfort?" then drilling again. It was the matter-of-fact application of pain. It worked. The woman began blurting out answers before Chung had finished asking the question. *Whap.* He hit her for answering too soon.

"Pain is a language that everyone knows." Mr. Minh was standing next to Hanson, gravely watching the interrogation. "Vietnamese, American, Montagnard, even animals understand," he said. "It is a way to talk when you want to be sure you are understood. No problem then. When I translate Rhade into American or French, sometimes a problem. One word, maybe, almost the same, but different. Maybe you say the wrong word. With pain, no problem. No mistake. They know what you are saying to them."

"Bring food to VC, I think," Chung said, almost as if he were talking to himself. "Only two have ID cards."

He handed Andre two laminated IDs the size of playing cards. They were stained and warped and split, a blurred photo in the upper left hand corner of each card.

"Too old," Chung said, shaking his head.

Hanson looked at one of the cards. The photo of the woman was yellowing and had that disturbing quality of all old photos, looking like a person from another time or dimension who is trying to tell you something important. He looked over at the woman, meeting her eyes, one heartbeat, before she looked away.

Chung pointed his stick at a pile of vegetables, spoke to the woman, then kicked her in the thigh. She rocked back from the kick but continued to stare at the ground. He hit her across the shoulders, *whap*.

"Too much food," Chung said, shaking his head.

Piled next to the potatoes and greens, there were plastic sacks of cooked rice, salted fish wrapped in newspaper, a plastic bag of salt, and a blackened pot with a handle made of commo wire. And there was a new pair of black pajama pants in a bag.

Lieutenant Andre, who had been pacing in front of the women, stopped as though he was listening to something. "We're going to have another contact," he said. "I've got that feeling. Just like when we picked up those trail watchers this morning. When civilians—" he began as a burst of rifle fire came from the other side of the temple, beyond the perimeter. There was more firing, then a heavier, slower pounding as an M-60 opened up.

Andre looked at Hanson with a tight smile. "When civilians show up out here, Charlie's around. Damn, I knew it."

They ran in a Groucho Marx duck walk back to the radio, bobbing closer to the ground after each new burst of fire. Hanson saw soldiers appear and disappear as they ducked and ran inside the tree line.

"What's that goddamn call sign?" Andre shouted.

"Bright Packs."

"Yeah, that's right, Bright Packs. Dumbass fuckin' codes."

"Bright Packs, Bright Packs," he said into the radio handset, "this is four six, over . . ."

"Four six, this is Packs," Silver said. "Go . . ."

"Uh, roger, we got—"

Hanson spun around in a crouch toward the quick burst of fire just behind them. A soldier was standing on tiptoe, one of the Indians, holding his M-16 high, firing down into a little ravine. He was wearing a green tiger suit and a red bandana. He looked like a lizard with red markings, rearing up on his hind legs. The spent brass floated out of his rifle, glittering in the sun.

"We got a contact here," Andre continued on the radio. "Don't know how big it is yet. They seem to be on two sides of us. I'll advise you of our situation as soon as I know more, over . . ."

"Roger that, four six," Silver's voice came from the radio, tinny and faint. "We'll be here."

Another of the Indians broke from the jungle into the clearing. He was brandishing an AK-47, shaking the heavy weapon with one hand above his head, whooping, leaping like a dancer, the muscles in his neck and forearms cording under his brown skin.

Chung ran over. "Two VC," he said, breathing hard. "KIA. Two weapon. AKs. Platoon leader say more VC run. Maybe WIA. We go check it out now."

"Wait," Andre said, and called the camp. "Bright Packs, things seem to be under control here, but there's still some movement out there. How about cranking up the four deuce and putting some stuff out there before we make a sweep. Anybody in there wounded is gonna be pissed off."

"Uh, roger, wait one . . ." Silver said. "Affirm. We can do that for you. Where do you want us to put it . . ."

Andre gave them a six-digit coordinate for the 4.2-inch mortar, Silver repeated it, and the radio began to hiss.

The five women were huddled together, looking toward the sound of the last rifle fire.

One of the Montagnards fired a grenade launcher in that direction, a clear metallic *tonk*, like the sound of a cork pulled out of a big aluminum jug. There was silence for two, three, four seconds, then the round detonated with a muffled concussion, distorting a patch of jungle like a furious wind, throwing up dirt and pieces of vine that slowly cartwheeled up and back down.

Silver's voice broke the radio static. "Four six, this is Packs. You want smoke first round? We're ready to lay it in."

"Negative, gimme HE first round. I don't want to give them any more time to boogie out of there. Put the high explosive on 'em."

"Roger, copy HE first round . . ."

The radio hissed, then the single word "shot" came from the speaker, and it began hissing again.

A faint whistling, more a presence, a pressure in the air, grew to a low muttering overhead, *whuwhuwhu,* and a flash of orange burst from the jungle, for an instant looking like the flame jetting out of the marine stove, then erupting with shredded leaves, bits of brown vine, and fat divots of earth and grass, all blotted out an instant later by a cloud of smoke and dust.

"Outstanding," Andre said into the handset. "Drop five zero and fire for effect."

Another murmuring whistle went over and exploded, then another and another, the concussions overlapping, the jungle and smoke violently frozen for an instant with each explosion, then boiling in on themselves again.

"Good, good," Andre said. "How about walking a few to the right, say a hundred meters, over . . ."

"Roger that."

They came more slowly, each one impacting a little farther ahead of the one before it, like the huge slow steps of an invisible giant.

Each woman watched silently, tight-lipped, the way a woman might watch from behind a police line as her house burned down, not knowing if everyone else got out in time.

"All right," Andre said to the radio. "Real fine. Cease fire, and we'll go take a look."

"Uh, roger," Silver said. "We try to do our best for the man in the field. We'll stand by the tube in case you need any more. Nice break from routine here."

"Uh, roger that," Andre said. "And can I get a chopper for ammo resupply and to pick up five detainees, over."

A different voice, the captain, spoke from the radio. "Affirmative. I've already got a bird en route to your location. They gave me a twenty-minute ETA. Anything else you need out there besides ammo? Over . . ."

"Affirm. How about a couple of cases of cold soda for the troops and a six-pack of beer for me and my man here? Put it on my tab, over . . ."

"Roger that, we'll send it out."

Two of the Indians were pulling a body out of the jungle. They'd tied a vine to one of his wrists and were dragging him on his back to the middle of the clearing. His arm seemed to reach, straining toward the end of the vine to hold on, the other arm flopping behind him. His head and heels bounced and jerked over the uneven ground like a puppet doing a jerky tap dance.

Hanson walked over and looked down at the body. It was badly torn up by M-16 rounds, but there wasn't much blood. He looked over at the women. They had been tied and blindfolded.

"Go ahead," Andre said.

"What?"

"Go ahead and put a burst into him. See what it feels like. Looks like half the platoon already did."

"I just wanted to have a look," Hanson said, his voice sounding strange to him.

"Go ahead. They had to be the people in the ambush this morning. Just picture him," Andre said. "Picture that guy there waiting for us. For you. He was laying there watching you this morning, waiting to turn you into something that looks like he does now. Same guy, right there.

"Hey," he said, in a different tone of voice, "look at that. The woman with the pants."

The dead man was wearing black pajamas. The top had been in good shape before the bullets went through it, but the pants were old and frayed.

"How about that," Andre said, smiling at the irony. "She was bringing her old man his lunch and a pair of pants.

"Picnic ends in tragedy for Vietcong couple," he said in a TV announcer's voice. "Film at eleven."

Later that afternoon they took a break on a hilltop at the northern edge of their area of operations, where the operational boundary for the 3rd Mech began. The terrain was rolling foothills covered with elephant grass, the uniformity broken only by a few backyard-size stands of trees and brush.

They could hear tanks. They couldn't see them yet, but

they could hear them, engines whining and gearing down like buses or garbage trucks climbing a steep hill. Then, one by one, they topped the crest of the hill two klicks away like drunken bugs, stopping, skidding around, then lurching off in a new direction.

They stopped at each clump of trees to engage in a "recon by fire," riddling the brush with heavy machine guns, then firing point-blank into the trees. From the hilltop Hanson could see the muzzle flash from the main gun, a burst of orange flame in the trees, then the greasy blossom of smoke. The sound reached him an instant later, a faint, paired concussion. They fired again and trees leapt from the ground and toppled slowly into the brush.

The tanks lumbered on from grove to grove and on out of sight as Hanson and Andre worked on their warm beers, but they could still hear the engines and the wooden, goofy-sounding *tat-tat-tat* of the .50-caliber machine guns.

"Loony tunes," Andre said. "The American war machine. Blowing up trees. Goddamn Third Mech. It's embarrassing. Charlie must think we're all fools.

"Big day, eh," he said to Hanson. "Pretty bizarre stuff, huh?"

"Pretty bizarre. Shit, I'm prepared to run into the three stooges out here. Larry, Moe, and Curly. The three stooges of Vietnam, barking and hitting each other in the head with sandbags."

"You're gonna learn to love it, I can see that already. You *appreciate* the insanity.

"I was in law school when I enlisted. You know, law school, you think you're gonna find out what the *rules* are, and things will make sense then. Because you know the law. So you've got statute law, which is slippery enough with all those clauses and exceptions and definitions, but at least it's there, written down. But then they throw case law at you, and it all goes out the window. So you take your exams, and it's mostly luck how you do, and you think, if they'd tested me on that *other* stuff, I'd have done better.

"I got tired of it and joined up. Special Forces, the whole

ball of wax, and I like it over here. If you're wrong, you're dead. Simple. No mistrials, no court of appeals. Things are final."

He finished his beer, flattened the can, and used it to dig out a hole beneath a rock he was sitting on. He slid the can under the rock, covered it with dirt, and brushed the area around it to hide any evidence of digging. He did it while he talked, as naturally as another person would throw the can in a dumpster.

"I was meaning to tell you," he said. "Don't trust Chung too much."

"You think *he* works for the other side?"

"No, not that. He hates the Communists. They killed his family. He's a little crazy that way. But he likes to run things out on a patrol like this, and he'll take over if you let him. He's probably a better field commander than I'll ever be—he's been at it for ten years—but we can't let him start running things. And you can't always trust his translations. If you're trying to tell a platoon leader something, or he's trying to tell you something, Chung is liable to translate it as what *he* wants to do.

"But he hates the Commies. Get him to show you his scars sometime. He used to be a company commander in one of the camps down south, and he thinks he's a great tactician. He'll take over the patrol in a heartbeat. You gotta let him know that you're the boss. His English isn't *that* good, either, and there are times when he'll tell you he understands when he doesn't know what you're saying. To save face. He'll never admit he doesn't understand. None of the Vietnamese will. They agree with almost anything you say because it's not polite to disagree. They'll say, 'yes, yes,' when they're thinking, 'no.'

"So it's a good idea to know enough Vietnamese—enough to pick out a few words here and there—and pay attention while he translates, then fake him out. Make him think you know more than you do.

"And you remember this morning, when I jacked him up about those M-60s? It wasn't really his fault, but you've got to do that. Get too friendly with them and they lose respect for you. Can't get 'em to do shit.

"Listen to me," he said. "I sound like some cigar-chewing

asshole from Alabama. I used to be a good liberal. Got tear-gassed in a picket line once."

He laughed and looked across at the smoldering patches of brush the tanks had shot up.

"Fire superiority and fear," he said. "That's how you enforce the law. That's why those people back in the States push that peace and love so hard. It's a real comfort to believe in the innate goodness of man. If you got that, hell, things are all right. You can sleep at night if you believe that."

It was after midnight when Hanson woke up. They had set up their night location in an abandoned apple orchard. The story was that some American missionaries had planted it years before, hoping the Vietnamese could get a cash crop out of it. The trees grew, but the apples didn't taste right. The Vietnamese wouldn't eat them, no one in the States would buy them, and the orchard had gone to seed. The air was heavy with the smell of rotting apples, and it made Hanson a little homesick. He didn't know what woke him up. Lieutenant Andre was still asleep on his side of the lean-to.

Besides the apples, there was the smell of rubberized fabric, wood smoke in his fatigues, and the sharp odor of insect repellent on his neck and face. But there was something else.

He touched the stubble on his cheek and stared into the dark. The far-away artillery sounded like old wooden windows banging in the wind. The volume of the radio was turned down, and the faint rushing sound of static reminded him of a TV set left on after the stations have signed off for the night.

Hanson looked at the silhouette of a tree against the dark sky, and the harder he looked at it, the more he felt that it was looking at him, defining and judging him. Something was going on out there. It was a feeling that would become familiar, but it was new to him then.

He recalled the time when he was five years old, when every night on his way upstairs to bed he had to pass a repro-duction of a painting of a French street scene. Some nights the shapes and colors in the painting would look to him like part of a hidden face, and he'd know then that he was in for a bad night. The headlights of passing cars would come in his bedroom windows, hit the mirror over his dresser, and circle the room, stretching and thickening as they passed across the walls.

Sixth sense is only the other five senses fine-tuned to threat. A shift in the rhythm of the silence that opens your eyes. A shudder in the pattern of shadow. The hint of some smell that brings your head up. Separately they would mean nothing, but together they are enough to lift the hair on your neck, to stir little bubbles of dread deep in the back of your brain, all of them forming like a forgotten name, right on the tip of your tongue. A group of men moving through the dark with plans to kill you gives off an energy you can feel if you pay attention to what your senses tell you.

Lieutenant Andre was awake and reaching for his rifle as Hanson heard the whisper of metal on metal, then a flash and an explosion. The firing started up like the little two-cycle engine on the lawn mower Hanson had been afraid to use as a kid, sputtering at first, then racing as though it would explode. He sat up as green and red tracers began blinking through the orchard, vanishing in the trunks of trees or glancing off them and droning away at random angles. He felt the thud of a claymore, its pattern of steel balls gnashing into the brush as he began to stand, and a trip flare popped in the black grass, hissing and smoking, burning with a silver magnesium flame that gilded what it touched and threw the rest into flat black shadow, turning the orchard two-dimensional and monochromatic.

The shelter half above Hanson snapped taut against its ropes, came apart, and vanished as something slapped him in the face, clubbed him in the chest. He watched himself lift and turn in the air through twinkling points of silver light, his ears ringing and roaring, his nose stinging, unable to get air. He watched it happen over and over, each time starting a little farther along, like a series of echoes fading out.

Then he was back inside himself, on the ground, heard himself grunt as he hit, his head and hip hurting. He stood slowly, testing to see if his body would betray him and collapse.

He found his rifle and Lieutenant Andre at the shredded shelter half. Bits of shrapnel had punctured the plastic stock of

Andre's M-16, and gouts of white Styrofoam oozed from the jagged holes. The shrapnel had driven through the rifle and into Andre.

Two men were running past in slow motion. They were silver and black in the flare light, glowing like phantoms, their eyes shadowed into empty sockets as they slowly turned and looked at Hanson, slowly tried to turn toward him as he fired his M-16 into them and they flinched and stumbled, wounds springing from their glittering khaki uniforms like tiny black hands and fists.

Hanson was sucked into another explosion that took his rifle and threw him down where he lay listening to his body, calling roll on his arms and legs, waiting for the precincts to come in. And he remembered the TV picture of Bobby Kennedy doing the same thing on the kitchen floor after winning his last primary in L.A., remembered seeing in his eyes the message the precincts of his body had sent him.

The firing was still going on, people were shouting, but it didn't seem very important. It was as if he were walking down a dark, empty street in a high wind, watching the street lights dim and brighten as the pitching wires arced and flashed above him.

He heard the helicopter and felt its rotor blast sting him with dirt and bits of gravel, surrounding him with violent sound. A gunship was putting out suppressive fire. The muzzle flash from the door gunner in the chopper that was coming down at him was a blistering yellow-white, a sourceless flame like a burnoff flare pipe in a refinery. The chopper was open-sided like a delivery truck, and in the flash of the gun Hanson could see the silhouette of the door gunner, and of the crew chief shifting his weight in the open door as the chopper side-slipped in. The aircraft-landing light on the nose came on, shuddering and arcing with the movement of the chopper, strobing, everything moving below it like footage in a jerky black and white newsreel.

He could see the reflection of green instrument lights on the face shield of the pilot and smell the hot sweet odor of jet fuel and gunpowder. The jet exhaust was a quivering cheery red.

Hanson smelled mildew, wet canvas and soil, creosote and rubbing alcohol. He woke up in a large bunker with gray concrete walls, the roof supported by rough-cut timbers. A shaft of light from the stairway writhed with glittering dust. He touched his face, feeling his nose and cheekbones, his lips and chin, then pulled his hand away and looked at his palm. He felt his crotch, slowly raised his head and looked at his legs, moving them alternately up and down. Above him a rat made its way along one of the ceiling beams.

He was more afraid than he had ever thought possible, not just an exaggeration of the fear he had known in his life before but a whole new emotion, an emotion as powerful and unexpected as love.

He got up, his legs still rubbery, picked up his rifle, and walked to the door. Looking out over the wire and gun towers, he remembered for some reason that Sunday afternoon long before, *Stand up, stand up and walk to your television set,* when Billy Graham had terrified him up and out of the chair he was sitting in.

He would begin volunteering for every operation as a means of beating the fear. Far better than waiting passively for his turn to come around again to go on operation. Attacking the fear, taking charge of it, was better.

It's not the round with your name on it you gotta watch out for, it's the one that's addressed "to whom it may concern," was the phrase that contained the two ways of looking at life and death in Vietnam.

Hanson *believed* in the round with his name on it, in a universe as ordained and relentless as the tracked passage of a locomotive. If he lost his belief in that bullet, he would be hostage to a random universe, to chance and sleepless fear, constantly trying to avoid the coincidence that would kill him, unable to do his job.

And besides, he thought, recalling the glittering silver soldiers he had killed, if he died now he would still be one life ahead. It occurred to him that the more people he killed, the stronger he would be.

And he was thinking, too, of Lieutenant Andre, who had

kept his body alive for Hanson, long enough to bring the choppers in.

The orders came through for Hanson's sergeant stripes and the thirty-five-dollar raise that went with them. Mr. Minh arranged a buffalo feast for the occasion.

The buffalo boys were between the ages of five and ten. They had picked out their bamboo clubs days before. The clubs were the size of Louisville Sluggers, but more flexible; the bigger boys had practiced until they could get a slight whipping motion when they swung, the club hissing through the air. Some of the boys were swinging bull roarers made of jagged artillery shrapnel, making a roar like a Phantom jet dropping its flaps, almost to stall speed, to lay out napalm.

"The young boys are happy for your stripes," Mr. Minh told Hanson. "You brought them a buffalo to kill. It is the way they can get power before they are old enough to kill men. When he dies, his power becomes theirs."

The water buffalo had huge curved horns and a back as broad as a small car. A black iron ring pierced his nose. He was tethered by the ring to a *llana,* a giant bamboo pole that had been cut and carried from the jungle, then pounded into the ground. The animal's large brown eyes rolled up and around, showing the whites, as he pulled against the ring.

"The power comes off him," Mr. Minh said, "like heat from a fire, power from the dying wood. And the one who kills him can feel it on his skin. It is the same when you kill a man, but a man has more power than a buffalo."

The first boy to hit the buffalo was ten years old. His father had been killed in the fighting a year before. The boy bowed to the *llana,* then shattered the buffalo's right front leg with his bamboo club. The animal grunted, almost fell, then balanced on three legs, straining at the ring in his nose and bellowing, moaning. The other boys moved in and broke his other front leg, and he dropped to his chest. They pounded his neck and ribs, and the animal emptied his bladder and bowels. The boys cheered, and the buffalo began breathing a bloody froth from his huge black nostrils. Dust and green flies rose from his dark hide as the clubs pounded him. One of the clubs smashed out a dark brown eye, another broke a hind leg and he toppled over, and the smaller boys were able to hit him in the head.

"I killed my first man, a Bru tribesman," Mr. Minh said, "with a bamboo knife. It was tribe against tribe, bamboo knives and crossbows. Then the French came, and they gave me a carbine, and I became squad leader. The world was different before the carbines. The rules of fighting were simple, everyone understood them, and not so many people died. How do you get power from a man killed by a gunship?"

The boys dragged the dead buffalo to a mound of sticks and heaved the carcass on top of it. The sticks were set afire, and Hanson could feel the heat of the fire and smell burning hair as the dead animal settled and sank into the flame. The buffalo's good eye stared up at the sky. His hide began to split, and the bloody ribs blackened in the fire. More sticks were heaped on top of the animal, and the carcass began to bloat and steam.

Part Three

_____

BACK IN NAM

". . . and remember," the chaplain said from the radio, "God has no problems, only plans," and his voice gave way to swelling organ music that suggested the inside of a cathedral, polished wood and flagstone floors, rays of blue and rose light splintering through the stained-glass windows and banks of gleaming organ pipes. Hanson's eyes snapped open. For an instant he thought he was back in the States. Then he remembered. Two nights before there'd been The Hustlers, and Blackie, and Quinn punching out the "college boy." Hanson relaxed and smiled. He'd kicked the bar over on the Spec 5 and passed out on the beach with Silver talking about men on the moon.

He rolled over and looked out the narrow screened windows of the ammo shed, over the rope-handled crates, past the perimeter bunkers, wire, and the raw, burned dead zone to where the paddy dikes gave way to foothills that built to mountains where the morning sun was burning the fog away. He smelled wood smoke, sandalwood, and the faint sourness of high explosives from the crates around his bunk. He heard a yapping howl and looked up to see Hose running, crablike, past the teamhouse.

He'd had a bad dream the night before. All his nightmares were about home now.

Hanson's first day back from Vietnam had begun with a perfect spring morning. His jeans and blue T-shirt had been folded in a drawer for eighteen months, and the track shoes felt weightless after a year and a half of combat boots. He was tanned from the Asian sun that had been burning down on him only two days before. When he walked out the door he still had that slight bounce that had given him so much trouble in basic training. The air was cool and fresh with the smell of cut grass and pine trees.

But by the time he'd walked the first block, it had begun to seem like a different kind of day. At first he felt just slightly confused, unsure of his judgment, like a hangover when you seem to be just a split-second behind the rest of the world. And the chirping in his ears seemed to be getting worse. The doctor at Fort Bragg had told him that a lot of people came back with high-frequency hearing problems, that it was no real problem, just an annoyance. But the sound, like the chirping of thousands of distant birds, made it difficult to pinpoint the source of sounds, as if he had lost some sort of auditory depth perception.

And there was so *much* sound: cars, and slamming doors, barking dogs, kids laughing on their way to school. A truck backfired and he almost threw himself to the ground, the adrenaline starting to pump. He dropped to a crouch and swung toward the sound, holding his hands as if there were a rifle in them, and found himself staring at a couple of high school kids across the street.

"What the *fuck* are you looking at," he yelled at them, suddenly enraged.

"Nothin', man," one of them yelled. "Don't sweat it."

Hanson stalked across the street. The two kids were about his size, and cocky, but as he got closer, they looked at each other and seemed less sure of themselves.

"You don't call me man, punk," Hanson said. "You don't say shit to me."

"Okay," the kid said, holding up his hands. "Take it easy."

"You don't tell me to take it easy, either. Get the fuck out of here before I kill your ass."

"Okay, okay, we're goin'."

They walked away, and as Hanson continued in the opposite direction, he heard them laugh. He almost turned to go after them, but stopped himself.

As he walked, he cut his eyes from side to side, high and low, looking for movement. At the same time he kept track of potential cover—trees, parked cars, ditches—hole-to-hole movement, he'd called it in Vietnam. On patrol he always knew where he was going to jump if the shooting started.

He looked for objects he could use as weapons: rocks, bricks, garbage cans, broken bottles, bits of lumber, lawn furniture, a garden sprinkler. When he passed someone on the sidewalk, his right fist was ready at his side, listening to the stranger's footsteps after he passed to be sure they didn't stop and swing around on him. There were people moving everywhere.

The cars were the worst. They made so much noise that he couldn't listen for sounds that might be "wrong." When he crossed a busy street in front of the staggered lines of idling automobiles, it was difficult for him not to break into a run. He kept rechecking to be sure that the light was green. Silently he chanted airborne cadences to keep his pace steady and glared at the drivers through their windshields. By the time he reached the quiet, manicured college campus, he was exhausted.

He sat with his back against a low brick wall and watched the students on their way to classes. The girls were pretty and clean. Impossibly clean. He wanted to walk up to one and smell her. The thought scared him. He might do anything, he thought, remembering the high school kids. He could have killed them.

A girl began walking toward him, and he didn't know whether to look away or run. For a moment he was terrified of himself.

"Oh, wow," she said. "How long have you been back?"

She looked at him and brushed a strand of blond hair back from her face, her smooth, white, perfect face that had no pockmarks or scars or running sores. Her green eyes were clear, and when she smiled, her teeth were dazzlingly white.

"Remember?" she said. "Suzanne?"

Then he remembered that she had been in some classes with him, and his words came out in a rush. "Sure, sure. Of course. Hi, Suzanne. Wow, I've been feeling a little weird. Jet lag, I guess. Yeah, I just got back. Last night." He laughed. "Huh."

"Far out. It must be great."

Hanson felt a little light-headed.

"Well," she said, "how'd it go?"

Hanson was smiling, but he felt embarrassed and a little frightened, like someone who has forgotten something simple —his birth date, or his name when about to sign a check.

"I don't know," he said, then laughed. "I guess I don't know exactly how it went. To *explain* it, you know?"

"I guess you're just happy to be back from there."

"Yeah," he said, trying to think of something else to say. "But I got to like it over there, in a way. It's a beautiful place. It's not all swamps like in the movies, you know, 'the green hell of jungle.' Up in the highlands they've got rolling grassy hills like Montana. No roads, no tourists. Well, occasionally you run across a few tourists, but you get to kill them over there," he said, smiling.

The girl didn't smile. "Hey," she said, "I've gotta run. Ten o'clock class. I'll probably see you around."

As she walked quickly away, Hanson inhaled slowly. He could still smell her.

The chirping in his ears was worse, and he felt a faint insistent wind against his face and chest, but the leaves around him weren't moving, and steam from the university physical plant was rising straight up. He sat there most of the morning, afraid he would fall if he tried to stand, trying to prepare himself for the trip back to his house.

"Goooooooood *morn*ing, Vietnam," a DJ shouted from the radio. "Hey, it looks like a beautiful Sunday morning, all the way from the Delta to the DMZ here *in*-country. This one's goin' out for the motor pool at Firebase Flora, and especially for 'Smooth' and 'Tip-in.' "

Hanson looked at his web gear and CAR-15 stacked against the wall next to his boots, up at the AK-47 and the canvas bag full of grenades hanging from nails. The wooden ammo crates were stacked neatly in the shed, their contents stenciled in crisp black letters on the raw wood.

He sat up and put his boots on, listening to a pair of Phantom jets off to the west, then checked the CAR-15. He dropped the clip out and pulled the charging handle back, ejecting a round from the chamber. He heard a burst of small-arms fire from the direction of the village, the tinny pop of an M-1 carbine, but no answering fire. He wiped down his rifle with an oily rag, reloaded it, and carried it with him to the door. Hose was running out the main gate, baying, chasing something only he could see.

Hanson stood in the doorway of the ammo shed and shouted, "Gentlemen. God has no problems, only plans. He does not *panic*. Gooooooooood *morn*ing, Vietnam."

Edge of the AO

Three hours before dawn it was cool out beyond the wire. Hanson and the squad of Montagnards slipped past the eastern edge of The Ville, where the local-force militia would be asleep, through the rice paddies that were blanketed with a thin layer of fog, and into the folds of the hills. The walk to the hills took them through the smells of camp, village, rice paddy, the air gradually growing sweeter and less acrid. The moon had set, and the darkness was thick.

Hanson slumped down against a hillock, shrugged his pack off, and took a Coke out. There was a frail smell of something like magnolia in the air, a sweetness that hinted at decomposition. In the distance harassment-and-interdiction fire was beginning to rumble, comforting as summer thunder. The H&I fire was preplotted each night on the routes NVA units might take to move supplies under cover of the night, and on the trails the VC would take to and from the villages where they spent the nights with their wives and families, leaving just before dawn like commuters to the war. A pink hand flare popped softly near the camp perimeter, showing the rice paddies as a green-black gridwork.

Hanson slipped the thick-bladed knife from the sheath taped upside down on his web gear at the left shoulder and used its point to drill a hole in the can of Coke, opening it silently. He sucked down the sweet liquid, and within seconds he could feel his body begin to burn the sugar. Sweat beaded his forehead and upper lip from the two-hour walk to the hills. Adrenaline and amphetamine burned the sugar from the Coke, and he could feel himself tuning in to the night, his sight and hearing beginning to focus. He pulled the starlight scope out of his pack, put the rubber eyepiece to his eye, and looked out over the paddy, village, and camp. The image he saw was foreshortened, two-dimensional, a grainy green picture of what lay before him, what a deep-sea diver might have seen if the valley were under water, if The Flood had come. He sat back, sipped the Coke, and smiled. This was what he'd come back for.

It was the hour when people were moving through the jungle, getting ready for another day of killing each other.

The 3rd Mech had been working the border of the camp's AO, and enemy units had been staying out of sight. Hanson had decided to take the small patrol on a three-day sweep of the AO's border. When the enemy discovered the boundary of two areas of operation, in this case the camp and the 3rd Mech, they often straddled it to avoid contact. It was necessary to establish AOs to prevent friendly units from shooting at each other, but it resulted in narrow corridors of safety for enemy units.

Rau moved silently over to where he was sitting, clapped him softly on the shoulder, and grinned. Hanson could see his smile in the dark. "Good you are back," he whispered.

Hanson smiled and handed him the can of Coke. "Yes," he said. "Good to be back on operation."

It turned into a hot day, like a day in August in the Midwest, very hot but far enough along into the summer that it seemed almost normal. There was a faint tremulousness in the air that suggested the possibility of a storm. During operations on such days, you just tried to keep moving, drinking the warm, iodine-tainted water that was gritty with river sediment. If you stopped to rest, you felt worse than when you were on the move, your muscles and tendons tightening and knotting up, and it was all you could do to heave yourself back up on your feet and start moving again. The passage of clouds overhead seemed to be the only evidence that time was passing at all.

Hanson wore a small compass like a crucifix on a chain around his neck, aligning him with the magnetic pull of north, anchoring him in those lines of force that girdle the poles. He kept easy track of landmarks in relation to his movement and to each other so that he always knew his position on the earth within a hundred yards. There were days on patrol when he felt that he was locked into the inertia and pull of the earth itself. The air he breathed, full of sunlight, fixed him as part of it all. And with his radio he could orchestrate the guns at the fire bases. While he walked along beneath the artillery fan, he had only to speak a few words into the black handset to make it happen, the combination of letters and numbers that singled out the map-grid locations like musical notation.

They took a break at the edge of an area that had been leveled by a B-52 Arclight, trees and foliage scythed away, rotting like a mammoth compost heap. They set up inside a bomb crater the size of a living room. As they climbed and slid down the crater walls, they set off small landslides, and breaths of sulfur rose about them.

Hanson eased his pack off into the soft red dirt wall of the crater and took out his marine stove. He found a stick of C-4 and pinched off a wad, using it to heat a canteen cup of brown river water, watching the silt and tiny debris boil up in little clouds. He dug around inside the pack, down in the bottom, found the yellow packet of Bugs Bunny lemonade, and poured it in the boiling water for hot lemonade.

The Bugs Bunny presweetened lemonade was contraband. A memo had come up from Da Nang directing all personnel to return any packages of Bugs Bunny lemonade to Da Nang because the surgeon general had found that it caused cancer in laboratory animals and could be hazardous to your health.

He sipped the hot lemonade, feeling it burn through the taste of sulfur on the back of his throat.

Rau tapped him on the shoulder, hissing, and pointed over the far edge of the crater, where he could see a soldier in khaki crawling toward the crater through the grass. It was an NVA regular, a fact that set an alarm pulsing in the back of Hanson's neck. NVA don't run around by themselves. Where there is one, there are sure to be more close by.

He pulled a smooth, cool, baseball-size grenade from his chest harness, lifting it from the harness ring and peeling off the electrical tape that held it there. He twisted and pulled the ring and cotter pin from the fuse, and the spring-loaded spoon throbbed in his palm. As he slipped into those simple, mechanical survival tasks, colors tightened, the smell of pollen and dust in the air grew rich, and he felt a tingling in his scalp and arms. The world was suddenly simple again, and real success, the possibility of staying alive, was in his hands and he was in control of his life.

He threw the grenade, and as he watched the green steel ball rise against the sky, small-arms fire began tearing and rattling along one arc of the crater, bullets kicking up dust and lashing the grass. A sheet of dirt and black smoke burst and spread where the grenade fell, and Hanson felt the concussion through the wall of the crater.

He barely heard the rattle of AK-47s and the sharper report of M-16s, the whine and snap of shrapnel. He was at the bottom of the crater, turning radio dials and watching the frequency numbers pop up and vanish behind the little plastic windows on the face of the radio. He was almost serene in the smooth equilibrium of adrenaline, and he radioed for gunships like a businessman making a long-distance call.

"Savage Names, Savage Names," he said, "this is five eight, over . . ." and the camp put him in touch with the pilots of a pair of Cobras that were in the air only minutes away. Hanson gave them his location, and the lead pilot said, "Uh, roger. Watch for us to come in from the east . . . looking for work," his words metallic through the radio speaker, his voice shivering violently with the vibration of the rotor blades.

A Cobra gunship looks like what it is, as simple as a wedge. It is a machine designed to kill people from the air, and every rivet and toggle switch in it is part of that purpose. It makes the kind of blunt, unapologetic statement that Hanson had learned to admire, cold simplicity, as unadorned as physics, without apology or qualification, requiring no "point of view" or situational perspective. It was like the inevitability of death or the existence of evil in human life, like part of a language that required no modifiers or metaphors, a language in which, when you said something, everyone knew exactly what you meant.

Hanson heard or felt them come, a stirring in the air toward the east. At the same time he saw the grass bending in the still air out beyond the edge of the crater. He took another grenade from the cluster in the canteen cover that hung at his hip and threw it, hearing clearly the tiny *ping* of the spoon flying off, the *snap* of the fuse like a kitchen match being struck. The grenade went off and he saw a body rise weirdly on all fours through the smoke and dirt, then vanish.

He saw the gunships, dots low on the horizon. "Redskin flight," he said, "I have you in sight. Turn to nine o'clock. I have a marker out."

The gunships got closer and louder, the thud of their rotors overtaken by the wailing of the turbojet engines. Hanson pulled the folded Day-Glo orange nylon panel out of his fatigue pocket. He opened it out, the size of a scarf, and snapped it open then crumpled it closed, open and closed, as the ships roared over, taking small-arms fire from the tree line, the glowing orange cone of their exhausts and blinking strobe lights clear against the bright sky.

"Mark, mark!" Hanson shouted.

"Uh, roger, we got you below us," the lead pilot said. "Orange panel."

"Roger the panel."

"Okay," the pilot said, "how do you want these runs to go in?"

"Make your passes from northeast to southwest. Bring 'em right up to the crater. They're getting close, and if they drop a grenade in here, we're in a lot of trouble."

"Roger that."

The gunships began to swing back around, their rotor blades slowing, digging in, straining against the ships' momentum, *whop-whop-whop.*

The lead Cobra looked more like a jet fighter than a helicopter, like a giant steel wasp, the long, delicate tail angling slightly up, tapering to a tip erect and poised like a stinger. The cockpit and nose drooped slightly, the revolving gun tub and grenade launcher like a heavy, low-slung jaw. Some Cobra units painted tooth-studded snarls across the gun tub, but they looked silly, redundant, an alligator wearing makeup.

They circled in and began their passes. The lead Cobra drove in from the northeast, its two crewmen behind their green blister canopy sitting in tandem, the gunner in front, pilot behind and slightly above him as if they were sitting in bleachers. There were only a few inches between their shoulders and the Plexiglas canopy, the gunner perched at the very nose of the ship, as exposed as a hood ornament, hurtling face-first toward the ground. The lead ship fired a cluster of rockets from the pods attached to the wing stubs just below the cockpit. The rockets streaked past the pilot and gunner, trailing jagged streamers of white smoke, accelerating ahead of the Cobra to detonate with sharp cracks in the tangle of bomb-torn jungle. The hognose, the automatic grenade launcher beneath the gunner, began to spit out grenades with a popping sound like an idling gasoline engine, firing the egg-size gold grenades from the snubnose revolving turret and, instants later, the grenades began to explode on the ground, throwing up shovelfuls of dirt and grass and people along their path.

A dozen khaki-clad soldiers rose from the grass and began running directly toward the oncoming Cobra, firing at it as they ran, knowing that the minigun was about to fire. By running toward the Cobra, into its field of fire, they were exposed to its minigun for less time than if they had stayed crouching in one spot.

As the last grenade exploded, the ship began to pull out of the dive, its rotor blades straining and popping. For an instant it seemed frozen, neither climbing nor diving, rigid in the tripod of force—the dive, climb, and turn. Only the little gun turret beneath the nose seemed to move, turning back toward the ground as the chopper began to bank away. The air was suddenly alive with the drone of the minigun firing a hundred times a second, pouring out tiny copper-jacketed bullets the size of pencil erasers that lose their stability on impact and begin to tumble end-for-end through muscle, six thousand rounds a minute, a sparkling caldron of red tracers in which people dissolve in a bloody mist. Hanson could feel the sound of the minigun like a file on his back teeth.

Red tracers filled the air like an electrical storm, skipping and ricocheting up, down, out; whining, snapping, droning, spreading to the lip of the crater and crackling over it like monster static. In the bottom of the crater Hanson began to laugh and shake the radio handset above his head like a trophy, just as the second ship, in its choreographed attack to cover the flank of the first, let go its rockets.

"Good, good," Hanson shouted into the radio. "Keep it coming." It was like calling lightning out of the sky. The gunships made pass after pass, shredding the jungle, sending shrapnel chirring and droning over the bomb crater, and Hanson knew he could not be touched that day as long as he kept his nerve, standing there in the fire.

A new voice came through the radio. The 3rd Mech had been traveling near the AO when they overheard Hanson's call for gunships, and they wanted to get into the fight. The enemy had managed to avoid their noisy tracked vehicles for weeks. The battalion commander, whose call sign was Green Hammer, low-leveled in his command chopper, took ground fire, and shuddered overhead and past the bomb crater, trailing black smoke.

As the Cobras, out of ammunition, headed back to their base, Hanson switched to the 3rd Mech radio frequency and heard Green Hammer calling for help to secure his downed chopper. The commander of a unit of APCs responded, saying that he was on his way. Hanson could hear the APCs squeaking and moaning in the distance, getting closer. Then he heard a dull *boom*, and a column of black smoke rose from the direction of the approaching APCs. There was shouting and confusion on the radio, calls for medivacs. An APC had hit a mine. Half the unit was left to guard it while the rest continued on.

Small patches of grass were on fire around the bomb crater, dense white smoke hiding the flame like ground fog. Except for the rumble of APCs and their random bursts of fire, it was quiet. Rau eased himself out, over the edge of the crater, and vanished into the smoke. A few moments later he appeared again, walking slowly and carefully, both hands over his stomach. "NVA," he said, almost thoughtfully, and sat down inside the lip of the crater. Some of the enemy out in the smoke and dust were still alive, and they would want to take as many with them as they could when they died.

Staring straight ahead, Rau said, "VC," grimacing this time, spittle dropping from the corner of his mouth. His hands were still clasped over his stomach, and Hanson tapped them lightly with his finger. Rau looked timidly down at his stomach and slowly opened his hands. The small hole in the middle of his brass belt buckle was a perfect circle, as if it had been punched out by a machine.

Rau looked on mournfully as Hanson, tenderly as a lover, tried to unbuckle the belt. But the bullet had wedged the buckle shut, and he had to cut the belt with his K-Bar. He unbuttoned the pants and pulled them down over Rau's abdomen. It was just a purple-black spot, like a bad bruise, smaller than a smashed fingernail.

Rau turned his head and vomited out the fish he had eaten that morning, matter-of-factly, like someone burping, but fear was in his eyes. His body was beginning to betray him. While Hanson called for a medivac, Rau reached over and gripped his hand.

They could hear the APCs in the distance, and the medivac was coming in from the south. The radio barked with excited voices. Hanson popped a yellow smoke, and the medivac identified it, pounding down into it, sucking the yellow smoke up in its rotors along with dirt and grass, its strobe lights sparking through the smoke that corkscrewed up and out of the rotors.

The yellow smoke bubbled and poured out of the canister, spreading over the bomb crater, then filling it. It was as if the atmosphere had turned to sulfur and jet fuel, wind and noise and the sour smell of vomit. And very faintly, beneath it all, the sound of people dying, of life lifting away with a sigh.

Hanson carried Rau out of the crater toward the medivac, the chopper fading in and out of yellow smoke, the world monochromatic, yellow and gray and black. The crew chief in the machine gestured at him to hurry, his mouth moving silently in the wind and roar, the chopper shuddering like a hallucination, its skids bumping on the ground.

Hanson hooked one of the Special Forces medical tags on Rau, the tag that would keep him alive, routing him to an American hospital rather than a Vietnamese facility where they would let him die.

There were scattered shots behind them as Hanson and

the crew chief got Rau on the chopper that was like a crude nuts-and-bolts time machine that would take him out of the smoke and noise and killing. The crew chief, his eyes hidden by a smoky bubble face mask, nodded, spoke into his throat mike, touching his throat like a man checking his own pulse. The helicopter rose and banked away as Hanson duck-walked back to the crater, the APCs roaring as they broke from the tree line, dragging lengths of vine, their tracks chewing up brush.

Hanson and the other Yards went on line, moving toward the APCs, searching the grass for dead and dying, firing bursts of high-velocity bullets into them, convulsing them with the withering fire, the muzzle blasts throwing up dirt and grass and blood.

A broken-legged body flipped over on his back, one eye full of blood, bringing his arm back. He bucked and shuddered in an explosion of dust and smoke, the grenade he had been holding going off prematurely, his uniform catching fire. The explosion shook Hanson, threw things out of sync for a beat, as if the earth had heaved up and slammed back down. A splinter of shrapnel blew past his head in the wind of the explosion with a droning, sucking sound, his ears popping in the vacuum. His nose and eyes stung as if someone had slapped him.

As his head cleared, another APC broke through the tree line, almost running him down. Quinn was riding on top, smoking a cigar.

"Well kiss my ass," Hanson screamed. "Tell those people to look out where they're going!

"Hey," Hanson screamed. "Hey! You want a souvenir?" His nose was bleeding.

The APC skidded to a stop as Quinn hopped off and hit the ground running with seventy pounds of equipment. "You all right there, little buddy?" he shouted.

"Yeah, yeah," Hanson grunted, wiping the blood off his nose and lip. "Look at this." He reached down and grabbed the smoldering body by the back of its belt. He heaved up, jack-knifing it at the waist, off the ground, holding the dead soldier easily. But the body had been opened by the grenade and a purple and silver load of guts fell heavily to the ground, trailing ribbons of muscle and membrane.

Hanson threw the body down. "Never mind. Never mind, goddammit. He's all fucked up. I'll find you another one."

The last thing they did was strip the bodies of negotiable war souvenirs, trading material. They usually left the packets of letters, the snapshots of parents and sweethearts. Hanson told Quinn that killing people, then stripping their bodies of personal effects was "a new, aggressive school of social anthropology." .

Twice he'd remembered to take an ear after a firefight, but neither one had worked out. He couldn't really get anything but the back part of the ear, not the little flap in the front, so they didn't really look like ears. He tried drying them on the tin roof of the teamhouse, but insects went after them, particularly a species of large red wasp. One of them spoiled during the rainy season, and the one that did dry wasn't recognizable as anything, looking like a piece of dried fruit, and Hanson threw it away.

Quang Tri

Moonlight bled through chinks in the longhouse wall and threw silver bars of light across its smoky interior as a flight of Phantom jets sighed high overhead like wind through the trees. A new tapestry was still on the loom, almost finished, the most recent of the weavings that reflected everyday tribal life like illustrations in a history book. It was done in the traditional dyes, the background blue, green jungle at the bottom, showing longhouses and moon-faced buffalo looking out from the foreground. Tiny human figures bent over a green-and-brown plaid of rice paddy, and off in one corner a tiger stalked into the green wool, snarling over its shoulder. A black Cobra gunship with jagged fangs stitched across its nose dominated the tapestry, blotting out all but the borders of the sky, looming like a thunderhead over the scene below. The pilot and gunner, their flat features woven in white yarn, looked full-face out the side of the canopy. Streaks of red yarn, indicating tracer rounds, were stitched from the nose of the gunship to the border of the design.

The Rhade word for "war" and the word for "bamboo knife" were the same, as tribal wars had been fought primarily with the long, elaborately carved knives. That seemed like a long time before, Mr. Minh thought, turning from the tapestry to the carved-ash and blood-painted pole in the center of the longhouse on which a rat had been bound with leather thongs.

The rat squirmed and squealed and tried to bite Mr. Minh's hand as he pierced its belly with a bamboo sliver, duplicating the wound that Rau had received at the edge of the bomb crater. Then he cut the belly open as the doctors had done to Rau.

In the days before the Americans had come, no Rhade had ever suffered that kind of wound and lived until morning. Rau should be dead, but he was being kept alive, his soul a hostage to the doctors who had cut him open. It was Mr. Minh's responsibility to free him.

He looked again at the tapestry. War was all there was now, he thought, but no one understood the rules anymore.

The moon set with the whistle and shudder of outbound gunships.

The 3rd Mech Headquarters Base at Quang Tri spread across the bulldozed and dusty flatlands like a boomtown. Roads and bridges leading to the base from the surrounding rice paddies and farmland were guarded by Vietnamese regional force militia. They were as ineffective as security guards in an American ghetto, paid poor wages to be afraid for as long as they were on duty. They seemed always to know when any VC terrorists were in the area and would vanish until things were safe again. They were ragged troops who lay smoking Salems in string hammocks beneath the bridges they were supposed to be guarding, Asian bridge trolls in castoff pieces of uniform. They lived in tents, cardboard shacks, sheet-metal lean-tos, and in crumbling French-built concrete pillboxes. They supplemented their wages by charging farmers a duty to cross the bridge, and seemed to be always cooking and eating whenever they weren't sleeping. When Hanson and Mr. Minh rumbled across the bridge into Quang Tri, the guards barely looked up from their pots and pans.

Hanson was wearing his trophy-trading outfit: tiger suit, beret, mirror sunglasses, and his folding stock AK-47, a costume designed to impress the rubes at the 3rd Mech camp. He was dressed to get the best price for the war souvenirs he had brought.

They passed an old French bunker taken over by Americans who had painted "Disneyland East" in three-foot letters along the sides. An aluminum Christmas tree stood on top, and even in the sun, Hanson could see that it had blinking lights. Christmas was less than a month away, and they were already playing Christmas Muzak in the PX in Da Nang, where they had an aluminum Christmas tree that snowed on itself. The trunk of the tree was a piece of aluminum tubing that sucked up bits of plastic snow from the reservoir at the base and blew it out the top with a noise like a vacuum cleaner.

Special Forces had produced their own Vietnam Christmas card, a painting of three soldiers on ambush with a single bright star, or flare, overhead. But Hanson and Quinn had had their Christmas cards made up in Florida, one of those mail-order places that usually prints group portraits of families with their dogs, posed in the living room near the tree. Their card incorporated a photo of Hanson and Quinn sitting on a pile of dead bodies, eating C-rations, bordered by the traditional holly design, and beneath them the word "Joy."

As they drove up to the main gate of the base, Hanson and Mr. Minh made an interesting contrast of energies in the battered, stolen truck. Mr. Minh, tiny, seeming to capture the light around him, wearing blue-black pajamas, a shadow independent of an object. He had been quiet on the trip down to see Rau, and to take care of tribal business with the Rhade who lived near Quang Tri.

Hanson was big by comparison, his sunglasses and the crest on his beret bright points of silver light, laughing and singing "Eve of Destruction" to himself. He felt good, good and mean. His mouth was a little dry, his skin tingled, and there was a tightness in the V of his ribs. When he felt good and mean he could *see*, like someone had finally turned on the bright lights, and everything he did seemed to go right, moving as easily as thought. Hanson had been trained to kill, it was the skill of his young life, and when he felt good, part of him wanted to kill something, the way another person might want to jog, or ski, or dance, or pick a fight in a bar.

At the main gate an MP was reading *Playboy* in the guardhouse. He was wearing the green triangle 3rd Mech patch on his fatigues. He barely glanced up when Hanson stopped the truck at the gate, then looked back at the magazine. A large sign on the gate stated ALL WEAPONS MUST BE CLEARED PRIOR TO ENTERING BASE.

Hanson honked the truck's horn and waited. He honked again, and the MP got up and walked to the gate. He strode out of the guardhouse with a cop's swagger, his fatigues starched and creased, wearing a white helmet and a .45 at his belt. He was startled for a moment when he looked up and saw the unusual couple in the truck, then slipped back into his attitude of bored irritation.

"He got an entry pass?" he asked, pointing at Mr. Minh, who was engrossed in studying the contents of his *katha*.

"What's that?" Hanson asked.

"A fuckin' entry pass, Jim. No gooks on the base without one."

"He's with me."

"He's gotta have an entry pass. And you better clear that weapon—in fact, you'd better leave it with me. Enemy weapons aren't authorized on base."

"Tell you what," Hanson said. "You just open the gate and go on back to your research there with the *Playboy* magazine. He doesn't have an *entry pass*, and I'm not gonna clear this weapon, and I'm sure not going to leave it here. People have been trying to *kill* me, funny thing, ever since I got to this country, so I always have a weapon with me. Why don't you just open the gate before I have to go down there and do it myself."

The MP moved his hand down toward the .45.

Hanson laughed. "You point that .45 at me," he said, "and I'll kill you. I don't like your looks anyway. You're just another dipshit Third Mech excuse for a soldier. I'll kill you and say that you went crazy and tried to shoot me. You know, they're gonna believe me because you'll be dead. It'll be *easy* for them to believe me. It'll be simpler to believe me because it won't involve so much paperwork. Anyway, either pull that gun or open the gate. I don't feel like fucking around anymore."

The MP stood there in the sun, thinking fast, and Hanson raised up in his seat a little, putting his hand on the stock of the submachine gun, the way he might lay his hand on a girl's thigh, a girl the MP had thought was his.

The MP opened the gate and stepped aside as Hanson double-clutched the old truck into first and onto the base, a little city of twenty thousand people, hundreds of Quonset huts huddling in the sun. There were barber shops, mess halls, hamburger stands, bars, theaters, and a PX shopping center full of liquor, candy, cameras, tape players, record albums,

Playboy magazines, wash 'n' wear civilian clothes, corn pop-
pers, and battery-powered shoe brushes.

The hospital had a small wing for Special Forces mercenaries, Yards and Nungs. The staff, American doctors and
nurses, watched Hanson and Mr. Minh with curiosity as they
walked the hall. They were a strange-looking pair, even in the
exotic culture of the war. Hanson enjoyed the impression they
made, but Mr. Minh seemed not to notice.

Rau was strapped to the bed, a plastic tube up his nose,
another sprouting from his stomach, draining yellow fluids into
a jar beneath the bed, a third dripping clear liquid into his arm
from a dangling IV bottle. He was in obvious pain, his eyes full
of terror, as if his soul was slipping away through the tubes, the
husk of his body kept alive by the indifferent machinery of
Western science.

Hanson had brought Rau a present to cheer him up, a
wind-up plastic helicopter. "For you," he said. "Baby gunship."
But Rau only stared up at the ceiling. Hanson wound the toy
up and held it out to him, the stubby plastic blades clicking
around. Rau looked past it and Hanson's smile died, the toy
twitching in his hand.

Mr. Minh sat on the floor and spread out the contents of his
katha. Hanson heard the faint sound of the teeth and stones
clicking and sliding across the tile floor as he watched jeep and
truck traffic through the grenade-screened window, raising
red dust out in the sun.

Three hours later he drove out the main gate and turned onto
Highway One headed north, passing a road sign that said
SPEED CHECKED BY RADAR. He was alone in the truck, having
left Mr. Minh to take care of his tribal obligations.

He had it all under a tarp in the back of the truck, the
stolen truck. Special Forces had a difficult time getting equipment because of the antagonism between them and the rest of
the Army, so all the trucks and jeeps at the camp were stolen.
Regular Army units often left unoccupied trucks running, and
it was simple to get a set of master keys for army vehicles. The
3rd Mech didn't have time for sustained investigations of
stolen trucks in the midst of the war, and the camp was far

enough away, isolated in enemy-dominated territory, that no one wanted to go there to look for stolen property.

Hanson had made a deal with the master sergeant in charge of unloading air-delivered supplies, wholesaling the entire truckload of war trophies to him for the supplies now under the tarp. There were fresh eggs, sirloin steaks, gallon cans of freeze-dried shrimp, steak sauce, milk, canned fruit and vegetables, canned bacon, Louisiana rice, fruit juice, packs of Kool-Aid the size of saddlebags, the perishables all packed in steaming dry ice. He'd gone to the PX for cognac, Chivas Regal, a Jimi Hendrix tape, and another tape Silver had asked for, *Bubble Gum Music Is the Ultimate Truth.*

It was noon in northern I-Corps, and Highway One was deserted. Gradually, miles back, the green rice paddies had thinned, dried up, and given way to silver salt flats. The nature of the heat had changed, becoming shrill, almost audible, pitched just above the whine of the truck's transmission. There were no shadows or shade, the sun burning down past anything in its way, then boiling back up from the salt. Behind the silver sunglass lenses, Hanson's eyes were pinpricks of black.

The truck had no roof or windshield, and the road grit collected in ridges below his sunglasses and in the sunburned creases around his neck. The can of 3.2 beer he'd drunk before leaving the base had settled into a flat coppery throb behind his eyes. But he was enjoying the trip, the momentum, feeling out the limits of the rattling truck, pushing her, building time like a shallow curve on a flowchart.

He rounded a banked curve and saw a small deer, compound fractures gleaming in both delicate hind legs, trying to pull itself upright, its legs collapsing at each attempt, yelping like a dog. The image of the deer appeared and vanished so suddenly around the curve that Hanson could almost believe that he had imagined it.

At the edge of a small village, the last one before the salt flats took over completely, he saw a child bathing in the shade of a doorway, smooth-skinned and wet, glistening in shadow.

A moment later he heard the bullet go past, just behind his head. He felt the little *snap* it made, its own tiny sonic boom, an instant of atmospheric disturbance behind his ear, and he drove on, out of range of the village sniper. He maintained his speed, thinking how he and the bullet had almost collided, shared the same square inch of space twelve thousand miles from the place he had been born, in a burning salt flat where he had come to be that morning through a lifetime of choice and coincidence. He shivered with sunburn, and for a moment the salt flats looked like arctic plains, white sand blowing across the blacktop like snow.

Up ahead, beside the road, a strange shadow took on depth as he rolled closer, into the smell of dust and motor oil and some other thing heavy and sweet for an instant, a pocket of odor. He saw the bodies clearly then, three of them, though it was difficult to sort them out, their arms and legs twined where they lay in a pile: three fat men—the bodies had swollen in the sun—with puffed-out cheeks, their faces covered with black and green bruises, looking as if they were in some hellish wrestling match, their teeth in snarls like dead dogs on the highway.

The bodies were stiffened and twisted into attitudes of revulsion, at each other and at themselves, arms and hands drawn back and clenched, heads cocked at an angle as if looking away in disgust. They were so swollen, they looked like enormous fat men bursting out of comically tight pajamas. Everybody loves a fat man, Hanson thought.

And the next instant they were gone, the salt flats ahead pristine again. Hanson looked in the rearview mirror, but all he could see was sand and salt. It puzzled him. There were no villages out that far, no military installations. What had they been doing? Who had killed them? Why? What side were they on? Had it happened at night or in the sunlight? He thought about it for what seemed like a long time. While he was thinking, the rat in the longhouse shuddered and died, and Rau's breathing stopped while Mr. Minh, walking a dusty road outside Quang Tri, touched his *katha*.

A jeep appeared alongside the truck, lurching dangerously, red lights flashing, the Vietnamese driver stiff-arming the horn, a 3rd Mech MP pounding the side of the jeep with one hand and jabbing his finger at the shoulder of the road, his shouts lost in the wind.

Hanson slowed and pulled the truck bumping to a stop off the road, and the jeep whipped around to a quick stop in front of him. The MP walked back toward the truck, stiff-legged, bent slightly at the waist as though walking against a wind, just a kid trying to look tough. He and Hanson locked stares as he got closer, and the MP's steps seemed less certain.

Hanson's face was stiff with sunburn and his eyes were hidden by the mirror sunglasses. He was wearing the beret and tiger suit, and he had the AK-47 in his hand. Except for the Vietnamese driver, there was no other living person for twenty miles. Hanson could kill them both and be on his way. The truck was stolen and so, technically, were the supplies. The kid paused, fear showing in his face, then came on ahead, and Hanson's eyes smiled behind his sunglasses.

"I've been back there following you for five miles, blowing the horn, trying to get you to pull over. Thought you were attempting to elude."

Hanson laughed. "Sorry," he said, taking off the sunglasses. "I didn't hear you. I was thinking about something else, I guess."

"Had you clocked at better than fifty, a solid clock. And this vehicle . . . Jesus. Where are your driving goggles?"

"I don't have any," Hanson said, shaking his head. "I didn't know things were getting so civilized around here."

"If the vehicle doesn't have a windshield, the operator is *required* to wear driving goggles. It's a good directive, and saves lives."

The MP checked the lights, turn signals, and emergency brake on the truck. None of them worked. "I don't even believe this vehicle," he said. "Where's your trip ticket?"

"My what?"

"Trip ticket. Trip ticket."

Hanson laughed and threw up his hands, one of them holding the AK-47. "I don't know what that means," he said. "I've never heard the term before."

The MP sighed, not knowing whether Hanson was baiting him or if he was stoned. "The form you filled out at the motor pool before the motor sergeant released this vehicle to you. What unit are you from?"

"We got a little camp about thirty miles west of here. There's ten of us Americans there."

"West of here? There's nothing west of here except NVA. I've never been this far west except in a convoy," he said, glancing up the road. "I only followed you this far against my better judgment."

"We're out there. We have a hell of a time getting spare parts for our vehicles. We don't have anything you'd call a motor pool, or a motor sergeant. I've been filling in as camp engineer since our regular engineer got shot up and medivaced. I guess that makes *me* the motor sergeant."

"Goddamn," the MP said, less defensive. "West of here, huh? I didn't think there was anything west of Dong Ha except gooks. What a fuckin' day it's been. Three accidents this morning, paperwork up the ass, and I haven't even started on it. Another hundred and seven fuckin' days left, and I'm gone.

"Look," he said, "I'm gonna drop the unsafe-vehicle charge I was gonna write you up for. If I charged you for everything that was wrong with this truck, you'd be in big trouble. Yeah, I'm only gonna charge you with doing forty. I don't like to fuck a guy over. But you get these deficiencies corrected as soon as possible."

He wrote out a DR, a military traffic citation, an original and three copies, each one a different color. He handed Hanson the green one.

"Well," Hanson said, "thanks for cutting me some slack. I'll watch that speed."

"Yeah," the MP said, smiling. "No sweat. Take it easy."

He hopped back into the jeep, and the driver whipped it squealing around back toward the east. Hanson leaned against the truck and watched them fade, bubble in the roiling heat above the road, and vanish. He looked at the ticket and began to laugh. He wadded up the little piece of green tissue paper and was about to throw it away, then realized that he'd need it as proof when he told Quinn and Silver that he'd gotten a speeding ticket. He stuffed it into his pocket, felt something there, and pulled out the toy helicopter. He wound it up and set it on the black asphalt.

The helicopter clicked and whirred, its little blades spinning as it rolled in one direction, stopped, spun around, then tracked off on a new course.

Up in the distance the mountains loomed cool and silent. Another hour and he would be through the pass, back where things made sense.

Mai Loc Launch Site

Hanson propped his rifle against the wall and piled his rucksack and web gear next to it, grenades hitting the floor like billiard balls. After five days in the field beneath the weight of the equipment, he suddenly felt as if he were floating. It was cool and dark inside the teamhouse, and it took a moment for his eyes to adjust to the light. Silver was sitting on a bar stool, his back to the bar, plucking notes from a ukulele he'd had a friend buy him during an R&R to Hawaii. "Aloha, waki, waki," he said.

"Who," Hanson asked him, "are those guys?"

There were five Americans sitting around the card table on the other side of the teamhouse. Strangers. They were all wearing hard-to-get camouflage Marine fatigues. On their left shoulders they wore the green triangle patch of the 3rd Mech.

Silver smiled broadly. "That's the U.S. Army."

"What are they doing in the teamhouse?"

"They're here to give us a hand, help us win the war. Hey, check out the fat guy over by the door, the one with the camouflage beret. Huh? Pretty neat. Never saw one of those before.

"What it is, see, there's a whole company of 'em down by The Ville where they're gonna put in some big guns. Which is okay, I guess. We'll make a fortune off beer and pop sales. But the captain said something about going on an operation with them."

"No way, GI. I don't associate with people like that."

"And," Silver went on, "you remember your man Grieson, back in Da Nang? He's due here pretty soon. Gonna put in some kind of classified radio relay bullshit. They're gonna be living here in camp. Captain isn't happy about it, but he says a lot of pressure is coming down to get us out of here and turn the whole show over to the Vietnamese and technicians like Grieson. Everything's changing."

Hanson walked around to the refrigerator and got a beer. "I'm taking this to drink in the shower," he said, heading for the door.

"Wait," Silver said. "Listen to this. I think I've got it." He picked out the beginning of "Hawaiian War Chant" on the ukulele, then grinned. "Hawaiian music is some awful shit, isn't it? What kind of weird people would, you know, *develop* music like that? Maybe it's what happens when all you eat is pineapple and coconuts."

That evening Hanson was sitting at the big mess table drinking French Cognac he'd bought at the Da Nang PX for three dollars a bottle, and reading the mail that had collected while he had been on operation. He drank out of a crystal snifter that Linda had sent him packed in popcorn.

There was a letter from Linda. They came irregularly because she only wrote him, apparently, when she was tripping on LSD. Her writing was hard to read, but even if he could make it out the letters never made sense anyway. "Don't ever change, even if you can," she wrote. "I stood at the window and cried one tear. I thought it would stop the war (I only promised you that I loved you and got high easy). I have heavy eyelids but my head goes on. Moon, sand, wind . . ."

"Well, well," Quinn said, sitting down. "Enjoying your mail, I see. Letters from home."

"Letters from Mars," Hanson said. "I don't know . . ."

The soldier with the camouflage beret, the one called Froggy, walked over to the table. "Hey, men," he said cheerfully. "What's happening?"

Quinn looked down at the magazine he was holding, glaring at it.

"Oh, not much," Hanson said. "Just looking at my mail."

"Yeah? I wish we'd get some mail. You know, we haven't gotten any mail for a week now."

Hanson nodded his head and looked back down at the letter.

"What's that, letters from your girl?"

"Yep."

"Wow. I wish our mail would catch up with us. My girl—"

"Look, pal," Quinn said, looking up with his flat, murderous stare, "I'm trying to read. Do you mind?"

"Right," Froggy said. "Sorry. Hey," he said to Hanson, "wait a second."

He walked to the other side of the room and pulled a plastic bag out of a box and brought it to the table. "Did you get yours?" he asked Hanson. "A whole box of these GI packs came in while you were out in the field. There's a lot of good shit in 'em. Here."

Hanson took the bag. "Yeah," he said, "we've gotten these before." He dug around in the bag, through the toothpaste and shoestrings and packets of catsup, till he found the little printed card inside, the one that said "First Presbyterian Church, St. Louis, Missouri, Ladies Auxiliary—We're behind you all the way!"

Hanson smiled. "Hey," he said to Quinn, who looked up angrily from his magazine. "Those ladies at the Presbyterian Church are still behind us all the way. I can see 'em now, you know, down in the 'activities room,' in the basement, sitting on folding chairs and stuffing these bags."

"If those cunts want to help," Quinn snapped, "let 'em come over here and kill gooks. That's the only kind of support I want. Fuck *this* bullshit," he said, grabbing the bag. He shoved it at Froggy's chest and said, "Why don't you take this shit and go on back to your unit out there. We need some privacy. Okay? Good-bye."

Froggy took the bag, said, "Okay. Sure." He walked over to the other four Americans, then all five of them left.

Silver had been sitting at the bar, playing with his ukulele. "That kind of attitude is going to cut down on our beer sales," he said.

"Fuck 'em," Quinn said. "They can buy it and drink it outside. Come on, bud," he said to Hanson. "Let's move to the bar and let Silver buy us a drink."

An hour later the captain came in the back door. He had been Lieutenant Andre's replacement, assigned to them six months after Andre's death. Now his tour of duty was almost over. He was a young captain, and it was easy to picture him as a college football star, tall and lean, blond crew cut, always ready with a gleaming smile. He had a face that was handsome but somehow bland, lacking the lines that come from worrying about problems that have no solution.

"Hey, *Di Wee,*" Silver called to him. "How about a beer?"

The captain smiled and walked over to the bar. "Well," he said, "my three favorite trained killers. How'd the operation go?"

"Number ten, *Di Wee.* Dry hole."

"Yeah. Not a lot of activity lately. Say, how would you and Quinn feel about going with some of these Third Mech people on a little road-clearing operation? Take a company of Vietnamese with you."

Silver rolled his eyes dramatically. "Vietnamese and Third Mech both. What a fucked-up operation."

"I thought we'd seen the last of the Vietnamese," Quinn said.

"Yeah, I know, I know," the captain said. "But we've gotta push 'Vietnamization' and the general over at the Third Mech wants his people to get some experience working with the little people. I'd appreciate it, guys."

"I suppose if it's a personal favor," Hanson said with a smile.

"Yeah," Quinn said, "I kind of enjoy watching the different ways the Third Mech fucks up."

"Good men," the captain said. "Get with me tomorrow, then, and we'll set it up."

"Hey, sir," Quinn said, "when are you gonna let the three of us go out on operation together? Back down at the river. We'd *get* some fuckin' kills. A body count to be proud of."

"Yeah, sir," Hanson said. "How about it? Personal favor."

"One good turn deserves another," Silver said, playing a little phrase on the ukulele.

The captain smiled uncomfortably. "Well," he said, "I'm afraid to let the three of you loose at one time. I'll think about it. I've been trying to get the Vietnamese captain, *Di Wee* Tau, to send an operation down there from the Third Mech AO, but all he says is 'Beaucoup NVA,' then changes the subject."

"That fish breath little cum bubble," Quinn said. "I wanta go down there and *kill* some motherfuckers, and it ain't even my country. And they think they're gonna 'Vietnamize' the goddamn war with people like that?"

"You read that bullshit about Vietnamization in the last *Time* magazine?" Silver asked. "Every general in the Army has got this push-to-talk button installed, and they just keep saying, 'Uh, yes. Yes! The Vietnamese are capable soldiers and ready now to take over the conduct of the war . . . clickclickclick. Buzz.' "

"Ain't no use in worrying about it," Quinn said. "The man in his office in Washington, D.C., has done decided how things are gonna go. He's laughing at us, man. Fuck these Vietnamese."

"Sir," Hanson said, "when the Americans leave, how long do you think it's gonna be before Charlie takes over the country? A month, maybe?"

"Well," the captain said, "it's hard to say . . ."

"You know," Quinn said, "I think I'd pay my own way back over here to fight with the Yards. Kill a couple busloads of ragged-ass ARVN. Huh? Blow that little turd *Di Wee* Tau out of his socks."

"What would be *more* fun, though," Hanson said, "would be to come back while the Third Mech was still here and blow *them* up."

"Right!" Quinn said. "Those worthless scumbags and their fuckin' *tanks*. Could we get a body count of those sorry-ass Third Mech legs or what?"

The captain finished his beer in a couple of quick swallows and said, "Well, guess I'll get some sleep. See you in the morning."

After he'd left, Quinn looked at Silver and Hanson with narrowed eyes and a tight smile. "The *Di Wee* couldn't handle that Third Mech shit, man. A little too heavy for the captain tonight."

"And nooooowwwww," Silver called, "let's hear it for . . . the *war!*"

The three of them began laughing, clapping, and cheering.

"Hey kids," Silver said, "I've got a great idea."

"Oh yeah," he said, turning to his right and assuming a different voice. "What's that?"

He turned back to his left and spoke in the first voice. "Why don't we . . . put on a musical comedy based on . . . the war in Vietnam?"

"Wow!" he said, turning to his right, "that's a swell idea. Wait'll I tell the guys about this. But . . . can we get some guns?"

"Sure. And we can use the vacant lot for rehearsals," he said, and went into a soft shoe, humming and grunting out a tune.

"All right, goddamn it," Quinn said. "Let's get serious," going into the speech they'd all heard a dozen times in the Army. "There's a time to fuck around—I like a good time as well as any of you men—but there's also a time to, uh, get serious. There's an appropriate time and place for everything. And we're talking about war here. About the lives of American boys. About Army regulations. Enthusiasm is fine, but at the right time and place."

"I've only got one question, Sarge," Hanson said.

"What's that, troop?"

"I just want to know," Hanson said, and paused, and in unison the three of them said in a slack-jawed Texas drawl, "Why . . . Vet-nom?"

They drank in silence then, until they heard Hose push open the screen door and come snuffling and wheezing across the room.

"Hey," Quinn said, "it's my main dog Hose. How's it hangin', Hose," he said, bending down to pet him. The dog bobbed his head back and forth like a punch-drunk fighter.

Quinn went to the refrigerator and got out a beer. He poured it into a bowl and set it in front of the dog. The four of them drank, alone in the teamhouse. Through the screened windows they could see the flash of distant artillery.

"Okay," Quinn said. "I think we should determine, once and for all, who is the best man with a handgun. The loser buying the next two rounds."

"Done."

"Okay. Although our flower child up there is shot up rather severely from the last time, I can see that her left tit is still untouched. The winner's gonna be the first man who puts a nipple on it."

Across the room there was a large poster tacked to the wall, a full-length image of a long-haired girl, naked, bending back as though caught up in a dance, her hair swirling around her. The girl was printed on the poster four times in four different colors, yellows and greens, the images juxtaposed on each other, producing a "psychedelic" effect.

"Wait one," Hanson said. "I'm tired of shooting her," and ran out the door. He was back in a minute with another, smaller poster that was black and white. "It came with a bunch of intel reports," he said. "I guess I'm supposed to put it up over the typewriter or something." He tacked it to the wall and stood back.

"Tricky Dickey," Silver cheered. "Our new main man."

Hanson stepped back and looked at the poster. "He looks like the founder of a shoe factory."

The portrait of Nixon was a bad reproduction, but it was him, the thinning hair, hard little eyes, the flattened nose and jowls.

"Me first," Quinn said, pulling the .45 from his belt.

Even though Hanson was expecting it, the report from the big automatic made him flinch, the shock in the closed room hitting him in the eyes and nose like a blow.

Hose hit the screen door running, knocking it completely back on its hinges.

"Grazed him," Quinn shouted, putting the pistol back in the Western-style holster he'd bought in Da Nang. Fat shiny .45 rounds ran the length of the wide black belt.

Silver fired his snub-nose .38, the kind of gun private detectives carry in the movies. They are inaccurate weapons, and he missed the poster completely.

"You know what I was thinking?" Quinn said, his words tinny in Hanson's ringing ears. "I wish everybody carried guns back in the States. You know, like the Old West? If you didn't like some asshole, you could shoot 'em. But they could shoot you too. Everybody just takes their chances, and the best guys win. That'd be all right."

"You're talking about the social contract," Hanson said.

"Go ahead and tell us about it," Quinn said. "I know you're gonna anyway."

"The fucking social contract," Hanson said. "In a Western democracy everybody supposedly agrees to give up a few rights in order to protect the rest. That's the contract. So I can't shoot some guy, or steal his shit, because I'm a party to this agreement. However, I do not remember signing any god-damn contract. I—"

"Freeze," Silver said. "Look," he said, slowly raising his hand and pointing over toward the far side of the teamhouse.

The back wall of the kitchen was lined with shelves of canned goods, and a rat was making his way across the top of a row of cans. He would dart ahead, stop, raise himself swaying on his hind legs, sniffing the air, then scurry on a foot or two farther.

"My shot," Hanson said, taking the combat magnum out of his shoulder holster, a gun powerful enough to shoot through car doors.

They had gotten used to living with rats. In the bunkers at night they scrabbled across the floor, squeaking. Sometimes they would jump on a bunk, thinking it was empty, and land on your chest, then scurry in panic, digging their little claws in, down your leg or across your neck.

Hanson's gun roared and a number-10 can of applesauce exploded beneath the rat. The rat jumped, flipping around in midair, and hit the floor running.

"Get him!"

The rat was trying to get to the back door, flattened against the baseboard, moving smoothly, terrifically fast, as if he were being reeled in on a line.

Hanson's ears rang like a harmonica.

Quinn fired, splintering the floor, and the rat slipped through a crack in the screen door like a gray wad of sewage.

They threw the screen door open in time to see the rat dive into a crack in one of the steps. Hanson got a flashlight and shined it into the crack. The rat's eyes glowed like tiny glass beads, bright red and absolutely motionless.

"He's in there."

"His ass is mine," Quinn said, putting the muzzle of his pistol to the crack. *"Die,* motherfucker!" he shouted, then fired twice.

When they shined the light back in the crack, the rat was gone.

"He got away," Silver said.

"Fuck it," Quinn said. "I don't have anything against rats. They just take their chances like everybody else."

"The social contract," Hanson said.

Highway 14—
Cua Viet Road

Hanson and Quinn went out with a company of Vietnamese to provide security for the small road-clearing unit from the 3rd Mech—two minesweeping teams, two Rome plows, and a deuce-and-a-half. Another unit was working down from the other end. When they linked up, the convoy would come through from Quang Ngai, bringing the guns for the new 3rd Mech fire base.

It was easy duty, and with a company of troops making enough noise to be sure they didn't surprise anybody into a firefight, safe enough. No hills to hump, no heavy bush to stumble through, just a two-day hike down the road. "A picnic," Hanson told Troc. "Same as a picnic."

"What is 'picnic,'" Troc wanted to know.

"Like, when you take food and eat it out in the woods."

"Same as combat operation?"

"No. There's no combat. It's—you do it in a secure area."

"Training mission then," Troc said, smiling.

"Yeah, sort of a training mission. Easy duty."

"Yes," Troc said. "I see. Picnic."

Even though the Vietnamese commander, *Di Wee* Tau, spoke English, Hanson had brought Troc along as an interpreter just in case. Troc was another of Mr. Minh's nephews and was the only Montagnard on the mission.

The operation was no picnic for the minesweepers. They had a rotten job. They worked in pairs, the lead man wearing hot earphones—fat foam rubber doughnuts—swinging the metal detector with one arm, back and forth, crossing and recrossing the road bed in shallow arcs. Occasionally he would stop, freeze for a second, as if he'd just had a terrible thought, then step aside and point to a spot in the road.

The man behind him would step up, kneel in front of the

spot, and gingerly probe the flint-hard red clay with a bayonet. It was slow going. The detector picked up anything made of metal—C-ration cans, spent cartridges, pieces of shrapnel, all the combat garbage from thirty years of war—and each piece had to be dug up.

Hanson spent a lot of time sitting back in the shade and at first felt a little guilty about how easy he had it compared to the minesweepers. He'd move a few hundred meters up the road, hack out a shady place in the bush, and wait for the mine-sweepers and Rome plows to catch up. The minesweepers would work past, never looking up from the road. They didn't pay attention. Even though Hanson was visible from the road, they never saw him, and instead of feeling sorry for them, he began to feel annoyed at them for their complacency and inattention. It was the way he'd come to think about most American soldiers. They were poorly trained and lazy.

At mid-morning of the first day out, a lieutenant colonel from the 3rd Mech Headquarters flew over and landed his little observation helicopter in the road. The lieutenant in charge of the road-clearing unit crouched in the rotor blast and saluted. He had a sparse mustache that made him look younger than he was.

Quinn took grim satisfaction in the landing chopper, another example of how fucked up the Americans were, letting everyone for miles around know where they were and that they were important enough to justify a command chopper.

"Watch," he said. "We're gonna get mortared tonight. Nguyen Cong and the boys are gonna drop some shit on us. The dumb fucks," he said, looking at the chopper. "I don't want to talk to 'em. I don't even want to go near 'em. It's embarrassing. Going on operation with them is like going to a dance with an ugly girl. I don't want anybody to know we're together."

Quinn walked away as the chopper left, and Hanson approached the lieutenant.

"Sir . . ." Hanson began.

"Yes, Sergeant," the lieutenant said, smiling, pleased at the rubbed-off authority he had gotten from the helicopter visit, a little patronizing.

"Sir, I know it's kind of tough when you're dealing with field-grade officers, but could you, you know, persuade the colonel not to drop in on us anymore? It kind of announces our location to anyone who's interested. It makes us look a little too important, too."

"Right. You're probably right, Sergeant."

"And sir, one other thing I've been meaning to mention . . ."

"Go ahead."

"I'd like you to tell your men not to carry their weapons with rounds in the chamber, and not to fire until you give the order. If we get into any kind of firefight out here, it's probably going to be a small-scale thing, but in the excitement our Vietnamese are gonna look just like the bad guys to your troops. And I'm a little worried about your guys firing across the perimeter—it's easy to do—and hitting our people by accident. I know it's kind of hard not to shoot back when you hear rounds coming in, but that's the safest thing. Trust *us* for your security.

"And I'm going to be moving around out there, too, checking out likely ambush sites. I'd hate to get shot by mistake."

"I'll talk to them, Sergeant."

The deuce-and-a-half truck rolled by, the land-clearing unit's rucksacks piled high in the back. Hanson and Quinn carried all their gear with them. They did it out of habit and were probably overcautious, but if something went wrong, they wanted to have all their gear with them.

They took a break for lunch, and Hanson and Quinn moved off from the main group to heat water for their freeze-dried rations. Troc went with them but sat off by himself, where he consulted his *katha*.

A young buck sergeant, the only NCO with the American unit, nodded as he walked past Hanson. Unlike the other Americans, he seemed to know what he was doing. It was apparent to Hanson in the way he moved, conserving his energy, and especially in the way he watched things.

"Hey Sarge," Hanson said. "Have a seat. Try some of this freeze-dried shit with us. It's made in Korea, and it looks awful," he said, holding up the plastic bag of tiny dried fish, their dried eyes flat and huge in brittle gray bodies, "but it's not bad. And it beats humping Cs."

Quinn nodded at the sergeant, indicating a spot to sit down. "How bad you gotta fuck up," he asked him, "to get stuck with a unit like this?"

"It's not so bad," the sergeant said. "I was down in the Delta with the Ninth Infantry, and this beats the shit out of that. At least I can keep my feet dry up here. These guys are just young and don't know what they're doing yet. That's all. They learn, but you gotta watch 'em close. But hell, they know more about this minesweeping business than I do. It's all new to me."

Hanson finished heating the water. He poured in the fish, added an extra packet of spices, and chopped in some pieces of bay leaf he'd picked earlier in the day, and let it simmer.

Finally he poured some in the sergeant's canteen cup, then watched him take a tentative sip.

"Hey," he said, "this is good. Tastes like gumbo. It's *good*. Those greasy Cs get kind of old."

"What'd you do back in the States?" Quinn asked him. He never said "back in the world," maintaining that only punks trying to sound salty used the term.

"Fucked up, mostly," the sergeant said, laughing. "But to tell the truth, I don't know what I'm gonna do when I get back there. It's got me a little worried. I extended to stay over here an extra six months so I could get out of the Army early, but part of it was that I'm not ready to go back home. I guess I could go to college or something, but I wasn't much good at that when I tried it before."

The private who called himself Froggy, wearing linked M-60 ammo across his chest, crashed through the brush and found himself looking at the muzzle of Quinn's rifle. "Hey," he said, in a voice so loud that it made Hanson wince. "So this is where you guys went, huh? How's it goin'?"

Even in a "secure area," eating lunch, Quinn and Hanson talked in low voices. An enemy squad in the bush could be eating, too, fifteen yards away.

"Hey," he said, "these Vietnamese are really something. It

must be really interesting, you know, living with them like you guys do."

"Yeah," Quinn said in a flat, nasty monotone. "They are wonderful little people. But we don't have to live with them."

In the silence that followed Froggy began looking at his hands.

"Why don't you go on back to the rest of the outfit, Spangler. I'll be down there in a few minutes," the buck sergeant said, giving him a way out.

"Okay, Sarge," he said. As he turned to go, he aimed a half-hearted kick at a rusty C-ration can sticking up from the roadway.

Hanson and Quinn were already lifting themselves off the ground as Froggy's foot began its slow arc down, and then they were in the air, throwing themselves backward, a silver spout of gumbo flaring over them as the kicked can jumped harmlessly across the roadway trailing a fine brown smoke of dirt and rust.

"Man," Hanson said, picking himself up off the ground, "you don't just kick things like that. If you didn't put it there, don't move it, don't touch it, don't pick it up. I don't care if it's a can or a rock or a pile of buffalo shit."

"But Sarge . . ." Froggy began.

"Everything," Quinn said, standing, the front of his shirt covered with tiny dead fish, "everything in this fuckin', fucked-up, goddamn gook country either bites or stings or blows up. And if you can't understand that," he said, the wide-eyed little fish dropping fitfully from his chest, "the next time you do anything like that I'll kill you myself."

"It's okay," Hanson said, stepping in front of Quinn. "Just remember it next time."

"Okay, Sarge," he said, nodding his head. He turned and lumbered off.

The buck sergeant smiled wryly. "Just young," he said. "He'll smarten up."

"If he doesn't get killed first," Hanson said, "or get you killed."

That afternoon they encountered a large grass fire that spread well beyond both sides of the old road. Charred stubble and clumps of greasy scorched brush extended to the perimeter of the fire, where white smoke bubbled over a sullen orange glow. Hanson sent two squads around the perimeter of the fire, but they found no sign of Charlie. Still, Hanson thought he had seen movement in the smoke, and even though it had probably been only the superheated air rippling, it made him uncomfortable. It was not a good omen.

"Number ten," Troc said, shaking his head. "Maybe no picnic."

Less than a kilometer beyond the edge of the fire they found some fresh one-seven-five craters, H&I fire from the night before. A dead Vietnamese was sprawled on his back amid the craters. The body had no visible wounds and had probably been killed by the concussion. Hanson imagined the dead man, hearing the shriek of incoming rounds, trying to decide which way to run.

His head was thrown back, his eyes and mouth wide open. Columns of ants passed one another as they marched in and out of his mouth carrying tiny white bundles. Occasionally an ant from one column would break formation to go over and touch antenna with an ant in the other column, then resume his place and continue to march.

The Americans were clustered around the body like spectators at a bad accident on a country road. Troc walked past them stiff-legged, stood looking down at the body, then spit on it and kicked it in the head, caving in its temple.

The Americans looked around at each other uncomfortably. One of them laughed, and the buck sergeant said, "Okay, let's get moving."

That night the Rome plow dug a chest-high pit as big as a garage for the Americans to sleep in. They built up berms around the edge of the pit with the excavated earth so the hole was deep enough to stand in without being exposed.

"Nice mass grave," Quinn said.

He and Hanson slung hammocks well away from the Americans. They were green nylon sheets that, folded, took up no more space than a pound stick of C-4. They slung them so that their backs just brushed the short grass when they were lying in the hammocks, and dug shallow fighting holes below them so they could roll out into their protection if there was any shooting. Before stringing the nylon parachute cord, they wrapped foil from their rations around the saplings used to support the hammocks. The foil would keep water from running down the tree, onto the cord, and into the hammock if there was a rain. It also kept bugs from crawling from the tree onto the hammocks, much like a rat guard on a ship's mooring line keeps rats from coming on board.

They lay in the hammocks and listened to the H&I artillery coming over, some of the rounds sending tremors through the earth, up into the saplings, down the parachute cord into the hammock. It was pleasant lying there, legs and shoulders aching from the day's long walk, face and neck sunburned, feeling the gentle pulse of distant artillery.

"Shit," Quinn hissed. "Goddamn," and Hanson laughed softly.

"What's so fuckin' funny?" Quinn hissed.

"You forgot about the elephant grass cuts on your hands when you squirted insect repellent on them to rub on your face. Stings like hell, doesn't it?"

"How the fuck did you know that?"

"Just listening. I can read you like a book, Quinn. Even in the dark."

"Shit."

Hanson laughed and pushed off the ground with one foot, making the hammock swing. "Hey, Quinn," he said, "is there any kind of decent hunting up there in Iowa?"

"What do you want to know that for?"

"Oh, man, come on. I was thinking that I might come up there and visit you sometime. Maybe we could go hunting."

"Naw. Deer season's about three days long. The fuckheads go out in the cornfields and murder these fat little deer with shotguns. But come on up anyway. We'll go to a bar and beat people up."

Hanson heard Quinn muffle a laugh, and he grinned in the dark. He closed his eyes to go to sleep but couldn't ignore the noise coming from the pit full of Americans. It had gotten louder, and one of them was playing a radio.

He swung out of the hammock and walked over to the trench, standing just beyond the lip. He stood looking down at them, his submachine gun in his hand, wondering if he could kill them all before any of them fired back. He'd have to change clips at least once, he thought, but he'd still have time. It would be easy if he threw in a grenade first. They were smoking and laughing and had two radios going.

Hanson crouched down at the lip of the trench and said, "Hey, guys. *Hey.*"

One of them noticed him, grabbed a couple others, and in a moment they were all standing quietly, looking at Hanson, the radios playing a tinny stereo.

"Better knock off the noise," Hanson said. "Charlie's gonna start dropping some mortars on us. Okay?"

They nodded and mumbled yes, looking like high-school kids who had been caught smoking behind the gym or torturing their biology-project frogs.

"Better get those radios off," Hanson said. Several of them dove for the radios and turned them off.

"Where's the lieutenant and your sergeant?"

"They're set up in the back of the truck with the radio."

"Okay," Hanson said. "Good night, then."

They muttered their good nights as he rose and walked away.

When he got back to the hammock, Quinn was asleep. Hanson lay in his hammock listening to artillery fire, staring up into the sky looking for shooting stars. He fell asleep with his boots on and his Car-15 cradled in the crook of his arm.

Sometime during the night he heard, far to the east, the sound of crying babies and the wail of Vietnamese funeral music. It grew louder and harsher, snapping Hanson wide awake, and then it was blaring from directly overhead, mixed with the clatter of rotor blades: a psychological operations helicopter playing funeral music and the cries of orphaned children.

It was hot the next day, the Americans listlessly swinging the metal detectors in arcs through the dead air, stopping to probe, moving out again.

A thunderstorm blew up that afternoon. Bamboo groves rattled and clacked in the wind. The rain swarmed down the road—they could see it come—and hit them. Hanson moved up against the side of a big tree that offered a view of the road and a little shelter, but the wind-driven rain worked through the leaves and branches, and he was soon wet to the skin, sudden furious gusts of hard rain stinging his face.

You don't move in weather like that because you can't hear. To be safe, you stop and wait it out. Hanson concentrated on a distant hilltop, imagining himself there, and soon he was watching himself from the hilltop, relaxed but alert, barely conscious of the cold. He sensed some disturbance and turned in time to see one of the Americans break through the brush below the road. His arms and face were scratched and he was shouting into the wind.

The minesweeping team hadn't known to stop when the rain struck. They had continued on down the trail, and the rain, puddled in a dip in the roadbed, had prevented the mine detector from picking up a booby-trapped artillery shell.

Hanson and Quinn ran after the soldier, splashing and slipping in the red mud, rain and brush lashing at them, their packs and ammo pouches beating at their backs and thighs.

The ponchos the Americans were holding over the road had the sheen of rain and gray light. The acrid stink of explosive still hung in the damp air. Two of them were lying in the road—the buck sergeant and one of the privates who'd been in the trench the night before. Quinn knelt to check the buck sergeant. "Dead," he said.

The private was lying in a puddle of muddy, blood-streaked water, and ponchos had been draped over his body like rubber blankets. Two soldiers were holding a poncho over his head to keep the rain off his face. He was almost bled out, his face a waxy yellow, his blond hair matted with mud and grit. It looked as though he were dissolving into the mud. Part of his right arm, ragged and torn away at the elbow, was sticking out from beneath a poncho.

One of the Americans whispered, "Look at his legs." Hanson knelt and lifted the edge of a poncho, sending little rivulets of water and blood running off, and looked under. Both legs were gone. What was left of them still hung together by scraps of muscle and skin and pieces of fatigue pants. One foot, untouched and still in the boot, was twisted around backward, dangling just off the ground from a thick silver tendon. Above the knees his legs were full of holes, the thighs bent and bowed. They looked like the legs of an old discarded rubber doll, gray and decomposed with age, gouts of muscle tissue sticking out of the holes in the skin like pinkish gray foam rubber.

"Hold that poncho down a little farther," the lieutenant said as he stood, just looking.

The one who had told Hanson to look at the legs said something else, and the lieutenant said, "Just shut up."

The wounded boy didn't seem to be in any pain.

The water was speeding the flow of blood out of his wounds and putting him deep into shock. "Okay," Hanson said, glancing at the lieutenant, "we gotta get him out of this water. Let's get around him, all lift together, and get him over there on that piece of high ground."

"Right," the lieutenant said. "Let's get him over there."

Behind him, Hanson could hear Quinn yelling at the Vietnamese to set up a perimeter.

"Okay. Ready. Lift."

Hanson lifted him by the hip and what remained of his left leg, but he couldn't balance it and dropped him. The lieutenant, who should have lifted the other side, hadn't moved. He just stood looking at the mangled leg, unable to bring himself to touch it.

Hanson saw Froggy standing back by himself.

"Froggy," he said, "come over here and lift him by the ass. I'll get his legs."

"Okay, Sarge," he said, and came over, past the lieutenant, and took hold.

The kid moaned as they lifted him, not because of the amputated limbs, but because of a small wound in his arm. The dangling foot kicked softly but insistently against Hanson's hip as they moved off the road. The mine detector, still connected to a battery in the boy's pocket, dragged through the mud beneath him.

Hanson tied off the amputated limbs with pieces of the mine detector battery cord. He pulled a canister of blood expander off his web gear, peeled open the canister, and removed a glass bottle of amber fluid, some IV tubing, and a large needle.

He had lost so much blood that it was difficult to find an artery in the arm he had left. Hanson stroked the artery inside the elbow and tried to slip the needle into it, but the flaccid artery kept rolling to the side. Hanson managed to pin it up against the inside of the arm, against the bone, and stick the needle in. He taped the IV to his arm, then got the blood expander, thick as honey, flowing down.

He handed the bottle to a skinny kid with acne. He was shivering, his thin, pocked face a pattern of blue and angry red. In a frightened, awed voice, as though he was having trouble remembering what it was he was saying, the skinny kid said, "Don't worry. You'll be okay."

But the wounded kid was looking directly up at Hanson.

"I know you won't let me die," he said slowly. "You won't. I'll be on my way home in a few days."

"What's his name?" Hanson whispered to the skinny kid.

"Dave, I think. He's a new guy."

"Yeah," Hanson said. "Just relax, Dave. I'll take care of everything. Medivac's on its way."

"I know, Sarge. You won't let me die. You know what you're doing," he said in a precise, almost disinterested monotone, as if he were talking about someone other than himself. "I don't even care about my legs. I'll make out. I still have a lot to live for," he said. Hanson could hear *Di Wee* Tau shouting in Vietnamese and the medivac pilot breaking static on the radio.

"My mom and dad," the kid said, "they're really great. You should meet them. My girl Ann. She loves me. It won't matter —about the legs. Just don't let me die, okay?"

"No way you're gonna die, Dave. Don't even think about it. I'm taking care of everything."

He smiled and closed his eyes.

Hanson took off down the road to look for a wide spot where they could bring the medivac chopper in, but he stopped for a moment and looked back to see the boy heave himself up on his one good arm and look down at his legs. His face was a combination of horror and utter calm.

Hanson found a bend in the road, skirting the river, where the trees weren't so high. The chopper, if it couldn't land, could at least get low enough to take on the casualties.

As he ran back to tell *Di Wee* Tau to secure the bend in the road, he could hear the lieutenant yelling, "Do I have to do *every*thing myself? Doesn't anybody else here have a brain? I've got a dead soldier and one that's al*most* dead to take care of, and nobody . . . I'm *gonna* have some people's *asses* when this is over. Try it *again*, Spangler."

Froggy and the kid with acne were trying to make a stretcher out of a poncho and two lengths of bamboo, but it just wouldn't hold the wounded kid's weight.

The lieutenant was pacing back and forth while Froggy and the kid with acne struggled in the mud to adjust the poncho beneath the wounded kid's back and roll it up on the bamboo. The kid looked scared. "Sarge," he said when he saw Hanson, "I'm not gonna die. Tell him," he said, looking at the lieutenant.

"Naw," Hanson told him, "I'll have the medivac drop a litter. We'll use that. No sweat, Dave. I got it all under control. No problem."

"Well *I* see a problem," the lieutenant said as Quinn stalked over. "What *I* see—" he continued, until Quinn wrapped a huge arm around his shoulders and lifted him to tiptoe.

"Sir," Quinn said, "I need a little help with the radio, if you've got a second. Let's ask 'em to drop a litter."

The lieutenant stiffened in Quinn's grip. Quinn whispered into his ear, and the lieutenant relaxed and walked along, his feet barely touching the ground.

The medivac chopper arrived on station, hovering, sideslipping, waiting. Hanson popped red smoke in the bend of the road, then crouched beneath a tree, covered his head with his arms, and hoped that the litter wouldn't hit anyone. The chopper came pounding in, tail down, sucking the red smoke up through its rotor blades, blowing it out pink, lashing Hanson with leaves, twigs, and wads of mud. The litter sailed down, hit the roadbed on end, and somersaulted into the brush.

Hanson ran back with the litter, where they rolled the wounded kid onto it and carried him to the road, struggling to hold the litter level.

"Froggy," Hanson yelled over his shoulder as he walked bowlegged, holding the litter with one hand and the bottle of blood expander with the other, "you two bring the sarge. Drag him. He doesn't care anymore."

At the bend in the road, the chopper hovered just off the ground, its blades chopping small branches off the trees. Hanson lifted his end of the litter up to the medivac attendants, handing them the still-flowing bottle of blood expander. The attendants and the door gunner had gleaming black bubbles hiding their faces. The huge flying machine hung in the air, and Hanson could feel the turbine shrieking in his back teeth.

They slid the litter the rest of the way over the lip of the open door, Dave's back and buttocks scraping as they pushed him in. The rotor blast blew blood and water down the tilted litter onto the faces and chests of the soldiers holding the bottom. They stood the buck sergeant up, raised his arms as if he were surrendering, and the attendants grabbed his wrists and pulled him in.

The chopper rose slightly, seemed to hesitate a moment, swept into the wind, and was gone. Hanson slapped Froggy on the shoulder, "Thanks," he told him.

Later that day they linked up with the other unit. A black GI came up to Hanson and said, "I know that buck sergeant who was KIA, but who was the other dude got his shit blowed away? Was he a brother or what?"

"Naw," Hanson said. "White guy. His name was Dave."

"Lotta Daves around. What did the dude look like?"

Hanson described him.

The soldier thought a moment, then brightened and said to another GI, "Hey, yeah. It was that 'cruit. That big blond-headed dude. He ain't been in-country a month yet. Ain't that some shit?"

By morning they had the company of Vietnamese strung out along the road at both ends of the bridge, waiting for the convoy to come through. As soon as it passed, they could start back for camp. The two American minesweeping units were camped together up the road.

The Vietnamese at the bridge were settling in for an easy morning, slinging their green hammocks and cooking breakfast. Quinn and Hanson found a shady spot near the bridge, and Hanson had his rucksack off, digging in it for a packet of coffee, when *Di Wee* Tau shouted from the other side of the road, *"Trung Si,* VC! VC!"

A noisy cluster of men formed, gesturing excitedly toward the river. Quinn and Hanson took their weapons and web gear and went over to see what was going on. *Di Wee* Tau turned to them, grinning. "VC go," he said, pointing.

On the other side of the river, barely within rifle range, four Montagnard farmers and a pair of water buffalo were fording a waist-deep inlet. They were moving slowly, obviously not having seen the soldiers. Their conical straw hats bobbed brightly in the sun. The river glinted and flashed as it broke past them.

"Now fini' VC," *Di Wee* Tau said brightly, nodding his head in agreement with himself. He said something in Vietnamese to a young soldier hunched over an M-60 machine gun, who grinned up at them, showing black teeth. Another soldier, squatting near the machine gun, was eating his breakfast; squeezing a little plastic rice bag until a yellowish gob, a mouthful, oozed up, then biting it away.

Troc, the Montagnard interpreter, Mr. Minh's nephew, watched from the tree line.

"Moc phut," Hanson said to the machine gunner. "Wait a minute."

The smile on *Di Wee* Tau's face tightened. Officially Hanson and Quinn were only advisers, but unofficially they were in charge. The situation presented a delicate relationship of "face," and by interfering with *Di Wee* Tau's order to the gunner, Hanson had insulted him, humiliated him in front of his men.

"Little fucker needs the body count," Quinn said to Hanson in a conversational tone.

Di Wee Tau was one of the many Vietnamese officers who had bought his rank in Da Nang. His boots were always spit-shined by his bat boy, his fatigues tailored ass-tight. Day and night he wore wraparound sunglasses, and the nails on the little finger of both his hands curved to yellow points an inch and a half long, a status symbol showing that he did not do manual labor. He used the nails to indicate routes and locations on field maps and to pick his nose and ears, imperiously probing them, examining his finds elaborately. He wouldn't accept advice; neither would he admit mistakes. The day before he had told Hanson and Quinn that they had flank security out. They'd checked and found that there wasn't any. When they told him there was no security, he refused to listen, stridently insisting, "Have security. I see. I know," then walking away.

"Well," Quinn said, nodding toward the river. "Free-fire zone over there."

"Yeah, but they're just some old Yard farmers. It's a nice day. I don't really need it today."

Quinn laughed. "Charlie eats their rice, you know . . ."

He was interrupted by a single shot from an M-16.

"God*damn,*" Hanson yelled, looking to see which of the soldiers had fired. "I said wait."

The farmers, hearing the shot, began to beat the buffalo with their bamboo rods, making them rear and plunge toward the other bank of the inlet. *Di Wee* Tau was furious, jabbing his fingernail at the farmers, screaming, "Vee-*Cee,* Vee-*Cee!*"

The first two farmers were already splashing through the shallows, making for the trees on the opposite bank.

The machine gun opened up, too low at first, ripping the water in front of the farmers, throwing up a curtain of spray, red tracers glancing and droning straight up from the river. One of the buffalo went down kicking. A farmer tripped in the rocky shallows, lost his hat, caught himself with his hands, and stumbled toward the trees. He started to go back for the hat, then changed his mind.

The men around the machine gun, many of them holding

bags of rice and steaming canteen cups, were laughing and
shouting, swinging their arms, shrieking with delight.

The machine gun chewed across the shallows, sending up
eruptions of pebbles and mud. The Montagnard who had lost
his hat seemed to rise lightly on his toes and then, as though
he'd been shoved from behind, threw his head back and
slammed spread-eagled to the ground, embracing the earth.

The water buffalo was still thrashing around near the
mouth of the inlet. The machine gunner walked a three-sec-
ond burst into him, jerking him around. The dead animal spun
slowly around as the current took it, pulling it downstream, a
hairy gray carcass darkening the water.

Di Wee Tau turned to them, grinning, hating them, and
made a thumbs-up gesture. "Number one," he said. "Kill VC.
Number one, number one."

Quinn laughed ruefully, giving him a parody of a salute.
"Yeah," he said, "number one."

The 3rd Mech lieutenant and two Americans ran up, out
of breath. "What's going on?" he asked.

Quinn jabbed a thumb at *Di Wee* Tau.

"Who shoot, *Di Wee?*" he asked him.

"We shoot, kill VC," he said, pointing across the river at
the dead farmer.

"Ah. Number one!" the lieutenant said. "Very good . . ."

"Hey," Quinn said to Hanson, "let's go finish making that
coffee."

Hanson pulled a wad of C-4 explosive off the end of a two-
pound stick and put the rest back in his rucksack.

"Who knows," Quinn said. "Those guys they just shot
could have been the ones who set that booby trap yesterday.
Them or their buddies. Those Yards ain't *all* ours."

"Farmers, man, just farmers," Hanson said. He scooped
out a small hole in the ground and set the half-filled canteen
cup over it. He took a piece of C-4, pressed it into a ball, and
pinched a little sail-shaped fuse on one side, then rolled it
beneath the canteen cup. The best way is to use several small
pieces, feeding them in slowly. That way you use less. He
touched a match to the C-4 and watched the orange flame

spread around and envelop the little white ball. C-4 consumes itself evenly, from the outside in, the surface liquefying, then boiling and burning away with a faint hiss. He dropped in another small piece, and another—the C-4 is soft and a little gritty, like sugary bubblegum—until the water was just beginning to steam, nervous little bubbles breaking on the dull gray bottom of the cup. If you heated it any more than that, the cup would get too hot to drink from. Hanson lifted the cup, and the bubbles stopped.

"Well," Hanson said, "what it all comes down to"—smiling now—"it raises just one question." He paused. Then they both said in an exaggerated Texas accent: *"Why . . . Vet-nom?"*

"Maybe *Di Wee* Tau will put us in for a medal for however many gooks he decides he killed," Quinn said. "I don't have one of those little green ones they give out. It'd look good on my khakis."

Hanson dumped in the packet of coffee and the one of sugar. The coffee hit the water, spreading out over the surface like a concussion blast. He stirred it with the little white plastic spoon he carried in his breast pocket and took a sip. It was just right.

Mai Loc—
Rainy Season

It had been raining for two weeks. The medical bunker had a foot of water in it, and the stolen jeep was sunk to its axles in the mud out at the chopper pad. The typewriter down in the command bunker was getting rusty. The O and P keys kept sticking, reaching up like cadaverous little arms, and had to be pushed back down each time they were struck. At night the rats ran across Hanson's legs and chest to stay out of the water in his bunker when artillery fire set off squeaking, mewling rat stampedes.

The rain stopped late that day and it turned windy and cold. The wire, the generators, and the mortar tubes had a dirty, dull sheen. Red mud was two feet deep in the road to the chopper pad. A pig was being slaughtered over in the Montagnard compound, its screams long and tapering, then silenced in mid-squeal.

The weather was too socked in to send out any recon operations, and Hanson was getting cabin fever. He decided to walk the mile and a half to the 3rd Mech's new fire base to compare intelligence reports with the major who was S-2 there. He and the major didn't like each other, and Hanson knew that the information the major gave him was mostly useless—though all military units were supposed to share intelligence so it could be more effectively exploited, each unit kept its best information to itself—but it was an excuse to get out of camp and take a walk.

On the way out of camp he met Troc. He had been down at the river fishing with hand grenades, and he was carrying a basket heaped with silver fish. Many of them were still alive, their gills working open and closed, so that the whole pile of fish seemed to be shrinking and swelling, making a faint whispering sound.

"Beaucoup fish KIA," Troc said, grinning. His teeth were black as coal, his gums the color of supermarket beef, from chewing betel nut.

As Hanson crossed the airstrip, he could see one of the 3rd Mech's 105 howitzers firing. He watched the big gun jump back and felt the concussion against his face and chest as white smoke poured out of the gun tube. The ammonia stink of high explosive hung in the damp air like refinery fumes. He was in full combat gear, with a canvas bag full of grenades slung over his shoulder. It was unlikely that he'd run into any trouble on the road to the fire base, but it was possible. The enemy owned everything outside the wire.

He passed the dumping area off to the right of the road. It flared with trash fires and oily smoke, and the ragged children who lived there watched him from their ammo-crate shelters.

He'd just passed the edge of the dump when he heard shouts and looked up the road at the crew of a 3rd Mech armored personnel carrier. One of them stood on top of the APC, the others just in front of it. They were jumping up and down, waving at Hanson and gesturing at something off the road.

Hanson looked in the direction they were pointing and saw a GI with dirty blond hair running away from the road, pumping his arms and stretching out, as if something was after him. He was doing a kind of broken field run, dodging the circular burial mounds of a cemetery, each of which was topped with a white pennant, like the flags you'd see on a golf course. They'd been staked into the mounds by the land-clearing unit after the Vietnamese had complained that they were digging up the graves of their ancestors with the huge bulldozers called hog jaws.

Darkness was coming on. The wind was pushing another storm front over the mountains. The white flags were whipping in the wind, and the GI was running desperately.

"Sarge," the soldier on the APC yelled at Hanson, "Sarge. He went crazy, Sarge. Jumped out of that jeep over there and started running."

"Well, let's get him," Hanson shouted and ran after the GI, the bag of grenades ringing, slamming into his hip. He kept the

GI in sight, not gaining or losing ground. The GI stumbled and glanced back, panic in his eyes, then plunged on, vanishing behind a hedgerow, part of a maze of bamboo and thornbush hedges as tall as a house and hundreds of meters long.

Hanson followed, but when he rounded the hedgerow, the GI was gone. Hanson turned to direct the others in an attempt to head him off and discovered that he was alone. He was alone and boxed in on three sides by hedgerows. The wind roared in his ears and stung his eyes with rain. He dropped to one knee, holding his rifle against his chest, and listened. He slowly turned his head, smelling the wind, cocking his head against it so he could hear. The hedgerows made a sound like thorns scratching glass. Palm fronds patted each other like fleshy hands, and the sound of his own breathing was thunderous. He made his way back to the road, moving a few feet, stopping to look and listen, then moving again.

"We couldn't leave the track, Sarge," one of the APC crew said from behind his machine gun mount. "The captain would have our ass if we left the track." The rest of the crew busied themselves inspecting weapons, talking without looking up.

"Right."

"Fucker was crazy anyway."

"Who was he?" Hanson demanded.

"Never saw him before, Sarge. He just bailed out of that jeep and took off. I mean, there it is."

"Must be some new guy. Who knows? It's a freaky war."

Hanson walked back up the road to the track unit headquarters building, but it was empty. He heard the crash of acid rock music coming from one of the big tents and walked toward the sound, the music twisting in and out of the wind. He stepped through the tent flaps into a faint odor of marijuana.

"What's happenin', Sarge," a soldier shouted to him against the music and wind. He was wearing a fatigue shirt with the sleeves torn off, and he had a tattoo of a peace sign on his arm with the words "Fuck It" below. One side of the peace sign was swollen, infected and scabbed over. The walls of the tent were decorated with posters of rock stars and Day-Glo peace signs.

"Where's your CO?" Hanson shouted over the noise, fighting the urge to empty his rifle into the stereo.

"I guess he's down at the motor pool looking at the deer. Him and every other swinging dick. One of the mechanics shot a motherfuckin' deer, man. They're gonna clean it or eat it or some shit. Not me, though, man. I don't eat the flesh of dead animals anymore. That's one thing I don't do. It's wrong, man, it's . . ."

As Hanson turned and went through the tent flaps, the soldier gave him the peace sign and said, "Later."

Two olive drab armored personnel carriers were parked in the motor pool, slab-sided and blunt as steel safes, shuddering in clouds of diesel fume, each of them mounting a pair of .50-caliber machine guns that could chop down trees two miles away. They had the green triangle of the 3rd Mech painted on their sides, and the names OHIO'S FORGOTTEN SON and STONED PONY. The APCs had a peculiar odor, mo-gas and hot metal, perspiration and urine, something half-machine and half-animal. Brown crates of C-rations and rolls of concertina wire were lashed to the tops and sides of the APCs, and stand-off wire was staked around them like little fences.

The deer was in the mud in front of the APCs. It wasn't a dog-size barking deer, the kind so common up in Northern I-Corps, but one as big as Hanson had ever seen, the size of a quarter horse. A GI walked over to it and, looking down at the dead animal, said, "He looks sick."

"Yeah," another soldier said. "Jimmy shot him in the head. Blowed his eyes out," and they both laughed.

The two of them cut slits on each side of the neck, through the thick hide and muscle, and one of them began shoving a warped piece of two-by-four through the slits. He had trouble forcing it through, and the muscled meaty gash surrounded by matted hair looked like a beastly vagina, the two-by-four a giant penis.

"Goddamn," he said, "I think I'm falling in love," twisting and shoving the bloody wood through the neck.

"Get passionate with that thing, Bobby," someone yelled as the wood tore through.

They hooked chains around the two-by-four and raised the

deer with a winch on one of the APCs, raising it so its hind legs were just off the ground. The carcass twisted in the wind, its head lolling to the side, pellets of feces dropping from the corpse.

Two soldiers took the hind legs, forced them apart and held the deer steady while a third ran his hand over the deer's belly. He worked a bayonet through the skin and muscle just beneath the ribs and pulled it down to the tail, opening the abdomen.

He jumped to one side, almost falling, as a glistening purple bubble as big as a beer keg popped out of the wound, hitting the mud with a wet thud, splashing him with blood and blue gouts of membrane.

The fully formed fetus, its fur matted, looked with pearly dead eyes toward the hills.

Hanson turned and walked away without trying to find the CO. He stayed off the road all the way back to camp and kept his weapon on full automatic.

Yankee Delta 528917—
NVA Field Hospital

Cabin fever was setting in at the launch site. Cross-border operations had been suspended for three weeks because of diplomatic gestures in Paris, the local-force VC weren't moving around for some reason, and things were slow. Quinn had gone into Da Nang to pick up supplies, and Mr. Minh had taken a leave to see some of his people. Officially he was in Dong Ha, but in fact he was somewhere up in the DMZ. Through talking to Mr. Minh, Hanson had come to see the DMZ as a sanctuary at the far end of the looking-glass of the war, where tiger and deer, cobras and hawks waited for the war to end, waited until it was safe to come out. All of Vietnam had once been like the DMZ, a place where, Mr. Minh said, the animals still talked like they did before men came.

Meanwhile Warrant Officer Grieson was getting on everyone's nerves, especially Silver's. He had been assigned to the camp to coordinate a highly classified communications system, and in that position had assumed the role of senior commo man. He didn't have Silver's genius with radios, but he outranked him. In fact, he outranked everyone at the camp except the captain, and he had a lot of unofficial clout through the 3rd Mech headquarters. The captain tried to run interference between Silver and Grieson because if their arguments got much worse, one of them would have to be reassigned, and that would be the junior man, Silver. The captain had tried, through unofficial channels, to get rid of Grieson, but he'd had no luck.

Grieson took things too seriously, especially himself. He was from Texas, tall and lanky, and he talked with a John Wayne drawl. He had no part in combat operations, but the push for "Vietnamization" was on, the new commo system was a big part of that, and the camp was stuck with him.

For some reason, Hose hated Grieson even worse than he hated the Vietnamese, snarling whenever he saw him. Grieson threatened to shoot the dog, and he and Silver had almost come to blows over it.

"Who says the world isn't predictable," Silver had said to Hanson and Quinn soon after Grieson came to the launch site. "I've never met anyone from Texas who wasn't an asshole. Not one. Not one swinging dick.

"Did I ever tell you," he went on, "that I spent a little time down in Texas? Huh? Yeah, I was down there playing drums with this for-shit band that called themselves Electric Apple. They broke up and I was stuck in Lubbock—Lubbock fuckin' Texas. Broke. So I got a job as a short-order cook in the Big-Eight Truckstop on graveyard shift.

"They had this sign you could see from the Interstate. A big neon number eight that turned all night long, kind of *grinding* all the time out in the parking lot. I hated that place."

Silver paused, as if he were listening to the sign, then said, "It was just like a Popeye cartoon," and looked back at Hanson.

"Remember Bluto?" he said. "The big guy with the beard in Popeye cartoons who's always throwing Popeye up against walls so hard that Popeye just sticks there like a wad of snot, then kinda, you know, *sliiiides* down the wall onto the floor? And then Bluto laughs. He has that laugh, real deep," and Silver hunched his bony shoulders over his skinny chest, squinted through his wire-rim glasses and smiled grimly, then laughed like Bluto, "Huh! Huh, huh, huh.

"Right? That's how Bluto laughs whenever he really fucks Popeye up. Okay? One night about two in the morning I'm cooking burgers and eggs, and grits. Grits! At the Big Eight Truckstop. This young guy comes in, skinny guy, about like me, I guess. He's a truck driver, but not a bad guy. He'd been in before. Anyway, he's been driving for about three days without sleeping, and he's *all* fucked up on speed. I mean, he's wired, he's about ready to chew on the linoleum tile.

"So he's sitting at the table having a beer, looking out at the parking lot with his twelve-gauge pupils, and he says, 'I can jump over that cattle truck.'

"So the conversation in the place sort of misses a beat, but starts back up until this one guy says, 'What'd you say, Jim?'

" 'I can jump over the cattle truck out there.'

"So some of the *boys* get him going. You know, one of them says, 'Naw, no way, Jim. You're full of shit.' Another guy says, like, 'Hey, *I* think he can do it. If Jim says he can do it, I'll take the man at his word.' Another says, 'No way,' and another offers to bet ten dollars that he can do it. Like that. They get him in a spot where he's all pumped up and has to perform. He's so wasted on the speed he doesn't even notice how they're all kind of laughing.

"So they all go outside. *I* go outside to see what happens. There's this cattle truck. You know, with the aluminum sides with holes in them. You can see the cattle in there, packed inside, grunting and mooing and shitting, banging against the side. Some of 'em got their heads turned sideways, looking out the holes with those big cow eyes. The Big Eight Truckstop sign is turning above the lot: there. Kinda, like groaning, *urrerrurr,* and Jim trots back to the edge of the lot—these guys out there are saying, " 'Good, Jim, get a good running start,' and laughing. Jim starts running, and they're all yelling, 'Go Jim, go. You got it, boy.'

"This guy Jim runs full-speed into the truck, about a foot off the ground when he hits it. Those aluminum slats go *whang,* the cattle inside go batshit, trampling each other in there, falling down, walking on each other. Jim is *all* fucked up. They gotta call an ambulance for him. And all these guys out in the lot are laughing, 'Huh, huh, huh,' just like old Bluto. It's life imitating cartoons. I don't know, man. What a shitty thing to do. Why do people act like such assholes?

"I got out of there pretty soon after that. I was drunk and got picked up by this chick who liked me for some reason. She was on her way to California, and I went with her. Stayed drunk for three days, and she dropped me off in L.A. Only thing I remember about her was that she had bad teeth and a purple GTO."

That morning there was a team meeting. The weekly meetings gave everyone a chance to make suggestions and air complaints about conditions and procedures at the site. The problems were usually about small things, but small things sometimes blew up out of proportion if they weren't caught in time. The camp, scraped out of the jungle, surrounded by mines, wire, the jungle, and the enemy, was a lot like a ship on hostile seas. Minor problems could quickly become serious.

After a breakfast of canned bacon, fresh eggs scrambled with ham, onion and peppers, papaya, orange juice, and home-made biscuits, Co Ba and her daughter cleared the big wooden picnic table. Silver reluctantly took off the stereo earphones he was listening to, and all the Americans sat around the table with coffee. They planned the next supply run to the air base at Quang Tri, worked out plans for stealing a jeep at the 3rd Mech base, and complained about the poor selection of movies they'd been getting on the mail chopper. Then Grieson brought up the mo-gas.

"Captain," he drawled, "those Montagnards have been stealing mo-gas. They claim it's to burn the shit in their compound, but they been taking a lot more than they need for that. They been gettin' blatant about it lately."

Silver looked at Hanson and rolled his eyes. He raised his hand and said, "Sir, I'm concerned about the gas shrinkage situation, too; we all are," he said, looking sternly at Hanson. "But it's tough to prove."

He looked out the screen window a moment, then said, "What we need to do is establish a standard unit of Montagnard shit, making allowances for diet patterns, protein content, and so on."

Silver pursed his lips, held a finger up, tapped the table. "I mean," he said, "does a turd that's primarily, say, canned mackerel burn at the same rate, with the same intensity, the same—efficiency as one that's mostly just rice? Somebody, perhaps *Mister* Grieson would volunteer, has to observe the Montagnard compound to determine the amount of fecal matter produced by the average Yard in a twenty-four-hour period . . . based on weight, I think, rather than volume, because, you know, density varies. Some float and others sink. And finally, we have to, uh, seize a shit sample and test it to establish the amount of fuel, hi-test or regular, it takes to oxidize a given unit of shit. We'll have 'em by the balls then, sir."

Hanson and the captain were both laughing. Quinn just glared at Grieson.

"Silver," Grieson said, "either that sarcasm of yours has to go, or you do."

"Jesus Christ," Silver said, his voice breaking on the second word, "who the fuck cares if they steal a little gas?"

"You'll sing a different tune when they sell it on the black market and it ends up being used against you."

"Used against *me?* How?" Silver asked, standing up. "They gonna sneak up and pour it on me and set me on fire? That's about all I can think of. Or does *Mister* Grieson here know something we don't? They gonna use the gas to attack us in taxi cabs, or . ."

"As you were, young sergeant," the captain said, seeing that things were getting out of hand. "Why don't you take a walk?"

Silver left the teamhouse muttering, "Sing a different *tune,*" and Hanson realized that it was time to plan some kind of operation to get Silver out of camp for a while.

Grieson had bought a TV set at the PX in Da Nang and installed it in one corner of the teamhouse, mounting it on a plywood shelf suspended from the ceiling. When the weather was right, they could get the AFVN station, which was mostly old sit-coms, panel discussions, and travelogues. Once, during some sun-spot activity, they'd gotten a Bangkok station that was showing an episode of "Gunsmoke" dubbed in Thai, where slow-moving Matt Dillon screamed at everyone in a high Asian singsong. But the main reason Grieson had bought the TV was so he could watch "Hee-Haw," his "favorite program."

The night after the team meeting, Silver was drinking beer and listening to his reel-to-reel tape deck on the earphones he'd ordered out of an electronics catalog. He was fanatic about what he called sound fidelity and kept replacing his earphones with a newer, improved set every time one came on the market.

Silver sat with the fat earphones on, glaring up at the TV across the room and at Grieson, who laughed at all the jokes. Silver watched the leggy hillbilly girls and the fat men in overalls popping up and down in the crepe paper cornfield. He watched Buck Owens strum his red-white-and-blue guitar. Finally, he took off his earphones and said, "I hate that phony hillbilly shit."

"Tough," Grieson said, never taking his eyes off the screen.

On the TV a hillbilly in a straw hat said, *"Marriage? Sure I believe in marriage."*

"How much did you pay for the TV?" Silver asked Grieson.

"Without marriage," the hillbilly said, *"husbands and wives would have to fight with perfect strangers."*

When he'd stopped laughing, Grieson looked at Silver and said, "I paid two-fifty. A good deal.

"And it's American-made," he added.

Silver walked out of the teamhouse followed by a burst of tinny laughter from the TV.

He came back a few minutes later with a wad of MPC, military pay certificates, in his hand. It was often called funny money, miniature bills of different colors bearing pictures of tanks, submarines, and jet fighters on their faces, like currency for some violent board game.

Silver began counting the bills out on the bar, mumbling to himself as he stacked them. When he was through, he aligned the edges of the bills by tapping them on the edge of the bar.

Grieson was pointedly not paying attention to Silver's performance.

Buck Owens was sitting in a barber chair on the TV, and the barber asked him, *"Have you changed much since you graduated from high school?"*

Silver thumbed the edges of the bills and looked at the TV.

"No, I haven't changed a bit," Buck Owens said.

"Not a bit? Are you sure?" the barber asked him.

"Heck no, I just graduated last month."

"You're right," Silver said, walking over and dropping the stack of bills in Grieson's lap. "Two-fifty *is* a good deal."

Buck Owens and the barber vanished. The TV twitched, rocked, and began swinging on its shelf, spewing gray smoke and silver dust. A tracery of blue fire played about the set as the screen imploded, turning white, then black again. The explosion that ended the "Hee-Haw" show and sent everyone in the teamhouse to the floor, reaching for their M-16s, left Hanson with an angry chirping in his ears, the sound of an overflight of vicious birds.

As they all looked up from the floor, Silver slowly lowered the big .45 in his hand, his voice sounding synthesized through the whine in Hanson's ears.

"At ease, everyone. At ease," he said as he holstered the pistol and walked out the door.

Hanson went through the agent reports and the top-secret radio-intercept logs, the daily intelligence logs, and the results of airborne radio monitors, then finally decided, on a hunch, to go south, to where the hills dropped off into the river valley.

In the absence of Mr. Minh, Hanson planned to take Sergeant Major's four Nung bodyguards along. Sergeant Major had sent them up from Da Nang for a little time out in the field to keep them sharp and mean.

As far as Hanson could tell, the Nungs were as close to being evil as a human being could be. They were Chinese mercenaries, loyal to Sergeant Major. They enjoyed hurting people. Or any living thing. They thought it was funny to shoot water buffalo to pieces in free-fire zones. But they were effective.

The Korean Marines were brutal too. The United States hired the Koreans to do the jobs Americans couldn't get away with, paid them four times what they would have made in their own country, plus all they could buy from the PX and sell on the black market, doubling and tripling their income.

The Koreans would sweep through a village and kill everything in it—men, women, children, pigs, dogs, buffalo, chickens, everything—then burn what was left to the ground. The smoke from the village would carry the smell of burning straw, rice, meat, and kerosene on the wind. And the American Military Command could say that the Koreans, our allies, had done it, not Americans, because Americans deplore such actions. Of course, the Koreans had been sent to the village by the American command because the Americans wanted the village wiped out.

But the Koreans were mere hired thugs, fraternity boys following orders, compared to the Nungs. The Nungs were as brutal as the weather, as a heart attack shooting up your arm. Once when Hanson had not been long in-country, he had stopped them from cutting the throat of a dying Vietcong who had shot at them from the edge of a village. The Vietcong was a middle-aged Vietnamese with a fist-size goiter on the side of his neck. His old Springfield rifle was held to its stock with wraps of wire, and he had only two bullets for it. Hanson had felt like a boy trying to stop farmers from bleeding a pig. The Nungs just looked at him, puzzled, and the VC died of his wounds there on the dirt in front of them.

The Nungs were as normal as the war around them, and Hanson came to admire the way they got the job done. Some of them shot up a mixture of opium dissolved in rice wine when they were in camp and things were slow, but it didn't seem to blunt their effectiveness out on operation.

It was hot that first day out. The dry elephant grass hissed and left a fine brown dust as they moved through it, its sharp edges cutting their forearms and faces, sweat making the cuts sting and washing the blood off their skin.

Sweat stung Hanson's eyes, and dust from the elephant grass tickled his nose. His face was a tight mask of sunburn and grit.

The Nungs in their black pajamas moved through the heat like shadows or hallucinations in Hanson's peripheral vision.

Hanson could feel the small compass he wore on a chain around his neck. As he moved, it tapped his chest lightly just above his heart. He didn't wear dog tags, not caring if his dead body was ever identified or not, didn't like the clicking pieces of metal at his throat like stamped zinc tags of ownership.

They crossed an open pasturelike area two at a time, the only way to do it. There was no safe way. As Hanson watched, squinting against the sun, looking for movement in the tree line beyond the clearing, the first two Nungs, one on each flank, moved across the clearing like black thoughts. Hanson, then Silver, crossed, each paired with a Nung. The two Americans didn't go across together because if one of them got hit, the other would have to coordinate gunships and medivacs on the radio.

Earlier that morning they'd had to hide from a group of women and buffalo boys who were collecting herbs. Hanson had felt at first foolish, then annoyed, and finally grimly amused at the possibility of a water buffalo stepping on him where he hid. The bandy-legged women had chattered happily and smoked their acrid pipes. It was a situation that had never been covered in the classes on patrolling back at Fort Bragg. Had they been seen, they would have had to abort the operation. Hanson was worried that the Nungs might decide to kill the women and boys, and the operation wasn't important enough for that.

They had all crossed the pasture and were edging through a stand of dead reeds, taller than a man, growing out of baked and broken mud, when they heard a voice. Part of a word. They froze and waited, listening, the smell of reeds around them like a cornfield. Hanson shifted his weight, and the shards of dried mud broke underfoot like rotten tile.

He saw the two khaki-uniformed men for an instant before they faded into the reeds. Hanson, Silver, and the Nungs crashed through the weeds after them, firing twenty-round clips of ammunition. The muzzle blasts from the weapons rippled the hot air with superheated gas roiling with dust, brown flakes of reed and red dust pulsing with concussions that Hanson could feel on his face and chest.

The two men vanished. They were able to track them for a short distance through the dust and dry grass, but the trail disappeared. Silver found a Ho Chi Minh sandal, the sole cut out of a U.S. Army truck tire, the straps from pieces of inner tube made in Akron, Ohio.

One of the Nungs spotted a khaki shadow slipping through the tan grass at the base of a hill but lost sight of it. At the base of the hill they got on-line and walked slowly, parting the grass with the barrels of their rifles. They found something that looked like an animal burrow, then discovered that the size of the opening was concealed by grass. After checking for trip wires, Hanson knelt at the edge of the tunnel. The faint stink of humans hung at its mouth. Silver called the camp and plotted some 105 artillery in case they ran into more than they could handle alone.

Hanson told Quan, a Nung whose forearms were mottled with sores from shooting opium and rice wine, to call for anyone in the tunnel to surrender.

"They will not come out, sir," he said to Hanson.

"Try it anyway. Maybe they will. We'll get a week's R and R in China Beach for a prisoner."

"They will not come out," he said again. "We have to kill them, I think."

"Just try it, okay? Tell them that we will not hurt them if they come out."

"I've seen this movie," Silver said. "Come out with your hands empty, Scarface," he said, imitating Humphrey Bogart. "Yeah, the party's over. Give it up. Your mother's here. We flew her out from the nursing home in Cleveland. Your mom doesn't want you to take the big sleep."

"Tell 'em to come out, Quan," Hanson said again.

The Nung crouched to one side of the hole and began to shout, but Hanson knew he wasn't telling them to come out. Quan didn't want to fuck around with prisoners. He knew he wouldn't get the trip to China Beach anyway, only Hanson and Silver would.

Quan looked up at Hanson. "I tell you, sir. They will not come out."

"Try again."

Quan shrugged and yelled some more.

Hanson took a concussion grenade from his harness and looked at Silver. "You know we're gonna have to smoke 'em," he said. "Quan's probably told them we're gonna cut off their balls and tear their hearts out."

"Yeah, well, I don't know about you," Silver said, "but I don't want to go down in there until we've Osterized the fuckers. I'm gonna want 'em pureed before Mrs. Silver's boy goes down there in a hole in the ground."

Hanson pulled the pin on the grenade and spun it into the hole. Four seconds later the ground shuddered beneath their feet and dust drifted from the hole, its edges collapsing inward, enlarging. Hanson and Silver stood looking down into the darkness. They threw in fragmentation grenades.

Hanson dropped his pack and rummaged through it, pulling out a stick of plastic explosive. He pulled it in half like a piece of bread dough, lit the end of one piece with a match, and threw it into the tunnel. The flame flickered, grew, then enveloped the fist-size piece of explosive. The yellow flame turned blue, and beneath the nimbus of flame, the explosive blistered and glowed black and red, revealing a narrow smoky tunnel. Fresh shrapnel glittered like silver where it was embedded in the walls. Silver looked at Hanson. Hanson shrugged and said, "Might as well take a look."

Two of the Nungs stayed on the surface to watch for anyone who might try to escape from other tunnel exits. Hanson eased himself into the tunnel, the short-barreled submachine gun in one hand, a red-lens flashlight in the other. Quan and another Nung followed, and Silver went in last. Moving through the tunnel was like reaching into a hole and feeling for a snake. Exposed roots pulled at Hanson's shirt as the walls of the tunnel turned, turned back, then opened out into a room.

The air was alive with gossamer creatures. Hanson felt them settle on his cheeks, then jump off. They walked across the backs of his hands. He felt one in his lips and spit it out. Breathing through his nose, he wiped them away from his nostrils. One as big as a hand landed on his neck and he snatched it away, slapping his hand savagely against his thigh to kill it. They weren't stinging, so he tried to concentrate on the darkness in front of him.

He thought he saw movement and fired a twenty-round clip. He turned off the light and hugged the floor, worried as much about getting hit by fire from the Nungs behind him as anything ahead.

He was right to be worried. Fire from behind snapped over him like deafening bursts of static in the smoky, dusty, dirt-floored chamber. It illuminated the room like strobe lights, making it difficult to tell what was movement and what was only flickering shadow. As he reached out, low-crawling, his hand sank into something warm and wet. He jerked his hand out and began beating at whatever it was he'd touched, smashing it with the metal stock of his submachine gun. In the yellow and blue flash of automatic fire it absorbed the blows like a tar baby. Then the green tracers flickered out and stopped. The red ones stopped, and all he could hear was the ringing in his ears.

With the flashlight he found a kerosene lamp and lit it. As they adjusted the flame, bodies took shape in the dark. Hanson spun around at the sound of a burst of fire and saw Quan standing over a corpse. There were bodies, parts of bodies, and bloody puddles of mud on the dirt floor of what Hanson realized must have been a small field hospital. His ears rang and buzzed from the gunfire and his eyes stung. He licked his lips, tasting dust and explosive.

Shards of parachute nylon purled and sideslipped in the dusty, reeking air. The earthen walls and roof of the room had been covered with parachute panels, and the grenades had shredded them. Greenish red tendrils of the cloth hung from the ceiling, undulating like kelp, stroking and tickling Hanson's ears and neck.

He backed into a bunk wedged in one corner of the room and turned to find himself looking at an emaciated corpse. But the corpse was still alive. He was so frail that he must have been in the hospital for TB or malaria, but he was riddled with fresh shrapnel wounds from the grenades. One of his legs was almost severed, white shards of bone catching the light. He was dying, glaring up at Hanson from beneath one propped-up arm. He worked his mouth, to speak or to spit at Hanson, but he could do neither.

As a reflex, Hanson held eye contact with him, trying to stare him down, feeling foolish and ashamed of himself but unable to look away. The soldier seemed to grow more powerful, taking Hanson over, taking control. He was dying and had nothing to lose anymore. Then, somehow, Hanson began to accept whatever it was in the soldier's eyes. It was not anger or hate that poured into him from those black eyes, but a kind of neutral strength that filled Hanson with energy, like deep breaths of pure oxygen.

And then the soldier died, and it was as if Hanson had to have taken whatever it was boring into him from those eyes before the soldier was able to die. A tiny sigh escaped the soldier as he passed on to death, and he and Hanson were, for a moment, alone somewhere—in space, in the desert, drifting on the ocean. Hanson could see himself watching the last light leave the soldier's eyes, deaf to any sound in the room because of the wail and chatter in his ears. His nose and throat burned with dust and gunsmoke, rubbing alcohol, high explosive and urine, blood and sweat. Everything but the soldier's eyes seemed out of focus until they went dark and flat, and then Hanson turned away, his heart pounding with murder and joy. In the yellow light he saw Quan watching him, smiling.

They smashed the shelves of medicine and stripped the bodies of valuables. Silver found a Chinese copy of a Walther PPK on one of the bodies, a pistol that would be worth a thousand dollars in Da Nang.

"I can see it in the hometown paper now," Silver said as he went through the pockets of a dead nurse. "Green Berets attack hospital. No mercy. Turn hospital into morgue . . . no, into *charnal* house. That's it. That's the word they'd use.

"Jesus," he said, "this looks like a cave-in at the hillside butcher shop."

It was late in the day when they got back to the launch site. "Okay," Hanson said into the radio handset, looking down at the camp from just inside the tree line, "we're coming into camp from the banana patch out here. Gonna pop a little smoke so you know it's us."

"Pop it," Grieson's voice said over the radio.

Hanson pulled the pin from an olive drab canister, the size and shape of a beer can, labeled in stark black letters, M-1 A-1 SMOKE/PURPLE. He side-armed it out into the clear killing zone that ringed the camp like a moat. The spring-loaded fuse snapped shut with a soft pop. Hanson held the ring and cotter pin he had pulled, spinning it on his finger as thick purple smoke began to billow, blowing back into the green jungle. He liked the purple and green together, like a landscape from another world.

"I identify purple smoke," Grieson said.

"Grape smoke, you got it. Goofy grape," Hanson said. "We're comin' on in then."

"Come on in."

"I'm gonna kill that fucking Grieson," Silver said.

They had a John Wayne movie that night, a Western. John Wayne was a hit with the Montagnards because he wore a Montagnard tribal bracelet that he had been given while filming *The Green Berets* a few years before. Whenever the Apache Indians rode across the screen, the Yards shouted, "VC! VC!"

Grieson was the projectionist. He'd hung a sheet across a line on the teamhouse patio for a screen. The Cinemascope lens was held onto the projector with a piece of string, and at times it would slip, turning the people on the screen fat and skinny, like a funhouse mirror.

The lights came on at the end of the movie, and the image of a cabin shaded by a live oak faded from the bedsheet screen. Hanson left the patio, where Quan staggered past him, muttering to himself, and walked to the ammo shed where his gear was stored.

Rope-handled ammo crates lined the walls of the shed, some of them broken open to the dull sheen of grenades, mortar rounds, and linked fifty-caliber ammunition. It was cooler sleeping in the ammo shed than it was down in a bunker. Sometimes there was a breeze. And he liked to sleep surrounded by the explosives. He felt safe there.

He took the heavy-barreled M-14 with the starlight scope off the wall, picked up a green bottle of cognac, and started out the door. He stopped, went back for his web gear, and slung it over his shoulder, then walked across the dark camp and sat down on the sandbags around one of the heavy mortars. The big mortar tube was down in a concrete pit, set in the center of concentric circles, painted aiming arcs. Clusters of aiming stakes were driven into the ground at the edge of the pit. It looked like the site of an exotic religion or a ritual sacrifice.

He put the rifle scope to his eye and scanned the perimeter. The scope made a tiny whine, like a mosquito near his ear. The scope revealed things in two dimensions only, so the rows of wire and perimeter bunkers seemed to be painted on a curving backdrop.

He laid the rifle in his lap and took a pull of cognac, listening to the ragged rise and fall of the generators and the rumble of faraway artillery. Shadows moved around the teamhouse. He took another slug of the burning liquor and looked up at the stars.

He thought he heard a noise and turned to see Mr. Minh sitting a few yards away, watching him.

"It is a good night," Mr. Minh said. "You can see all the stars. They are only a short look away tonight."

It was a warm night, and the moon moved in and out of the few high clouds. Hanson remembered that he'd had the dream the night before, the one about killing the rabbits and goats. Mr. Minh had told him that dreams are as important as things that happen when you are awake. Sometimes they are the same thing. Dreams can be about the past and the future, because everything is always happening at the same time. Dreams can be a memory of the future.

"A long time ago," Mr. Minh said, "my wife and children were killed. The Vietnamese bombed my village and killed them. They said it was a mistake. I saw the planes coming, but what could I do? A man cannot make the dead live again. They were all KIA," he said, using the military term for "killed in action," the term he used for all the dead, no matter how they died.

"So I began to walk," he said. "I walked for three days and slept at night, places I had never been before. At the end of the third day the night came, but I still kept walking and the earth began to sweat in the dark. The dark began to close up. It was —what is the word for it?"

"The fog?" Hanson asked.

"Yes. Yes, the fog came and made everything seem very far away. I came to a big river I had never been to before. I could not see it with the—the fog, but I could hear it. It sounded like a giant man, a monster breathing in the dark.

"I listened to the river breathing and thought that maybe I would jump in and let the river kill me.

"What could I do? I had no power. I could not stop a plane or bring my wife and children back to life. The fog was very close. It was like being inside a cloud at night. There was nothing but me and the river breathing. We were alone.

"And then I thought, the river does not care if I jump in or if I don't jump in. It will not even notice if I do. The river is an important man and a busy man. It is too busy being a river and it does not matter to the river how I feel. I was not important to the river.

"What should I do, I thought. The river does not care. Maybe I should live. But I was already too old to care about starting a new family. Should I use rice wine and opium every day the way the Nungs do? That is the same as being dead.

"Maybe I would go crazy, like some have. I cannot farm anymore. I cannot live by hunting. The Vietnamese and the war stopped the hunting. I cannot be a husband or a father anymore. I thought, why should I go to bed at night and wake up in the morning?

"I sat down and listened to the river and it told me. I can fight. I can kill Vietnamese. So that is what I do now. I am like a good farmer or a good hunter, but what I do is kill Vietnamese. It is all there is now," he said. "It is my work. A man can live if he has work to do."

Hanson realized that there were fireflies in the air around him, pulsing like lazy yellow eyes. He couldn't remember ever having seen fireflies in Vietnam before.

Mai Loc
Launch Site

The night before the ground attack, Hanson saw strange lights to the north, glowing blues and greens just above the horizon, some kind of electrical storm, he supposed. And Hose was acting stranger than usual.

Later that night the five enlisted men who had been assigned to work with Grieson on the new commo system had come to the teamhouse for the first time. One of them looked in the door and smiled. He had a chipped tooth.

"Uh, hi," he said. "We were wondering if we could buy a few beers from you guys."

Quinn was working over his web gear. He looked up and glared at the five soldiers with the green 3rd Mech patch. "Technicians," he muttered, and went back to his web gear, saying, " 'You guys,' " mocking the soldier's East Coast accent.

Hanson looked at the soldiers, looked back at Quinn, and grinned. "Oh, gosh, pardon me," he said. "Is it all right with you, Sergeant Quinn, sir, to sell these young servicemen a beer?"

Quinn ignored him.

"Come on in," Hanson said. "Pay no attention to that bad person over there. Have a beer. First one is on Sergeant Quinn," he said, marking five checks next to Quinn's name on the team roster.

"I hear you," Quinn said, not looking up from his work. "You're feeling real froggy tonight. But I ain't gonna let you get me goin'. Yet."

Hanson took an armload of beer cans out of the battered refrigerator and set them on the bar. "Allow me to open them for you," he said. "A courtesy. A small gesture of interservice fraternity."

He opened one for himself. "A toast," he said, "to you, the men of Mister Grieson and his magic radio work.

"Yes, just ignore mean Sergeant Quinn over there. I'm more representative of the young NCO you'll find in the elite corps of Green Berets, the well-known fighting soldiers from the sky."

Dawson laughed.

"Easy derision, racist laughter," Hanson said. "Pay him no mind. That's Dawson, our Afro-American NCO. Up for a visit from Da Nang."

"Han-sun, I don't know *who* you a representative of. I ain't seen any more like you. I believe you had yourself a little taste of that army-issue speed for dessert, you so froggy tonight."

"No, that's not it, Sergeant. I never touch that dangerous drug. What it is," Hanson said, creeping around the bar, walking in a crouch toward Dawson, "is that I'm worried that Charles is sneakin' around out there in the dark, sneakin', sneakin' to get you before you leave, talking in his inscrutable gook language, 'ching-chang, yip yip, gettee buffalo soldier . . .'"

"I'm liable to shoot somebody like that," Dawson said, picking up a Thompson submachine gun and pulling the bolt back.

Hanson laughed and backed his way to the bar. "You see," he said to the soldiers, "Dawson's going back home tomorrow, 'back to the world,' as they say, after two tours. He just came up for a visit, see if he could kill a couple more people before he goes."

Dawson laughed. "I had to see you people before I left."

"Anyway, Silver bet him a case of beer that the camp would get hit before he left—that *mystery* battalion out there we've been getting some intel on.

"*Mystery* battalion, *mystery* battalion," he sang to himself.

"Hey," he said to the 3rd Mech technician, "how'd you break that tooth?"

"Playing cricket," he said. "Really. I lived in England for five years. Cricket. Funny game."

"How much longer till you guys get all the right lights to

blink over there in that green mobile home?" Hanson asked him.

"Couple days. Couple of weeks. Who knows? It's the humidity here. They designed the damn thing in a lab somewhere, controlled atmospheric conditions, and they expect it to work over here. And they say it's 'air droppable.' A good kick against the door blows circuits."

The "green mobile home" was a highly classified air-conditioned, humidity-controlled radio room that had been shipped as a single unit. It was part of a complex airborne and ground electronic network to be used to locate enemy troop concentrations so that air strikes or artillery could be used against them. It was part of the "Vietnamization" effort to replace U.S. troops with machines so the war could be turned over to the Vietnamese. It was designed to replace recon units, like Hanson's, who patrolled enemy-controlled areas in the hope of discovering enemy units, a strategy Quinn referred to as stomping through the bushes until you step in shit.

"How do you like working for Grieson?" Hanson asked, and Quinn even looked up from his work at that.

The soldiers looked at the ceiling, then looked at each other. One smiled, shaking his head. The kid with the chipped tooth glanced toward the door and, lowering his voice, said, "If he'd just leave us alone, we could get the work done a lot quicker—"

"But the son of a bitch couldn't do that now," another one of the five interrupted, "could he? I'm so sick of listening to that phony fuck tell us how great he is . . . He doesn't know *anything* about that unit out there."

The kid with the chipped tooth laughed. "That's Pierce," he said, nodding at the other soldier. "He knows what he's doing out there and he makes Grieson look bad."

"Hey," Quinn said, looking up from his gear. The five soldiers looked quickly over at him.

"When I was down in Da Nang, I heard that Grieson got relieved down there because too much of his information was bullshit. A couple of recon teams got shot up because of it. How about that?"

"Yeah," the one named Pierce said. "That's what a couple of my buddies down there told me."

"Hey, Dawson," Quinn said. "What time is it?"

"Gettin' on toward ten," he said. "That's close enough to midnight, don't you think?"

"Yeah, let's break out that case of beer."

More beer was passed out, and Hanson asked the kid with the chipped tooth, "How'd you end up here?"

"Like I said, I was over in England. In school at first—I'm a rich kid. Then I started bumming around, and my draft notice caught up to me."

"But what are you doing *here?* In 'Nam. How bad did you have to fuck up to get sent over here?"

He laughed. "I volunteered. See, you've never been an electronics repairman at Fort Bliss, so you can't know. You sit in a little room all day. There was a neon light over my desk that made a high little hum like a bug. I was going nuts trying to look busy under that light. The damn thing flickered, like it had an electrical tic. I tried to kill time debating things with myself like the, uh, relative merits of two different kinds of radar-scope image configurations.

"So I decided to come to Vietnam. You know, does it really look like the six-thirty news? My generation's war. If I ever have any grandchildren I can tell them I was here."

They drank in silence for a few minutes. Then Hanson looked up at the ceiling and said in a monotone, "Uh, this is Defcon, Body Count."

Quinn was polishing the bolt of his Swedish K.

"Body Count, this is Defcon, do you *copy*, over."

Still polishing the bolt, Quinn said, "Uh, roger-roger Defcon, I copy five-by-five, over."

"What is our situation here, Body Count? Do we have max H&I concentrations this location? Are we operational? Please confirm."

"That is most affirmed. Max H and I. Fire Base Bruise and Peggy Lee on call with selected ordnance to include Willy Pete, HE, uh, photo-flash, flare, BLU-10 Brave Firecracker, and nonpersistent CN nausea, and smoke. One-o-fives, one-five-fives, and eight inch."

"Uh, roger, Body Count. Have you made contact with Colonel Fang's phantom battalion—the *mystery* battalion—and, if so, have you deployed as planned, Op-plan Blue Tango?"

"That is most affirmed, Defcon."

"Real fine, Body Count. We have the Grieson mobile home here, calibrated with blinking lights. You may anticipate Max saturation, your location."

"Roger that, Defcon," Quinn said.

Then Silver, who was standing just inside the door, said, "Uh, roger-roger. We have the ordnance, the technology, and, Body Count and Defcon, we *have* the motivation. Good fortune surrounds us." Then he hissed through his teeth, sounding like radio static.

"Ah, good fortune," he said, walking toward the refrigerator, where he got a beer. He took a sip, then said, "Hey, Commander Hanson, lemme borrow your tin whistle."

Hanson walked to his footlocker, took the tin whistle out of his pack, and gave it to Silver.

Silver sat down on a rope-handled ammo crate on which black words were stenciled across the raw wood: PROJECTILES/HE/105—LOT 177321. He bent his head, paused, then began to play, a slow, frail piping that seemed to confirm the possibility of joy while rejecting it, sad, and so eerie that Quinn stopped polishing the machine gun bolt and looked up.

When Silver had finished the piece, the kid with the chipped tooth said, " 'Banish Misfortune.' I haven't heard that in a long time. Stay where you are," he said. "I'll be right back," rushing out the door.

"Couldn't sleep," Silver said. "Figured I ought to come up and have one of the beers I'm gonna win from Dawson. Shit, I got radio watch in an hour or so."

The kid came banging back through the screen door. "Now," he said, "sure the beer is fine, but I happen to have this bottle of Irish"—setting a green Bushmill's bottle on the bar—"and," he said, a little out of breath, "I happen to have this," and he pulled a dulcimer from beneath his arm.

"First," he said, holding up one finger, "a taste of the Irish."

They passed the bottle around and drank from it.

"And now, sir," the kid said to Silver, "would you happen to know a little air, a favorite of mine, 'Sir John Fenwick was the flower of them all'?"

Silver nodded his head, smiled, and they began to play together, the dulcimer, the tin whistle, and the song about a knight who was brave and thoughtful and honest, gentle and kind enough to be remembered as the Flower of Them All. The teamhouse was silent for the music. Quinn looked up from his gear, his cold little eyes almost thoughtful.

When they'd finished the song they passed the bottle around until it was empty.

The kid with the chipped tooth said, "Thanks for the hospitality," as he and the other four got up to leave.

"Not at all," Hanson said.

"Our pleasure," Silver said. "See you tomorrow."

Dawson smiled and said, "Later," and even Quinn nodded and said, "Yeah."

After they left, Quinn said, "Fuckin' Third Mech radio plumbers. Shit!" He was walking to the refrigerator to get another beer when they heard a whining and snuffling at the door.

"Hose," Quinn said, "come on in and have a beer." While he looked for Hose's beer bowl, Silver walked over and opened the screen door.

Hose swaggered in, his head held high, carrying an arm in his teeth.

"Jesus!" Silver said, shocked in spite of himself. The other three froze for a second, then Quinn said, "Come and get it, Bud," setting the bowl of beer down on the floor.

The dog dropped the arm, walked over to the bowl, and began lapping up the Carling's Red Label.

"It's a gook," Silver said, crouching next to the arm. It had been blown off at the shoulder, but the force of the explosion had driven the fabric of the fatigue shirt into the flesh, so the arm was clothed in a khaki sleeve. The fingers were dirty and clenched, but untouched. Only the ragged shoulder was bloody.

"What's that insignia?" Hanson asked. "I've never seen that."

There was a red circle patch on the shoulder of the shirt sleeve.

Quinn kneeled to look. "A sun?" he said. "A red sun?"

"Fuck," Silver said, "let's get that mother out of here, over the first row of wire, anyway. We can send it down to Da Nang in the morning. I mean," he said, beginning to laugh, "I don't want that fucking thing in here while I'm on radio watch."

Hanson picked up the arm by the sleeve and carried it out the door. It was heavy and it flexed at the elbow as he walked to the inner perimeter wire.

He slung it over the first row of concertina wire, and as he watched it arc heavily away, the clenched fist opened into a reaching hand, the tendons in the arm having been loosened by the force of the throw.

It was almost 2 A.M. when it started to rain. The sappers, wearing only loincloths in order to slip through the wire more easily, pushed long bamboo tubes ahead of them. The bamboo was filled with explosive and would blow paths through the wire for the assault troops.

The sappers had covered themselves with ash so they would not reflect light, and it gave them a ghostly appearance. In their loincloths they carried foot-long sections of engineer stakes and short lengths of wire with loops twisted in both ends. As they slithered through the wire, they used the sections of engineer stakes to prop up the tanglefoot wire so they could crawl under it. When they came to the coils of concertina, they hooked one looped end of the wire they carried to a section of concertina, then pulled it back and hooked the other end to another section, parting the concertina wide enough to crawl through. Freckles of blood began to appear through the ash as they nicked and cut themselves on the wire.

They moved very slowly, feeling ahead of them for trip flares and claymore mines. They turned the mines around so that they faced the camp even though they themselves would be in the camp if the mines were fired. When they came to pebble-filled beer cans that were hung on the wire as noisemakers, they simply dropped in a handful of dirt to muffle them. The North Vietnamese sappers were brave soldiers who were very good at a dangerous job. An elbow or ankle could trip a flare, ruin the attack, and ensure their deaths in the bubbling smoking silver light of the magnesium flares.

Once the sappers had the bamboo charges in place, they entered the camp and began throwing satchel charges into bunkers. Others detonated the lengths of bamboo, and the assault troops poured through the wire, some of them dragging small trees, like Christmas trees, behind them. There was a satchel charge tied to the peak of each tree, and the troops jammed the trees, peak first, down the entrances of perimeter bunkers. The Montagnard troops in the perimeter bunkers could not push the trees out before the charge went off, the tree branches jamming the narrow bunker entrance like a plug.

Support troops began to mortar the camp when they heard the first of the satchel charges go off, hoping that the Americans and Montagnards in the camp would think that *all* the explosions were mortars, hiding the fact that NVA troops were already in the camp blowing up bunkers. The assault troops moved steadily through the gaps in the perimeter wire, some carrying bamboo ladders, many of them dying from the explosions of their own mortars.

Silver was on radio watch as the sappers came through the wire, monitoring headquarters in Da Nang and listening to a football game in the States on a transistor radio. It was Saturday afternoon in the States, and the announcer's voice was tiny and tinny as he screamed, "And it's the twenty-five, the twenty, the fifteen, and Parker is *down* on their own fourteen. Yessir, folks, it's that kind of ballgame here today." And Silver could hear the crowd cheer, a faint wail, the sound an insect might make as it burned to death.

Then the B-40 rocket came through the teamhouse door, driving a sliver of shrapnel into the back of Silver's head, and he fell across the bank of radios. He wasn't dead, but he couldn't move. He could still hear the radio. ". . . and it looks like Nebraska is really going to have to get their defensive machine moving against the Missouri Tigers if they're going to have any chance at all . . ."

Quinn burst through the door, his rifle in one hand, web gear slung over his shoulder. He saw Silver and ran to him, checking for a pulse. When he found one, he laid him on the floor and discovered he was conscious.

"Hey," he said to him. "Are you okay? What's wrong?"

Silver looked up at him as though he were a stranger.

"Can you hear me?" Quinn demanded. "Can you hear me, man? Blink your eyes if you can hear me."

Silver fluttered his eyelids, then tried to talk, but all he could do was make senseless, guttural noises. He tried again to speak, tried harder, but the noises only grew louder, more out of control. His eyes were full of fear and confusion, like an animal hit by a car on the freeway.

Outside the first of the satchel charges went off. A few green tracers hissed through the rain.

Quinn checked Silver for wounds and found nothing but a cut on the back of his head. "You're okay," he told Silver. "It must be just a concussion. You're all right."

Grieson banged through the screen door and Quinn almost shot him. Grieson was wearing only his pants and boots. He was wild-eyed, his hair wet and matted. "What are we doing?" he yelled. "What'll we do?"

Quinn heard the distant *tonk tonktonk* of mortars being fired. "Shit," he hissed, and unconsciously began counting off the seconds—"one thousand, two thousand . . ."—waiting for them to hit the camp, picturing the little cast-iron bombs arcing up through the rain. *"Tonk. Tonk."* Two more.

Quinn began to drag Silver across the floor toward the kitchen. "Come'ere," he ordered Grieson. *Tonk.*

"Shit, shit, shit," Quinn said to himself.

In the kitchen he pulled open the door of one of the big floor-level cupboards and began pushing cans out of the way.

The first two mortar rounds, then the third exploded out in the wire. Short rounds. The NVA gunners would adjust their fire for the next ones. "Come'ere!" Quinn shouted to Grieson.

"They're in the wire, I know it," Quinn said. "I gotta get out to the Quad-fifty. Here's what you do. Slide Silver into the cupboard here. Get rid of these fuckin' cans. Close the door and tip the table over in front of the cupboards. That's all we can do. Okay? Okay, okay!"

"Okay," Grieson said. "What then? What're we gonna do?"

"I'm gonna kill me a bunch of slope-head motherfuckers, that's what," he said, starting for the door. "Take the shotgun," he said, pointing to a .12-gauge pump hanging on the wall, a bandolier of ammo looped over the stock. He froze for an instant, glaring at Grieson. "But get Silver in there . . ." Two more mortar rounds exploded, inside the camp this time. "You're responsible for him," Quinn said, spinning and going out the door, hoping that the sandbags on top of the teamhouse would stop the mortars.

By the time Hanson was out of the ammo shed, the camp had begun to fire illumination rounds from their mortar tubes. The illum rounds burst high overhead, hurtled earthward like shooting stars, then were pulled up short by their parachutes, pink stars swinging with the wind, dripping sparks, throwing black-green shadows.

A green fan of machine gun tracers swept in from the west, the wedge of heavy rounds popping as they passed overhead. The rain dripped down Hanson's face, and he tasted salt and dust on his lips.

On the top of the TOC bunker, Dawson had taken the cover off the M-60 and was looking for a target. He found one and began firing six-round bursts, the muzzle flash lighting up his cheekbones and eyes. The recoil and muzzle blast from the gun pulled at his T-shirt like a heavy wind, puffing it out at the small of his back, plastering it against his ribs.

"*Get* some, brother!" Hanson yelled.

Without turning his head, Dawson pumped his fist up and down.

Out on the southwest corner of the wire, a trip flare burst with silver glare and dense white smoke. Hanson thought he could hear it burning, like boiling grease, but of course it was too far away.

Then, near the point of the camp nearest the trip flare, he heard the hesitant popping of a small gasoline engine being started. The popping rose, then steadied into a cheerful flutter like a lawn mower on Saturday afternoon.

The little engine was the power source for the Quad-fifty machine gun. Hanson paused, staring through the dark and rain toward the sound. It was very dark, the only light from muzzle flashes and an occasional flare. Hanson's pupils were black and huge.

The gun showed then like a movie scene flashing suddenly on a dark screen, the sound out of control. Linked-brass rounds flickered in the muzzle flash, snaking toward the gray slab of the breech blocks of the four yoked guns. The Montagnard gun crew moved in the strobe light of the four barrels like silent comedy stars trying to do something hilarious and impossible while there was still time. They fed cans of ammo to the gun as the four barrels wove tracers smoothly crossing and recrossing the perimeter. Then one of the barrels burned out and raveled the pattern with a mad counterpoint of plunging red tracers.

Hanson crossed toward the Quad-50 position, where he knew he'd find Quinn. He moved in a heavy lope, his web gear shifting and pulling at him, a canvas bag of grenades at one hip, his weapon down at a low port arms. He saw a thin, naked man in the wire and fired at him. Pink flares, red and green tracers reflected in puddles and across tin roofs.

Quinn had on asbestos gloves and was changing the burned-out barrel when Hanson got to the gun. He heard AK-47 rounds and ducked as they popped past the gun. The old barrel still glowed faintly red in the dark as Quinn threw it down in the mud, where it hissed and steamed.

"Fire slow," Quinn was shouting to the Montagnard gun commander. "Fire slow."

"Hey," Hanson shouted up at him as he jammed and twisted the new barrel into the gun, "let's get to the TOC bunker and find out what the fuck's happening."

Quinn told the gun commander one more time to fire slower and save the barrels, then jumped down into the mud. "Let's go, little buddy," he shouted. "I got Silver stashed in the teamhouse. He got all banged to shit by a B-40. I had to leave him with Grieson to get this gun going."

Getting back to the TOC bunker was like running through

heavy traffic, across a series of freeways at night in the rain. Tracers were like taillights, flares and muzzle flashes the high beams of out-of-control head-on traffic. The enemy were everywhere, skinny, dark-faced little men, many of them naked except for loincloths, appearing, then vanishing in the shifting light. Hanson and Quinn saw three of them staggering off with a heavy machine gun and tripod, a strange tableau strobing in and out of the dark. They each lobbed a grenade at the struggling men, pitching them underhand, like softballs, then threw themselves onto the ground. Hanson felt the vacuum in his ears, like a sudden change in altitude, the slap of an explosion, and another. One of the three was still alive, pinned by the heavy tripod, flopping in the silver flarelight like a fish in a trap, his body patterned with blood. They both shot him and ran on.

They were running in step, splashing through multicolored puddles, their eyes dilated and black, charged with something very close to joy.

In the light of a flare they saw Mr. Minh running toward one of the perimeter bunkers. He had a rope around his waist and was dragging a cluster of palm fronds behind him. The flare sputtered out, and darkness closed over him.

"I don't know what he's doing," Quinn shouted, "but I hope it works. Those little fuckers are all *over* the place, little buddy. If we don't come up with something we're gonna have to E&E out of here."

Hanson almost stumbled over one of the bodies in front of the TOC. They emptied their weapons into the bodies, making them quiver and splash in the mud, then threw the empty clips aside and reloaded. Hanson inhaled and smelled gunpowder and sweet blood. He could taste it on the backs of his eyeballs. He felt as if he had aligned himself with the fault lines beneath the earth. He could point his finger and tracers would appear. His gestures set off explosions.

Dawson was down at the bottom of the stairs with a shotgun. "Fools won't come in," he shouted. "Third Mech says they won't come in until we've secured the camp. Say they're under orders from Da Nang not to come in. If they don't, man, we're gonna *have* to E&E out. I'm gonna need some help down here destroying files and equipment."

"Fuck *me*," Quinn said. "I'm gonna die in this stinking gook country because the fucking Third Mech won't fight. We don't *need* their asses if the camp's secure. And Silver can't E&E."

"I better start popping thermal grenades and get ready to blow the E&E routes through the wire," Dawson said. "Shit. It was *my* idea to come up here for a visit. I wouldn't talk to anybody dumb as me."

All the file cabinets and radios in the TOC bunker had dusty, beer-can-shaped thermal grenades set on top of them. They were crude but effective devices for destroying files. Once they started to burn, there was no way to put them out, and they would smoke and bubble through metal and classified documents until they reached the earth.

A burst of fire, then another exploded at the top of the stairs.

"Look out," Quinn yelled. "Grenade."

Hanson heard it bumping down the stairs. It fell into the grenade sump and went off, shaking dust from the beams and walls.

He got on the radio to the 3rd Mech, which was waiting just down the road for word that the camp was secure.

"Green Eagle, Green Eagle," he called. "This is Strange Names, over."

"Go ahead, Strange Names."

"Ah, roger . . ." Another burst of fire from the top of the stairs interrupted him.

"Let's get persuasive," Quinn said. "Shit's getting heavy."

"Enemy units have fallen back," Hanson continued. "The camp itself is secure, but we need some assistance to help us firm up the perimeter, over."

"Strange Names, this is Green Eagle. I copy your transmission that the camp is secure. I still hear a large volume of automatic weapons fire your location. What is your situation? Over."

"I say again, the camp is secure. There is still some contact beyond the wire south of camp. We need assistance in holding the perimeter until dawn, over."

"I copy the camp is secure. What are your initials, over."

"Initials are Charlie Kilo Hotel, over."

"Copy Charlie Kilo Hotel. We're coming in."

"We better keep our asses down here," Dawson said. "Those people are gonna be shooting anything that moves when they come in."

"I gotta get Silver," Quinn said, turning to the tunnel exit.

"Let's go," Hanson said, then to Dawson, "Can you handle the commo by yourself?"

"I got it. Go get Silver, but watch your ass," Dawson said, sliding the tracked steel door shut on the main entrance. "Let me know on the radio when you're coming back down. I'm gonna start blowing claymores in that stairway. Don't want those people out there to try a shaped-charge on this door."

As Hanson and Quinn climbed out of the tunnel behind the TOC bunker, they heard the rumble and whine of the 3rd Mech tanks moving toward the camp. They moved toward the teamhouse, crouching and freezing in the shadows, sprinting, then stopping again to listen to the squeaking tracks and the crash of the outer perimeter gate as it was flattened, engines straining against the wire.

When they kicked in the door of the teamhouse, the air inside was heavy with the smell of Vietnamese, sweat and fish sauce and wood smoke. But they were gone. Silver was lying on his back in the kitchen, where Quinn had left him with Grieson. His throat was cut clear to the spine, his own dark blood an inch deep around him, already drawing flies.

The coaxial heavy machine gun on one of the tanks in the wire was pounding.

"Grieson," Quinn said. "He left him alone."

Then, to Silver, "I'm sorry, man." He turned to Hanson. "I had to leave him," he said. "The Quad-fifty is my responsibility. They were in the wire . . ." He spun and went out the door, Hanson after him.

Tanks were coming through the wire on-line, 3rd Mech infantry behind them, and Quinn headed for Grieson's bunker. A red fan of tracers from the closest tank swept past them, followed by poorly aimed M-16 fire. Quinn stopped, took a white phosphorus grenade from his web gear, and threw it at the tank. It made a metallic *clang* against the body of the M-60 tank as it bounced off, then exploded in a fountain of silver-white bits of phosphorus and dense smoke that hid Hanson and Quinn as they ran on. Hanson threw his own WP grenade and they ran on to find Grieson's bunker empty.

They heard the sound of a shotgun from the radio relay unit, the green mobile home, and they ran there and rushed the door.

The relay unit had its own power source and glowed green inside from the oscilloscope screens. It stank of gunpowder inside and burned-out wiring. Grieson was standing with the shotgun at his side, his pants ripped, his legs bloody. Hose lay on the floor dead, gunned to pieces, shreds of Grieson's pants in his jaws. The single-sideband radio barked and warbled. Quinn killed Grieson with two short bursts from his Swedish K.

At dawn it was like the morning after a bad fire, everything burned and sodden, the time when survivors sort through the debris for whatever might be left. Outside the wire, dead Montagnards hung on ropes from tree branches. White flare parachutes draped their bodies, and warnings were written on the chutes in Vietnamese promising death to anyone who helped the Americans.

They found the captain and two Yards in the mud at the bottom of a trench, riddled with AK rounds. One of the Yards was Rau's son, the kid who had gone on his first operation the day Hanson had, with Lieutenant Andre. He'd turned into a good soldier.

They carried Silver's body to the ammo shed, one at each end, pulling against each other so his back wouldn't sag in the mud. They covered him with a poncho, very carefully, so the flies couldn't get to him. Quinn tucked the poncho under his feet as if he were tucking a child into bed.

A pile of North Vietnamese bodies, a busload, was heaped in front of the teamhouse, arms and legs tangled, some of the limbs already stiff and sticking out from the pile. As Hanson watched, a Montagnard dragged another body to the pile, dumped it, kicked it in the face, then walked off.

"Come and take a look at something," Quinn said to Hanson, and they walked around the teamhouse and past the TOC bunker.

"Every one of them," Quinn said. "They got every one of those sorry fuckers."

All five radio technicians were sprawled in the mud, spread out in a line not more than five meters apart, without weapons or boots. It was clear that they had all run out of their bunker in panic, barefoot and without weapons, with no idea of where they were going, and Charlie had shot them down one by one.

Hanson found the one who had played the dulcimer. No boots, no weapon, no shirt, his pallid skin torn by ugly purple holes. He'd fallen face-first into the mud, and it was packed into his nose and mouth. "Aw, man," Hanson said, looking down at him.

Two olive drab tanks were parked in front of the TOC. They had the green triangle of the 3rd Mech on their sides and smelled of electricity and mo-gas. One of them made a low grinding moan and the sullen gun turret swung the main gun in a short arc, stopped with a click, then swung back to the original position like an animal interrupted for a moment in the midst of feeding.

Naked sappers hung in the perimeter wire like dead fish. One of the tankers had put a cigarette in the mouth of one of them and had his arm around the body. Another tanker was taking his picture with an Instamatic camera.

Quang Tri

The scrawny, dung-stained chicken squawked and shook off dust as Mr. Minh drove the long needle into its neck, then went limp as the needle severed the spinal cord. Mr. Minh split the breast, pulled the ribs open, and watched the beating heart, the blood pumping into earth-colored organs. Like everything, the chicken was part of the system of things, a model of the workings of the universe in which patterns could be seen, like the needle of a seismograph sketching a shudder deep within the earth, or a barometer moving with the first inhalation of an ocean-borne storm.

He lightly touched the heart and liver, slipped two fingers into the intestines, feeling the warmth and subtle movement of the blood. It was not magic, just knowing how to read the signs, the way sailors can look at the sky at dusk, smell the air, and tell what kind of day will follow.

All life moves with the breathing of the universe, all the way to the end of life and back to the dream time when the world was first imagined.

Now the women were weaving gunships and Phantom jets into their tapestries where birds and tigers used to be, tapestries that traditionally told of the past, present, and future of the tribe. Crops were dying in the ground, and many of the Rhade children were stillborn.

Mr. Minh pulled a blade of grass from the ground, breathed on it, and the chicken's heart hesitated, quivered, and stopped dead.

A gray dawn rose with the sound of artillery.

CONFIDENTIAL

021502 BS 987602 Sensor indicated movement in area. Engaged W/50 rounds 175 artillery. Movement

*ceased. A/4-21 checked area at first light, found one
NVA uniform, one pair of US fatigue pants, and some
human internal organs lying on the ground. The
uniform and pants were evacuated to HQ Intelligence.*

*Security classification to be downgraded at seven-
year intervals.*

CONFIDENTIAL

*From the daily intelligence bulletin of the 3rd Infan-
try Brigade (Mechanized)*

At 8 A.M. the thirty officers in the air-conditioned briefing
room talked and laughed like students before the beginning of
class. The room was long and narrow, like a small movie theater, with a raised stage at one end. A podium stood at the right
side of the stage, and the wall at the back of the stage was
partly covered by a large window shade with the word SECRET
painted across its face.

The walls were paneled with shellacked plywood, and
plaques hung along the walls, bearing the crests of the sub-
units in the brigade, cartoonlike paintings of dangerous animals—tigers, dragons, coiled snakes—and clumsy Latin
phrases that declared such things as "Never Falter," and "All
The Way."

Two strange totems flanked the stage. The one on the left
looked like a brass cigarette urn, the kind you see in hotels,
filled with sand. It was a 175-millimeter artillery shell, en-
graved with the words "50,000th round fired by the 1st Artillery, 3rd Infantry Brigade (Mech)." The shell gleamed in the
light from the stage. A thirty-two-year-old staff sergeant polished it twice a day.

The totem on the right appeared to be a giant green car-
rot, two feet long, with green plastic leaves sprouting from its
base. It was a sensor that could pick up vibrations in the
ground. Dropped from a helicopter, it stuck into the ground
like a fat dart and gave off radio signals if anything moved

nearby. Quang Tri fire base would then bracket the area with artillery fire and send out a unit to sweep the area. They rarely found anything but craters and sometimes pieces of the sensor. The sensors, however, had a reputation for being effective. This was because whenever they indicated movement in an area and artillery was fired, the indications of movement ceased. No one ever mentioned that often this was because the sensor had been destroyed by the artillery fire. The fact that there were no bodies found after the fire mission would be explained by the enemy's practice of removing any bodies to frustrate American body counts. The 3rd Mech got around that by estimating how many were *probably* killed. It was very scientifically done with mathematical tables and flowcharts.

A lieutenant at the stage door gave a signal, and the talking and laughing stopped. A moment later the lieutenant announced, "Gentlemen, the commanding general."

General Frederic Hart entered the room. He had command presence, the kind of charisma that some movie stars and politicians have. He was a handsome man with silver-gray hair who could have been cast in a movie as a general. He looked over the officers who had snapped to attention as he entered the room, then nodded his head, smiled slightly, and said, "Good morning, gentlemen. Please take your seats."

As the general sat down in his leather chair in the center of the front row, the rest of the room *sat*, just half a beat behind him, hitting their chairs in unison.

"Good morning, sir," Major Long began, standing behind the podium, while his assistant, Staff Sergeant Martin, stood at attention with a pointer that was tipped by a .50-caliber bullet.

"Good morning, Major," the general said. "Gentlemen," he said, turning his head slightly to indicate the room full of officers behind him, "let's begin."

Sergeant Martin raised the "Secret" map cover and pulled down the first of the transparent overlays. As the daily briefing continued, he pulled down others. One overlay illustrated enemy positions, another showed friendly positions, others portrayed "incidents" and "contacts." The symbols, flags, boxes, and arrows were drawn in fluorescent grease pencil and glowed beneath an ultraviolet light. The light gave a slight purple tint to Major Long's short blond hair, like a matron's blue rinse.

The major and Sergeant Martin had choreographed and rehearsed their briefing in the dark hours of early morning. Their presentations were always sharp, military performances. Each time the major indicated a location, saying, *"Sir,* at this location, *sir . . ."* Sergeant Martin would slap the pointer against the correct plastic overlay without appearing to look, making an audible *snap* with the pointer. They moved from situation to prediction, cataloging data and options with the rhythm and timing of TV weathermen.

Meanwhile the rest of the officers listened—listened aggressively, eyes narrowed, jaws thrust forward, as though the major knew what he was talking about, as though it was the real goddamn thing, as though it mattered. All the while they mentally rehearsed difficult questions and satisfactory answers for the general, should he call on them.

"Up there in the northeast," the general said. "Captain Spike's AO. What's the situation there?"

"Sir. The Bang Son Delta region reports very little verifiable enemy activity for the past two weeks. The 242-D Sapper Battalion appears to have relocated to the south."

"Paul," the general said, looking at the map.

"Yes sir," Captain Spike said, standing up from one of the folding chairs behind the general.

"Do you have anything to add to that?"

"No sir. It's been quiet lately. We haven't been mortared in ten days. I think we've got the AO under control."

"It's been my experience," the general said, "that when the enemy stops harassing you, it means that they're comfortable with your presence. That you're not hurting them. If I were in command up there, I'd question whether my patrolling was aggressive enough."

"Yes sir."

A smile appeared in the general's eyes. You have to keep these new captains on their toes, he thought. Had the camp *been* mortared, the general would have asked why Captain Spike's patrols could not prevent it.

"Major Long," the general said, "that battalion up there by the DMZ, the Three Eighteenth . . ."

"Yes sir."

Snap.

"Now, Bill, is that the Three Eighteenth, or is it the People's Red Moon Batallion, as you had it identified last week? What kind of unit is it? What's its mission? What are its organic weapons? What is its *name?*"

"Sir, we don't know for certain at this time, sir. The only information we have comes from radio intercepts. It may be a combined unit, a different unit entirely, or the unit may simply have changed its nominal designation."

"Are they the unit that ambushed our people on the fourteenth?"

"We don't know yet, sir."

"Let's find out, Major."

"Yes sir," the major said. For the first time he was aware of a faint chirping in the air-conditioner. He made a mental note to have it fixed.

General Hart sat at his desk looking out the window of his trailer. A silver cargo plane was taking off in the distance and the heat made it look as if it was warped, bent in the middle.

One of the pictures on his desk was of his daughter at her high school graduation. She was at an expensive eastern college now, and refused to answer his letters. It must be tough, he thought, to be the daughter of a general these days. He recalled a night, years before, when he'd tucked her into bed, then gone back downstairs to work on some sort of feasibility study. He'd almost gone back up to kiss her good night, hesitated at the bottom of the stairs, then decided against it, glad that no one would know how indecisive he had been over such a foolish thing. He wished now that he'd gone back and kissed her. Not that it would have made any difference in how she felt about him now. He just wished that he'd done it.

He looked out the window at the rows of tanks and APCs and slowly shook his head. This was no war for tanks. The terrain was all wrong. They bogged down in the Delta, and in the rolling hills of the highlands the unmuffled roar of the twin diesels gave the enemy a half-hour's warning before they arrived. A heavy machine gun bullet could pierce their light armor and ricochet through the tank like a red-hot hornet.

So all the troops rode on top of the tanks except the driver, who knew that if they hit a mine he would, at the very least, lose his legs. He sat with his shoulders and head outside the hatch, his legs and groin tingling each time they went up a new trail. The tanks heaved on their suspension like powerboats in rough water, chasing men in sandals made out of Goodyear truck tires that left tread marks in the mud, little men carrying plastic bags of rice and grenades made out of mackerel cans. Chasing them with million-dollar Sheridan tanks that fired 150-millimeter guns aimed by electronic sights that rarely worked because of their complexity, the humidity, and the jarring recoil of the big gun. One of the shells weighed as much as a Vietcong soldier.

The tanks and APCs were worse than useless in the fluid jungle war, but if the military had equipment, they used it, and by its use justified the production of more. It was good for the economy. Congressmen wanted to maintain and increase jobs in their districts so they would be reelected, and the Pentagon wanted to keep the goodwill of Congress so they'd pass military appropriations bills. And if a brigadier general like Frederic Hart wanted a second star, he'd damn well better use the equipment and use it with enthusiasm.

And it all came down to four high-school kids in a million-dollar tank chasing a couple of kids in black pajamas. In the past year the 3rd Mech had gotten more high school dropouts than ever before. Anybody with any brains was hiding out in college or the National Guard. They were getting recruits who were illiterate criminals and drug addicts who wouldn't follow orders. The company grade officers weren't much better. Some of the new OCS second lieutenants didn't have the leadership to manage a 7-Eleven store, much less a combat unit.

The general reached over and buzzed for his aide, Ed Freeman.

Captain Freeman was an athletic officer, an "outstanding individual," as they say in the military. He had Airborne and Ranger patches on his fatigues, and a West Point ring on his hand. He was on his second tour in Vietnam. As a lieutenant, he had been an adviser to a Vietnamese Ranger unit. After his second purple heart, he had been reassigned as the general's aide.

"Sit down, Ed," the general said. "What did you think of the briefing?"

The captain glanced out the window, then said, "We don't have any idea who that unit is up there, that 'Red Moon' Battalion. We can drop a thousand of those electronic carrots and they won't tell us. All they have to do is change their name and we're at square one again."

"You know, Ed," the general said, "you've got probably two more wars ahead of you. I hope that they're better than this one. This is the last one I'm going to have, I'm afraid.

"I was talking to General Baker down in Saigon—we were plebes together at the Point—and he told me that we'd better get something moving up here in I-Corps if I want a second star. Something big that gets in the papers, that makes it look like we're finally on to a winning strategy. That means the whole nine yards—sensors, artillery, tanks, APCs, something we can call an 'armored assault force.' That sounds good. Sounds like WWII. Like we're winning.

"If I don't get that second star I can plan on spending the rest of my career somewhere in North Dakota or Oklahoma."

The general opened a drawer of his desk and pulled out a torn and stained khaki shirt. It had a red circular patch on the shoulder.

The general held up the shirt and tapped the red patch with his finger. "I want this Red Moon outfit," he said. "It's been causing us problems and, Ed, it's a name people remember. A nice name. Romantic. *Mem*orable. I want people to remember that I destroyed the Red Moon Battalion," he said, putting the fatigue shirt away.

"Ed, I want to defoliate the shit out of their area of operations, then move some big units in. Fast. And I want it kept quiet until we are on the damn *ground* up there. The Vietnamese barbers in camp know about our operations before the company commanders do.

"There's nobody working in that area except some Special

Forces recon unit farting around. I'm not going to jeopardize an operation this size by clearing it all the way through channels so some flaky Green Beret outfit gets the word. I don't like those people anyway, Ed. That kind of so-called elite unit has no place in the Army. It's a lot of wasted talent that ought to be spread around. But the worst thing is that they start thinking that they're a law unto themselves. They think they can do anything they want.

"But you've heard my opinion on that before, haven't you?" he said, laughing.

"Get to work on it, Ed. And keep it quiet."

After Freeman left, the general looked up at a photograph on the wall. It showed him as a second lieutenant standing in front of a large tent with three other men. Two of them were dead now, and the third was a major general. The picture was grainy, overexposed black and white, but the eyes seemed almost alive. The February light was weak, and they were all bundled up in the winter-issue gear that was never warm enough.

The general looked at the L-shaped scar on the back of his hand, then back at the photograph. The thing about Korea was that it had been so deceptive, the terrain. You could never predict what the terrain was going to be like up ahead by what came before. And by the time they'd gotten good maps and warm clothing, it was over.

He remembered the staff sergeant who had died next to him early one freezing morning beside a steaming river they'd crossed in inflatable boats. He'd held the sergeant's hand with his unwounded one while he died, the two of them discussing his imminent death as though it were a poor business deal or a bad hand of poker.

Red Moon
Battalion

The day before there had been a fierce rain, a two-hour cloudburst, the kind of storm that would stop interstate traffic back in Kansas and set off the tornado sirens. It was impossible to see or hear anything out in it, difficult even to breathe. It was a freak rain for I-Corps. The monsoon season was weeks away, and the Asian sun came back out hotter than ever, making the grass and red clay steam.

"The earth is sweating," Mr. Minh said. "The storm was hard work for him."

And then the termites appeared, flying termites with bodies like baroque pearls and wings like flower petals. Millions of them swarmed out of their burrows in the baked red clay that the rain had frosted with a layer of mud. They rode the steaming air like pollen or blowing snow, the silver-blue wings sticking to Hanson's face and forearms and chest. And then they died. The mud glittered with their twitching bodies.

Somehow they had gotten through the screened windows of the teamhouse, and at supper Hanson and Quinn swept them off the table, brushed them away like an unexpected dusting of snow at a picnic. The powder from their wings made a white paste on the back of Hanson's hand.

Mr. Minh had never seen such a thing happen before, and he was worried. Clearly, it was a powerful omen.

Hanson stepped from the shade of the teamhouse and walked to the command bunker, the TOC, a concrete slab with only a hooded doorway showing above the ground. He stopped on the stairs and waited for his eyes to adjust to the shade. He smelled creosote, mildew, wet canvas, and the delicate scent of electricity. Three pairs of claymore mines were mounted along the sides of the timbered stairwell, facing him like sets of stereo speakers.

Down in the bunker the banks of radios hummed and warbled as he rolled an office swivel chair out from the long plywood desk and up to the wall covered with the intel map. The single sideband receiver was on, making the strange hollow barking sounds that Hanson called space dogs, imagining them adrift in some fourth dimension of radio waves. A sawed-off shotgun stood propped in the corner. A Thompson submachine gun, bandoliers of ammunition and satchels bulging with grenades hung from nails on the rough-hewn teak walls.

He heard Sergeant Major on the stairs behind him, favoring one leg slightly. Sergeant Major had come up to the camp after it was overrun to try to get it back into operational shape.

"What do you see there, young sergeant?" he asked from the stairs.

"I think the Three Eighteenth up there, the Red Moon Battalion or whatever they're calling themselves this month—the Jane Fonda Liberation Unit—it's cranking up for something." He flipped an overlay down on the map, then another, and rolled the chair back for perspective. The overlays showed a pattern of secret radio intercepts that radiated from a central area near the DMZ, a good indication of enemy buildup. "Look at that," he said. "Maybe we could put in there, a couple klicks west of them, inside the border there, move toward them from their side of the border . . ."

"You and Quinn and Mr. Minh and a couple of Mr. Minh's boys, right?"

"Good idea," Hanson said, grinning. "You and me think a lot alike. I'd like to take Troc and one other guy. Troc's been feeling bad about Rau's son getting killed."

"Are you going to win this war all by yourself, then?" Sergeant Major asked.

Hanson swung around in the chair, laughing. "Don't tell anybody, but I don't think we're gonna win. It's just that I've grown to love the work."

Sergeant Major smiled. "Sketch out an operations plan. I'll see what I can do."

"Why," Hanson asked him, "do we bother to sanitize these

operations? They know we're crossing the border, and we know that they know, so why bother with all this sterile equipment? Everybody knows what's going on. It's in the *news*papers."

"It's sort of like fooling around with another guy's wife," Sergeant Major said in mock seriousness. "Now, neither of you wants to fight over her. She's been whoring around on both of you just like these little pissant countries over here. But he knows that everybody else has been hearing the rumors, so he's got to confront you to save face. So he asks you if you've been fucking his wife and you tell him no. You both know that it's a lie, but it takes care of the situation. He's just got to say something, like, 'I'd better not hear that you *are*,' then both of you can go back to doing more important things. Besides," he said with a smile, "we love those black helicopters and all that spook stuff."

After Sergeant Major left, Hanson studied the map, planning where to fly in and where to walk out, imagining what the terrain would look like from the air. He saw himself moving across the surface of the map itself, over the hills whose contour lines looked like huge fingerprints, around the white spaces of rice paddy, crossing black grid lines and elevation numbers, past the clusters of tiny black squares that were deserted and destroyed villages, and down the loose blue river lines.

He swung his legs up onto the desk, stripped a piece of red clay from between the worn black boot tread, rolled it into a ball between his thumb and forefinger, and looked back at the map. He aimed like a dart player and lobbed the mud at the map. It stuck to the plastic just across the border, north of the red highway that slipped through the fibrous contour lines like a blood vessel through a bundle of nerves.

Hanson could imagine himself on the hillsides, feel the ground underfoot, smell the heat and dust, gun oil and grass and his own sweat. He could feel his breath in his chest and throat as he moved down the slope toward a stream, stopping every few yards to listen for anything that seemed wrong, turning his head so the breeze didn't slip sound past him, moving into it at an angle so it would bring the sounds to him, smelling the wind like a man listening for faint music.

He was calm and happy sitting alone in the command bunker with the map of the AO, the rectangular section of the earth that was all his, whose contours were as familiar to him as the lines on his palm and fingers and knuckles. He studied his hand and imagined himself leading a patrol across it.

Outside the bunker the two-cycle generator roared and paused like a stricken pulse. Hanson felt as though he were inside the brain of some larger organism. The generators were its heart and lungs, the map a diagram of its arteries and organs, and the radios its eyes and ears. Hanson himself had become the consciousness that directed it.

The two troop-carrying helicopters were flat black and had no markings. They throbbed like shadows on the linked-steel airstrip, the rotors turning lazily with a sound like bone hitting muscle—*whop-whop-whop*—the sound of a smiling, patient, professional interrogator matter-of-factly hitting a suspect with a sap.

The door gunner, his face hidden behind his tinted helmet shield, was slouched in the exposed, wall-locker-shaped position behind his gun. When the engine whistled, wailed, and began to rev, he shook his arms and head like a runner in the blocks, loosening up as he waited for the starter's gun.

Hanson looked over his shoulder. Quinn's back filled most of the open door, Troc looking like a child next to him. Hanson smiled at Mr. Minh and at Krang, another of Mr. Minh's nephews, sitting on either side of him. He began to laugh as the chopper throbbed beneath the rotor blades, then lifted a few feet off the ground, shifting and sideslipping as it hovered. It was like a carnival ride, the Tilt-a-Whirl or the Octopus, where you paid your quarter and the tattooed carnie with bad teeth and dilated pupils locked you in and shifted the car a few feet up, where it rocked above the tents and booths of the midway and you began to wish you had stayed on the ground.

Reaching between his feet, the door gunner pulled a brass belt of ammo to the breech of his swivel-mounted machine gun, flipped the stamped steel breech cover up, then slammed it down over the first rounds in the belt. With his right hand, palm up, he pulled the cocking handle toward him and let it slam back, like a clerk pumping the handle of a massive credit card printer.

The helicopter was as dented and scraped as a dump truck. The gunner had bolted a beer can to the breech of the gun so the ammunition would feed smoothly over the curve of the can, the kind of homely, matter-of-fact modification that made the war seem as normal and civilized as suicide, an occupation where men dress up in funny clothes and kill each other with machines.

Off to the side of the airstrip, two Cobra gunships, stream-lined and wasplike, seemed impatient to take off, their skids bumping and sucking in the mud.

The two troop-carrying slicks began to move sluggishly forward, nose down, seemed to hesitate, then banked suddenly toward the hills. Hanson caught a glimpse of Sergeant Major smiling behind his sunglasses, giving him the thumbs-up. Then he and the airstrip became a blur as the chopper banked away and gained speed, and the twin points of silver light from Sergeant Major's sunglasses vanished. In the mountains to the east Hanson could see a waterfall full of rainbows. The pounding of machine guns startled him as the door gunners test fired their weapons, gun oil burning off the barrels as a blue and yellow nimbus. Below and behind them, the Cobras skimmed down the strip, tails up like poised stingers. They rose quickly, easily overtaking the slicks, and positioned themselves on their flanks.

The sun was low in the west. The slicks and Cobras, the clouds and sky, the trees and streams and blinking rice paddies below moved against each other like parts of a solar system, wheels within wheels, and Hanson felt his muscles and eyes working to move it all together as if he were the center of the universe. A patchwork of rice paddies, like panes of variously shaded green glass, blinked and flickered below.

Hanson's legs hung out over the side of the slick, blown back and up by the eighty-knot wind, held at an angle by the slipstream. The slick banked to the right, then leveled off and tipped slightly back. Centrifugal force, gravity, pure physics moved Hanson in response to it as he looked out and down at the jungle, his trouser legs flapping, cold now at altitude.

The Cobras banked away as the slicks began to descend across the border, the sun sinking with them. It was almost twilight. The pilot pointed down as they passed over their ultimate destination, and Hanson recognized a saddle-shaped hill and a stream from the map in the command bunker. They were going through the looking-glass of the map.

The two slicks touched down, then rose as they moved west, like flies too nervous to settle, camouflaging their true destinations with simulated landings. It was almost dark as they headed back east to the saddle-shaped hill, and Hanson tightened his hold on the scarred aluminum lip of the door. He braced one foot on the landing skid, then noticed an exposed bolt on the floor and shifted his hips so he would not tear his fatigues when he slipped away.

The slick went in with its nose slightly up, like a horse reined in. The other troop carrier, the empty one, passed above them to mask the sound of their descent. The dull red of its exhaust lapped through the rotor blades of Hanson's ship, showing the blowing elephant grass in flickering bars of red and black where it whipped and broke like waves. Once over the edge, there was no turning back, and little chance of rescue before dawn. No one knew what was down there. There were no options, no past or future to consider, only that instant, that euphoria of adrenaline and fear, as he slid off into the stroboscopic bars of red and black, the prop blast like a great wind at his back.

He hit the ground off balance, on his heels, the impact snapping his head back, his heavy pack almost pulling him over. He regained his balance and looked at the departing choppers, their blue-red exhausts bobbing and growing smaller. He and Quinn chose a compass course away from the LZ and followed it for half an hour. When they came upon a grove of bamboo and thornbushes, they gingerly worked their way inside to wait until dawn.

Hanson lay on his back, looking up through thornbushes at the scudding clouds, and smiled in the dark. He was eight thousand miles from home in the middle of a thorn patch, illegally across the border, surrounded by the enemy, and he was happy. There was fear, of course, but he was as happy as he could imagine ever being. All he had to worry about was staying alive. If he failed, he'd be dead, and his troubles would be over. At the very most, he had to plan only three days ahead.

The enemy soldiers unloading the trucks were wearing khaki uniforms and jungle hats. Hanson noticed that as in any army, individuals and small groups wandered off in an attempt to avoid work details. He looked down on them most of the day through binoculars he had braced on a log, well hidden above them in high grass, and he became familiar with individual soldiers and gave them names.

The map on the ground in front of Hanson was a pattern of pale green ovals shading off into brown as the elevation contour lines grew closer together, mountains piling up higher and steeper in the west. He inked in a blue dot on one of the slopes, marking the truck park below, then placed a plastic protractor on the map and drew a blue line from his position to the dot. He drew another blue line down the length of the valley. That was the way the air strike would come in.

At dusk he set up the bombing beacon, assembling the olive drab radio components like pieces of a puzzle.

"How does the damn thing work?" Quinn asked him. "You need at least two known points for a heading. How do they lock in on just one?"

Hanson shrugged. "I just push the right buttons, the pilot feeds the information into the little black box in the airplane he's driving, and he locks on. Radio signals? Satellites? Magic!"

He flipped a toggle switch and a low humming grew to a whine that made him think of insects and dentist's drills, the electricity building a charge. The dials began to glow. Frequency numbers popped up and disappeared behind their thick little windows as he clicked the dials around.

"All set," he said, standing up. "When the plane locks on, this little light here starts to blink. As long as it keeps blinking, we know he's on course."

"Gentlemen," Hanson said, imitating an Army instructor, "if you can get yourselfs a can of Coca-Cola outta the machine in front of the 7-Eleven store, you are qualified to operate the *bombing*"—he spun and jabbed his finger at the radio—*"beacon!* You are limited in its use and application only by your imagination. This equipment is the finest in the world."

Behind them they could hear the clicking sound made by Mr. Minh as he sorted through the contents of his *katha*, trying to work out the omens as darkness settled into the mountains.

"Strange Address, Strange Address, this is Ringneck three eight, over . . ."

The words came from the radio speaker, rasping like a file on sheet metal. Not a human voice. The voice of one machine talking to another.

"Ringneck three eight," Hanson said, "this *is* that Strange Address, how do you copy, over."

"Lima Charles, Lima Charles, how me?"

"Comin' in good, over."

"Uh, rodge. What have you people got for us tonight?"

"People and trucks," Hanson said. "You prepared to copy?"

"Roger. Send it."

Hanson sent the data and the voice replied, "Roger. Good copy. I read back for possible correction," and he repeated the strings of numbers and letters like an algebraic chant.

"Wait one," the radio said, "while I do my thing here."

And then they saw him, a blinking red and green light high over to the northwest, floating slowly toward them, bobbing slightly in the dark sky.

The small red light on the beacon began to blink.

"Strange Address, this is Ringneck three eight. Am locked on and beginning my run. Will give you 'mark' at eight miles and five miles. Give me a 'go' or 'no go' on my mark, over . . ."

"Strange Address rogers that."

"Mark."

"Go."

The red light blinked insistently, like an alarm on the radio beacon.

Hanson could hear Ringneck three eight, the faraway roar seeming to have nothing to do with the delicate lights floating in the sky. In the cool early fog of evening, he could smell the soil, centuries of mulch, the elephant grass, the slightly metallic smell of thornbushes.

The anxious little light on the bombing beacon was as irritating as a facial tic.

"Mark."

"Go."

Hanson watched the lights and imagined the pilot and the radar intercept officer, behind and just above him, in the green instrument light of the cockpit, breathing raw bottled oxygen through rubber tubing.

"Bombs gone . . ."

A rippling line of orange flashes bubbled and burst along the base of the ridgeline, fading out but consuming themselves slowly, the dull thumps reaching Hanson only after the hillside had gone dark again. The concussions stuttered through the air, puffing against his cheeks, an instant later moving up from the earth, gently patting at the soles of his feet.

"Strange Address, this is three eight. All ordnance expended. Good coverage on that ridgeline. Some crispy critters down there. Hey, we enjoyed it. Come on down and see us next time you're at our place. We'll buy the first round, over."

"Roger that, Ringneck. Good show. Thank you much."

"Our pleasure. You all step careful down there."

The Phantom jet passed over them on the way out, a low shadow against the sky, a concentrated piece of the night trailing flame and seeming to suck the air out of their lungs. After it had passed, there were secondary explosions in the valley, and flames sprang up. By the light of the flames Hanson could see soldiers running in and out of the dark. The Red Moon Battalion.

They couldn't know it, it hadn't gone through channels, but on a morning not long before, two silver C-123s had leveled off nearby, flying low, one to the left and slightly behind the other. Giant crop dusters. Their shadows had flashed, onetwo, across the jungle floor. And then, silently, thin silver trails of Agent Orange appeared behind the planes, spinning out like spiderweb. They seemed to hang in the air for a moment, then turned to mist.

In the days that followed the jungle below began to snap and shatter and crack, branches swelling and tearing free, falling end-for-end onto the dying undergrowth and splintering tree trunks. It was growth gone out of control, like a factory or an assembly line speeded up beyond any recall. Triple canopy jungle that had taken centuries to grow broke and fell to pieces as though caught in a slow forest fire without flame. The cells of the trees and plants grew until they ruptured and died, like the inner cities of America, the spirit-killing suburbs, the urban freeways and commuter air corridors, as if America's passion for growth had been concentrated into the oily mist that made the jungle swell like a cancer, burst, and die.

In the midst of it, tiny barking deer ran in confusion and panic. One of the last tigers coughed, bellied down into the dying grass, and slunk off. Gray jungle rats began gnawing their own flanks and eating their young. And down in the centuries-old loam of the jungle floor, centipedes stiffened, arched, and stung themselves to death.

"You think we're across the border yet?" Hanson whispered.

"Beats the dogshit outta me," Quinn said. "I don't see no broken yellow line that says 'Border.' "

"I think we came this way before," Hanson said. "Didn't we?"

"Here," he said, pointing at the map. "It's good cover all the way across this stream, and by then we're less than a klick from the border. Remember? Then there's this hill here."

"Yeah, I remember. That was the time . . ."

They heard a single shot, back from the direction they'd come from.

"Shit."

"Trail watcher," Quinn said.

"Do you think they know we're here, or are they just guessing?"

"I don't know, little buddy, but my military mind tells me we better beat feet outta here and across that stream. Fast. They're gonna be pissed off about last night."

They checked the map again and moved on to the border crossing area they had used before and were familiar with.

"What the fuck . . . Over," Quinn said.

"This is it," Hanson said. "We're there. There's the hill. There's the stream."

"Where the fuck is everything else?" Quinn said.

It was as though some kind of chemical forest fire had swept through, up and down the stream as far as they could see. Decayed foliage drifted down like ash. Leaves and brush were black and slimy with decomposition. Black-orange dust rose in puffs with each step, stuck to their sweaty skin, and got into their eyes, ears, and noses. Nothing seemed to be alive in the area. The only sounds were their footsteps, their labored breathing, and the creak of their web gear. It was like walking through a graveyard or ground zero. The black-orange dust hung in the sunlight around them, malevolent, with a smell of kerosene.

"Somebody defoliated the border," Hanson said, "and forgot to mention it to us."

Mr. Minh was horrified. He had seen the tiger's tracks. "This is very bad," he said. "The tiger has left his home. It is all killing itself. There is no time to go around."

The stream reached up to their armpits in spots. It was sluggish and smelled like kerosene, choked with rotting leaves and dead fish. The bloated body of a small monkey drifted past, its eyes eaten away. Something moved against Hanson's foot beneath the water and he jerked his foot away, almost losing his balance and falling into the stinking stream.

They crawled into a peninsula of brush and bamboo to wait for dusk before sprinting across the dead jungle to the first of the foothills where they could wait out the night. Hanson pulled leeches off his stomach and ankles, soaked them with insect repellent, and set them on fire. As they swayed and twitched in the saffron flame, he thought about the pictures of the monks in Saigon who had doused themselves in gasoline and set fire to themselves for peace.

They moved out at dusk, feeling exposed and foolish, but there was no other way to go. They had barely begun when they saw them, eight soldiers coming over the hill to their left. Then there was another group of six or eight, and another, all wearing fatigues and packs and helmets, silhouetted against the orange sky. The only enemy soldiers who dressed that way were Main Force North Vietnamese Army troops.

"Oh shit," Hanson said, as though he had just remembered an important missed appointment. "Gotta be at least a company there," he said. "Look at those uniforms. That's hard-core NVA. They must have just slipped over the border. Bad luck. Bad fucking luck."

Quinn turned the radio frequency dials to contact the only fire base with guns big enough to reach them. He thrust the handset at Hanson and said, "Talk fast, little buddy. Those guys up there see us."

Hanson glanced up at the hills, then spoke into the handset. "Bright Names, this is Strange Address, over . . ."

"Address, this is Names, go . . ."

"Bright Names, this is Strange Address. I gotta have a fire mission fast. We got at least a company of Main Force NVA at coordinates . . ."

He looked down to where Quinn was pointing at the map. "Coordinates Yankee Delta five seven niner, two three three. Go ahead and shoot it. We don't have time for . . ." Dust began to kick up from the ground around them. An explosion threw dirt and stones and hissing bits of steel from an M-79 grenade launcher. They were *American* weapons, M-16s and M-60 machine guns, the brass-jacketed rounds snapping overhead, each making its own little *crack* of a sonic boom as it passed. Krang ran toward the firing, waving his arms, and Quinn yelled at him to get down, but a burst of small-arms fire caught him full in the chest, throwing him onto his back, dead.

"Bright Names," Hanson said, speaking slowly and distinctly into the handset, "it is friendlies. We are being fired on by an American unit."

The rounds began coming in lower, kicking up orange dust that shimmered and stank of kerosene, the Americans getting their range. Hanson, on his stomach, unconsciously shifted from side to side as if he could burrow into the dirt. He winced, imagining one of the bullets hitting him in the top of the head, then forced himself to stop thinking of possibilities like that because it only invited them. He dug the fingers of his free hand into the dirt, the way a person grips the armrest of a dentist's chair during the drilling.

"Strange Address," the voice on the radio said, "that's a negative. There are no friendlies in your AO."

The black and orange flash of an M-79 shredded one of Troc's legs and tore at his side. He fell, then propped on his elbow, looking mournfully at the stump as it bled out until a burst of machine gun fire slapped him back.

"Sonofabitch," Hanson snarled into the radio handset, "it's fuckin' friendlies. Get on their push and tell 'em to stop firing. They're killing us."

"I say again, negative . . ."

A second voice, angry and full of authority, interrupted the first on the radio. "This is the Bright Names *One*. There are no friendlies in your AO. You *will* use no more profanity on this radio net. What are your initials? You are already in big trouble, soldier . . ."

Hanson laughed. He was dead for sure this time. God-*damn*, though, he thought, I just hope it doesn't hurt too bad.

"Shit," Hanson said, glancing at Quinn, pushing up off the ground, "let's *go*." There was a fold in the hill two hundred yards away that would shelter them until the Americans discovered their mistake.

As Hanson came up on his toes, like a runner in the starting blocks, he looked over Quinn's shoulder and saw Mr. Minh go down. He tried to get back up and the machine gun knocked him down again. Mr. Minh had told Hanson that when the soul leaves the body it becomes a bird and can see everything from the sky. His body quivered and jumped as another burst of fire raked it, smoke ooozing from the wounds the tracer rounds made.

Hanson took one step and was straightening up, striding into another, when the concussion from another M-79 round clubbed him on the side of the head, clapped his ears ringing and droning. His nose stung and his eyes watered with points of light. Quinn drove into him, bucking as he took hits from the machine gun, slamming him to the ground where tiny funnels of dirt and dead grass erupted around them.

He rolled out from beneath Quinn, the wind knocked out

of him, enraged by the concussion as if he'd been sucker-punched and jumped from behind. He turned and looked up at the hill where the fire was coming from, muzzle flashes blinking dirty yellow, saw the tiny red blips of tracer rounds grow to golf-ball size as they soared glowing past him.

"Goddamnit," he shouted, standing up again. "God*damn* it."

He was already dead, he thought, as he reached down and took hold of Quinn's fatigue shirt, stood him up, leaned into him, and lifted him onto his shoulders. "If they kill us, they kill us," he shouted, talking to Quinn over the pop and whine and hiss of small-arms fire. "Not a fuckin' thing we can do about that. But we're not gonna play the fool for 'em," he yelled, walking steadily through the tracers, pebbles and dirt stinging the backs of his legs. "Fuck 'em," he said. He stumbled and almost fell with Quinn's weight, got his balance and looked back at where the fire was coming from. "Fuck *you!*" he shouted.

"Something like this was bound to happen," he muttered to Quinn, "with those dumb fuckers. Gotta be the Third Mech up there. They can't read a motherfucking map. Shit," he said, trudging through the fire, shrugging Quinn more solidly onto his shoulders, moving as steadily and mechanically as he did when he shuffled the length of a C-130 to parachute out the open, roaring door.

An M-79 jarred them and something burned into his arm. "God*damn* it," he said. "Fuck your pissant little shrapnel."

"Fuck 'em, you know," he said to Quinn. "And the man says I'm in *big* trouble for saying 'shit' on the radio. There it is, 'big trouble.' Is this some kind of fucked-up war or what?"

The fire slackened, less accurate in the growing gloom as Hanson reached the fold in the hills, kneeled, and rolled Quinn onto the grass.

It took Quinn less than a minute to die. The color in his face faded layer by layer as regularly as a pulse until the face was dead except for the eyes that looked at Hanson, and then they were dead too. The skin seemed to settle around his eyes and cheekbones, its color fading under layers of gray like a photograph that has been overexposed in a developing tray.

He was alive and then he was dead so quickly, but it didn't seem quick to Hanson. It was like watching someone you love turn his back to you and walk away in long deliberate strides and knowing that nothing you do or say can make him stop and turn around, but thinking that there must be something if only you could think of it in time, and then it is too late because he is gone, because in all that long time you watched him walk away, you didn't do whatever it was you should have done, to say what it was he needed to hear so he could stop and come back.

It was almost dark, and Hanson was still alive behind a little peninsula of rock, crouching next to Quinn. "I'm sorry, man," he said, placing the palm of his hand on Quinn's chest and speaking softly into his ear. "I know you can still hear me. You're still in there." His arm stung just behind the elbow where the tiny piece of shrapnel had struck him. "I wish you could do this with me. They won't send a patrol down here before dawn. You know how they are. They're afraid to move around in the dark." Quinn's chest was still warm.

"Listen. *Listen*, I'll see you soon, or whatever the fuck happens, and Silver too." He was crying now. "I don't know. What the fuck do I know. *Believe* me that I'm gonna kick some ass. I wish you guys were here." He patted Quinn's chest lightly. "You've been great. You were just great.

"I'll see you soon," he said, lifting his hand. Quinn's blood on Hanson's fingernails was translucent, like thin nail polish. "I'd better borrow this," he said, taking the silenced Swedish K slung over Quinn's shoulder. "It's payback time."

It was some time later before he killed the first of them. Security around their night position was sloppy, as it usually was around American units. He cached the radio and extra equipment, and crawled up the hill toward the 3rd Mech, feeling for trip wires as he got closer. He passed several claymore mines and turned them around so they would fire into the Americans if they triggered them. He thought about the time Mr. Minh had taught him the VC trick.

A metallic *snap*, the sound of a grenade fuse or trip flare, froze him, then someone nearby said, "What you got?"

The *snap* of another can of soda being opened was followed by a voice that said, "Fuckin' orange pop. When we gonna get some Cokes? I'm *pissing* orange pop."

"Fuckin' CO don't give a shit about us," yet another voice added. "I ain't seen Coke *one* in weeks. CO don't care about nothing but fuckin' body count."

"There it is."

Hanson worked his way around them, stood up, and approached them from inside the perimeter, "Hey, what's happenin'," he said to them. "I fuckin' got turned around out here. Which way's the TOC?"

"You're turned around, all right. It's way the hell over that way."

"Right," Hanson said. "Hey, what's the skinny on those fuckers we shot up down there?"

"Platoon of VC. Twenty-five or thirty of 'em. Killed most of them. Where have you been?"

"I was out on a little recon patrol on the other side of the hill. Missed the whole thing."

"Hey, they fuck with us, they die."

"All right!"

"There it is."

Hanson walked toward the Tactical Operations Center, past APCs and tanks whose crews were listening to rock music and laughing, through pockets of marijuana smoke. A soldier stumbled backward into him, spun around, and demanded, "What the fuck's your problem?"

"No problem, your honor. Just looking for the TOC."

He moved on, toward the sound of the generators. When he found them, next to the TOC, the command center, he took a grenade from his web gear, taped the spoon down with electrical tape, and pulled the pin. He dropped the grenade in the generator gas tank and walked off. It would take the diesel fuel about half an hour to dissolve the adhesive on the tape, allowing the grenade to go off. He'd be ready by then.

He waited in the dark, just outside the perimeter. Four

perimeter guards were bunched together nearby, eating and talking.

"Naw, man, it's gonna be a Charger, a hemi-head Charger. I don't have no use for no Ford. When I get back to the world, first thing I'm gonna do—after I get drunk and laid, by a white woman—is buy a Charger. Dark green. Hey, I owe it to myself, right? That's what this whole fuckin' year is about. At least I'll have something worthwhile to show for it."

"Yeah," another voice said, "that McQueen flick back at Camp Carroll. The dude driving the Charger? Was that cool or what? The way he just snapped on his seatbelt and punched that big Hemi. You could tell he had a low impedence air cleaner on that baby. I don't believe McQueen could have caught him in that Mustang."

"I don't know. You put you that big Cobra V-eight in . . ."

The generator blew up with a quick double explosion, a sheet of burning gas illuminating the camp like lightning. Hanson cut the four guards down with the AK-47. The green tracer rounds from the Chinese weapon fluttered and bounced through the camp. Hanson changed clips as he sprinted for a gully fifty yards away, hearing the claymores he had reversed go off, sending their pattern of ball-bearings gnashing through the grass into the American position.

The whole perimeter opened fire in all directions, most of it too high to hit anything. A red fan of .50-caliber tracers slapped past Hanson, the pattern spreading, then silently winking out, point by point. Another grenade went off inside the perimeter, one that must have been dropped or bounced off a tree, and there was more shouting and confusion until the officers began to get the panicky firing under control, whole clips of M-16 rounds arcing straight up into the night sky.

Hanson pulled out the fat, foot-long starlight scope, attached it to a mount on the AK-47, and scanned the perimeter, seeing it as a grainy green TV picture that reminded him of the TV pictures of the moon walk, remembering that night on the beach with Silver. He watched soldiers duck-walking and low-crawling, officers and NCOs waving their arms. One soldier lit a cigarette and stood out as though he were spotlighted, the cigarette tip bright as a flare in his mouth. Hanson aimed for the cigarette and it spun away like a little comet.

He swallowed a capsule of speed and lay back, listening to the chaos behind him and looking up at the stars. He felt good, as if this was the job that had been waiting for him all his life. He didn't plan to live through the night, and that gave him a big advantage. He could do anything now.

The Americans were amateurs, more concerned with survival than with killing the enemy. Most of them had never learned the lesson that aggression will save you when caution won't. Most American units went out only in company-size and larger operations, and the smaller, lighter-armed VC units rarely did anything more than harass them with snipers and booby-traps. The Americans were not used to being attacked.

Hanson smiled. By now the Americans would have radioed that they were taking heavy hostile fire from a platoon or larger unit. He moved around to another section of the perimeter and studied the position with the scope. Three soldiers were moving a machine gun under the direction of a fourth. They glowed and sparkled emerald green in the scope, as if they were radioactive. The picture in the scope was two-dimensional, and Hanson had to estimate the distance, using trees that he could make out against the sky. He took out two baseball-size grenades from the canteen cover at his belt, threw them overhand at the four men, fired a burst of green tracers behind them, and flattened on the ground.

The thud of the grenades rocked him, and the night position was visible for an instant in the yellow blast, the men frozen, two of them in the air, caught as if in a snapshot, and then it was black again. Red tracers snapped over and past Hanson, hitting the ground and glancing up, deflecting off bushes and leaves, boiling through the grass.

Hanson began laughing, probing the position at will, making it twitch. They'd start popping flares now, he thought.

Mortars coughed, sending their rounds up with faint red nimbuses that moments later burst into spiky points of light, their small parachutes opening with gentle *pops*, the flares swinging beneath the parachutes like fiery pendulums, dripping sparks, *pop, pop*.

They gave off a dead white light that didn't show color or depth, lighting the hilltop in black and silver-white, objects flat and deceptive as plywood stage settings. They threw shadows in conflicting directions, dizzying, confusing, and Hanson ran through the grass and froze, changed direction, ran, froze, just another shadow.

He unstrapped Quinn's Swedish K, its fat silencer designed to hide the gun's muzzle flash. Hanson ran, froze in a crouch, and when the shadows converged on him, he fired a burst, the only sound the dry clicking of the bolt, and soldiers fell. He slipped in and out of the perimeter like a wraith. The Americans could hear him laughing, hidden by the light from the flares, like strobe lights at a rock concert, overlaying movement and shadow and darkness. By then some of the Americans, in panic, were firing across arcs of their own perimeter, shooting each other in the back, and those accidental casualties, perceived as the result of enemy fire, threw them further into fear and confusion.

They'll be calling in artillery, he thought, scrambling and sliding down the hill to where he'd left the pack and radio. He sat with his back against a tree in a depression that hid him, and watched the hilltop, occasional fans of tracer fire spreading gracefully above him. He felt detached from the situation and wished only that Quinn were alive there with him. And Silver. They'd all be laughing.

He covered himself and the radio with a poncho and turned it on. Dim yellow lights began to glow, and the ocean-surf rushing sound of static grew. Using the red-lensed penlight, he checked a list of radio frequencies that the 3rd Mech might use to call in artillery from their fire bases. Beneath the hot rubberized shelter, in the dim yellow and red light, he began changing frequencies like a man trying to find a radio station that played just the kind of music he liked.

". . . heavy contact all around our position," an excited voice said, and then began calling in the coordinates of the hill, requesting eight-inch artillery fire.

"Shot. Over . . ." a voice from the fire base said, indicating that the first round was on its way.

"Shot out," said a voice from the hilltop.

The round blossomed against the base of the hill, setting the tall dry grass on fire, throwing shrapnel into the trees above Hanson, red-hot twisted shards of cast iron the size of human hands, ripping branches loose. Then he could hear spent pieces of shrapnel falling to the ground around him, *thunk, thunk,* where they hissed in the dew that had begun to form on the grass.

Hanson keyed his microphone, cutting off the voice from the hill, and said, "That looked real good. Add one hundred and fire for effect." The added hundred yards would put the fire on top of the hill.

"Shot. Over . . ."

"Shot out."

The next three rounds came in together, roaring over like low-flying jets in close formation, screaming into the hill, into the American position.

"Looking good," Hanson said. "Keep it coming. Fire for effect."

Another salvo of three rounds roared in, setting off secondary explosions from ammunition and gasoline on the hill, then three more. Trees and grass on the hillside were in flames as Hanson walked back down the hill to the bodies of Quinn and Mr. Minh.

He chopped down two wrist-thick lengths of bamboo and used them to make a litter with nylon line and a poncho. He placed the two bodies on it and began dragging it away by a shoulder harness rigged out of the green nylon line. The hilltop behind them danced in flame and smoke and shadow, the sound of grenades, small-arms fire, and heavy machine guns rising and falling as the surviving Americans fought the empty darkness, the fury fading as Hanson trudged toward the river, until finally he was able to hear the hiss and thump of the bamboo poles and his own heavy breathing.

"I don't know," he said to the bodies. "It wasn't as much fun as we thought it would be. Too easy. Seems like all my life I've made myself do things that seemed difficult so I could say, 'Hey, look what I did.' And then when I've done it, it doesn't seem like it was difficult at all. It was easy."

He walked in silence for what seemed like a long time,

feeling the weight of the bodies, the flex of the bamboo on his shoulders.

"I wish I knew," he said. "You guys are dead. All those dumb fuckers back there are dead. It was *easy*. What are we gonna do now?"

By first light they had reached a tree-covered bend in the stream, out of the defoliated zone, and Hanson called for an extraction chopper. He cleaned his friends' wounds with water from the stream, wiping the black blood away from the ugly entrance wounds, purple punctures like bruises, then began to work on the ragged exit wounds, the compound fractures.

"I wish I could have brought Troc and Krang," he said to Mr. Minh, "but I couldn't take everybody. They'll understand, won't they?"

He cupped Mr. Minh's *katha* in his hand, then slipped it over the little Montagnard's head and put it around his own neck.

It was still cool, bands of pink clouds on the horizon, when he first heard the choppers, like faraway thunder, a troop carrier and two gunships.

The air was full of angry radio traffic. The American unit had been calling in medivacs and resupply choppers during the night, and now they were trying to explain what they had been doing on the hilltop, why they had not cleared the operation with Hanson's launch site and the other units in the AO.

When Hanson spotted the extraction choppers, low on the horizon, he directed them over his position and popped a Day-Glo signal panel, the panel snapping like a flag in the wind. The choppers wheeled and came back, hovering at treetop level. Over the radio Hanson told them to drop the Stabo gear. The ships shuddered above him, huge machines suspended in the air. The glowing orange cone of their exhaust and their blinking strobe lights were bright against the early morning sky.

"There's a clearing. Just to the south. We can set down there," the crew chief said, his voice metallic through the small radio speaker. "No need for the gear," he said, his voice quavering with the pounding rotor blades.

Hanson looked up at him, leaning out the side of the chopper, his face covered by the round black visor, reflecting Hanson and the bodies.

"Negative," Hanson said, jabbing his weapon at the chopper, then at the ground. "I want the Stabo gear."

The lines and harness of the Stabo gear came out the door and uncoiled as they fell, snap links and buckles tumbling through the pearly morning light. Hanson hooked up Mr. Minh and Quinn, talking to them beneath the roar of the chopper. He hooked himself in, then gave the crew chief the thumbs-up. The slack was taken up and then the chopper pulled pitch and they were in the air heading east. Hanson looked up into Quinn's dead face, the prop blast stinging him with flurries of oily blood.

He saw smoke and debris on the hilltop three klicks away, and he smelled burning mo-gas, but as the chopper climbed, the air was cooler and sweeter and the horizon expanded and spread out before him—the green of the jungle, the lighter green of bamboo, raw red bomb craters, the silver winking of rice paddies below where, for a moment, he watched the reflection and the shadow of the chopper and the three bodies chasing behind, the reflection bending and jumping crazily across the paddies, the shadow racing alongside, black and relentless. He saw round graves, trails webbing a riverbank, a powder blue pagoda, dark mountains, and the morning sun. The taut cable angled up from his shoulders to the black thorax of the helicopter.

Anyone watching from below could have seen that only one man in the rig was alive. The other two hung almost horizontally, spread-eagled and limp, rolling and kicking in the wind.

Hanson gripped the submachine gun across his chest and looked east, past the sun, to where he knew the ocean would be if he could only see farther. And he knew, he'd always known, he thought, that no matter what he did, and no matter how many others died, he was doomed to survive the war.